CURLY

Lilly Atlas

Copyright © 2021 Lilly Atlas

ISBN-13: 978-1-946068-38-5

In case you haven't caught on, first in series always goes to my husband, who has encouraged me every step of the way.

<3

Travis Bryant, known in the biker world as Curly, spent thirteen hard years behind bars for a heinous crime he didn't commit. When the truth finally sets him free, nothing remains of his previous life. Curly doesn't know how to live without the brotherhood of a club. After visiting the Hell's Handler's MC, he's given the go ahead to open a charter in his home state. Claiming an ol' lady is the furthest thing from his mind until he meets Brooke, the beautiful, hardheaded, dog trainer bent on ending a violent dog fighting ring near her home.

After ten long years married to an abusive narcissist, Brooke vowed she'd never live under another man's thumb again. Accepting help doesn't come easy, but when abandoned dogs begin popping up with fatal injuries, she'll do anything to put an end to the fighting ring responsible. Even enlist the assistance of the most attractive man she's ever met, and his outlaw MC brothers.

From her feisty, independent spirit to her shapely legs, Brooke appeals to Curly on every level. He can't keep himself away, but he's been burned before, and has no plans to tie himself to a woman. Brooke is in the same boat, having promised herself no man would ever have control over her life again. Unfortunately, she can't kick the curly-haired man in the biker boots out of her head or her bed.

As Brooke and Curly grow closer and danger strikes, will they be able to overcome their past traumas and find strength in each other? Or will they remain stubborn and stick to their guns as their lives crash and burn?

Table of Contents

Prologue

14 years ago

"Ladies and gentlemen of the jury, have you reached a verdict?"

"We have, Your Honor."

Travis Bryant sat as motionless as a marble statue and just as cold. Beside him, his attorney shifted papers on the desk while squirming in his seat. If he'd been able to move, Travis would have smacked the fucker upside his head until he calmed, but handcuffs and shackles around his ankles prevented most movement.

Chained like a fucking animal.

That's how the world had seen him for the past six months. But people had viewed him like a rabid animal for far longer—the chains and locks only fortified people's pre-formed opinions.

No one knew or cared he had a college degree.

No one gave a shit that he rescued dogs and donated to the local children's hospital.

No one cared how he'd taken care of his grandmother until she'd passed.

All they saw was his loud motorcycle, leather clothes, and tattoos.

Okay, fine, they saw a load of laws broken by his one-percenter motorcycle club. The club he led. He sure as fuck wasn't a saint, but he wasn't an animal either.

"Please deliver your verdict to the bailiff." The pinched-faced judge's expression never changed. Her mouth looked like a clenched asshole resisting entry.

"Yes, Your Honor." The jury foreman, a rail-skinny man with thick glasses overtaking his entire face, passed a folded paper to the bailiff with a trembling hand.

That's right, motherfucker. You should be scared of me.

Or at least fear the rest of his motorcycle club. Travis was pretty confident he'd be spending the rest of his life behind steel bars. But no one fucked with his club and got away with it. Revenge for this bullshit investigation would rain down on everyone involved, from the DA to the grunt of a beat cop who'd first arrived at the murder scene. And that included each of the twelve jurors if they voted to convict.

The stern judge glanced at the paper, nodded once, then handed it back to the bailiff. Then, like a good little sheep, the uniformed bailiff returned the form to the foreman.

"Please announce the verdict," the judge ordered.

Travis had spent more than a few nights in jail over his thirty-two years. First time had been a few nights in juvie when he'd gotten pinched swiping cigarettes from a gas station. He'd been fourteen at the time. That judge assumed he could scare Travis straight with a formal arrest and a few nights away from home. It hadn't worked. From there, his rap sheet read like a laundry list of typical biker crimes. Assault, battery, drug possession—they'd tried for intent to sell on that one, but somehow his lawyer pulled a miracle out of his smarmy ass and knocked the charges down—illegal possession of a firearm and a few additional charges.

Murder of a minor was a new one for him.

Curly

One that would fuck him right in the ass. Hopefully, only figuratively. But the sinking feeling in his gut had him sure he'd be showering with his back to the wall for many years to come.

"In the c-case of the State of Florida vs. Travis Bryant, we f-find the defendant, g-guilty of murder in the first degree." The sound of rustling paper accompanied the foreman's voice as his hands shook so badly, he couldn't keep from crinkling what he read. Not once did he shift his focus from the page.

Could he feel the burn of Curly's gaze on his face?

Gasps of both pleasure and shock went up in the courtroom with murmurs and a few shouts of furious disbelief from his brothers.

Guilty.

As the judge banged her gavel and bellowed for silence, Travis didn't twitch.

A guilty verdict.

He blinked.

Huh, he'd expected to feel more. To stand up and rage against the injustice of it all. To scream at the twelve assholes in the jury who'd fallen for this sham of a trial. To shout promises of retribution and the fires of hell on everyone who'd participated in framing him. He'd expected to fear his impending time behind bars. This was different than the past. This was permanent, as in for the rest of his miserable life.

Hell, he'd assumed he'd feel *something*, anything, but there was nothing. His insides were hollow as he sat there with chaos erupting around him.

Of course, his brothers were outraged by the verdict. They screamed obscenities and threats at the jurors, stomping their boots and promising death. If they kept at it, the entire jail would be full of unruly bikers that night.

Travis gazed across the courtroom aisle where Joy Lane's family expressed their relief and elation at what they thought was justice with long hugs and tears. As Detective Lane held his sobbing wife to his chest, his gaze connected with Travis's. As the city's lead homicide detective, he'd had to step aside on this case because his daughter was the victim, but that didn't mean he'd kept his nose out of the investigation.

No, the man had had it out for Travis for the past decade. He'd had it out for the True Outlaws Motorcycle Club, where Travis went by the handle Curly due to his long, curly hair. He also happened to be the MC's president. Though the detective didn't have a lick of proof, Curly knew deep in his bones that Lane played a significant role in framing him.

Over his wife's shoulder, Detective Lane smiled a smug, victorious grin. Travis swallowed down his hatred for the bastard who'd ruined his life. Shackled and in a courtroom, he may not be in a position to exact revenge, but he'd get it. No one fucked with the True Outlaws and lived to talk about it. The arrest of the club's president for a gruesome crime he damn well didn't commit wasn't only an attack on Travis. It was an attack on the entire club. If he knew his club, and he sure as fuck did, the whole police station would go up in flames in a matter of hours.

Bang, bang, bang.

"There will be order in my courtroom, or I will have each of you held in contempt of court," the judge shouted as she glared over Travis's shoulder, no doubt at the members of his club still railing against the verdict.

"Get the prisoner out of here." The judge waved to the armed guards hovering only a few feet away. That dismissive wave irked him more than the damn verdict. Fancy judge treating him as though he were nothing more than an irritating gnat in her courtroom.

A guard hauled him to his feet by his upper arm with as little care as possible. Travis ground his molars together. He didn't much like being touched, something that would only intensify behind bars, and the instinctive urge to fight whoever put their hands on him flared to life. He'd had decades of resisting those urges and managed to keep from swinging his cuffed hands into the guard's fat face.

"Let's go, Curly-q," the guard said with laughter in his tone. As security tugged Travis out of the room, he focused on his furious brothers. The violence-promising scowl on his VP's face let him know the club would be in good hands during his absence. His VP, Mutt, nodded once, which Travis returned. Then he shifted his gaze to his former sergeant-at-arms, Prick, and like a sucker punch to the gut, his air whooshed out in a painful exhale.

Prick wore the same self-satisfied smirk as Detective Lane. As though Travis's conviction was a personal victory.

And then Travis understood. He'd figured out exactly how the police had framed him. Prick had been banging some bitch on the police force for the past year. She was a young cop with a penchant for being fucked hard by biker cock. In exchange, she passed along info, which had kept their club one step ahead of the cop's bullshit for quite a while.

But then Prick had gone and stuck his dick in Travis's ol' lady as well.

That's right. He'd fucked his president's ol' lady. Travis and Jana hadn't been the stuff of fairytales, but he'd loved her in his way. More importantly, he'd trusted her with his heart and his club's livelihood. She'd shattered that trust, as did Prick.

It had fucked with his head more than he'd been willing to admit. More than he could think about right then.

After kicking his ol' lady to the curb, Travis had stripped Prick of his SAE title, and they'd been on the outs ever since. Prick hadn't been silent about his newly developed hatred of Travis. His attitude had become so toxic for the club, Mutt recently suggested meeting to vote on booting out him from the club altogether.

But it appeared Prick had been quicker to draw blood. The vengeful bastard had helped the cops frame him. The betrayal cut deep into Travis's flesh.

And then it came. The reaction he'd expected when the jury declared him guilty. White-hot rage flashed through him, taking his anger nuclear. Self-restraint flew out the window. The only two people who existed in the courtroom were him and the soon-to-be lifeless Prick. "You motherfucker," he shouted as he sprung forward, slipping out of the guard's grasp.

"Oh, shit." The guard barked as he dove for Travis, regaining his hold with ease. "What the fuck, Curly?"

"You're dead!" Travis screamed as he wrenched his body in all directions, trying to shake the guard loose again.

"A little help here. He's lost his shit." Another guard rushed over, and together they dragged him backward by his arms toward the exit.

"Fucking dead, you hear me!" Travis screamed.

Prick turned until his gaze met Travis's. He lifted his hand and wiggled his fingers in a cheerful wave.

"Fuck you!" Travis shouted as he thrashed against the guard's hold. He'd have bruises from their iron grip and the metal abrading his ankles and wrists, but he didn't give a single fuck. All he wanted was Prick's blood coating the courtroom floor.

"Christ, man, calm the fuck down." The guards struggled to keep a hold of him as he fought like hell.

A sharp jab to his kidney had him doubling forward as pain spread from his back into his gut. The guards used his momentary slackening to drag him from the room.

Once in the quiet hall, the pissed-off guards started berating him for being as stupid as he was ugly. Travis let himself go limp. Why bother making their job easier by trotting along like the dutiful prisoner he'd been so far?

Sentencing would be held in a week or so. Then his life would be over. No way the murderer of a police officer's kid would get anything other than life without parole.

It didn't matter how loud he'd proclaimed his innocence or the fact it was true.

Curly

He'd committed almost every crime in the book at some point in his life, but even he had a moral code. There were three things he didn't stand for. Three lines he'd never cross.

Rape, beating on his ol' lady, and killing of the innocent.

He'd spent most of his childhood listening to his father violate and pound on his mother. Now, as an adult who most of the world feared, he had no tolerance for that shit and no problem booting someone from his club for mistreating their ol' ladies.

And as for killing the innocent? Well, it didn't get much more innocent than a twelve-year-old girl with her entire life ahead of her.

Like that poor murdered child, he had no future. But he did have one thing she didn't, and that was the hope of revenge. Travis's reach was vast. Even from prison, he could wreak havoc on the men who'd set him up to take the fall for this vicious crime.

And he'd do just that.

Not only for himself, but for Joy Lane and her twin sister Holly.

Chapter One

Present Day

Curly lingered at the bar, nursing a beer as the Hell's Handlers Motorcycle Club partied around him. The pint had warmed a while ago and no longer held any appeal, but his mind wouldn't quiet. Having something to hold in his hands helped give him something to focus on besides his spiraling thoughts.

"Hey." Someone bumped his shoulder, and he turned to find a cute young blonde smiling at him with genuine affection. "What are you doing over here all by yourself?"

Holly Lane, the twin sister of the girl he'd been convicted of murdering, scooted onto the barstool next to him. She was the reason for his second chance at life. As a child, she'd never believed him guilty of murdering her twin and best friend but had been powerless to do anything about it. As an adult, she'd been integral in exposing her father's corruption and facilitating Curly's recent release from jail. He owed her his life. There were no lengths he wouldn't go to to ensure that happy expression remained on her face for the rest of her life.

"Hey, Little Miss," he said, smiling back at her. In the eight months since his release, Holly had become one of the most valuable people in his life.

The daughter he'd never had.

And never would have.

Bitter at the world and forty-six years old, he sure as fuck wouldn't be having kids of his own.

"Where's your ol' man?" He sipped the tepid beer then grimaced as the flat warmth went down.

Holly raised an eyebrow. "You couldn't possibly be implying that I shouldn't be wandering around the clubhouse without LJ, could you?"

Sweet as the baked goods she was famous for, Holly wasn't a pushover. Curly raised his hands as he spun her way. "Never. Just used to the big guy following you around. He's worse than your dog."

The lovesick smile she beamed warmed him. Despite losing her twin at an early age then finding out her father was a dirty cop who used his daughter's death for personal gain, she was remarkably well adjusted. Much of that was owed to her ol' man and the family she'd found in the MC. "I'm sure he'll be along soon. I just wanted to check on you over here brooding all by yourself."

More often than not, over the six or so months he'd been staying with her and LJ, she called him brooding or antisocial for hovering on the outskirts of the group. He couldn't help it. One of the most challenging aspects of re-entering the world had been socializing. After thirteen years of speaking only with corrections officers and angry convicts, he'd lost the skills to shoot the shit with anyone and everyone. Being the center of attention sucked, and loud parties made him want to cower in a corner and scan for attacks. Sitting at the bar with his back to the entire room took a massive amount of effort was a huge step forward. But he kept all that to himself. No one needed to hear him cry about the shitty hand life dealt him. Especially not Holly, who already lived on a mountain of misguided guilt. "I'm not brooding, honey, just waiting to chat with Copper about something."

"Oh?" Her blue eyes lit up. "Does this mean you're finally going to patch in with the club?" She practically squealed with glee.

Since the moment he'd arrived in town on a mission to find and thank Holly for her role in his recent freedom, she and her club's president had been trying to get him to patch in with the Handlers.

He'd been hesitant, to say the least.

It'd been almost fourteen years since he'd last been part of a club. And that sure hadn't ended well. After multiple betrayals, false imprisonment, then spending over a decade behind bars, trust wasn't exactly his thing. So while Copper ran a close-knit club, whose members were more a family than anything else, Curly couldn't stomach the idea of putting his complete confidence in another man to serve as his president. Even a man as solid as Copper. Nothing personal, just a product of his life experiences.

"Not sure," he said, stretching the truth a bit. "Just got some shit to talk to him about."

With a roll of her eyes, Holly snorted. "That's pretty much biker speak for mind your own business." She mimicked a deep, gravelly voice, making Curly snicker. The women here had their men's numbers, that was for damn sure.

"That's not what I meant. I—"

"Hey, sugar." LJ appeared behind his woman. He wrapped a long, thick arm around her waist, squeezing her lush hip.

As happened every time she was in the presence of her ol' man, Holly practically glowed.

"Copper's ready for you, brother," he said to Curly.

Holly pulled out of her man's arms as Curly stood. She grabbed his forearms. "Is everything okay?" She'd curled her long hair and wore a hunter-green dress that emphasized her eyes.

She was such a pretty girl, and her sister would have been the same had her life not been uselessly stolen.

Curly

"I'm good, honey. Swear it." He pressed a kiss to the top of her head before passing her off to her old man. "Take good care of her."

"Always," LJ responded with a nod.

Curly slapped the huge man on the shoulder as he walked by.

He'd been staying in their finished basement since he came to town half a year ago. As much as he loved Holly, there were times being around her spurned a pang of irrational guilt in him. Not that he'd ever tell her. Her tender heart would break. He'd had nothing to do with Joy's death—the murder had been committed by a drifter passing through town who'd then committed suicide in his cell. Although those truths had been covered up by the police, he still felt the weight of responsibility.

Maybe because of his conviction and wearing the false title of murderer for so many years. Or perhaps it stemmed from her father's hatred of his old MC, but on occasion, being around Holly dredged up feelings of shame and remorse.

Another reason for his desire to speak with Copper.

Curly had an inkling LJ sensed his inner turmoil, but thankfully, he'd kept his thoughts to himself. Last thing he wanted was to make Holly feel worse than she already did for the unfortunate turn his life had taken.

"Knock, knock," he said as he reached the open door of Copper's office. It had taken more than a few minutes to worm his way through the bustling clubhouse.

"Curly, hey, come on in, man." The ginger-headed, bearded giant waved him into his office. "Grab a seat. Want me to have a prospect grab you a drink?"

"No, I'm good."

Lowering himself into a chair opposite Copper's desk, Curly scanned the office as he always did when in Copper's space. Back in the day, his own office had a desk, a shelf with a bunch of liquor bottles, and a few chairs.

Copper, on the other hand, had a basket of kids toys in on corner, pictures of him and his club brothers on the walls, a framed wedding picture of him and his gorgeous bride on the desk, and no less than ten hand-drawn pictures taped to the walls right about the height a five-year-old could reach.

The stark contrast between the offices was the perfect representation of the differences between their clubs. The True Outlaws MC had been just that. True fucking outlaws. They'd participated in just about every illegal operation there was. Drug, guns, money laundering, theft, prostitution, you name it, they had their grimy hands in it. He and his brothers had been cocky, thought themselves above the law, and didn't give a shit about anyone other than themselves. Sometimes they didn't even give a shit about their supposed brothers.

Curly had been as guilty as of being a world-class jackoff as any of them. Maybe more so since he led the club.

Copper's club didn't run that way. They had several profitable legal businesses as well as some less than legal ventures, but they kept their noses cleaner than Curly ever had.

And the men had each other's backs one hundred percent. Even the women were close. Sisters more than friends, which was mind-blowing. If his memory served him right, the women associated with the TOs were catty bitches who'd claw each other's faces off at the slightest provocation.

"So," Copper said, steepling his fingers. "You asked for this meeting. What can I do for you?"

"Shit, sorry. Been lost in my head a lot lately."

With a shrug, Copper leaned back in his chair and stroked his beard. Early on, LJ informed him that their prez did it when deep in thought himself. "You finally thinking about patching in?"

Same question as Holly.

"No," he said, cringing when Copper frowned. "Not exactly. Copper, I'm gonna try not to sound like an ungrateful fucker here because you and your club have welcomed me in a way I never expected, but I don't think I can stay here and be one of you guys."

Curly

Copper's hand stilled on his beard before he dropped it to the desk. "You're thinking of leaving town?"

Hearing Copper say it helped solidify the decision as the right one. Much as he'd enjoyed his time in Tennessee with the Handlers, it wasn't where he belonged. "I am. Nothing against your leadership, but I'm not sure I can be part of a club and not be the prez. I'm sorry. I suppose I have good reason, but I've got trust issues coming out my fucking ears."

"Hmm," Copper said. "I'm not even gonna pretend to understand the shit that must have gone through your head every day since the conviction. That kinda thing would destroy most of us. You've more than earned the right to have problems trusting. Feel what you're gonna feel, man. We're not big on judgment around here."

"Yeah, I've noticed." And that acceptance was one of the things that impressed him most about the club. "Actually, watching you with your men has given me an idea, which is what I was hoping to talk to you about."

"Okay? Shoot." Copper leaned back in his chair and folded those massive arms across his chest. His was of settling in to listen.

Curly swallowed down a torrent of nerves he hadn't noticed until right then. He only had a few years on Copper's almost forty-one, but it seemed like a lifetime with what he'd gone through over the past decade. He felt like an old, bitter, has-been compared to the vital and commanding Copper.

Curly had been like that once and mourned those parts of himself.

But maybe with the right motivation, he could get them back. He cleared his throat. "I'm thinking it's about time I head down to Florida."

Copper's face morphed into a dropped-jaw expression of shock that made Curly chuckle. Wasn't often someone got one over on the big guy. "Back to where…it all happened?"

With a last huff of laughter, Curly said, "Yeah. Surprised me too, but I can't get it out of my head. I've got a place there. Not much else, though. Cops arrested most of my club brothers shortly after I was locked up, and the others scattered around the country. The majority of my family dropped contact after I went away." Not that he'd ever been close to them. He'd been an only child of a deadbeat alcoholic and a mom who'd passed young. "Had a cousin who kept in touch somewhat. But, uh…" He swirled a lock of hair around his fingers. It'd taken eight months to grow it from the buzz cut to chin-length. Back in the day, it'd been well past his shoulders and a mess of curls, hence his handle. Of course, it'd also been jet black without all the grays, but he could blame the stress of prison on that one.

He shrugged. "It's my home. Where I grew up. What I know." And he had an increasing need to prove he wasn't what every single person in his hometown thought of him.

A loser.

An animal.

A child killer.

"Hey," Copper said, drawing Curly's gaze. "I get it. You've got unfinished business. You feel you got something to prove. Even if it's only to yourself."

Huh, maybe Copper did get it.

"Yeah, that pretty much sums it up." Never one to beat around the bush, Curly stared Copper straight in the eye. "What would you think about opening up a charter in Florida? More specifically, me opening a Hell's Handler's charter in Florida?"

If he thought he'd surprised Copper with news of wanting to return to his hometown, he'd been mistaken. Now, the president's eyes nearly fell out of his head.

Curly laughed. "You need to work on your poker face, man."

Copper joined in the laughter, back to rubbing his beard. "Shit, man. Wasn't expecting that at all. You caught me off guard. I fucking hate surprises."

Curly

"I know. And I'm sorry. I'm not real good at easing into shit. Find it better to put it out there." Not to mention his basic social skills, at least for polite conversation, had suffered after spending thirteen years surrounded by nothing but angry felons and embittered prison guards.

"No, man, it's all good. I'd rather you give it to me straight." He ran a hand down his face while huffing out a rough chuckle. "Shocked the shit outta me." He cocked his head. "Just so you know, you don't have to prove shit to anyone—even yourself. What went down with your arrest and conviction wasn't your fault. You're a victim like any other."

A victim. Since meeting Copper, Curly considered the burly president wise beyond his years. But in this, he was dead wrong. "I may not have had shit to do with Joy's death, but you can't exactly call me innocent." He shrugged as though not bothered by the facts that kept his mind churning long into the night. "My club wasn't like yours. You got good people here. Hard-working, moral—even if it's your own code—you've got a fucking family. My club was a rowdy band of common criminals and thugs with a handful of nastier fuckers thrown in there. Way I see it, those thirteen years were the universe's way of getting back at me for all the other fucked-up shit I did."

The drugs he'd sold.

The deadly weapons he put into men's hands without a thought of their use.

The shit he'd stolen.

The people he'd threatened, assaulted, hurt.

Hell, if the universe were just, he'd still be rotting in that cell. But for some reason, he wasn't. Now it was time to take the gift he'd received and do...something with it.

Copper leaned his massive form across the desk. "Come on, man. Doesn't work that way. If it did, I'da been right there in the cell next to you. So would most of my men. You know who spewed that same bullshit?"

Curly lifted an eyebrow instead of responding.

Copper wore a fierce expression of indignation. "Holly's fucking father. No way I'm gonna let you get away with thinking of yourself the way he thought of you."

Fuck.

Curly ran a hand through the hair which had given him his name. One day it'd be long again, and he'd feel more like himself. Or so he kept promising himself. In reality, he feared he'd never be entirely comfortable in his skin again. It was as though someone had hit the fast-forward button on a movie everyone had seen but him. Thirteen years was a long time. People died, others were born, jobs were had and lost. Hell, multiple presidents held office. He'd stepped into the prison in one era and out in another. For fuck's sake, he'd been looked at like he was from another planet when he hadn't known who Mark Zuckerberg was. Why the hell did he think regrowing his hair would fix any of that?

"I hear you, man. Just takes a while for the words to sink into my bones. Know what I mean?"

Nodding, Copper relaxed back in his chair. "I do." He crossed his arms over his chest. They bulged in a way that probably intimidated the hell outta most people. Those who didn't know that beneath the leather, muscles, and gruff expression lived a family man with a very pregnant wife and a daughter who had him wrapped around their pinkies.

"Now," Copper said. "Let's talk about this idea of yours because I'm starting to think it's a pretty fucking good one."

Chapter Two

Curly secured the strap on his saddlebag then gave the decades-old leather an affectionate rub. The smooth glide of leather beneath his fingers felt almost as heavenly as the wind whipping past his face as he rode. Such a simple thing, but those saddle bags, which were the first he'd ever purchased at eighteen, represented independence, choice, the openness of the wide world. All things he'd been denied for long, lonely years.

As soon as the prison released him, he'd had the bike shipped from the storage unit where his meager important possessions gathered dust for thirteen years.

While locked away, he'd missed his Harley more than most guys missed their wives. It wasn't until his ass finally hit the worn seat that he felt free after his release.

And the first time he'd flown down the highway after so long? Fucking nirvana.

After sex, riding was his absolute favorite activity. At least he'd had his hand to provide sexual release in prison.

He hadn't had a single thing that came close to mimicking the thrill of riding.

Now he and his baby were about to cruise down to Florida. It was time to scope out potential properties for a clubhouse and begin recruiting members for the Florida chapter of the HHMC.

Settling back into the home he owned was high on the list as well. Hopefully, he'd be able to breathe life back into the house. For all he knew, it lay in a pile of rubble. More likely, squatters, snakes, and those rabid Florida termites inhabited it now.

He'd find out soon enough.

"Curly Whatever-your-last-name-is!" Holly stormed out of her house wearing sweatpants and what had to be her ol' man's T-shirt because she got lost in the thing.

Curly's lips twitched at the fury on her face. She marched down her driveway, waving an envelope and giving him the same glare he'd seen take LJ down easily. Speaking of, LJ appeared in the open doorway wearing an amused grin and a pair of charcoal sweats. He folded his gigantic arms, leaned against the door frame, and settled in to watch the fireworks.

"What the hell is this?" Holly shouted as she stomped his way.

Curly sighed. He'd planned on being halfway out of town before she found the envelope. Guess it wasn't his lucky day. Hopefully, this wouldn't be an omen for the rest of his trip.

When she reached him, she shook the envelope in his face. "I asked you a question."

He bit his upper lip to keep it from quirking. Laughing would make him a dick, but she was so damned cute in her anger, it was hard to take her seriously. "Let's call it rent."

Holly frowned. "Rent?"

"Yeah." He shrugged. "I've been living with you two for the past six months. It's well past time I contributed."

A head shake joined her frown. The familiar smell of brown sugar wafted off her. He'd miss the scent that never left her home from how she spent her days baking delicious pastries.

"Curly, we've told you a million times we don't want rent money from you. I've loved having you stay with us." Her voice hitched. "We both have."

Oh, shit. If she brought out the waterworks, he was screwed. He sent LJ a SOS glance.

"Honey…" LJ wore a what're-you-gonna-do-now smirk.

Curly

All of a sudden, her blooming sadness transformed back into anger. "And one hundred thousand dollars? Are you out of your freaking mind? Who pays one hundred thousand dollars for six months of rent? That's ridiculous. Take this back right now." She shoved the envelope and check against his chest, but he didn't budge.

The money wasn't rent. It was a gift. A gift he wanted them to have with all his being. Fuck, he'd have doubled it if he didn't think her head would blow right off her shoulders.

"Curly!" She half whined when he didn't move to take the money back.

They stood there for a few moments, locked in a standoff of stubborn will. Of course, the poor kid had no way of knowing waiting thirteen years for one's freedom made a few minutes of stare-down laughable.

Finally, her shoulders sagged, and her arms dropped to her sides, limp. "It's too much," she whispered, defeated. Tears filled the baby-blue eyes he'd come to care for as though she shared his blood.

With a grunt, he tugged her into a fierce hug. She was everything any man could want in a daughter. Her parents were the worst kind of fools for throwing her away in favor of hatred and lies.

"Please," he whispered against the top of her head. "You and LJ have so many dreams for this little house. With his talent and a little extra cash, you can make all of them a reality." Late one night, after they'd moved into the small three-bedroom house, Holly had clued him into the vision she had for the place. A new kitchen to fuel her love of baking, a massive deck in their sprawling backyard with gorgeous views of the Smoky Mountains. LJ wanted to knock down the wall between the two adjoining rooms turning it into a large master, and then add a second story for when they filled the home with children.

Curly couldn't imagine anything better than seeing little clones of Holly and LJ running around, driving their parents bonkers. Since Holly's parents were out of the picture, Curly felt it not only his responsibility to help take care of her but also a great honor. Her father's hatred of him and his old club was what drove the man to commit heinous acts and drive an unpassable rift in the family. This gift was the least of what he owed her.

Maybe some of his generosity came from guilt, but that part he'd keep buried deep inside. She didn't need anything adding to her unjustified self-blame.

"It's still too much," she said against his chest.

Too much. Hell, after the court overturned his conviction, his tale began to hit the news and make the rounds on social media sites. Copper and a very talented attorney worked their asses off to spin the narrative. To the world, the police department in his hometown bungled the investigation, and he got screwed in the worst way. No one beyond the HHMC and the guilty parties knew what had actually happened. He and Holly's ol' man wanted to spare her the crippling loss of privacy that would accompany the world, learning her father had framed Curly for Joy's murder—directing the story where they wanted it to go kept her father out of jail and Holly off the media vultures' radar. Detective Lane was now living a lonely life under an assumed name in a tiny town in Montana. His wife had left him, his children didn't speak to him, he had no job and no prospects, and that would have to be punishment enough.

Embarrassed by their police's apparent inability to conduct a proper investigation, the State of Florida was quick to throw a disgusting amount of money his way to keep him from blabbing to every reporter who came sniffing his way.

Little did they know, the last thing he'd ever do was whine about his unfair treatment to a bunch of nosy strangers. Fuck, the entire event was traumatic enough without having the world weigh in thirteen years later. Still, he had nothing but bitterness and animosity when he'd left prison, so he'd gladly taken the seven-million-dollar settlement.

Now he was a rich man who didn't want or need a fraction of that money but was spiteful enough to keep it. Maybe hanging on to the cash was more self-preservation than spite. If his past ever repeated itself, if shit ever hit the fan in such a fantastic way again, he'd have the funds to save himself. Whether that meant hiring the best lawyer or fleeing the fucking country with a new identity, he could manage either with plenty to spare. There was a comfort in financial excess.

Plus, after so many years in prison, he was tired. He had no interest in being a lazy piece of crap who refused to work, but knowing he had the fiscal padding to avoid a typical nine-to-five job and still be comfortable gave him a sense of security he'd never experienced.

"It's not too much," he said, moving her back so he could look into her eyes. "You know I got a shitload in the wrongful conviction settlement. I only chose this amount because I knew you'd never accept more. Take it, Holly. Take it and make an incredible home with that man up there. All I ask is that you name your first-born Travis."

A watery laugh bubbled from her before she glanced over her shoulder at LJ, who still stood watching the interaction. Her face lit up as it always did when he was around. "Thank you seems so inadequate," she said once she faced Curly again. This time her eyes shone with emotion. She clutched the envelope to her chest. "I can't believe you're leaving. It won't be the same around here without you."

"You and that man of yours better get your asses down to Florida for a visit before long," he said as a tickle made his throat thicken.

"You'd really want us to visit you?" Her smile made his heart soar in a way he'd never experienced.

He glanced away from the affection she sucked at hiding. Fuck, his chest ached.

Having genuine affection and love for someone wasn't familiar to him, and he had no idea how to express his feelings to her. She meant more to him than anyone ever had, but he didn't have the first clue how to tell her. He'd hoped the money would speak for him and they could avoid any awkward or overly emotional goodbye.

"Of course I want you to visit, Holly. You and LJ have become, uh, important to me." He stared at his feet. Her tender gaze had his skin itching. "You, uh, you feel like family," He grumbled, staring at the concrete driveway.

Before he knew it, surprisingly strong arms wrapped around his waist while she rested her head on his chest. "I love you, Curly. You've become like a father to me. Or a really great older brother. Thank you. We can't wait to visit."

Curly's gaze found LJ's once again. The big man wore a smile and gave a nod of agreement.

"Love you too, Little Miss." He gave her an awkward pat on the back. Even after all these months of living with her, her spontaneous bursts of physical contact threw him.

They held each other for a few moments. It seemed like as long as he had Holly's affection, all the tangled emotions and anger over his past took a back seat to his desire to be a better man. Hopefully, once he landed in his old town, he wouldn't revert to the man he'd been before the conviction. Bringing a Handlers charter to Florida would ensure a connection to this place where he'd found peace and had begun to shed the intense resentment he'd harbored for years.

"I need to get on the road if I want to get halfway by dark," he finally said.

"Yeah, I know." Holly released him and stepped back. Her cheeks were wet with tears, and his T-shirt now had a dark gray spot soaked in. "Sorry," she said as she pointed to it.

"Five minutes on the road, and it'll be dry." He tried for a cheerful smile, but it wasn't exactly his thing and probably looked like he was constipated instead. After swinging his leg over his bike, he gave one final wave to LJ, then looked back to Holly. "See you soon, Little Miss."

Curly

Not goodbye.

Never goodbye. She was as much a part of him now as the blood in his veins.

That got her smiling. "See you soon." She blew him a kiss.

Once his helmet was secure, he coasted out of the driveway then hit the throttle, gunning his baby down the street. After a quick stop at the clubhouse, he'd be on his way to Florida. Unfortunately, the night before, Holly and LJ had thrown him a goodbye party, and he'd accidentally left the clubhouse with the wrong phone, so he needed to return it and retrieve his cell.

As he pulled into the clubhouse parking lot, he found Scott leaning against the building, smoking a cigarette. He was Chloe's brother and not exactly a huge fan of the MC, but he came around frequently and made nice because he loved his sister. At least that's what Rocket, Chloe's ol' man, had told Curly.

"Hey, man," Scott said when Curly cut the engine. The Green Beret pushed off the wall and strode over with that classic special forces swagger. Aviators hid his eyes, and the trim, muscular body and buzz haircut gave away his all-American good boy status. "Sorry you had to make an extra stop."

"Don't worry about it." Curly pulled Scott's phone from his pocket, and they made the swap. "How long are you hanging around?"

Scott rubbed the stubble on his face. He probably only got to let it get so scruffy when on leave. "Just through the weekend. Gotta be back on base for PT Monday morning. So, I hear you're bringing the Handlers to Florida."

With a nod, Curly stowed his phone in the pocket of his brand-new Hell's Handlers leather jacket. "That's the plan. Club voted it in last weekend. They patched me in, and I'm heading down to get started on the legwork."

"Hmm." Gaze cast downward, Scott toed a rock with his boot.

Tilting his head, Curly asked, "Something on your mind?"

After blowing out a breath, Scott pushed his sunglasses up on his head. "Yeah, actually. Haven't told Chloe yet, so I appreciate it if you keep this to yourself, but I'll be getting out of the Army soon." As he spoke, his shoulders seemed to stiffen more with each word. "Anyway, I'm looking for a place to land. Thinking maybe Florida's it."

Interesting.

"You don't want to base yourself outta Tennessee? Be close to your sister?"

"Nah." He cleared his throat. "Not now, at least. Maybe at some point."

Curly studied him for a moment. There was a story there. A reason he didn't want to live so close to Chloe. He'd bet his newfound freedom on it. But it wasn't his business. He had enough of his own shit to wade through, so he didn't bother asking Scott to tell his tale. But he was curious about one thing.

"You saying you're interested in club life?"

"Think so, yeah." He said with a sheepish half-grin.

This conversation got crazier by the second. From what he'd heard, Scott flipped his shit when he found out his sister was involved with a biker. "For real?" Curly arched an eyebrow. That would be quite the one-eighty if it were true. "Word around here is you think as highly of MCs as you do a wart on your ass." If it came out a little gruff, Scott would have to ignore it. Being a biker was all Curly had ever known or wanted.

And it'd been ripped away from him.

Now he'd lived as a biker and a wrongfully convicted felon. Both labels held stigmas he'd never shake.

Scott grimaced as he went back to rolling his boot over a jagged hunk of gravel. He rubbed the back of his neck. "Yeah, I may have been a little harsh on my judgment when I first met Rocket. A lot was going on with Choe back then, and I mistakenly believed Rocket was responsible for it."

Took a big man to be able to admit when wrong. It was a quality Curly admired.

Curly

"I've hung around here a lot over the past few years, and it's changed my opinion. Maybe not of all MCs, but I have no issue with the Handlers. In fact, I've come to have a lot of respect for these guys and think it's a pretty sweet setup here. I just need a little separation from prying family eyes."

As he gazed at the sprawling clubhouse, a huge cabin-style building, Curly experienced the same bizarre warmth he'd been feeling in his chest for months. "Yeah, this club is pretty damn special."

Scott ran a hand across the back of his neck. "You hoping for something similar in Florida? I just, uh, I heard your old club was a little different back in the day. I'm not interested in a lot of the shit I've been hearing about it."

With a grunt, Curly planted his hands on his hips. "My club wasn't anything like this. We spouted bullshit about being brothers, but we weren't. Not like these guys," he said, lifting his chin toward the clubhouse. "To answer your questions, yes. Copper wouldn't let me use the Handler's name if I planned to take the club in the opposite direction of what he's built here."

Scott nodded. "Didn't think so."

"I'll never be a completely straight arrow, but I'm not trying to spend another minute behind bars. If you're looking for a place to land when you discharge from the military, I'd love to have you, but you need to accept that. We aren't gonna be running drugs or guns, but I'm not looking to start a Boy Scout troop either."

With a snort, Scott stared off into the distance for a minute. "I don't see the world in black and white, Curly. Not anymore. Spent too much time in the gray zone ever to be called naïve or idealistic. I want a brotherhood. It's what I'll miss most about the military. And I want a group that isn't gonna judge if I'm a little broken."

Their gazes met, and Curly saw Scott in a new light. All he knew of the younger man's story was that he was active-duty military, special operations. Whatever shit he'd seen and done in his time must have left a deep mark. What he saw before him was a man who understood pain, knew the darker side of life, and hadn't quite found what he needed to heal.

"Pretty sure being broken is a requirement of this kinda life. I'm sure as hell not in one piece anymore." Fuck, he'd fragmented before he hit puberty. Happened to a kid when his parents sucked. His father had hated him before he'd been born, demanding his mother abort him. Thankfully, he'd had a tough-as-nails grandmother who'd put her foot down on her daughter's behalf. After his mother died, Curly's grandmother tried to help, but his father didn't make it easy. Still, she'd been the only stable force in his life until she passed when he was in his early twenties.

Finally, Scott smiled and lost some of his tension. "Anyway, I'm out in about a month."

"Shit, you meant it when you said soon."

"Yeah."

"Chloe know?"

Blowing out a breath, Scott shook his head. "That's why I'm here, though. Gonna fill her in on my plans this weekend."

"Well, you can get my contact info from Rocket. If you're serious, give me a call when you're out. I wanna start with a core group who will be the exec board. Think you'd be perfect for it. From there, we'll look for guys to start prospecting."

Scott's eyes popped. "You'd give me a seat on the board?"

"Fuck yes," Curly said, and he meant it. "You're exactly what I'd want in an enforcer." He already had a choice—perhaps hope was a better word—for a VP, though it might take fucking miracle for the guy to sign on.

"Well, shit, thanks, man." Scott held out his hand. "You'll be hearing from me in a few weeks."

Curly shook his hand. "Looking forward to it."

Rare excitement simmered in his gut. The fluttering should have been pleasant, but a man never had anything to get enthusiastic about in prison. Not one goddammed thing. Even when he'd learned of the overturned conviction and settlement from the state, he hadn't gotten excited. By that point, it'd been so long since anything good had happened he'd thought he'd lost the ability for happiness. Relief? Yes. Nerves? Fuck yes. But not joy.

His world lost all joy the day a drifter murdered a twelve-year-old girl in his hometown.

Now, closing in on a year back in society with people who supported him and didn't cast judgment, his emotions were finally beginning to normalize.

For the past few weeks, he'd been stressing over his desire to bring the Handlers to Florida.

Could he find enough men?

Good men he'd want to call brother?

Men who didn't believe the lies about him?

A few times, he'd come close to calling Copper and scrapping the whole thing.

But Scott's interest solidified his commitment. Maybe he could pull it off and start up a Florida HHMC charter.

With a broad smile, another infrequent action, he rode out of the parking lot and began the journey toward his new life.

His free life.

One where no one would cage him ever again.

Chapter Three

Why was it the doorbell only rang the second Brooke stuffed a huge bite of food in her mouth?

It had to be the universe's cruel way of shaming her for her high-calorie breakfast choice.

"Mph, cming," she attempted to yell around a mouthful of chocolate chip muffin. Dusting her hands on her frayed denim shorts, she made for the front door. She didn't have any clients scheduled for a few hours, and those appointments weren't at her home, so there shouldn't be anyone darkening her doorstep. Especially not at seven on a Monday morning.

"If this is a solicitor, I'm siccing you on them, Ray," she muttered to her five-year-old German Shepherd, who merely twitched an ear in her direction. When she'd first rescued him as an eight-month-old energetic puppy, he'd charge the door whenever the wind blew too hard. To the outside world, Ray was passive, even lazy, for not reacting to the doorbell.

But Brooke knew from experience that Ray was fully aware of his surroundings and alert no matter how chill he appeared. If she opened that door to any kind of threat, her fierce protector would spring from his bed and make anyone who dared threaten her sorry as hell.

Curly

He'd done it before, and it had saved her life. No one should ever interpret his relaxed posture as apathy or lethargy.

"David," she said with a genuine smile for the town's vet and her best friend's husband. "What are you—" Her gaze immediately landed on the dog lying still in a wagon beside him. His truck sat in her driveway. Her heart sank, and the muffin she'd consumed threatened to reappear. "Oh no, another one?" She pressed a hand to her stomach.

The grim set of David's mouth said it all. "I'm sorry I didn't ask before bringing him here. It's been an insane day, and it slipped my mind. But, he's stable, and you have more room here than we do in our kennel, so I thought it'd be good for him to stay here a few days."

"The poor baby." She rushed forward then dropped to a crouch next to the wagon. "You know you never have to ask. I'll take whoever you have for me." If she didn't have the space to house a dog he needed assistance with, she'd give up her own room. "Where did you find him?"

"A trucker dropped him off pretty late last night. He got lucky. I'd gotten a call from the security company and had to run to the clinic to reset the code. Normally, I would never have been there at that hour on a Saturday. I didn't even have time to tell the trucker this poor dog's injuries were more than my clinic could handle before he was hopping back in his truck and speeding off. He yelled through the window that he found the dog on the side of the road real close to here." David spoke with hatred thickening his voice.

"I didn't think he'd survive the thirty-minute trip to the closest twenty-four-hour ER, so I called Nance, and she rushed over. We did what we could to save him." Brooke's best friend Nancy happened to be her husband's veterinary assistant. It was how they met eight or so years ago, and their connection had been instant.

The story made her insides ache with sadness. "This is the third one this month," Brooke whispered as she ran her hand over the injured Cane Corso's muscular body with the gentlest of touch. He didn't react to her at all.

"Careful, Brooke. This one's real aggressive and not a fan of people. Even though he was bleeding out all over my office, he was ready to go to battle with me last night. He's sedated now, but I'm not sure what to expect when he comes around. I'd like to get him in a kennel before he's alert enough to take a chunk out of either of us."

Bite marks and deep scratches littered the poor dog's body. He would have been a handsome boy when not drugged and injured: shiny black coat, impressive musculature, fierce face. As foolish as it would be, Brooke couldn't stem the urge to gather the injured dog in her arms and rock him back and forth. How someone could allow this to happen, how someone could use a dog for this very purpose, she'd never understand. Nothing riled her like those who abused innocent animals. If she could put the sadistic bastards down, she'd do it in a heartbeat.

"You had to amputate his leg?" she asked, voice cracking as she stared at the bandage wrapped around what remained of his right front leg.

"I did. It was mangled beyond repair. He'll suffer much less this way than if I had tried to repair the damage."

"We need to find these fuckers," Brooke said, glancing up at her friend. As a popular dog trainer and frequent fur foster parent, she had a close working relationship with many veterinary clinics in the area, but David was by far her favorite. He shared a true and deep love of all the animals he cared for. He was also the type of man who'd spend half the night trying to save a dog he hadn't planned on treating.

He dragged a hand down his handsome yet weary face. A good few years younger than she was, David and his wife lived in the loving relationship she wished she'd had at their age. But stupid decisions and even stupider actions hadn't allowed it.

At least you're settled and happy now.

Yeah, but with thick emotional scars and a personal promise to avoid relationships.

"I'm on my way to file another police report," David said as he squatted on the other side of the wagon.

Shit, she hadn't meant to get so morose in her head. The past crept up on her every so often, no matter how much she valued her current life situation.

"You mean you're about to waste another hour of your time," Brooke grumbled. "They don't give a shit about dead or injured dogs." The last two dogs concerned citizens had brought to David's clinic hadn't survived. One had died on David's operating table from internal bleeding while another hung on for a week before succumbing to a severe infection.

"Well, unfortunately, we don't have too many other options."

Brooke stood. "You said this guy was found near here, right?"

David flicked a green-eyed glance her way, then went back to adjusting the dog's bandages. "Yeah. Just up the road, actually. Maybe a quarter mile."

"Huh." She wiped sweat off her brow. A little after seven a.m. and the morning sun had already heated the air to near ninety.

With narrowed eyes, David rose to his feet. "What's going on in that head of yours, Ms. Williams?"

After tapping her finger against her lips, she pointed toward her backyard. "All three of the dogs were found bordering the farm, weren't they?"

"The old Miller place? Right behind you?" he asked of the extensive farmland her property butted up to.

She snapped her fingers. "Yes, I can never remember who'd owned it. I'm pretty sure it's been abandoned since before I moved in here." The farm was about two hundred acres, and her property bordered the back. As far as she knew, there was a large barn and impressively sized farmhouse, but they were toward the front of the property, meaning she didn't have a view of either from her house.

"It's not abandoned anymore. I heard someone purchased the property about five months ago." His pale skin flushed pink from the heat as it always did.

Her jaw dropped. "What?" She hadn't seen anyone taking care of the overgrown property. "I've never seen anyone, and it's still such a mess."

David used the hem of his shirt to wipe his sweaty face. "Yeah, I don't know much, just rumors from gossipy pet owners. Supposedly some guy who's lived in the trailer park for several years purchased the land and moved in a few months ago. Don't think he's started farming anything yet. And I haven't been called out to attend to any animals, so he's either using another vet or doesn't have any livestock. Word around town is the guy's a bit of a loner and not the friendliest sort."

Not the friendliest sort. That was David's overly kind way of calling someone an asshole. His wife would have called it like it was, but then, Nancy had always been the saltier of the pair.

"Oh, my God, David!" She grabbed her friend's arms as a daunting idea hit her. "Maybe he's running a dog fighting ring out of there." It made perfect sense. "The timing lines up, the location is isolated, and the dogs were all found near his property. We should go check it out."

With a laugh, David shook his head. "Check it out? Brooke, take a breath. It's not a bad theory, and I'll mention it to the cops, but let's leave the detective work up to the professionals, okay?"

"Uh-huh." She nodded, barely hearing his words, as she released his arms and watched the sleeping dog's belly rise and fall with each peaceful breath. Gnawing her lower lip, she allowed her mind to run wild with possibilities of who and what was happing on that farm. Eight years ago, Brooke learned to trust her gut in the most powerful way possible. Now, it was screaming at her that she was on to something. There was no way in hell she'd allow some violent asshole get away with hurting innocent dogs if she could help it.

"Brooke." The warning in David's tone yanked her from the rabbit hole her mind had jumped down.

"What?" she asked, shielding her eyes from the rising sun so she could see his scowl.

"Promise me you aren't going to go all cowboy on me and charge over to that farm flinging accusations. Nance will blame me if she has to bail you out of jail."

He knew her too well. "David?" She planted her hands on her hip and gave him her most harmless smile though he'd never buy it. "Do you really think that's something I'd do?"

Laughing, he tugged the brim of his Tampa Bay Rays ballcap. "Don't even try to pull that innocent crap with me. You don't take shit from anyone. We both know storming that farm is exactly the type of thing you'd do."

Actually, it wasn't. First, she'd research anything and everything she could learn about the buyer, then she'd sneak over and snoop around until she uncovered something useful. Then, if her theory proved true, she'd lose her shit.

With a roll of her eyes, she huffed. "Okay," she said, lifting her hands in surrender. "I promise I will not go over there and make a scene."

"You'll let the police do their job?"

"Yes, David. I'll let the cops do their thing." She'd just aid them as much as she could.

Slyly.

Stealthfully.

He studied her for a few more seconds as though trying to determine whether she meant her vow. Finally, he nodded. "All right. Let me help you get this guy settled. I've already been on the phone with the pit rescue, and they'll be picking him up on Tuesday.

"Okay. Let's put him in the quarantine kennel since we don't know how he'll react around other dogs."

"I vaccinated him for a bunch of diseases, but you know that takes time to be effective, so I think this is best," David said with a nod.

"Just gotta grab my boots. Be right back." She darted into the house.

Tim, a buddy of David's, ran an incredible pit bull rescue foundation about four hours away. They rehabbed and re-homed some of the most aggressive and abused dogs she'd ever encountered—dogs most would consider terminally unsafe and recommend putting down. The man was a freakin' miracle worker. She swore he had canine blood running through his veins. It seemed the only explanation for the way he got these mistreated and damaged dogs to trust him. She had rehabbed a number of mildly aggressive and reactive dogs, but fighting dogs were in a class of their own. Many bred these dogs for the sole purpose of battling other dogs. They were isolated and trained to fight their entire lives. Given the rest of her skittish menagerie, it was too dangerous to have those animals roaming around her place. Thankfully, Tim never turned down a dog, no matter how precarious the prognosis.

After she'd shoved her unsocked feet into her rubber boots, they walked around the back of her house, where she'd had two structures for her fosters. The biggest held six eight-by-ten-foot kennels where she could house any size dogs. The smaller was the size of a shed and held one kennel, which she'd coined the *quarantine kennel*. She used it if she was fostering an ill dog or one awaiting vaccinations. In this case, it'd be perfect for a dog who needed to be isolated from the others for safety reasons.

The land behind the kennels—the rest of her six-acre property—was designed to be dog heaven. Fully fenced in, the pups had plenty of space to run free, obstacles to jump on and run through, toys galore, and even a built-in dog water fountain. There was also a smaller circular fenced-in area she used for training.

What could she say? She took her job seriously.

Curly

Really, she just loved dogs to distraction and preferred their company to people's nine times out of ten. David and Nancy were the few exceptions.

She unlocked the temperature-controlled shed and stepped in. One corner held a large dog bed, while another housed a pile of toys. Large windows at a dog's eye level along the back allowed them to see the world even while quarantining.

"Help me lift him?" David asked as he pulled the wagon into the building. "I'll take his head just in case. I'm pretty sure he'll be zonked for a few more hours, but you never know."

"Gotcha." Brooke moved to the hind end of the dog. She carefully worked her hands under his injured body then squatted, prepared to lift the dead weight.

"Okay, on three," David said from his end. "One...two... three."

Brooke straightened her legs and hefted her portion of the dog. She was no slouch, yet the muscles in her arms bunched and strained under the dog's bulk. "Wow, this is one big boy," she gasped as they shuffled sideways to clear the sides of the wagon.

"Yeah, he is solid muscle. Only good thing about some of the fighting dogs is that they are fed the best food to keep them fit and strong."

Yeah, solid was a damn good way to describe the heavy beast.

"Ready to lower him to the bed?"

"Uh, yes. And I think I need to bump up my workouts."

Laughing, David nodded. "I hear that."

As best she could, she bent her knees to keep from wrenching her back while they set the dog on the plush bed. He let out a little sigh as though he already felt more comfortable. She sure hoped her home could provide some measure of ease for the poor guy.

"There you go, buddy. We're gonna take good care of you." Brooke ran her hand over his massive rump once before straightening. She ignored the cracking of her knees and the slight ache in her back. At forty-one, she wasn't close to old, but she certainly didn't feel as limber as she once did. "I wonder what his name is."

David shrugged. "Don't think we'll ever know that. He's not chipped and didn't have a collar." He brushed his hands on his jeans then grabbed the wagon handle. "Okay, I'll be back later to check him over and give him his meds. Depending on how alert and agitated he is, I might need some help subduing him."

"I've got a few trainings later this morning, but I should be home by three the latest."

"Okay. Good if I swing by around four?" He pulled his ballcap off and ran his hand through his sweaty red hair.

"As long as you bring Nancy this time. You know she's the only reason I tolerate you, right?"

Laughing, he shut the shed door started back around the house with her at his side. "Trust me, she's the only reason I tolerate myself most days."

"Phew." Brooke fanned herself. "Sweating already. Gonna be a scorcher today."

"Make sure you hydrate while you're running around with the pups all day."

"Yes, Doc, I will. Speaking of hydrate, you and Nance wanna stick around for a drink or two tonight?"

"You bet." He collapsed the wagon then shoved it in the back of his large SUV. "See you at four?"

"I'll be here."

Brooke stood in the driveway and waved as he drove off. He and Nance only lived about two miles away. When the trip wouldn't melt her face off, she loved to take Ray and jog over for a visit.

Once David's car was out of sight, she sighed. As much as she'd love to head inside and luxuriate over a second cup of coffee, there were chores waiting. Dogs to feed, kennels to clean, and clients to visit.

Curly

Opening the front door, she called out, "Come on, Ray." Her faithful buddy trotted out the door and toward the gate leading to the backyard. He knew the routine. They'd been at it long enough.

As Brooke went about feeding the four dogs she was currently fostering, her mind drifted to the wounded pup sleeping away in the quarantine kennel.

She had a soft spot ten miles wide for all dogs, but the abused and neglected ones spoke to her heart. Even as injured as the Cane Corso appeared, the wounds on the outside of his body would heal with time and proper care. It was the ones on the inside that took longer if they ever fully went away.

She knew that firsthand. Even after years of therapy, she still had internal wounds that felt gaping at times. Animals didn't have the benefit of being able to talk through their trauma, and have someone tell them what they were feeling was not only okay, but it was also normal. She understood the agony of keeping the pain deep inside as well. It'd been a long time before she'd opened up and sought help for her own suffering.

In more ways than one, she felt a kinship with these mistreated and abandoned animals. And if all she could do was give them a safe place to stay, food to fill their bellies, and lots of love, she'd damn well do it.

Though in this case, maybe there was something to be done. Something that could prevent more gravely injured animals from ending up on the side of the road.

And the first step involved some research time on her laptop.

Chapter Four

The second Curly stepped foot in the tire shop, it was as if he had been transported almost fourteen years back in time. Not much had changed as far as he could tell. The old registers were gone, replaced with sleek computers, but aside from that, the place was as he remembered the last time he'd been there. Four days before the cops pounded on his door and arrested him in the middle of the night.

"Welcome to Ty's Tires," a man said from behind the counter. He had his back to the door as he erased a name from a schedule on a whiteboard. The same whiteboard Curly used to leave inappropriate drawings on when he'd been younger. The place might have computers, but that didn't mean Tyler would use them. He'd always preferred pen and paper to anything higher-tech.

Curly cleared his throat. "Hey," he said.

"Anything I can help you with?" Tyler turned, and his eyes widened to a comical width. "Travis," he whispered.

Growing up, the two of them had been inseparable. Cousins with sisters for mothers, they'd seen each other at least five days a week throughout their entire childhoods, even after Curly's mother died. Both had developed a love of motorcycles early on and, all through high school, had pledged to patch into the True Outlaws together. They'd been a team.

So at twenty-one, they'd prospected. Curly had fit right in, taking to the rough and gritty lifestyle like a raccoon to trash, but Tyler could never get past some of the acts committed by the club. He'd bailed three months into prospecting.

The difference in opinion on the Outlaws MC had driven a rift between Curly and his cousin. Despite it all, Tyler had been the only family member to write Curly in prison. The letters had been few and far between but receiving them had given Curly hope for a future reconciliation.

Looked like the future had finally arrived, which explained the nausea and inability to eat breakfast that morning.

A handful of letters to a felonious family member were one thing. Getting Ty to agree to Curly's in-person proposition was another thing entirely. Curly hadn't realized just how vital this reunion was until Tyler stood in front of him. How much he wanted to rekindle the friendship they'd once had. Guess he'd find out just what his cousin thought of him.

"Hi, Tyler."

His cousin still stared at him as though he were an alien landed on earth. "I—" He shook his head then strode forward. "Shit, it's good to see you, man." He enveloped Curly in a back-slapping hug that lasted longer than any he'd ever received from a family member.

"You too, Ty." Understatement of the century.

"Um, I, uh..." Tyler cleared his throat as he released Curly. After a step back, he shook his head and rubbed his chest. "Sorry, I sound like an idiot. Think it's safe to say you shocked me to a near heart attack."

Curly smiled. "Sorry. Thought in person would be better than a phone call."

"I'd heard you'd gotten out." Ty ran a hand through his hair. "Wondered if you'd get in contact."

That made Curly wince. Maybe he should have called as soon as he'd gotten out. "I always planned to. Just needed…time to get my head on straight."

Similar in color to Curly's, Tyler wasn't gifted the chick-magnet mop of curls. Still, it was dark and shaggy, and when combined with his muscular form, plentiful tattoos, and a deep tan, he'd never had trouble nabbing a girl.

"Yeah. Can't imagine." Ty cleared his throat. "Never thought I see you again, though. Figured you'd stay as far from this place as possible. Is everything okay?"

"Everything's good with me. Real good." With a heavy sigh, Curly shrugged. "Staying far away was the original plan. Shit changes, though. Probably doesn't make sense, but I just needed to be here."

They stared at each other for a moment. What was Tyler thinking? He'd been warned that despite the overturned conviction and confession from Lane of the police department's role in framing him, not everyone would automatically believe his innocence. Even if they did, some people would fear him after he'd spent so many years in a maximum-security prison with other convicted murderers.

"Well, shit, cuz, it doesn't need to make sense to me." Tyler rubbed his chest as though it ached. "I can't even begin to imagine what you've been through. I know it doesn't mean shit, but I'm fucking sorry for what happened to you. Never believed you did it, you know? Back then, I tried to tell the cops it just wasn't possible, but the evidence…"

He met Ty's somber gaze. "Yeah." The manufactured and planted evidence that stole his fucking life.

They fell quiet for a moment, probably both lost in the horrifying events of the past. Finally, Tyler broke the silence. "So, what's your plan now? You need a place to crash or anything? My house is yours. Anything you need."

"Nah, believe it or not, I still got the house."

Curly

"No shit?" Ty asked with a laugh. "Damn, cuz, had I known, I'd have made sure it wasn't falling to pieces over the years."

Curly joined him in chuckling. "Yeah. It's a shithole, obviously, but I had a company deep clean it yesterday while I started on some yardwork. Figure in a few days I'll have it looking livable again." He'd owned the small two-bedroom house since he was thirty. It'd sat untouched for more than a decade, and the overgrowth was insane at this point. He had the money to do whatever the hell he wanted to renovate it, he could sell the thing and buy something a hundred times nicer, but he wasn't ready to make that decision. He needed to get his footing, make sure he could pull off starting a club, and determine if he genuinely wanted to stay in the area long term before making any decisions about a more permanent living situation. For now, the tiny house was more than enough for him. Hell, anything bigger than a seventy-square-foot cell still felt like a mansion these days.

"How about I come help you out this evening? I'm done here about five this afternoon. We can get a few hours of work in while the sun's not so high, then grab some dinner. I could kill someone for a burger and a beer."

As Curly was about to agree the idea sounded damn good, Tyler paled.

"Oh, fuck," he said, running a hand over his mouth. "I'm so sorry."

Curly scrunched his face. "For what?"

"For what I said. For running my fat mouth."

Again, he tried to figure out what Travis said that might have been offensive. Then it hit him.

I could kill someone for a burger.

Waving away his cousin's concern, he said, "Ty, it's okay. Seriously. If I flipped out every time someone made a dumb figure of speech, I'd lose my shit fifteen times a day."

"But you must be so angry. How could you not be? I think I'd hate the whole fucking world."

41

Curly snorted. "Oh, I'm fucking angry. Trust me." He shrugged. "But I figure I've already lost more than a decade of my life because of those bastards. I'm not willing to let them take another fucking minute from me."

That wasn't entirely true. He had his dark moments when the desire for revenge took over, but he'd been able to curb the impulse to go rogue and gun down anyone involved in his wrongful incarceration.

"Well, shit Trav, look at you getting all mature and shit."

"Had to happen sometime, I guess."

They laughed, and the years of not being around each other melted away, leaving two boys who were related by not only blood but also the best of friends.

A bell rang out, indicating the arrival of a customer. "Give me one sec," Ty said as he turned toward the guest. "Hey there, help you with something?"

Curly took a step back and watched his cousin in action.

The twenty-something who entered blushed at the attention from the two large, tattooed men. "Uh, I have an appointment to repair a flat and for an alignment."

"All righty," Tyler said. He waved the young woman to the counter. "You Erin Marx?"

"That's me." She fluttered her eyelashes and arched her back, sticking her tits out. It didn't escape Curly's notice the way Tyler's eyes slid over the woman's form. Not much had changed.

Three minutes later, Erin made her way to the waiting area in the back, and Ty was returned to chatting with Curly.

"You still ride?" Curly asked his cousin.

"Fuck yes. Every chance I get." Tyler's eyes lit with excitement only another motorcycle lover would appreciate.

Huh, maybe this would work. "Wanna run something by you."

"Okay?" Ty tilted his head.

"I want to start a club. A new MC."

Tyler stiffened. A muscle in his left cheek twitched as he probably ground his teeth to dust. What was he thinking at that moment? Were the memories really that shitty?

Stupid question. Looking back on their past, when they'd prospected with the Outlaws, Curly could confidently say, yes. The memories of the stupid shit they'd done to prove themselves to a group of disloyal assholes were fucked up.

"Christ, Trav," Tyler finally said. "Seriously? You ain't had enough of that life?"

Shaking his head, Curly lifted a hand. "Hear me out. This is different. I've spent the last half-year with a club that's nothing like the Outlaws. They're a real fucking family. Brothers who'd do anything for each other. Good damn men. Hard-working, loyal, solid earners. It was what we thought we'd be getting with the Outlaws. Their prez has endorsed my idea to open a charter here."

"They one-percenters?"

With a chuckle, Curly shrugged. "Well, they're not Boy Scouts."

Tyler scoffed. "You spent thirteen years behind bars, cuz. How can you even think—"

"They ain't about that. No guns, no drugs, no fucking robberies. They've got legit businesses like a gym, a diner, working on opening a garage. But, yeah, they also earn from loan sharking, some muscle for hire, few gambling rings."

Tyler stared him down for a long, tension-filled moment. He wanted it. Curly could feel it. They'd grown up with a strong bond but had shit-all in terms of additional family. Tyler's old man had ridden with a club a few states over. He'd blow into town once or twice a year, toss some cash at Ty's mother, and zoom back out with his club.

As an adult, Curly realized what a shit father the man had been, but damn, he and Ty had idolized the guy. He'd been a huge, dominating presence with a boisterous laugh he was quick to share. Both he and his cousin fantasized of growing up to be

Tyler's old man who'd let them drink their first beer at ten and laughed his head off when they'd both spit it out. The stories he'd shared of his club had fueled their young dreams and solidified their love of motorcycles and club life.

"It's still a risk. You could always get a job. I can offer you something here until you find something more your speed." The argument was weak at best, and Tyler knew it. He knew Curly, how he thought, what he wanted from his life. Knew he'd never be satisfied with a typical job.

"You know I can't do that shit, Ty. Spent too many years in a club and then a cell to work in an office or live a nine-to-five life." The thought of a regular routine, same thing day in day out, made him shudder. There wouldn't be steel bars, but it was another prison all the same. "Can't work under anyone either. Too many fucking trust issues." At least he was aware of his head problems. That had to count for something, right?

"Loan sharking, huh?" Tyler rubbed the back of his neck.

"For one thing. Got a few other ideas." He had Tyler on the hook. His cousin regretted not patching in with the Outlaws even if he'd have hated the life. At least he would have had some form of brotherhood.

"Where the fuck we gonna get cash to loan out? Will the other club front you?"

"I got that under control." Though Tyler was one of the two or three people Curly trusted, he had no plans to share his financial status with him. Not yet. If he agreed to help Curly with the club and pledged an oath, eventually, but not now. That kind of money changed things. "I want you for my VP."

Tyler's eyes widened, "You're shitting me."

"Dead serious. Need someone I trust. And like I said, there ain't many."

Finally, Tyler's uneasy expression gave way to a smile. "Fuck it. I'm in. Shit, cuz. I'm one hundred percent in." He held out a hand and walked toward Curly, who sucked in a sharp breath.

Curly

Until that moment, Curly hadn't realized just how important it was for him to have his cousin by his side and in his club. It was then he also realized just how much he wanted this to work. How badly he wanted to be a part of the Hell's Handlers family and bring that to his hometown. "Fuck yes," he said as he grabbed his cousin's hand and hauled him in for a quick hug and a slap on the back.

Pressure eased in his chest. It felt like the first time he'd taken a true full breath since he sat in Copper's office and proposed the idea.

Tyler pounded his shoulder with a booming laugh. The same way his father had. Curly would never forget him even though the man had been killed in a motorcycle accident almost two decades ago.

"You're ol' lady gonna be on board with this?" Curly asked of Tyler's wife as he stepped back.

With a snort, Tyler shook his head. "Fuck that. I got shot of her about two years after you went away."

Thank fuck. He'd never liked her. She was a whiny, manipulative shrew who'd run around on Tyler since day one.

"Guess we got a lotta work to do now, huh?"

"Damn straight," Curly said. "I'll catch you up on everything tonight. Sound good?"

"Hell yeah. Where you off to now?"

Curly smiled. "I'm off to get myself a best friend."

Chapter Five

Brooke hefted the first of three fifty-pound sacks of dog food from the back of her Jeep. "God," she muttered to herself as she staggered backward under the weight of the bag. "I swear these get heavier each time."

With her arms wrapped around the bag, she hoisted it higher and settled it on her hip as though it were a heavy child. At least she got some use outta those hips of hers. By the time she'd sweated her way through her large yard to the kennel, her arms ached, and the thought of going through that two more times had her groaning. If she were smart, she'd get a wagon to lug the food instead of straining, but she used this chore to justify skipping the gym.

The dogs yipped and bounced around their kennels as she ripped open the bag. A huff had her peeking over her shoulder. "Hey, Ray," she said to her German Shepherd. Most of the time, he stayed in the house while she was out, but today he'd been insistent on hanging out with the rest of the dogs. He seemed to have fallen head over paws for a little lab/boxer mix she'd rescued a few days ago. The pup had been left outside David's clinic with her leash tied to the door.

With a shake of her head, she squashed the anger threatening to rise. If she allowed herself to get pissed every time someone abandoned a dog at the vet clinic, she'd spend most of her time in a furious state. But, over the years, she'd learned to turn that anger into motivation. Now she used it to fuel her in fostering as many dogs as possible.

David guessed this pup to be somewhere around eight or nine months. From a note tucked in her collar, Brooke had learned the puppy's owner had passed, and no one in his family wanted the dog. She couldn't figure that one out to save her life. The puppy was an adorable chocolate color with two white toes on a back paw and a little strip of white fur on her head. She was also smart as hell and sweet as could be. Ray certainly seemed to think so, even if she had boundless amounts of energy.

He sat outside the pup's kennel whining as he thumped his fluffy tail. "Give me a minute," she said as she managed to dump the contents of the bag in a food storage bin. "I'll let your girlfriend out as soon as I get the rest of the food in here."

Ray whined again.

"Seriously, buddy, chill. Don't you know us girls like a little bit of chase? You can't seem too eager, or she's gonna get bored with you."

Another whine.

She laughed as she shook the food bin to even out the kibble. "All right, all right. Geez, can't imagine what you'd be like if you actually had your balls."

"I imagine he'd be a whole lot happier."

Brooke yelped and spun around to find a man standing in the open door with a bag of dog food under each arm as though they weighed five pounds instead of fifty. Ray sat at his feet whining, not in distress or because an intruder threatened her space, but because the man didn't have a free hand to pet him.

"Us guys tend to appreciate our balls."

"Uh, what?" Her face heated to molten hot. She could do nothing but stare at the round bulge of the man's tanned biceps as he stood just ten feet away. A vein ran down the left one while the right had a tattoo ringing it. Some sort of saying she couldn't make out from her distance.

"Where do you want these?"

"Huh?" She blinked. Had he asked something?

"You want this dog food over by you? I can just drop them here if you want."

Her gaze finally went to his face—more specifically his mouth, and she sucked in a breath. Those lips. Holy crap, those lips were smooth and surrounded by a light layer of dark gray, near black stubble. Then there were his eyes, a deep mesmerizing blue. Atop his head was a mop of curly hair.

Oh, my God, that hair. People would kill for that kind of thick, natural curl.

She had a flash of sinking her fingers through those coils and yanking his head from one of her breasts to the other. He'd open his mouth wide and suck—

He cleared his throat.

The tips of her ears burned. "Oh, God. I'm sorry. Yes. Please set them over here." She stepped to the side. Too bad she couldn't become invisible. Then she could hide from the man who'd turned her stupid, and he wouldn't have to see the humiliation turn her face into a tomato.

Also, she could keep staring and drooling over the sexiest man she'd seen in years, if ever, without his knowledge.

Geez. She ran a hand over her hair, wincing as she discovered much of it had fallen free of the messy bun she'd shoved it in earlier. Here she was talking to a man who was hot enough to melt iron, and she was a hot, sweaty mess.

Oh, my God. What the hell was wrong with her this morning? In the five years since her divorce, she'd never looked at a man with more than a stray thought of, *huh, not bad*. Her libido picked a helluva time to wake up and join the party.

The man's perfect lips quirked as he strode toward her, still carrying those bags as though they were full of feathers. "Here?"

he asked when he was so close, she had to step back to avoid bumping him.

"Yeah, that's perfect."

Don't smell him. Don't smell him.

She inhaled as he bent down to release one of the bags.

Her eyes nearly rolled back in her head as his clean, fresh, outdoorsy mixed with a bit of leather scent hit her.

"Are you Brooke?" he asked in a rough voice after setting the sacks down next to the food bin.

She'd have slapped herself to get with the program if it wouldn't have made her look even stupider. Clearing her throat, she nodded. "I am yes. Did we have an appointment?" Trying to remember what she'd written in her planner would be pointless, seeing how her brain had left the building.

"Nah, we didn't. Sorry to show up unannounced. I stopped by the pet store in town yesterday, and someone mentioned you were the person to see about getting a dog."

Ray trotted over then plopped his fuzzy rump right down at the stranger's feet. The traitor. So much for being a fearsome guard dog.

The man crouched down, stroking his large hand over her dog's head. "Well, aren't you a handsome boy," he crooned to Ray, and Brooke nearly melted in a puddle as that raspy voice seduced her dog. Ray's tongue lolled out, and he rolled to his back, presenting his belly like the attention whore he was.

In Ray's defense, there probably wasn't a creature out there, male or female immune to this man.

"I've got a few fosters right now who are ready to adopt and lots of connections with shelters in the area if I don't have what you're looking for."

He glanced up at her from his low squat next to Ray. "Pretty sure you have everything I'm looking for."

If she didn't know, better, she'd have sworn he meant *her* and not a dog.

But that would be insane. She was a forty-one-year-old divorced woman who hadn't been touched by anything other than silicone and her own fingers in over five years. She needed a push-up bra to keep her full Cs anywhere near where they used to live, and her ass had always been a bit plumper than she'd liked. It'd been at least a good seven months since she'd worn a touch of make-up, and her idea of fancy was jeans that didn't have holes in them and a premium cotton T-shirt.

Men didn't flirt with her. And not just because she didn't put herself in many situations where single men would have the opportunity to pick her up.

This guy probably had to beat off perky twenty-somethings with daddy issues everywhere he went. He could have his choice of women without putting in an ounce of effort—no way in hell she'd do it for him.

"Uh, so what kind of dog are you interested in?"

Rising to his full height of...maybe six-two, he shrugged. "Not sure. Just kind of hoping I'll know it when I meet 'em. Just know I'm not looking for something too small."

It'd been a long time since a man had this effect on her, and she wasn't sure she liked it. Actually, that was the problem. She didn't like that she *did* like it. He towered over her five and a half feet, making her feel small and delicate, vulnerable even.

Brooke didn't do vulnerable. Not anymore.

Squaring her shoulders, she fought off old feelings of inferiority. This was her turf, her home. She was the expert here. This man hadn't done anything to humble her. He couldn't help his height and its effect on her. Damn her ex-husband and his mind games.

"Well, let me let the crew out, and you can meet them and watch them running around playing. You can see if any of them steal your heart."

"Sounds good," he said as he held out a hand. "I'm Curly."

Yes, you are.

"Brooke," she said. "But I guess you already know that." She placed her hand against his, and as the callused fingers closed around her palm, she fought to repress the shiver that tried to run up her spine. Those hands were so...masculine. So strong and rough. If she hadn't guessed it before, she'd know now that he was not a man who lived his life behind a desk. He must do something outdoors if his tanned, gritty hands were any indication.

She liked that. She'd never cared for men who had office jobs or inactive lifestyles.

Okay, that was a lie. She'd been very attracted to one once, but that had certainly blown up in her face.

As she pulled her hand from his, she frowned. Shit, given that she worked outside training dogs all day, her hands were probably as coarse as his. What man wanted a woman with beat-up hands?

Note to self: buy hand cream.

Not that she planned on getting with this or any man in the near future. Still, it wouldn't kill her to take a little better care of her skin.

"Nice to meet you, Brooke. This town speaks highly of you."

"Are you new here?" she asked as she opened the first kennel and let the little eight-pound terrier out. He yipped and yapped a circle around Curly's feet before jetting outside.

"Born and raised," he said as he mimicked her actions and opened a kennel, releasing a senior golden retriever. "But I've been away for over a decade. Just moved back a few days ago."

What the hell? Did he think she couldn't handle the kennels herself? For fuck's sake, she'd been managing it on her own for years. "I've got it," she snapped as he reached to open another door. Quick as lightening, she grabbed for the latch herself, opening it before he had a chance to.

Frowning, he took a step back, stuffing his hands in his pockets. The move made him look smaller and less powerful. "Sorry, didn't mean to step on your toes. Just trying to make myself useful. Didn't want to be rude and stand around while you did all the work."

Brooke's cheeks burned. Maybe she'd read that wrong. She wasn't used to having a man around. "Well, um, welcome back. Bet a lot has changed since you moved away."

"You have no idea," he muttered half under his breath.

By now, she had all the dogs out of their kennels. They were surrounded by wagging tails and lapping tongues. Brooke laughed and tried to usher them out into the yard. "Come on, gang. Let's let the man breathe," she said as she herded them outside. It was impossible for her to feel anything but joy when in the presence of happy dogs. Knowing the safety, happiness, and comfort she provided was the only kind treatment some of these dogs had ever received provided her with a tremendous sense of pride.

"You coming?" she asked over her shoulder as she realized the large man in the sexy jeans was no longer directly behind her. When she turned to look for him, her stomach flipped.

He sat cross-legged on the floor with a huge grin on his face while the boxer/lab mix puppy made him her personal jungle gym. Was there anything hotter than a big gruff man being sweet to an adorable dog?

No. The answer to that was a clear no.

"Looks like you may have found the one," she said as she leaned against the door frame.

Curly laughed. "Pretty sure she found me." He gently shoved the puppy away, and she came bounding right back, so he did it again. And a game was born.

Brooke couldn't keep the smile off her face. "I was told her name is Harley, you know, after the motorcycles."

Curly's expression lit. "No shit?" He rubbed under the puppy's chin and as she flopped on her back into his lap. "If you'd seen what I rode in on, you'd know that's pretty damn perfect."

"You ride a motorcycle?" Good Lord that would be a sight.

Curly

"Yep."

"Um, well, the vet thinks she's about nine months. Her owner died suddenly, and no one wanted her. We're told she's half chocolate lab and half boxer. Gonna have a lot of energy so make sure you're up for that if you decide to adopt her."

"I'm not looking for a lazy lap dog. I want one I can take running with me and who will like to play." His big hands rubbed the puppy's belly with vigorous strokes.

"Harley will be that dog."

Ray hovered nearby like a protective big brother sizing up his kid sister's new boyfriend.

Curly snorted. "Your boy seems to have a thing for her, huh?"

"Oh, uh, yeah. You might have to bring her around every once in a while." Her face heated. "I mean because I'm pretty sure Ray's sweet on her. I'm always available...."

Curly raised an eyebrow as a teasing smirk crossed his face. "I think that can be arranged."

"I mean available for the dogs to play." Oh, my God, did it sound like she wanted him to come see her? Did he think she was hitting on him? Always available? Ugh, she might as well have told the man she was single and lifeless. Clearly, she needed to get out and socialize with other humans more.

How embarrassing. The guy would probably have a good laugh with his twenty-five-year-old girlfriend after he got home. His girlfriend who could bend in ways Brooke could only dream of. And who didn't have an ounce of cellulite or a wrinkle in sight. And who didn't need to disguise gray hairs at the salon.

Ugh. Seriously? Five years and nothing. Not a flicker of interest in anyone. Now a gorgeous man walks into her yard, and her brain had utterly rebelled.

Time to get control over herself. Chances were, the moment he took Harley home, she'd never see him again. And that would be for the best.

"Well, if you're serious about this, I can get you the adoption paperwork. I do a two-day hold for a background check, and

53

when that clears, I'll come see where she'll be living. If that's good, she's yours."

He frowned. "A background check?"

"Yeah, I'm a little over the top when it comes to the safety of the dogs I foster." The way he asked the question had the back of her neck itching. "Is that gonna be a problem?"

Her inquiry was met with a heavy sigh. "Guess we'll find out."

Her forehead scrunched. What the hell? She'd be running that background check as soon as possible. "I'll be right back." She darted into the house with a million questions running through her brain. First and foremost was whether she was safe to be alone in her yard with Curly. Ray sure seemed to like him, and at least she had him as her backup should things go south.

After grabbing the paperwork, she made her way back outside. Harley was frolicking with the rest of the dogs while Curly stood gazing into the quarantine kennel. "Who's this guy?" he asked as she approached.

How the hell did he know she was behind him? She hadn't made a sound.

Brooke kept some space between them. "Not sure what his name is. A trucker found him bleeding on the side of the road last night. The vet is a friend and brought him to me until he can be moved to a proper pit rescue organization."

"A friend?" he asked in a way that sounded more interested than he should be.

"Yes. Anyway, we've found a few injured dogs lately. Stereotypical fighting breeds. I'm pretty sure someone is running an illegal fighting ring around here."

"Bastards," Curly said with venom in his voice. He pierced her with an icy glare. "You ever find out who it is, feel free to let me know. Trash like that needs to be taken out."

A chill ran down her spine at the threat in his tone, even while his reaction set her at ease in a strange way. Somehow, she knew that despite whatever she'd find in his background check, this man would never harm his pet. "Here's the paperwork. If you don't want to fill it out now, you can email it to me later."

"I'm good to do it now if you have the time." His fingertips brushed hers as he took the pen and papers from her. Sparks shot off under her skin.

Maybe it was time for her to try out one of those online dating sites, even if the thought of it made her want to hide under her bed.

"Feel free to have a seat at the table near the pool." She pointed to the lanai enclosing her pool and outdoor furniture.

"Thanks."

A horn honked from her driveway, indicating the arrival of David and hopefully Nancy. "I'll give you a few minutes."

He winked, and she nearly giggled like a schoolgirl. Good Lord, she needed to get it together. Must be the damn heat because the last thing she needed or wanted in her life was a man. Some mistakes were learned and learned well the first time around.

As he sauntered off toward her patio, Brooke bit her lower lip. The man filled out a pair of jeans like no one she'd ever seen. Maybe he knew a clothing designer who'd literally made the things for him, they fit that damn well.

Ugh, she was losing her mind.

Nancy waved as she walked into the yard. Her blond hair hung halfway down her back in gorgeous, silky waves despite the humidity. Lucky wench.

Hopefully, her friend could talk some sense into her.

"Hey, girl." Speak of the devil. "Um, who the hell is that fine specimen, and what is he doing in your yard?" Nancy said under her breath as she walked up to Brooke

"What was that?" David asked when he reached them a half-second later.

"Nothing, honey." She flashed her husband a sweet and innocent smile. "Just telling Brooke how hot you look today." She raised a blond eyebrow as Brooke snorted out a laugh.

David rolled his eyes. "Nice try, babe." He narrowed his eyes Curly's way. "Who's that at the table?"

Great, now they were all staring at the guy like some kind of creepy panel of judges. "He's interested in adopting Harley."

"He could adopt me if he wanted," Nancy murmured as Curly rose and began to head their way, papers in hand.

"Cute, Nance," David said with another roll of his eyes. He was more than used to his wife's lack of filter.

Curly kept his penetrating gaze on Brooke. That stare did funny things to her insides. Made them all quivery. She swallowed and refused to let anyone see on the outside how affected she was inside.

"Hmmm," Nancy said as she tapped her coral-painted lip. "He is yummy."

"Is he?" Brooke's face felt like it was on fire. Damn Florida sun.

"Oh please," Nancy whispered. "If you don't think that man is sex on legs, we're taking you to the doctor tomorrow. Look, even David thinks he's fine as fuck."

With a laugh, David said, "She's got a point, Brooke."

"Shut up, you two," she whispered as harshly as she could. Curly was going to hear and think they were insane.

"All done," he said when he reached her. "I'll be waiting for your call."

Was it her imagination, or was his voice even more gravelly than before? "Uh, great. Curly, this is David," she said, pointing to her friend. "He's the vet who checked Harley over."

"Hey, man," Curly said, extending a hand.

Nancy reached him first, palm against Curly's. "And I am Nancy, his wife. Ohhh, that's a strong grip. Bet you can do some magic with those hands, huh?"

"Jesus," David muttered under his breath while Brooke snorted out a laugh.

"Babe, leave the man alone. He came for a normal dog, not one in heat."

Curly

"Hey!" Nancy smacked her husband's stomach.

"Sorry about them," Brooke said when Curly's eyes widened. Most men didn't know how to take Nancy when they first met her. She came on strong and had no problem blatantly flirting with someone right in her husband's view. Brooke swore it was some kind of foreplay for the two of them, but she didn't need to know anything more about that. "I'll call as soon as I hear back," she said to Curly as she lifted the papers. "In the meantime, no one else will be able to adopt her, so there are no worries there."

He nodded. "Thanks."

Brooke couldn't help but notice David's eyes narrow as he took in Curly.

After a quick goodbye and some slobbery attention from Nancy and Ray, Curly strode toward his bike. Brooke forced herself to keep her gaze on his broad shoulders but happened to find them nearly as enticing as his ass, so the effort was a waste.

"Holy shit," Nancy said as Curly threw a leg over his bike. "I knew I'd seen him somewhere. Is that—?"

"Yup," David said with a curt nod. "Pretty sure it is."

Brooke frowned. "Who?"

"I forget his real name," Nancy said, "but he goes by the handle Curly. He used to be the president of the True Outlaws Motorcycle Club. He got arrested, oh what was it? More than ten years ago, I think."

David nodded his agreement though his gaze remained on Curly.

"Arrested? What for?"

"Murdering a twelve-year-old girl."

Brooke's blood ran cold. "Shit," she whispered. "I read about that. Wasn't he just released after like thirteen years in prison? Turned out the cops fucked up the investigation and arrested the wrong man. He never committed the murder."

"Yes," Nancy answered. "That's him. That man must have a lot of bitterness hiding behind those sexy eyes."

"Watch yourself around that one, Brooke," David said, serious as death. "He may not have killed that girl, but the True Outlaws were about as bad as it comes. He might be innocent of that crime, but he's not innocent of much else. You don't want a guy like that want hanging around."

"Don't worry. He won't be hanging around. All he wants is a dog."

Her gaze remained glued to Curly's back as he rode further away. Thirteen years behind bars for a crime he didn't commit. How did he make it through each day without resentment consuming him? The knowledge that the system could fail someone so completely had her stomach roiling.

Then again, she knew firsthand how easy it was for the system to crash and burn. And she understood somewhat what it meant to live in prison. Hers was constructed of gold and silver instead of iron, and her bars had been metaphorical, but they'd held her captive nonetheless.

It'd be best if she put Curly out of her mind. She had enough of her own issues to deal with. Adding worry for a damaged biker to the pile would be a mistake. Tomorrow she planned to pay a visit to the farm she suspected of being used for dog fighting. She'd need her head in the game, not in the clouds, if she wanted to scope out the farm without being caught.

Man troubles were the last thing she needed, now or ever.

Chapter Six

Curly glanced around the vast open space spread wide before him. Damn, Prick owned a lot of land. Of course, the asshole hadn't done a damn thing to take care of his property and probably never would, but with a bit of effort, this place could be gorgeous. Plenty of space for a dog to run and play. Hell, he could get twenty dogs if he had this much land.

Someone like Brooke would love all this land for her squad of dogs.

Thoughts of the pretty dog trainer had him smiling. He liked a woman with spunk. Had this been fourteen years ago, before his arrest and his ol' lady'd shattered his trust in relationships, he'd have been all over a woman like her. Though back then, he tended to go for the stereotypical patch bunnies. Maybe Brooke only caught his eye because of those fourteen years of challenge and change.

Not that any of it mattered. She was a supplier for a pet. Nothing more.

He had enough on his plate without a woman, that was for damn sure. For the past thirteen years, Curly had imagined this moment countless times. Not a day went by where he hadn't dreamed about confronting Prick over the role he played in destroying Curly's life. In the beginning, he'd been out for blood, and nothing short of Prick's death would have satisfied him. As the years behind bars crawled by, the fantasies grew less violent, but never once did they end in forgiveness or renewed friendship.

From what he'd pieced together, Prick had been one of the few Outlaws who still lived in Florida and stayed out of prison after Curly's trial. Seemed as though he'd been granted immunity for his crimes by aiding the police in fucking Curly over. The only positive to come from the entire clusterfuck was that Prick's evil plan backfired. He'd hoped to slide into the Outlaw's president's chair and lord over the club, but after Curly's conviction, the club crashed and burned in a major way. Those who escaped arrest fled town to avoid future incarceration, and the ones who spent time in jail hadn't returned post-release. Even Prick had left town for a while, but the fucker had returned almost a decade ago.

Nicknamed for his thorny personality, Prick now ran with a small crew of bikers who didn't have the numbers to call themselves a club. Just a rag-tag group of ex-cons and assholes who had nowhere else to land. It'd been simple enough to sweet talk a county clerk into giving up Prick's address. She had no idea his involvement in Curly's arrest. They'd all gone to high school together, and all the woman remembered was a close friendship between the two back in the day. Curly remembered her having quite the crush on any man in leather, which seemed to stick all these years later. She'd been more than thrilled to help reunite to club brothers.

So there he was, climbing off his bike at a farm that looked like no one inhabited it for over a hundred years. He'd thought his abandoned house had been in bad shape, but a pricy cleaning company and a few days of grueling yard work had brought it back to life. Razing this farm might be the only way to make this property worth something. Off to his left, the large, faded barn had a gaping hole in the roof as well as three smashed-out windows. The wood boards were warped and rotted from lack

Curly

of care. A silo could be seen in the distance, crooked and neglected. Straight ahead, the large main house seemed to be in slightly better condition, but even that needed a serious pressure washing and few coats of paint at the very least. What once had been a sprawling white colonial-style home was now a dingy gray with a sloped second-story porch and cardboard over two of the front windows. Who knew what the inside looked like, and if the foundation would hold up much longer.

"Prick's done well for himself," he muttered with a snort as he strode toward the house.

Though he'd dreamed of this moment, the second he raised his fist to knock on the door, all words fled. He'd long gotten over the impulse to pound Prick to a bloody pulp as soon as they came in contact. The main reason for this visit was to let the fucker know he was back and he wasn't going anywhere. Lithia would become Hell's Handler's territory. Prick would have no choice but to respect that no matter how much he fucking hated it. Curly was older, wiser, more intelligent, and wouldn't fall prey to a devious plan this time around.

Squaring his shoulders, he pounded on the door. Flecks of faded blue paint flittered to the ground along with a thick cloud of dust. Seconds ticked by without anyone opening the door. Curly couldn't hear any movement or activity inside either. He sighed. Guess it would have been too easy to have Prick open the door and bow down to Curly's presence.

As he began to head back to his bike, a faint yelp had his spine snapping straight. He strained his ears and held his breath. This time the bark of an unhappy dog caught his attention. The sound came from behind the barn. Then there was another yelp, definitely human, definitely female. As the barking began in earnest this time, Curly took off in jog toward the barn.

The barking grew rowdier with each step until a voice he'd recognize anywhere shouted, "Shut the fuck up!" A chain rattled, followed by a dog's whimper.

Fucking Prick seemed to be as big a piece of shit as ever.

"Hey!" yelled a female voice. "Stop that!"

Curly's eyes narrowed. She sounded familiar. He pressed himself against the short side of the barn and crept toward the edge. Hopefully, the entire barn wouldn't crumble to the ground.

"If you kick that dog again—"

"You'll what? What the fuck're you gonna do about it, bitch?"

"B-back up." The words sounded like they came through clenched teeth. Forceful despite the slight tremor of fear.

Time for Curly to step in. He rounded the corner of the barn to find Prick crowding a woman much smaller than him against the side of the barn. All he could see were two bare legs and beat-up Converse. Prick's wide body blocked the rest of her. At the other end of the barn, a large tan and white pitbull tied to a metal post with a thick metal chain sat quiet and quivering.

"The fuck you doing on my property? You come here for me? For this?" One of Prick's hands disappeared between his legs.

Fucking charmer.

Curly widened his stance but kept his posture relaxed. Ready for whatever might come, but not showing aggression. Then he cleared his throat.

Prick whipped around then froze. His bloodshot eyes flared wide. "Holy fuck," he whispered. As though staring at a ghost instead of his old president, his face went deathly pale. Then again, when he'd betrayed that president and expected them to spend the rest of their life in a cage, having him pop up at your house fourteen years later had to be shocking.

Curly couldn't keep the satisfied smile off his face. Felt damn good to have the upper hand back. "Hey, *brother*," he said, mockery dripping from the word.

The woman shoved Prick with her shoulder. "Get the hell away from me," she muttered as she freed herself then came to a standstill as well. "Curly."

Brooke.

No wonder the voice rang familiar. He should have known she'd be the feisty type that would confront a psycho on her own. The reminder of the position he'd found her in had him scowling. "Get behind me, Brooke."

"I'm not done with him yet," she growled as she turned to face Prick as though she'd stood a chance of intimidating the man.

Curly wrapped a hand around her arm and tugged her out of Prick's reach. If the asshole was as unpredictable and volatile as he used to be, she needed to be out of swinging distance.

"Hey!" she grumbled.

"You can say your piece." Curly murmured once she was at his side. "Just don't trust that motherfucker for shit." Her silky skin teased his fingertips, practically begging them to stroke and explore.

She studied him with uncertainty in her brown-eyed gaze as though deciding whether to argue her independence and capability. After a brief moment, she nodded.

He gave his attention back to Prick. The years hadn't been kind to the once muscular biker. The six-pack he'd taken pride in had been replaced by a jiggling gut that hung over his jeans and stretched his T-shirt. If Curly wasn't mistaken, Prick had a yellowish hue to his skin and not as many teeth as he'd once had. Petty as it was, Curly felt damn good about keeping his own body in tip-top shape over the past decade. Then again, if he hadn't gone to prison where working out was one of the only enjoyable activities, he might have turned out as slovenly as Prick.

"I heard you bought this shit hole. Figured I'd swing by and let you know I'm back in town. For good."

"Yeah, um, I heard…" Prick pulled his ball cap off and ran a hand through his thinning blond hair before replacing the hat. "I heard you were released. That the whole case was bullshit. That's uh, great, brother. We should grab a beer. Catch up."

So that's how he was gonna play it. Pretend he hadn't broken an oath by plunging a knife in his president's back and destroying the entire MC. Curly tilted his head. "You're brave."

"What do you mean?" Prick fidgeted as though unable to stand still under the scrutiny of a man he'd fucked over.

"You're brave to risk having a drink with me. To risk me smashing my bottle against the bar and slitting your throat with a shard of glass."

Brooke sucked in a breath while Prick's throat worked up and down in a hard swallow.

He'd probably shocked the hell outta her and killed any chance of adopting a dog off her, but Curly couldn't help himself. He'd hungered for the opportunity to witness this exact fear in Prick. He might not want to return to the gritty club life he'd lived in during his time with the Outlaws, but he wasn't soft. And he wasn't stupid. Never would be. Life had made sure of that.

A betrayal like Prick's wasn't something he could overlook.

Prick knew it too. He'd be sleeping with one eye open for the foreseeable future. And that fact was almost as pleasurable as a good fuck.

For one hot second, he imagined a naked Brooke spread out on his bed with that mane of brown hair tousled and a sated look in her eyes.

All right, this was a distant second to a good fuck, but damn fun nonetheless.

Running a hand over the scar on his throat, Curly smirked at Prick. "Or maybe I'll show up one night while you're sleeping with a toothbrush I sharpened against my bed and use that to slice you up. Just to even the score a bit."

From the corner of his eye, he caught Brooke's mouth hinge open. No doubt she'd noticed his scar and wondered about it but would never have guessed its cause in a million years.

He could feel her stunned gaze on him, heating his skin as he watched Prick's reaction.

"Shit," the other man said. "That how you got, uh…" He motioned with his finger, drawing a line across his own throat.

"It is. About a month in. I was in a pretty shitty head space when they first locked me up, as you can imagine. Mouthed off to the wrong person."

Prick cleared his throat and scratched his rounded stomach. "Yeah, uh, I can imagine. Being innocent and all."

Tension filled the space between them as quiet ensured. Brooke seemed to sense it and react. She stiffened as though on high alert. The feel of her flesh against his palm kept him grounded. If she wasn't standing beside him with her slightly citrus scent wafting his way, he was likely to wrap his hands around Prick's neck and rejoice as the man turned various shades of purple.

Curly had reached his limit of making nice. "How about we cut the bullshit, huh?"

"Wha—"

He released Brooke and stepped toward Prick. "I'm chartering a new club here."

Prick's eyes lit as though he thought he had a chance in hell of patching in.

"This is now Hell's Handler's territory. You aren't welcome in it, and neither is the shitty little group of boys you ride with. So fair warning, in case you plan on wearing colors of any kind."

Look at that. He didn't even need to strangle the guy to see his face turn a deep shade of purple.

"Prez—"

Curly lifted a hand. "I ain't your fucking prez anymore." Walking backward, he stopped beside Brooke. "You made that bed, and now that I'm back, you gotta lie in it."

Prick might be a motherfucker, but he was smart enough to keep his mouth shut at that moment. Later, he'd get his merry band of dickwads together and bitch and moan to them.

"Now," Curly continued. "I believe the lady had something to say to you."

Her gaze shifted to the pitbull sitting off to the side, quietly watching the exchange, not like an obedient man's best friend but like a mistreated animal afraid of its owner's wrath.

She straightened, which had the effect of lifting her tits. Damn, the woman had a nice rack. And strong, shapely legs. And an ass he'd love to grab hold of. Shit, with those thighs wrapped around his hips and his hands full of that ass, a man could die happy and satisfied.

Fuck, another ten seconds of those thoughts, and he'd pop a boner Prick would notice. He'd gotten laid a few times right after he left prison, but it'd been like scratching an itch and only mildly rewarding. Might be time to remedy that situation and find himself a good fuck he could repeat a few times. Brooke's attitude screamed *hands off,* though, even if he'd seen a flicker of interest in her gaze.

"There have been three injured dogs found on the outskirts of this property in the past six weeks," she said in a firm voice.

Half of Prick's mouth quirked up in a smug as fuck grin. "Yeah?"

"Yes," she said, curling her small hands into fists at her sides. "Two died, and one lost a leg."

"The fuck that gotta do with me?" Prick spat a brownish glob on the ground between them all.

"Charming," Brooke muttered, making Curly cover a laugh with a grunt.

The woman had sass coming out her ears.

"If I find out you're running a dog fighting ring—"

Prick laughed, making his gut jiggle. "You'll what? Snoop around my property again? Pretty sure you don't want to do that a second time. Next time you might not have someone around to save you."

She stepped forward, bold as could be. "Did you just threaten me?"

"Brooke," Curly began as he reached for her arm again.

This time she jerked away before he could reach her. "The police have been made aware of my suspicions. It won't be long before they're knocking on your door."

"Oooh," Prick said with a mock shudder. Then he laughed, making Brooke seethe. "Ain't never been much of one to give a shit what the cops thought. Always been on their good side. Just ask your friend." He jerked his chin in Curly's direction. Then he turned and strode to the dog and unhooked the chain. After giving it an unnecessarily aggressive yank that had the dog whimpering, he started to walk away.

"Oh, hell no," Brooke shouted as she lunged forward.

"Whoa!" Curly caught her around her waist and lifted her off her feet.

She fought against his hold, shouting at Prick and threatening to return to take his dog.

"Shit, woman, retract those claws."

"He's an asshole who doesn't deserve to own an animal."

"I get it," he whispered against her ear. "I really do. But you can't attack him. You'll be the one behind bars, and who will take care of your pups?"

Even if he hadn't had a personal beef with Prick, he wanted to strangle the fucker. Men who abused and preyed on helpless creatures made him sick. Even in a maximum-security prison among the worst of the offenders, there'd been a code. Those who'd victimized the weak didn't receive any mercy.

With a defeated sigh, Brooke sagged against him. Her lush ass brushed his dick, which had no choice but to perk up. It was unavoidable.

Just as he was about to release her before she discovered what was poking her, Prick turned around. "Hey, Curly," he shouted, now far enough away to need to raise his voice. "You need help getting a leash on your bitch, you know where to find me."

"What did he just call me?" She thrashed against his hold once again. He got a face full of sweet-smelling hair, which did nothing to dissuade his interested dick.

"Settle down, woman!" he said to avoid a groan as her ass rubbed against him again.

That was the wrong thing to say.

"Don't you woman me," she barked as she tried to pry his arm from around her waist.

Thankfully, he had a good eight inches and dozens of pounds of muscle on her. But, fuck, her nails were sharp.

"That guy's an asshole. An asshole!" she shouted at Prick, waving her arms as though she could propel them forward.

"And we're done here." Curly gritted his teeth as he hauled the thrashing woman around the side of the barn. Every jerky movement she made bounced her ass against his cock. Christ, he wanted to press her against the barn and grind himself all over her until she eased the ache in his balls. Then he wanted to bend her over and spank her ass red for such a stupid move as showing up here alone and unprotected.

Instead, he set her on her feet and crowded her against the barn, sure to keep a good few inches between his needy cock and her wriggling body. Then, he boxed her in by slapping his palms on both sides of her head.

Thankfully, the barn remained standing.

Brooke jumped as his palms smacked the barn, then closed her eyes and breathed hard. Her chest rose and fell giving him a tiny peek of cleavage from the V of her T-shirt every time she inhaled. Most of her hair had come loose from the ponytail, and a few strands clung to her lower lip.

She didn't seem to notice.

While he admired her passion, knowing exactly what Prick could and would have done had he not shown up had Curly seething.

"Do you have any idea how fucking stupid it is to be slinking around this place by yourself?" he growled down at her. "Do you have any fucking clue what he would have done to you if I hadn't come by?"

Curly

"I'm sorry," she whispered, slightly breathless as she shook her head. "I know it was stupid, but I'm about ninety percent certain he's running a dog fighting ring out of this barn."

Jesus Christ that made it even worse.

"So you decided to play amateur cop and investigate that shit yourself?"

Eyes still closed, she blew out a beath.

"Did you know Prick once did time for beating a man who cut him off on the highway? The guy spent three weeks in a coma. Did you know an ol' lady he had years ago kicked his ass to the curb after he broke her arm? For the second time."

Brooke paled.

"Give me one good reason why I shouldn't drive you home and tie you to your bed?"

Her eyes opened, wide and searching as she fought to steady her breath. As she stared at him, he swore he saw a flicker of interest in her gaze.

Shit. He'd meant so she wouldn't get into more trouble, but fuck if it didn't sound sexy as hell. Did she think so too? Was that why her breath hitched, and her nostrils flared. Did she like the idea of being bound and at his mercy? To do with as he pleased. All that sexy skin his for the taking.

He almost groaned out loud.

At the very least, he needed to hit a bar and find someone to suck him off before he did something idiotic like fuck this little canine vigilante. Brooke was a good woman, and good women steered clear of men like him.

"Because the idea of him hurting dogs makes you as sick as it makes me."

"What?" he growled as her words dragged him from his dirty fantasies.

"You shouldn't tie me up in my house because the idea of Prick running a dog fighting ring makes you as sick as it makes me," she said as the courageous woman poked him in the chest.

Well, shit, she had him there. She could add mind reader to her list of skills because there was no way he'd tolerate Prick abusing animals on top of all his other sins.

Chapter Seven

Tie her to the bed?

Tie her to the bed!

Clearly, the man hadn't meant anything sexual. A man like him wouldn't go for someone like her who lived in jeans and tanks and couldn't flirt if her life depended on it. He was trying to demonstrate that he could remove her from this situation and keep her from returning, but her sex-starved mind went straight to the naughty.

She'd never tried the tying up thing before. She'd met her ex-husband her first year of college, and he'd been the only man she'd ever slept with. Sex with him had been vanilla at best. Was there something blander than vanilla? Bran, maybe?

Yeah, sex with her husband had been bran. No sparks, no heat, no flavor. Even in the early days, she often felt like nothing more than a vessel he used to get off in. Not once had sex been about her pleasure or even *their* pleasure. Shared intimacy hadn't existed in their relationship. The second Evan came, he'd rolled off and passed out no matter where she'd been or what she'd needed. Of course, he'd been getting serviced on the side, so what the fuck did he care if it wasn't great between them? But she'd been left wondering if that's just how sex would be for her or if there was something…hotter.

Her ex had done his part and then some to destroy her self-confidence both in and out of bed, so she'd never had any rebound sex or wild fling post-divorce. As the years passed, her confidence dwindled further with continued inexperience. Now, at forty-one, she was practically re-virginized, self-conscious about her body, and still had only ever had bran sex.

No wonder the thought of this rugged, slightly dangerous man tying her up and doing things to her had her long-neglected body going haywire and acting so out of character.

And the things he'd do would be dirty. Hell, the man probably skipped dirty and went straight to filthy. The kind of things she read about alone at night.

"You're right," he said as his shoulders relaxed.

Brooke blinked. "Huh?" Oh, God, how embarrassing. Caught practically drooling over the man.

Again.

His stubbled face hovered just inches above hers. "It does make me sick. Prick is the lowest kind of shit, so it doesn't surprise me he'd abuse animals, but I do fucking hate it."

Her shoulders sagged. "The cops don't seem to care. David, my vet friend, filed a report after he received each dog. He also told them our suspicions about this place. So far, they don't seem too concerned." Disgust filled her. If a dog had attacked a child, the cops would be on it in a second. Why couldn't they extend the same courtesy to the injured animals?

"You can file a thousand reports. Cops around here won't do shit."

Her heart sank. "You think?"

Curly nodded. "Prick's got an in with the local police. Least he did back when I knew him better."

"You were friends?" she asked, trying to envision the two of them hanging out but couldn't see it.

He must have heard the disbelief in her voice. His gaze darkened. "We ran in the same circle."

Curly

The motorcycle club. After David and Nancy left yesterday, the urge to Google Curly had been nearly impossible to resist, but she'd managed. Any moment now, a thorough background check would land in her inbox, and she'd have accurate information on the man. Not inflated, overblown, or downright falsified reports from the Internet. If anyone knew how events could be twisted, embellished, or lied about then spread through social circles, it was her.

Curly lifted a hand from the wall, and the next thing she knew, his finger was on her face. The coarse pad stroked her cheek, near the corner of her mouth, eliciting a full-body shiver. "W-what are you doing?" she asked, unable to keep the breathlessness out of the question.

"You had hair stuck to your lip. Just getting it for you."

"Oh". She touched the spot on her face, still tingling from his touch. "Thanks." Time to get this back on track before she grabbed him by that sexy hair and begged him to teach her how sex should be. "So, uh, going to the cops is a waste of time?"

Curly pushed off the wall with a huff that sounded like pure frustration and gave her his back. After staring across the field, he faced her again. "You're not going to let this go, are you?"

Shaking her head, she remained against the barn. "I can't." Her passion for rescuing animals ran deep. Once, her therapist had suggested she took in abandoned and abused animals as a projection of her traumatic feelings of rejection and neglect. No one had rescued her. No one had helped her escape her own hell. She'd done it on her own and now had a compulsive desire to help creatures less capable than her. That had been the last session with that therapist. Not because their accusation had been wildly out of line, but because they'd hit the nail a little too close to the head, and she hadn't been mentally prepared to deal with the truth then.

"How long before you do something stupid like this again?"

Despite his serious question and the hard set of his face, Brooke couldn't help but chuckle. "Honestly? Not long. I'll need to figure out my next move, but I'm not walking away from this until I'm certain I'm wrong about the dog fighting or until I shut it down."

She and Curly knew nothing about each other beyond a similar love of dogs, but for her, it was more than that. She'd rescue every dog in her power and make sure men like Prick paid for their crimes by whatever means necessary. No matter what it said about her psyche.

Curly studied her for so long she squirmed against the wall. That gaze of his was too intense. As though he could see beneath her skin to the heart and soul powering her actions.

"Look," she said as she reached up to adjust what remained of her ponytail. "Thank you for the save today." She'd never admit it, but for a few moments, she'd been closer to scared than concerned when Prick had her cornered. He'd happened upon her while she'd been peeking into the barn. Just dumb bad luck.

Years ago, she'd vowed no man would ever physically intimidate her again, and with the help of self-defense classes and the pepper spray she kept in her purse, she'd kept that promise. But today, she'd left her purse in the car, and it had been a while since she'd practiced her martial arts skills, so when confronted by a large, angry man, she'd suffered a flash of paralyzing panic.

"I will make sure I'm more careful in the future, but the cops not caring doesn't mean I'm not going to care. There's blood on the floor in there," she said, pointing her thumb over her shoulder at the barn. "I don't know where he keeps the dogs or if he even has any of his own. Maybe he just organizes it, but I'd bet my house that he's using this barn for fighting. I'm going to find out for sure, and I'm going to put a stop to it no matter what I have to do." Her blood heated with each impassioned word. Fuck Prick and fuck his connections to the police. That wouldn't stop her.

Curly opened his mouth, and she raised a hand to keep him from butting in.

"I won't be stupid," she threw in for good measure. "I have no desire to go all psycho on him. Don't worry. I'll play it smart. Now, I'm sorry to have interrupted your day. I'm gonna get going."

She stepped away from the barn, headed in the direction of her car, which she'd parked a good quarter mile down the road. As she walked past him, Curly snagged her arm. Why was it every time he touched her, no matter how platonic, every nerve ending in her skin erupted in tingly zings?

"Wait," he said in that gravelly voice that made her stop and listen even when her instinct was to balk at being bossed around. "Twenty-four-sixty-three Breakview Drive. Seven p.m. tomorrow if you're serious about this."

She sucked in a breath. "You want to help?" Maybe he'd be open to Nancy and David joining as well. With four heads to put together, they'd come up with something.

He nodded. "But only show up if you're serious."

"I am." How could he not see that?

"No, I mean serious about doing this without the cops. Because we won't be involving them. No matter how it plays out. No matter what goes down. I don't do cops."

That'd be a no on David and Nancy then. While fantastic friends who'd do anything to help a human or animal, they lived in a world brighter and shinier than Brooke's. Neither of them had experienced the darker side of the universe yet. Neither had the someone they loved fail them in ways that altered their entire view on the world, and Brooke refused to be the one who dirtied the lens through which they viewed humanity.

"Think about it," he said, giving her arm an affectionate squeeze before releasing her.

"I will." Think about it? She'd do nothing but think about it for the next day and a half.

The entire walk to her car, his gaze burned into her back. Wearing her favorite denim shorts and a ribbed coral tank top, she wasn't remotely dressed up. Over and over, she warned herself to keep her gait as steady and ordinary as possible. Yet her stupid body overrode her good sense, and within seconds, she had her hips swaying in a way designed to draw attention.

"You're an idiot," she whispered to herself as she reached her car. A quick peek over her shoulder revealed him standing in the road, watching after her. That weird feeling in her chest was in no way affection for the man who stayed to make sure she made it to her car safely. Nope, it was just adrenaline from the insanity of the morning. For all she knew, he observed her out of distrust, not concern.

Without glancing in his direction again, she started her car, blasted the air conditioning, and flipped a U-turn in the homeward direction. "Dammit," she whispered, as the temptation grew too strong to resist. She checked the rear-view mirror.

Curly was gone. Wherever he'd parked his bike, she hadn't seen it.

Halfway home, her phone rang through the car's Bluetooth. "Hello?" she answered after hitting the button on her dashboard screen.

"Brooke, it's Aaron. I've emailed the background check you requested."

She frowned. Usually, he just sent it once it was complete. This was the first time he'd phoned to let her know. "Thanks, Aaron. Everything all right with it?"

He snorted. "Wanted to give you a heads up on this one. He's got a rap sheet, and it's as long as a football field."

After speaking with David and Nance, she'd expected it, yet hearing the news officially had her stomach twisting. "I'll read through the entire report, but do you mind giving me the highlights?"

With a bitter laugh, Aaron said, "That might take all day. But here goes. He patched in as a member of True Outlaws Motorcycle Club at twenty-one, but he'd been hanging around them for years before that. At thirty-two, he took over as

Curly

president. Did some digging into the club, and they were bad news, Brooke. I'm talking drugs, guns, prostitution. A slew of suspected murders. You name it, these guys had their grubby fingers in it and Travis Bryant, or Curly, ran all of it for a number of years."

Frowning, she tried to reconcile the man who'd saved her ass with the one Aaron described. "You said you dug into the True Outlaws. Are they still around?"

"No. The club disbanded more than a decade ago. Curly has several arrests for a multitude of charges, but almost fourteen years ago, he was arrested and convicted of murdering a preteen girl. The club fell apart after that. Many went to prison, and those that didn't left town. Curly was sent to prison near Tallahassee but transferred to Kentucky after a few years. Some kind of budgetary issue. Here's the kicker though, a little more than eight months ago, the case blew wide open someone discovered information about a man who'd confessed to the killing. Turns out it was a drifter with severe mental illness who killed the girl then killed himself. Details are a little fuzzy, but DNA evidence proved it. The police department mishandled the case, big time. Curly served thirteen years behind bars for that crime. Sucks he got put away for something he didn't do, but if you ask me, he probably shoulda been there for something anyway, so it kinda comes out in the wash."

Sucks he got put away for something he didn't do? Was Aaron for real?

"That's not how our justice system works, Aaron," she shot back before thinking. They weren't exactly friends, just business acquaintances despite the fact he'd asked her out a few times. She'd always turned him down. "We don't just put people in jail and say, 'I'm sure you did something to deserve being there.' That's thirteen years of a man's life." Just thinking about it had her aching to right the wrong that Curly suffered. But how did anyone give years back to a person? No matter what had been

77

said or done to compensate for the mistakes made, nothing could give him back those years.

And that broke her heart.

Shit, she needed to shut up before she made an enemy of Aaron while supporting a man she'd met twice. Why the hell did she feel so compelled to defend him anyway? She and Curly certainly didn't have any kind of friendship. Hell, he couldn't even be considered an acquaintance.

But he was the man who'd agreed to help her put an end to the dog fighting.

"Our justice system? Come on, Brooke. You can't be that naïve?"

"No, I left naïve behind years ago. Look, Aaron, I gotta run." It was time for this conversation to end before she needed to find someone else to run her background checks.

"Brooke, I didn't mean—"

"No hard feelings, seriously. I just have a crazy day ahead of me. Thanks for running the check and sending it on over. I'll be thorough when I read it." She hung up before he had a chance to respond. Her mind had already jumped ahead.

Thirteen years in prison for a crime he hadn't committed. She couldn't even wrap her mind around it. What must have gone through his head day in and day out as he served someone else's sentence?

In a way, she did know, didn't she?

Maybe not a wrongful incarceration, but she knew helplessness.

She knew fear.

She knew despair.

Had it been the same for him? Trapped in a place he didn't deserve to be? She'd walked willingly into her hell of a marriage, whereas an unjust conviction had blindsided him. Perhaps she shouldn't compare the two, but for some reason, the knowledge of his ordeal had her feeling a kinship with him.

The rest of his story she wasn't so comfortable thinking about.

Curly

Motorcycle clubs?

Drugs? Prostitution?

Multiple arrests?

After learning of Curly's background, there was only one question left to ask. Was she still willing to let him help her take down Prick?

Yes. She was.

She'd do anything to keep assholes like Prick from abusing innocent animals.

Chapter Eight

He needed to nail down a location for a clubhouse, and he needed one fast. Preferably something with more property than he had so his new pup could run around. If Brooke decided to let him adopt after seeing the background report, which would undoubtedly be full of interesting information, both true and false.

Curly glanced around his tiny kitchen, packed to the brim with six large men, including himself. Apparently, Tyler had connections all over the damn area, and those connections led to guys who were interested in MC life.

His cousin strode up to him, holding out his favorite beer. That he remembered after so long was amazing. It also gave Curly a sense of belonging he'd been searching for since moving back.

Ty's guys had brought a few cases of the brew, which probably meant they planned to hang for a good few hours. Not a bad idea if they were potentially going to be brothers. Might as well get to know each other and see if they'd mesh.

"Sorry to spring the guys on you like this," Tyler said with a wry grin. His green T-shirt had streaks of oil on it as though Ty had come straight from work.

"No, it's all good." Curly accepted the beer and took a long pull. Damn, that was tasty.

After slogging through the same routine day in day out for thirteen years, rapid change overwhelmed him in a way it ever used to. But prison also taught him how to keep his internal shit from showing on the outside. So, he swallowed the beer along with his discomfort and spoke the truth even if not entirely settled. "I told you we'd need men, and you delivered. I've been gone been so long I hardly know anyone in town." He tilted his bottle in Tyler's direction. "I trust you, cuz."

Tyler clinked their bottle necks as he smiled. "I gotta tell you. My head's been spinning since you walked into my shop. Gotta keep reminding myself this is real."

"Tell me about it," Curly replied with a grunt. He'd been doing the same thing multiple times per day for more than eight months. But, reminding himself, this was his life now.

Free to make his own choices.

Two of the men Tyler brought shared a story that had the other two cracking up. They didn't all know each other when they first arrived, but in just fifteen minutes, they seemed to have clicked.

"They're good men," Tyler said. "Wouldn't have let them set foot in your home if I didn't trust them and think you could, too."

Nodding, Curly said, "Tell me about them."

"That's Fin. He owns a tat shop called Ink Layer," he said, pointing to the animated man covered in ink, who'd taken over the story. He had emerald green eyes and jet-black hair. Shaved bald on the sides, he wore the top of his hair in a buzzed mohawk. At least six of his fingers had rings, and his nails had been painted black. Metal in his nose, eyebrow, and ears completed the badass look. "Damn good artist. Personable, too. Swear to Christ he could befriend God and the devil at the same time."

Good quality to have since people skills weren't Curly's strong point. "I've walked past his shop. Thought about popping in a few times to get some ink touched up." A handful of his tats had been done in prison and needed some love at the very least.

"Let him know. He'll get you right in. He goes by the name Tracker because he volunteers for Florida Search and Rescue. Got some stories of rescues from the Everglades that'll shrivel your balls. Think he's somewhere in his mid-thirties."

Shit. Tracker sounded like a damn solid guy.

"Let's see, the shaggy blond goes by Jinx. His real name is Conrad. He's been working for me at the tire shop for a few years. The guy spends all his free time at the beach. He's a damn hard worker. Young though. Twenty-four, I think. Good personality, funny. We call him Jinx because he's superstitious about all sorts of weird shit."

Curly nodded.

"Quiet one there with the brown hair is Jake. He's thirty and owns a locksmith shop. Think he inherited it when his old man kicked it. Don't know much about him, but Gabe, who's the clean-cut guy next to Jake vouches for him. Gabe's a thirty-two-year-old trauma nurse. Met him when I wrecked my bike about eight years back. Fucked myself up good. Gabe's good people. Be nice to have someone with a little medical knowledge as well."

Something dark twisted in Curly's stomach. His cousin could have died, and he'd never have known. No one would have told him because once he'd gone away, thoughts of him had dropped from everyone's heads. He was nothing more than the family embarrassment who shouldn't be named.

"Hey." Tyler nudged his shoulder. "I imagine it's gonna take some time, but I'm here for you. Whatever you need."

Slapping his cousin on the shoulder, he said, "Thanks, Ty. I mean it. Just got a lotta shit going on." He tapped the side of his head. "Shit, I thought I'd moved past."

"Yeah, I imagine being here's gonna dredge up the past a lot."

He had no idea. "One day at a time, right? Don't they say some shit like that?"

With a snort, Tyler nodded. "They sure do." His gaze clouded for a moment which had Curly frowning. "Easier said than done, though, ain't it?"

Though not something he was proud of, it was easy for Curly to get lost in his own problems, given what he'd endured. He'd have to consciously remember that thirteen years of Tyler's life had passed by as well, and from the look on his cousin's face, they weren't all sunshine and good times. Hopefully, they'd get to the point over the next few months where they could sit with a few beers and spill their guts on their pasts.

For now, they had plenty of shit to deal with in the present.

He clapped Tyler on the back. "All right, let's do this."

Together they moved to the table. The guys fell silent as he approached. He remained standing, mainly because all the seats were occupied.

Definitely needed to find a clubhouse.

"Gentlemen," he said, garnering a few snickers and elbow jabs. "I'm assuming Tyler has already filled you in a bit on what I'm trying to build. My name's Travis, but I go by Curly." He pointed to his head. "If you can't figure out why, please see yourself out."

That one got a genuine laugh out of all the guys. Even Tyler, who stood with his back against the refrigerator, chuckled. Curly smiled. So far, so good. "I'm sure you all know who I am and where I've been. I'll say a few things, then I won't say shit about it, okay?"

The guys nodded. "Yes, I was the president of the True Outlaws who was wrongfully imprisoned for murdering a kid. Yes, the last thirteen years sucked. Imagine it, then multiply it by a hundred. That's how bad it was. Yes, I sometimes get fucked in the head about it. The story you know from the news is not the correct story. I'll tell you what really happened sometime soon. Until then, the most important thing to know is that I didn't do it. No, I'm not hellbent on some violent revenge scheme, though there are a few people I don't plan on sending Christmas cards to. While I'm not gonna go out of my way to get vengeance, I never have and never will shy from a fight. Got it?"

They all voiced their understanding.

"Great. Moving on. If you're here, it's because Ty told you I'm planning to charter an MC. An MC, not a church group, but not a gang either. I'm not interested in drugs, guns, or sex."

Tracker snorted.

Curly's lips quirked. "Selling sex. Is that better?"

"Fuck yeah," Tracker said with a wink. His pierced eyebrow glinted in the light. "Worried there for a second that thirteen years without a woman broke you."

The entire group of them cracked up. And that's when Curly knew without a shadow of a doubt that he could make this dream a reality, and this was the group to get it done. "Anyway, you want in, you'll need a bike. A Harley eventually, but anything will work at first. I'm tagging Tyler for VP, and I've got a guy named Scott who's getting out of the military who I want for enforcer. That leaves me in need of a sergeant-at-arms, a treasurer, and a road captain. We can figure that shit out soon enough. Also, we need a clubhouse, so if you have any ideas, let me know. Today isn't any kind of official club meeting, and I won't discuss potential revenue sources until we all swear an oath and patch in. I'll tell you now, though, club comes first, and we do shit our way. That way might not line up with what others think is right."

"Meaning the cops," Gabe broke in. He was the only one sitting stiff and wearing an expression of uncertainty.

Curly nodded as he folded his arms across his chest. "For one. That gonna be a problem for you, Gabe?"

A grain of rice falling would have boomed through the room at that point. If Gabe couldn't get on board with this most basic tenet of MC life, he had no future there. Given his career as a trauma nurse, chances were Gabe came in contact with the cops frequently. Hell, he might even be friendly toward some, which was fine, but when it came down to it, he'd have to know where his loyalty laid.

And that would be with the club no matter what.

Curly would accept nothing less.

Not after the last time.

After what felt like an hour delay, Gabe finally shook his head. "No problem. And you can call me Pulse. Did a tour as Navy corpsman and went by Pulse."

"Pulse. I like it." Curly made a note to question the guy further. He'd be vetting each of them before swearing them in. Tonight was for making connections and getting to know each other, not a deep dive into anyone's background.

"You gonna make us prospect?" Jinx asked. The guy was freaking huge. He probably hauled those tires around Ty's shop like they weighed nothing more than a sack of feathers.

Curly unfolded his arms and rubbed his hands together as he met Tyler's eye. It shouldn't be his decision alone, but his cousin would be of a like mind. "I'm thinking no for the seven of us. It's a good place to start. Anyone else will have to. You got someone in mind? We'll let 'em hang around a bit, then take it to the table for a vote on letting them prospect. Maybe just two hang arounds at first. Until we're sure it all jives."

They chatted for a while about Curly's vision for the club and the basics of how it would run. Dues, legit business opportunities, partnering with the club on business if necessary. Curly had money to spare and a deep interest in investing in the community, but he wasn't going to toss his cash around without thought. Nor was he quite ready to admit his financial situation to these guys.

Lip service was great, but loyalty would only be proven with time. After all, he'd been through, trust wouldn't be handed over in one meeting no matter how many promises they made or how well they all clicked.

After a while, the conversation shifted from business to random bullshit, and Curly found a few rickety folding chairs in his garage so he and Ty could sit with the guys. They drank and laughed, already comfortable with each other.

Jinx was the only man who didn't already own a bike, but Tyler had a hookup for him, so he should have that settled by the end of the following week.

"Any of you guys try out that new strip club?" Jake asked after passing another round of beers out. "The one on State Street." He'd told them all to call him Lock as his friends and family had called him by the nickname for years.

Tracker nodded. "Been there a few times. They got some quality dancers."

Jinx frowned as he looked at Tyler. "That the one your mom works at, Ty?"

Curly snorted, almost shooting beer out his nose. Damn, that guy had some quick fucking wit.

"Cute," Tyler said, flipping Jinx off. "You come up with that all on your own?"

"Sure did," Jinx said with a laugh.

The only one who'd stayed relatively quiet was Gabe. His behavior didn't qualify as standoffish, but he didn't jump in as the others did. Maybe he was just reserved, or maybe he wouldn't be a good fit. Only time would tell.

The doorbell chimed, killing the conversation.

Tyler frowned. "You expecting anyone else?"

With a glance at the clock, Curly frowned. "Shit." Seven on the dot. With the unexpected presence of his new club members, he'd forgotten he'd invited Brooke. What would the sexy little dog trainer think of the crew of burly bikers overflowing his house?

As Curly rose to his feet, Tracker jumped up as well. "I got it, prez," he said with a wink, then darted for the door as though they'd known each other for years rather than a few short hours.

Curly

"Don't be an ass," Curly called out, which was followed by Tracker's laugh.

The rest of the guys at the table sat with raised eyebrows and curious gazes. When he invited Brooke, they'd only expected to be getting together with Ty, but here they all were, buzzed and acting a fool.

"Well, hello there, gorgeous," came from the door, followed by a low growl.

"Quiet, Ray, it's okay. Um, hi. I hope I don't have the wrong house. I'm looking for Curly."

Brooke was there.

She'd showed up, which meant she wanted his help. Surprising since he assumed her encounter with Prick would only ramp up her desire to go all Lara Croft and take the guy down herself.

She intrigued him with her feisty independence, her ballsy take no prisoners attitude, and those caramel-colored eyes he could have stared at all day. The second she'd snapped at him for helping with the dog kennels, she'd earned his respect and his genuine curiosity.

A woman like Brooke was so different than the women he'd spent his former life with. She reminded him of many of the Handlers' ol' ladies who were in complete contrast to the needy, manipulative, status-hungry club girls he'd been with as the Outlaws' president.

Still, he needed to keep his eye on the prize: putting a stop to the illegal dog fighting ring. A woman didn't factor into his life plan in any way beyond a bit of stress relief. Certainly not a relationship.

Been there, had the thick scars to prove it.

Chapter Nine

Brooke couldn't decide whether the man who'd answered the door terrified or intrigued her. Ray seemed to be just as ambivalent. His ears drew back, and he stood at attention with a slight forward tug on the leash. She patted his head to let him know everything was fine.

For now.

Covered in tattoos, the man who stood in the doorway wore a T-shirt with the sleeves ripped off and tattered jeans along with scuffed work boots. A strip of inky black hair ran down the center of his scalp—his tattooed scalp—while the rest of his head was smooth and hairless. Two silver rings glinted from one of his nostrils along with a ring in his eyebrow. Each ear had a gauge at least a half-inch wide, and finally, a silver hoop clung to his lower lip.

If it wasn't for the amused grin and sparkling green eyes, she might have turned and fled back to her car. Guess the four bikes outside the house should have clued her in that Curly wasn't alone.

If she'd gotten the right house. Part of her hoped she hadn't.

"That's a handsome bodyguard you've got there. I'd give him a scratch, but I'm afraid he'll take my hand off." The inked giant winked.

His easygoing smile and apparent charm disarmed her but not Ray. He wasn't yet convinced there were friendlies in the house. And that's why she'd taken him along. Sure, Curly hadn't done anything to make her feel uncomfortable, but he had a sketchy past.

Compared to the passive and meek woman she'd been during her marriage, she was damn strong and able to handle whatever life threw at her. Still, walking alone into the home of a man she didn't really know, a man with violence in his history, without caution, would be stupid. And she wasn't a stupid woman. She still had the potential to freeze up or be overpowered. Making the trip to Prick's farm alone had reminded her of that frustrating fact, but she'd been too worried Prick could have aggressive fighting dogs on premises to take Ray.

"You've come to the right place, sweetheart. Come on in. I'm Tracker, and your man's in the kitchen. Straight down the hall." He took a step back and held the door wide.

"Oh, no, he's not my man," she said, but Tracker had already turned his attention from her. "Okay," she whispered. As she and Ray made the short trip to the kitchen, she couldn't help but take in the place. The house was small but relatively neat and clean though sparsely decorated. It seemed the perfect size for one single man.

Curly was single, right?

Most of the furniture was outdated, as was the general style of the place. Paint peeled from a few walls while others appeared to have received a fresh coat. She couldn't find any feminine touches, suggesting he didn't live with a woman. Had the house sat abandoned the entire time he'd been in prison?

"Right through here," Tracker said, sweeping his arm in a dramatic gesture as she passed by.

"Thanks." She entered the dimly lit kitchen only to halt at the sight of a bunch of large, gruff men crammed around a tiny round table. Ray growled with intent this time, and she didn't shush him.

Curly immediately stood and made his way to her despite the snarling shepherd at her side. By the time he'd taken two steps in her direction, Ray recognized him and eased off the vicious dog routine. Tension on the leash disappeared, and his fluffy tail wagged as though she'd just offered him his favorite treat.

She tended to trust Ray's instincts, but this instalove was a bit ridiculous. If she wasn't careful, he'd be humping Curly's leg and slobbering all over the man she'd thought about way too much in the past few days.

"Hey," she peeped, then cringed at the weakness in her voice. Her husband's abuse had been of the psychological and emotional variety, not physical. Well, except one time at the end, where he'd snapped and attacked her. He'd slapped her so hard her head spun like that kid in The Exorcist. She hated that all it took was a few bigger and slightly menacing men to have her squeaking like a mouse. She rarely spent time with groups of men and was sorely out of practice in terms of socializing. For all she claimed to be tough and independent, part of her couldn't escape the instant discomfort.

"Hey, Brooke, sorry about the kids," he said as he crouched down to give Ray the attention he demanded. "Their mothers were supposed to pick them up by now, so I'm not sure what's going on. Hi, Ray. Such a good boy, looking out for your mama."

The other guys booed and heckled him as he winked at her while he still loved on Ray.

Brooke could have kissed Curly at that moment. Not only because he looked so yummy in a snug olive-green T-shirt with jeans riding low on his slim hips, but he seemed to sense she needed some levity to set her at ease.

"Hey, guys," she said, lifting a hand in an awkward wave.

"Hi, Brooke!" They chorused in a dramatized greeting, all wearing big cheesy grins.

She laughed and blew out a breath. Okay, whoever these men were, they didn't come off as a threat to her or Ray.

Curly

"Bunch of jackasses," Curly grumbled, earning him a smile from her. "Want a beer?"

"Yes," she said. "Please." A few.

He straightened to his full height, then placed his hand on her lower back and gave her a gentle nudge toward the table. She wanted to wiggle around and get that hand to rub all over her and maybe slip under her tank top to find her bare skin. Instead, she forced herself to step away from his touch. Her body reacted to him in ways it had never responded to a man before, and she had no plans to encourage it or him, no matter how wild her thoughts ran. She wouldn't be fooled into a man's trap by hormones and muscles.

"Take my seat, and I'll grab you a drink."

"Oh, no, I don't want to steal your seat."

"Brooke?"

The way he said her name, in a commanding but also respectful tone, had her knees weakening. "Yes?"

"Take my seat."

"Okay." But only because she didn't want to make a scene in front of the rest of the people.

As she approached the table, a blond guy kicked the chair out so she could sit. She bit off a laugh. Must be some form of tough-guy chivalry.

Another man grunted. "Classy, Jinx. No wonder you don't have a woman." He held out his hand. "I'm Tyler." He thumbed over his shoulder to Curly, who was pulling a beer from the fridge. "His cousin. Beautiful dog you got there."

"Thank you. I'm Brooke," she answered. "And this is Ray. Lie down, buddy." He plopped down next to her chair, resting his head on his front paws.

The other four guys introduced themselves as well. By then, Curly had deposited a chilled bottle of beer in front of her. "Thank you," she said as he propped his ass against the cream-colored wall next to her. Heat wafted off his body, practically searing her with its intensity. "I'm sorry I'm crashing the party."

"Nah, no party," Tyler said. He seemed to be around Curly's age, which she guessed was a few years older than she was. Maybe mid-forties. "Just working on getting the new MC up and running."

"Oh, wow." A new MC? She cut a glance Curly's way to find him studying her with dark eyes. Bending some rules to get his help with the dog fighting ring was one thing but partnering up with a man who had a hand in everything she knew him to have been involved in changed her comfort level.

Sliding her chair back an inch, she glanced down at Ray, who still seemed chill as could be. Maybe it was time to go.

"We can bug out so you and your woman can have some time," the one called Gabe interrupted her escape. He seemed the most serious of the men even though he told her to call him Pulse, which she wasn't sure she could pull off.

"Oh, no, I'm not his—" she said at the same time Curly said, "Stick around a few more minutes."

She waved at him to speak again as she reached for Ray's leash. "Sorry, go ahead."

He winked then said, "Don't run away just yet. I want to run your situation by the guys if that's okay?"

What was she gonna say? No? She was on his turf, surrounded by six large bikers all staring at her. "Sure, of course, it's okay." She dropped the leash and forced herself to relax in the chair.

"Brooke is a dog trainer, and she runs a small rescue operation from her property."

Tracker snapped his fingers then straightened in his seat. "You know, I knew you looked familiar. I do SAR for Find Me, Inc. and I think you've worked with some of our pups."

Well, small world. "Yes!" she said with a smile. "I've trained quite a few dogs for you guys. It's a fantastic organization." She loved training working dogs and their search handlers. It was such a satisfying experience.

"Yeah, we've done some good in the world."

Curly

Some good? That organization alone was responsible for finding over one hundred missing people in Florida just last year. What on earth was he doing hanging around with drug dealers and weapons traffickers?

Tracker looked up at Curly. "Sorry to interrupt, prez."

"All good." He reached down and stroked his big hand over Ray's head. Her dog let out a sigh of pleasure. "Anyway, several injured dogs have been found abandoned close to her house recently. All seem to be breeds typically used for fighting."

"Motherfuckers," Tracker said while the others wore expressions of equal disgust. Gang members who sold drugs, moved guns, and sold women but had a soft spot for abused dogs. Something didn't quite add up. She couldn't decide whether to run for the hills or stick around and see how they could lend a hand in ending the dog fights.

"You go to the cops?" Pulse asked her.

She nodded with a frustrated *mm-hmm*. "Yes, a friend filed a report after each one. Either the police don't care or have too many 'real crimes' to deal with. So far, no one's followed up with me about any of them." Countless dogs, alone and powerless, suffering at the hands of money-hungry abusers.

She shifted. She'd been one. A two-legged victim of a greedy social climber. No one to listen, no one to help her but herself. She refused to let those animals live in lonely misery as she did for so many years.

"Sounds about right," Jinx said, shaking his head.

"I have a good idea of where the fights are held," she said. "There's a farm that abuts the back of my property. It's sat abandoned for years, but it seems someone purchased it recently. I didn't even realize anyone was living there because my land runs along the back field, which is acres away from the house and barn."

"I think I know where you're talking about," Tyler said. He paused, running a hand over his mouth. "Out near the edge of town, right?"

She nodded. "That's right."

Tyler fingered his lower lip before his eyes widened. "Oh fuck." His gaze went to Curly's. "Prick bought that land. Cuz, you said this wasn't about revenge."

Brooke's forehead scrunched. Aside from Tyler, the rest of the guys seemed as clueless as she was. Sure, she'd known Curly hadn't held any love for Prick, but revenge? What the hell was that about?

"It's not," Curly answered with a lethal tone she'd yet to hear from him. As though to combat the grave turn of the conversation, he stepped up behind her and placed his hands on her shoulders, stroking her skin with his thumbs. She jumped at the initial contact, but the move was so smooth and natural any of the men there would think he'd been touching her for years. Brooke fought to keep her eyelids from dropping as the heat of his palms warmed her shoulders. How could such an innocent touch feel so good? She wanted to arch her back and let out a purr. No wonder Ray was such a slut for rubs from this guy. His hands were incredible.

Revenge? "What does he mean, revenge?" she asked around the thickening in her throat.

As he answered, Curly stared down at her. The rest of the men faded away until they were the only two remaining in the kitchen. Brooke shivered. If he ever turned that intensity on her in a more sensual manner, she'd combust on the spot.

And she'd be in massive trouble because, without a doubt, she could not handle a man like Curly. Hell, she couldn't handle a rich mama's boy when she had him. What the hell would she do with a dangerous man like Curly?

Though in her defense, her ex had been a raging narcissist with anger issues.

Still massaging her shoulders as though he belonged there, Curly said. "Prick was my club brother, and he participated in framing me for Joy's murder. He's one of the main reasons I spent thirteen years caged for a crime I didn't commit."

Brooke lost the ability to breathe. "Framing?" she whispered. Nothing she'd read indicated someone framed him for the girl's murder.

The statement landed like a bomb in the room, exploding the men into action.

"What the fuck?" Jinx yelled as he shot to his feet. "You fucking serious? That's some bullshit. He was your goddammed brother."

He'd filled Ty in on this, but still, his cousin practically shook with fury.

"Fucking hell," Tracker shouted.

Even Lock, who hadn't said much of anything, expressed his outrage with a shout.

Eventually, Curly lifted a hand, and the group settled. When his palm landed back on her shoulder, she nearly moaned in relief. The loss of contact had shaken her almost as much as his admission. "I don't want to get into all the details right now, but the lead detective on the case framed me. Prick had a hand in feeding him info about me and the club."

Her jaw dropped. Framed? Holy shit that is so much worse than what she'd read, and what she'd read was horrible.

A storm cloud passed over his handsome face. The rest of the men noticed and seemed to understand what she did without further explanation. He didn't want a million questions at that moment. Didn't want to rehash the nightmare.

She wished they could go back forty-five seconds ago when his hands were on her, and she didn't know he'd suffered in such an egregious way. What the hell was happening to her? This was absolute insanity. How could she be so attracted to a man who participated in things she abhorred? It had to be some weird chemical reaction. Pheromones or whatever. Maybe her body was going haywire because it'd been so long since she'd been in such close contact with a man who wasn't David or a client.

"I said I wasn't going to seek revenge, but I also said I wouldn't back down from a fight. The dog fighting ring needs to be stopped. If I get to fuck with Prick as we take it down, so be it. Icing on the cake I was going to eat already."

Well...that made sense for the most part.

Tyler smirked. "Sounds perfectly reasonable to me. What's our first move?"

"It's gonna be hard for you or me to get close to him in any way. He knows us both and hates me by association."

"I have no fucking idea who Prick is," Jinx said. "Why don't you point me in his direction, and I'll engage him. See if I can get invited to a fight."

"I'll do it with you," Pulse added.

Jinx frowned. "I'm up to the task."

Rolling his eyes, Pulse flipped Jinx off. "I'm not saying you can't do it. Just saying I'm tagging along."

Brooke's gaze ping-ponged between the men as they began to argue. Big as he was, Jinx had a baby face and seemed considerably younger than the rest of the men. Made sense he'd want to prove himself as an equal.

"Jinx, this isn't a commentary on your ability. I wouldn't let any of you go alone. Never turn down backup."

"Yeah, all right. I hear ya." Jinx nodded at Curly then relaxed back in his chair.

Clearly, these men respected Curly and his authority if they heeded his advice so easily. Brooke tried to reconcile the man standing above her with the one she'd read so many terrifying articles about when she'd finally broken down and Googled him.

The man who'd run a drug ring.

The man who'd sold weapons all up and down the east coast.

The man who broke laws as a hobby.

"You know," Lock said, finally letting his voice be heard. "That farm would be a great fucking place for a clubhouse. It's in shit condition now, but we could turn the barn into a few apartments, and his guys could renovate the farmhouse into a clubhouse. Maybe our goal should be to run Prick out of town."

Run him out of town? Brooke shifted in her chair as the conversation took a turn she wasn't entirely comfortable with. Curly must have sensed the change in her. He squeezed her shoulders but didn't steer the discussion away from talk of taking Prick's home from him.

She zoned out a bit as the men went back and forth with details of where Prick hung out, how to approach him, and gain his trust. At least if the cops arrested her, she could honestly say she hadn't paid attention to exactly what they were planning, right? Maybe this was a huge mistake, and she should focus on ending the dog fighting ring herself. Prick's furious face floated in front of her vision, and she nearly groaned out loud. As capable as she was on her own, there was a time to admit when she was in over her head, and when dealing with a man like Prick, she was way out of her depth. With the cops' apathy, this seemed her only course of action for now. To save those dogs, she'd do damn near anything. Even risk her soul by tying herself to a gang of bikers.

Next thing she knew, all the guys were rising from the table, and she was blinking herself back to the room.

"Nice to meet you, Brooke," Tracker said as he came around the table then patted her shoulder. "Looking forward to seeing you again soon."

Her face heated. This time she didn't bother to state how she and Curly weren't anything to each other, so they probably wouldn't be hanging out. She was too busy being amazed at how sweet and kind these gruff-looking men had been to her when her ex-husband's polished and perfect-on-paper friends had never been anything but judgmental snobs. Some had been downright antagonistic. And had her husband ever made her feel included, important, or wanted?

Hell no.

He'd laughed along with his friends when they questioned her taste, made fun of the small town she'd grown up in and whispered behind her back.

But it wasn't the time for a trip down memory lane.

"Guess I better get going as well," she said when the last man had filed out the door. A loud rumble of motorcycles kicked up. Her eyes widened, which made Curly smile.

"Beautiful music."

With a laugh, she shook her head. "Guess you get used to it."

"You come to crave it."

She'd have to take his word for that one. Just as she was about to call Ray to her, Curly opened the fridge and pulled out two more bottles of beer. "Sit for a bit. Wanna make sure you're good with all this."

"Oh, I, uh…"

I should not stay.

She was already blurring the lines by being attracted to him, listening to him open up about his past, and letting him help her.

I should definitely not stay.

"Okay, I'll hang out for one more beer."

"Follow me." He flashed her a sexy grin complete with sparkling blue eyes that basically had her trotting after him the same way Ray shadowed her.

Once in his den, she perched on one end of his couch. He took the other. "Make yourself at home," he said, so she forced herself to relax against the worn cushions.

She curled up, tucking her feet underneath her bottom, then pivoted to face him. He sat angled in her direction as well, with one ankle propped on the opposite thigh. Ray sidled up to Curly and rested his head on a small spot next to the man.

Traitor.

This was the first time she'd seen him with his mop of curly hair pulled back into a man-bun, and she'd be lying if she didn't admit it looked sexy as hell. Longer hair on men wasn't her thing, but it fit him so well, and every time she thought of it, she couldn't help but want to feel it sliding through her fingers.

"I got your background check," she blurted, then winced—way to kill the relaxed mood.

"Ahh," he said as he rubbed the soft spot between Ray's ears. Her dog's eyes drifted closed in bliss.

Double traitor.

"I'm guessing that's why you brought this guy along?"

Was it her imagination, or was that a note of disappointment in his question?

If she were as bright as she professed to be, she'd say yes. Let him think he alone was the reason she'd brought her dog along. But it'd be a lie. At least a partial lie. Picking at the label on her bottle, she shook her head. "Not entirely. It was more that I don't know you at all and I was going to your house alone in the evening. I'd have done it with any man."

"Smart," he said to which she shrugged. "So, am I getting that puppy, or did my past change your mind?"

Aside from his past, everything checked out. He'd been thorough on the application, listing a veterinarian, agreeing to shots, and spaying the pup. He'd agreed if there were any reason he became unable to care for the dog, he would contact her before rehoming the pup himself. He owned a home with a fenced-in yard—all the checks in all the boxes.

Aside from the outlaw motorcycle club history. Despite that fact, she knew deep in her bones he'd make an amazing dog parent.

Brooke met his gaze, and they held like that for a solid twenty seconds before she nodded.

He tilted his head to the side. "Is there anything you want to ask me?"

Only somewhere around a million questions. But none of it was her business. What right did she have to ask him about a history that had nothing to do with her? None at all. So she shook her head. "No. No questions." Probably best not to know.

Otherwise, she'd lie awake all night obsessing over his past and why she was still attracted to him. Because no matter what he confessed, she'd still feel this out of character pull to him.

"Okay, then. How about you tell me what made you so passionate about rescuing dogs?"

Well, shit. And well-played by Curly.

She sipped her beer then let out a sigh. "Can I change my mind and ask you the questions instead?" Delving too deep into her past gave her hives.

His lips quirked, and his eyes smoldered as he slowly shook his head back and forth. "Nope. You missed your chance. I get to conduct the interview."

She didn't discuss her past with anyone. Nancy knew the bare minimum required to maintain a close friendship, and she assumed David did as well, but no one knew the gritty details. The humiliation, the years of having her self-worth torn down, the helpless, trapped, desolate existence she'd endured. Then the lonely years since where she'd fought to climb out of that pit of despair. Untangling herself from a ten-year marriage had been so much more complicated than she'd ever expected. Walking away was only the very first step. A hard one for sure, but no more dificult than everything that came after.

The financial concerns.

The living arrangements.

The legal complications.

The job situation.

The pitiful glances from supposed friends and family.

None of it had been easy.

Curly's gaze held no judgment. Though he hadn't heard her story yet, she had a feeling when all was said and done, he still wouldn't judge her or find her lacking.

She'd done plenty of that herself and couldn't handle it from someone she considered…what? A friend? An acquaintance?

Not really either, but it didn't matter. Suddenly the weight of what she carried insider her pressed down on her shoulders like a million-pound blanket. She needed to shed it before the load crushed her. The man sitting before her was the absolute wrong man to flay her soul open for. He'd been a large-scale criminal and seemed to be diving back into that life, but still, the words burst from her mouth.

"I have a passion for rescuing abused and neglected animals because I know what it means to be one."

Chapter Ten

A man couldn't spend the first decade of his adult years with an outlaw MC and the second decade in prison without hearing just about every fucked-up story out there. Nothing shocked Curly anymore. Not recounting gruesome murders, not torture, not even people with no sense of right or wrong. He'd heard it all, witnessed almost as much, and had done things that would keep most men awake with nightmares. It took a shit-ton to get a reaction out of him, but that's precisely what Brooke's statement did.

Someone had abused her.

He balled his hands into fists beside him on the couch. His instinct demanded he launch himself at her and shake her until the name of the asshole fell from her beautiful lips. But he'd learned restraint while in prison. It was one of the first and most lasting lessons. Rash behavior often led to a shiv in the side.

Or a sharpened toothbrush across the neck.

So instead of following his instincts, he said, "Tell me."

Brooke blew out a breath as her gaze moved to Ray's head resting next to his thigh. He automatically rubbed the dog's fur, which drew a smile from her. "He likes you."

"The feeling is mutual."

"He was my first rescue. I'd never owned a dog before. As a kid, all I ever had was a fish. So I was clueless as to what to do with him when I found him. My..." She lifted her gaze. "My husband never wanted one."

Husband.

He swallowed hard as a bubble of rage began to creep its way up from his gut. These kinds of stories were never pleasant but hit harder when the abused was someone known to him. And if she hadn't left the bastard, Curly might lose his mind. "Ex-husband?"

Her eyes widened. "Yes. Sorry. Yes, definitely ex." A visible shudder ran through her. "Anyway, I went for a run one day, and Ray followed me the entire time. He was under a year at the time and so thin I could see his ribs."

A faraway look came into her eyes as a half-smile tilted her lips. "To be honest, I was afraid of him when I first saw him. You never know how an abused animal will act. But Ray was so sweet, just trotting along beside me. When I ended up back at my house, and he was still there, I couldn't leave him. We had some leftover chicken from the night before, so I put it in a bowl for him. He looked up at me with these big soulful starving eyes, and it broke my heart." Her voice hitched. "The poor guy was famished, yet he waited until I encouraged him to eat it before he dove in."

A glossy sheen coated her eyes. Curly couldn't tear his gaze away the sleek lines of her throat as she lifted the beer to her lips and took a few swallows.

"I took him straight to a vet to see if he had a microchip, but he didn't. The vet told me to get as thin as Ray had been, he'd have to have been neglected for quite some time. He was also filthy, and his hair was so matted a groomer had to shave him down. After I took him to the vet and a groomer, I brought him home with me." A slightly sad laugh erupted from her. "There were some growing pains in the beginning, but we figured it out and became the best of friends. After that, all I wanted to do was rescue dogs."

If he were placing a bet, he'd guess she left out more than half of that story. As much of an animal lover as he was, all he wanted to know was the story of her husband.

Ex-husband.

Instead of asking, he leaned forward and grabbed her bare feet, pulling them onto his lap. A small puff of air left her as she leaned against the arm of his couch. He just held her feet, connecting them.

Brooke blew out a breath. "I married when I was twenty. Divorced at thirty-five."

"Thirty-five? Shit, I thought you were younger than that now."

She snorted out a laugh, which had him smiling. A small victory.

"You're a good liar. I'm forty-one. And I look every day of it."

Forty-one? Shit, he'd never have guessed she was that close to his age. He grunted. "Babe, you look damn younger than that. Not that forty-one is old. I've got five years on you."

Her soft smile made his insides do some strange flip-flopping. Not that it mattered. Nothing could happen between them, no matter how hard she made his dick. He had priorities, and getting involved with a woman wasn't one of them. His ol' lady sleeping with Prick was the first in a chain of events that fucked up his entire life. He couldn't help the adverse visceral reaction to the idea of a relationship. Regular sex and daily company weren't worth it.

Starting a new charter for Copper was.

Investing in lucrative businesses was, too.

And yes, making Prick pay was high on the list. He claimed to not want revenge, but something dark and primal inside him couldn't pass up the chance to make the man pay for his sins.

Getting involved with a forty-something-year-old divorcee with baggage didn't even blip on his radar. Not matter how hot she was.

"You look at least ten years younger," he said, despite his brain screaming at him to shut the fuck up.

Brooke's laugh was long and genuine. "Oh, that's a good one. Shit, sometimes I feel twice my age."

"I hear that." Sometimes he felt as though he'd aged seven years for every one spent in prison, just like the dogs she trained.

Something about this simple statement must have resonated with her.

"Okay, here's the thirty-second tour through my life. I grew up poor as shit. Met my husband while I was working as a bagger in a grocery store. I was eighteen and *dying* for more than living as a nobody in a small town. He was ten years older, swept me off my feet, and dazzled me with a world I'd only seen in movies. Cliché, right? We were married within six months and before our one-year anniversary I realized the extent of my mistake."

"Did he hit you?"

She huffed out a laugh. "No. That kind of behavior would be far too low class for him. His brand of abuse came in the form of control and psychological manipulation. Before I knew what had hit me, I'd dyed my hair bleach blond, lost twenty pounds, painted my face with gallons of make-up each morning, and wore clothing that wasn't only uncomfortable but made me look like a clone of every other Stepford wife in his lavish world."

Curly remained quiet, allowing her to process her thoughts and share her story on her terms. He'd met men like her husband. Wealthy assholes who viewed their wives as property. As a trophy to do with as they pleased. Polish it up and put it on a shelf to look pretty and remain silent and obedient until they were ready to play with their prize.

"I know it sounds like a poor little rich girl story, but—"

"It doesn't," he cut in. One thing she'd learn about him fast is that he held no judgment for other's journeys. He hadn't been the only innocent man in that prison. Everyone had a story. Some were luckier than others, but he hadn't met a single soul who'd made it through life unscathed. "I've learned that damage you can't see can be much more caustic than bruises or blood. And money and privilege can't always save you. Especially when it doesn't sound as though it was ever *yours*."

"Yes," she whispered. "Crazy as it sounds, I used to wish he'd just haul off and hit me. Then at least everyone would have been able to see what he was doing to me. Bit by bit, he stole me from me. He controlled all the finances and wouldn't hear of me working. I wasn't allowed to go to college or have friends outside his social circle. My way of doing anything was always incorrect. By the time I realized I was living in a gilded cage, I was trapped. I'd cut contact with my family and had no friends to confide in. He'd convinced me my low-class family would only drag us down. That no one would take him seriously if we associated with them. It sounds hard to believe now, but he had a way of twisting things and making me doubt myself that made all his bullshit believable."

"A narcissist."

"Yes," she said with a nod. "I know that now. You know, he even complained about the way I answered the phone. Said that my 'hello' sounded too uneducated. Can you believe that?"

He believed it all right.

"The one time I tried to speak to a friend about how lonely and worthless I felt, Evan was waiting for me when I got home. He took my car keys, wallet, and phone. He also changed the Wifi password. For a week, I was his hostage. And it wasn't the last time he pulled that trick. I lived in a bougie, very expensive prison."

Evan. Now he had a name—what a piece of shit.

After she spoke, she sucked in a breath and covered her mouth. "Oh, my God. I'm so sorry. I shouldn't have compared what I went through to being in prison. I know it can't come close to what you went through."

Curly stroked his thumb along the top of her foot. "Sweetheart," he said, "your husband was a motherfucker who deserves to have his balls cut off. You may not have had steel bars, but it was a prison nonetheless."

Though the circumstances were entirely different, they shared a bond born of powerlessness. She knew as he did what it meant to feel worthless and have no control over her life and how vital it was to cling to it once she'd regained autonomy. "I understand what it means to be at someone's mercy and forced to live in a way I didn't want to. In some ways, what you endured sounds even worse than being in jail. For me, the sentence was designed to be a punishment. You were supposed to have found your happily ever after."

She bit her lower lip as she blinked rapidly. He didn't call her out on the teary eyes. Quickly he was learning Brooke didn't want to appear weak or helpless in front of anyone. Made sense considering what she'd suffered. Being criticized and insulted daily would stunt anyone's emotional health. So he gave her a moment to collect herself while he sipped his beer and continued rubbing her foot.

A few moments passed before she spoke again. "He did hit me once."

His hand stilled on her foot.

She'd spoken so low. Had he heard correctly?

The bleak expression on her face told him he had.

"Tell me."

"It was the night I found Ray. Evan was late getting home from work. He never bothered to let me know if he was going to be late but still expected a hot and ready dinner waiting for him. Something had happened at work, I don't even remember what it was anymore, but was in a foul mood. One of his worst. He'd been nasty and cutting about my outfit and hair, the reheated dinner, the cleanliness of the house, my ability as a wife in general. I stayed quiet and took it like I always did. Twisted as it now seems, I wasn't worried or afraid of him. His volatile moods had become my normal. I had nowhere to go, no one to turn to, so I just lived in my normal. Anyway, he'd been hollering, slamming things around, and getting in my face for a while when Ray barked from upstairs, where I'd set him up in our bedroom. I'll never forget the expression of shock and rage on his face."

She jolted then blinked as though she'd forgotten she'd been sharing the story with another person. Her cheeks turned pink. Embarrassment was the last thing she should feel. Strength, pride in no longer being in that shitty situation, happiness for living the way she wanted now.

Those were the things he felt for her.

Never shame.

But that was so much easier to tell someone than to have them believe it and live it.

"Keep going. Get it out."

After a few seconds, she cleared her throat. "Evan sprinted out of the kitchen and up the stairs screaming about how the noise better not be what he thought it was. I ran after him, begging him to stay out of the room. To please not hurt the dog. God, I tried so hard to keep up, but he was so much faster. When he threw our bedroom door open and saw Ray sitting there…"

Her shoulders drooped, and she shook her head. "I couldn't think of anything but my fear of Evan hurting Ray. I grabbed his arm and yanked him back into the hallway. It was a reaction. Instinct. No thought involved. It was also the first time in ten years that I stood up to him. I'm not sure who I surprised more, him or me." Her chuckle was heavy and sad.

"Evan whirled around and slapped me so fast, I didn't even feel it for a few seconds. Then he grabbed my throat and slammed me against the wall. He was screaming the entire time about what a horrible wife I was and how I didn't love him. I don't remember all of what he said because I was clawing at his hand, trying to get it off my throat instead of paying attention to his words." Her hand lifted to her neck.

Was she reliving every second of the pain and fear?

Jesus Christ. Curly ran a hand down his face. Evan. He needed a last name because there was no way in hell he'd let this fucker have a pass. "How'd you get away?" he asked, voice ragged.

A small huff slipped from her as she pointed to her dog. "Ray."

Curly glanced down at the Shepard whose ears twitched each time his name was mentioned.

"I swear he sprouted wings and flew out of the bedroom. He latched onto Evan's arm with this snarl that still makes my blood run cold to think about. Evan had no choice but to let go of me. Well, I guess he could have chosen to lose his arm. He fell to the floor screaming for me to call nine-one-one and clutching his mangled arm to his chest. I called Ray to me, grabbed my purse, and we ran. My first stop was a nearby Walmart. I took out as much cash as I could and bought whatever I thought we'd need for the next few weeks before Evan had a chance to cancel my cards. Then I drove a few towns over and got a motel room."

"And a divorce?"

She snorted. "That was a little more difficult. As I was lying there in the motel room that first night, stunned, sore, and terrified, I remembered the cameras in our house. Evan had them installed a few years after we were married. He claimed it was for security, but I'm pretty sure he only wanted to monitor me. I downloaded the app on my phone and guessed his password. It took me days to get it right, but I eventually did. The camera in the upstairs hallway had a perfect view of the door to our room. Everything that had happened that evening was there. Him punching me, choking me, screaming at me. I downloaded the footage and used it to get myself a divorce and enough money to start over. This was about five years ago. I've been on my own ever since, and that's how it's going to remain permanently. Well, not totally on my own. I've got Ray, huh, buddy?" She smiled at the dog who'd saved her life.

Curly scratched the dog behind his ears. He'd bring the dog a steak next time he saw him.

"I'll never give someone that kind of power over me again."

"Shit, Brooke…"

"I know," she said as she pulled her feet from his lap. "I'm sorry for dumping that all that on you. I don't know why I did."

"You are one badass woman."

She stilled in the process of slipping her feet into her worn flip-flops. "What?"

He scooted closer then tucked an escaped strand of hair behind her ear. "Smart, brave, resilient, strong, independent." He let his fingers linger on the soft skin beneath her ear.

"No, I…" she whispered, breathless. Her eyes fell closed.

"Badass." When she shook her head again, he said, "Brooke?"

She met his gaze, and he saw the deep-seated vulnerability she hid behind her independent nature and feisty spirit.

"Bad. Ass. Incredible."

This time her mouth pressed into a flat line. "Thank you." Her shoulders straightened, and her gaze lost its openness. As though a steel door into her psyche slammed shut, her gaze lost its openness. "And thank you for listening to all that crap. I should, uh, get home. It's past Ray's bedtime." She stood.

Yeah, she needed to get home before he threw her back down on the couch and didn't let her up until she'd come screaming his name.

A few times.

The thought of it, of hearing his name called out at that euphoric moment when pleasure turned to ecstasy, had his dick throbbing with need. As soon as she left, he'd need to take care of that, or he'd spend another miserable night hard and wanting.

"Does Saturday work to come pick up the dog?"

He tilted his head. "So I still pass muster?"

"Yes, Curly, you do."

"Saturday is perfect." He leaned in and pressed a kiss to her cheek, and if she noticed, he let his lips linger and his nose brush against her skin, she didn't say anything. But he swore he heard the slightest intake of breath when he made contact. "Drive safe," he said. "Text me when you get home."

"What?" She laughed, but it was stiff. "Remember when I said I was forty-one? Been driving at night for many years."

He shrugged and resisted the urge to smile at her prickliness. Like a hedgehog whenever he showed her kindness. "I'll worry."

Her eyebrows drew down. "Why?"

Laughing, he said, "How about you just text me as a favor, okay?"

"Sure. I guess." She shrugged. "Good night, Curly. Come on, Ray. Let's get on home."

"Good night, Brooke. Bye, Ray," he said, giving the dog one last pat on his head. Ray hurried along beside his mama but cast a pitiful look over his shoulder.

Don't worry, buddy, I'll be by soon.

Curly watched from his open doorway as she loaded Ray in her car then climbed behind the wheel. With a brief wave, she was off, backing out then heading down the street. He remained in the doorway for a solid five minutes, staring down the road and wondering what the hell was going on with him.

His head might be fucked for the moment, but two things were certain.

Prick's operation was going to meet with an unfortunate end.

And Brooke no longer had to look after herself alone. She now had the Hell's Handlers Florida Chapter standing behind her.

Even if it was a foolish move on his part.

Chapter Eleven

Around noon on Saturday, Brooke sat outside her quarantine kennel talking to the dog David had brought her earlier in the week. Tim from the pitbull rescue was due any time, and she'd wanted a moment alone with the dog before he moved on to the next phase of his recovery. It'd been difficult to get close to the dog. Only his inability to walk at the moment kept him from attacking her.

"They're gonna take good care of you, you hear?" she said. Inside, the dog snarled as he did every time she checked on him, fed him, cleaned the kennel, or interacted with him in any way. God, she hoped Tim could work his magic on this one.

"I know how scary it can be to go somewhere new where you don't know anyone and start over." Man, did she know that. "But you have a whole team of people who want to help you." So much more support than Brooke ever had. "Don't try to bite them, okay? They just want to help."

They'd be sedating him for the car ride. No need to stress him out when he still had so much healing to do.

A horn honked twice from her driveway. With a heavy sigh, Brooke pushed to her feet. She tapped patted the side of the kennel, wishing she could do the same to the dog, but he'd never tolerate it. "Be well, my friend," she whispered. "I hope we meet again under much better circumstances."

It wasn't possible to follow up long term with all the dogs she'd fostered or rescued over the years—there were just too many—but sometimes one wormed its way into her heart in an extra special way. Though this guy hadn't been with her long and the interaction had been minimal, she'd be calling Tim often to see how he was faring.

Half an hour later, she sat on the edge of her bed with tears streaming down her face. Why on earth did she let these dogs get to her so much?

Because you feel a kinship to them.

Just like she'd confessed to Curly a few nights ago. He'd been such a focused listener while she'd spewed her entire life story to him. God, how embarrassing. She couldn't even blame it on the alcohol because two beers did nothing to her. But, for some reason, she'd lost her mind for a bit and told the poor man more information than he bargained for. And afterward, she'd felt... good in a strange way. Lighter.

Suddenly she had the insane urge to talk to him again.

Thankfully, her phone chirped with a text before she could do something stupid like calling him.

Nancy: Bet you're crying right now. I'll be over in half hour to distract you with an afternoon at the pool. Your pool.

She laughed. Leave it to Nancy to cheer her up. She and David didn't have a pool and had a standing invitation to use Brooke's anytime at all.

Brooke: You should be my wife.

Nancy: You couldn't handle all this.

True story. Nancy was a force. But already, Brooke smiled and felt sunnier.

"Excuse me," Nancy said an hour later. Revulsion dripped from her voice. "What the hell is this?"

Brooke glanced over her shoulder from where she was digging through a drawer for the sarong she'd sworn she'd stuffed in there. "It's a bathing suit."

"Are you sure? Because it looks more like a potato sack."

Straightening, Brooke barked out a laugh. "Shut up. It does not. It's a normal one-piece bathing suit."

"With a skirt." Nancy held it by the strap with two fingers as though it were a dead rat rather than a floral bathing suit."

"Yes, with a skirt. What's wrong with that? I'm forty-one."

"Ugh, exactly!" Nancy tossed the bathing suit on the floor between them. "You're forty-one, not ninety-one. You are not wearing this. I won't allow it."

Brooke bent to retrieve the perfectly appropriate bathing suit with a laugh, but Nancy kicked it out of reach.

"Oh, it's on, bitch." She dove for her friend.

Nancy danced out of reach as she cracked up. "Wait! Don't attack. I come bearing gifts." She had her long blond hair pulled up in a high ponytail that made her look youthful and fun. When paired with her trendy swim coverup and designer sandals, Nance could be on the cover of a swimwear magazine.

"Gifts?" Brooke asked as she stopped the attack. "What gifts?"

After a quick rummage through her pool bag, Nancy pulled out something small and teal. "I'm tired of looking at your geriatric bathing suits, so I bought you...this!" She held up two scraps of material. "It's a bathing suit."

Her forehead wrinkled. "Is it for a toddler?"

With a roll of her eyes, Nancy asked, "Judgmental much? No! It's for you. Two pieces like someone with a hot bod should be wearing."

"Are you crazy?" Brooke lifted her hands and took a step back. "Oh, hell, no. There is no way I'm wearing that unless I have at least two layers of clothing over it. Did you not just hear me say I was forty-one?"

Nancy stared at the ceiling as though looking for strength. "Girlfriend, you are insane. Who the hell ever said a gorgeous forty-whatever-year-old with a banging body couldn't wear a bikini? I wear them all the time. And don't you tell me your husband would never have let you wear something like this because we both know he was a stupid fucknugget, and you can't believe a damn thing he said."

Well, it was true. Evan would have flipped his shit if she'd worn something so skimpy. Even in the privacy of their yard. He'd have had plenty of choice words about sluts and whores.

But if that were the only issue, she'd have jumped into the suit just to spite that asshole. "Um, I'm gonna give David a call and ask him to take you for a vision exam. There is something seriously wrong with your eyeballs. And you are thirty-two. That's nine fewer years of gravity dragging things down. And nine fewer years of collagen loss shriveling things up. And nine fewer years of donuts making things jiggle." When Nancy opened her mouth, Brooke held up a hand. "The wrong things."

Nancy's arms dropped to her side, and her mouth took on a disapproving frown. "Brooklynn Paige Williams, you will put this bathing suit on, or I will body slam you to the ground, strip you down, and put it on for you. Do you understand me?"

It took all her strength not to laugh at Nancy's fierce exasperation. If it were anyone else, she'd sigh then put on the one-piece, but Nancy was crazy enough to do as she threatened. "Yes, ma'am," Brooke said, though it came out as more of a garbled chuckle.

"Thank you." With an exaggerated roll of her eyes, Nancy handed over the thing she called a bathing suit.

"I feel bad for David," Brooke said as she examined the stretchy material. "You're scary."

"Don't you forget it." Nancy winked. "But I give a damn good BJ, so it all works out for him in the end."

Barking out a laugh, Brooke shook her head. "Scary and crazy. I'm gonna put this on now before you come at me."

"Good idea. I've already got mine on under this." Nancy indicated her adorable white coverup dress. "I so need a day to lounge by the pool. Work has been beyond crazy lately, and I haven't had a chance just to chill."

"I hear that," Brooke said as she walked into the bathroom. She shut the door and stripped out of her T-shirt and yoga pants. "What's David up to today?" she called out.

"Golfing with the boys. Blech."

Without peeking in the mirror, she finished undressing and stepped into the bathing suit bottoms. Huh, okay, they weren't *too* bad. The waist came up pretty high, giving a slight flattening to her stomach pooch. Brooke ate pretty well, exercised, and didn't hate her body. She just wasn't twenty-five anymore, and it showed. Also, after years of being told she was always too heavy, followed by too masculine when she would ramp up her workouts, then disgusting and gaunt once she lost dropped some weight, having a positive body self-image wasn't easy. Evan had found flaws in her figure no matter what she'd done or how hard she'd tried to earn his admiration, including sticking to his strict diet and exercise plans.

Nothing she'd done impressed Evan or met with his approval. Of course, now she knew it was more about his issues than how she looked or what she did, but the cutting words still played in her head now and again. He'd taken the most offense to any signs of aging. A wrinkle here or gray hair there would set him off on a tirade about how he'd shackled himself to a lazy wife who refused to care for her body and forced him to seek out other women.

A shudder ran through her. "That's over," she whispered. "Nothing he thought matters. Stop thinking about the loser."

"You say something?" Nancy asked.

"Just talking to myself," she called back as she tied the halter strap behind her neck.

"Talking about how hot you look?"

"Ha. You're hilarious. Okay," Brooke whispered to herself. "On three." She counted in her head, blew out a breath, then turned to the mirror with a hand over her eyes. Then she counted to three again and spread her fingers.

Well, she looked…pretty good. She let her hand fall to her side. She had pretty good-sized boobs. A thirty-six C. Over the years, they'd begun their downward journey, but this suit gave her lift and cleavage. A lot of cleavage. And the high-waisted bottoms kept her abdomen smoothed out. Of course, the little bit of cellulite on her legs would show whether she wore a one or two-piece, so that was a sunken cost.

All right, this was passable, especially since it would only be her and Nancy lounging by her pool for the next few hours.

"Time's up. Get that fine ass out here."

Oh, her ass. She turned and craned her next to look at her bottom in the mirror. This bathing suit lifted everything. "Coming."

She opened the door and stepped into her bedroom to a low whistle.

"Damn, Brooke. You are absolutely insane to put yourself down. You look amazing. I'd kill for those boobs. Look at these boor itty bitty titties," she said, staring down at her small chest.

Nancy was crazy. She had a body women killed for. Or paid thousands and thousands of dollars to achieve artificially. "Okay, the rule for the day, no self-body-shaming. Out loud or in our heads."

A smile broke out on Nancy's face. "Done. Let's get some drinks and soak up some harmful sun rays."

Twenty minutes later, they were lounging on chaises beside Brooke's pool. A small table between their chairs held a pitcher of margaritas as well as a bowl of chips and guac. Yes, I was only one in the afternoon, but it was a Saturday, and they deserved a treat.

"I'm pretty sure the only time I'm going to move for the next few hours is to flip over. Does it work for you if David swings by to pick me up at four when he's done golfing?" Nancy wore a sunny yellow bikini with a much slinkier cut than Brooke's.

Round white sunglasses took up most of her flawless face as she lay on her back with her arms dangling off the sides of the chaise.

The sun warmed Brooke's skin and relaxed her muscles to a state of drowsy bliss. Moving seemed a monumental and unnecessary task. "Yeah, that's perfect. I've got someone swinging by at six to adopt one of the dogs, so that'll give me time to get everything ready for him." Speaking of the dogs, her crew was scampering around the yard playing with each other and generally having a fantastic day. Ray supervised the other pooches from a shady spot beneath the covered area she'd had built for the dogs to escape the brutal summer sun. She'd turned on a sprinkler, and the water-loving pups ran around in the spray, happy as could be.

Nancy's head popped up. "He? That convict guy from the other day?"

With a frown, Brooke turned her face toward her nosy friend. "Don't call him that. He spent thirteen years behind bars for a crime he didn't commit. Can you imagine living through something like that?"

Propping herself up on her elbow, Nancy slid her sunglasses down her nose then pierced Brooke with a slightly intimidating look. Even though her friend couldn't see Brooke's eyes through her mirrored sunglasses, she felt raw and exposed. Transparent.

"What?"

"Awfully defensive of some random dude who's adopting a dog from you. Some guy who has a history of leading a criminal motorcycle club that did some terrible shit back in the day."

"He's not a bad guy." God, she was defensive of Curly, but she couldn't help it. The time she'd spent with him the other night only made her want to learn more about him. To hear his story, as ugly as it might be, and understand what made a man like him tick. "He doesn't deserve to be judged for something that wasn't his fault." Sometimes, one choice set off a chain reaction of events that changed someone's life, whether or not they deserved it. She sure knew that.

"Mm-hmm." Nancy laid back down.

"What?" Ugh, that didn't sound nearly as aloof as she'd hoped.

"I think someone's got a little crush on a bad boy," Nancy sing-songed. "Gotta say, I did not figure you for the tough-guy type. I was thinking when you finally woke up and looked at a man, it'd be someone who liked nature walks and granola. Maybe a vegan with a love of hemp and sprouts who rides a bicycle. Not a leather-wearing motorcycle sex fiend."

"A vegan?" Brooke laughed. "My favorite food in the entire world is Carne Asada tacos. What would I do with a vegan?"

With an unrepentant shrug, Nancy reached for her margarita. "I don't know. Eat tofu? You love to be outside. You like to garden and get dirty. To romp around with animals. Made sense in my head."

Brooke arched an eyebrow. "And a sex fiend? Way to stereotype, Nance, and to get back to your original statement, I do not have a crush on anyone."

"Your face is red. Excuse me if my imagination turned that hot biker man into an insatiable sex maniac."

Brooke pressed her palms to her warm face. "It's the sun. Keep this up, and I'll be advertising for a new best friend." She wasn't touching that sex maniac comment with a ten-foot pole.

Nancy snorted and almost spat her margarita all over herself. After she set the glass back on the table, she propped up on her side. "At the very least, you've gotta admit the man is studly as fuck. All those muscles and tattoos?" She shivered. "I bet he can do astonishing things in the sack. Like stuff that hasn't even been dreamed up yet by porn writers."

Rolling onto her stomach so she could grab her drink as well, Brooke said, "I'm sorry, did you forget about a man named David? He's about six feet, sweet as hell, handsome, and...oh, your husband."

Nancy pressed a hand to her heart. "I could never forget my hunky hubby. I was looking for you, my dearest friend. These are purely objective, clinical observations for your benefit."

Brooke rolled her eyes behind her glasses. God, she loved her wacky friend. "Weren't you the one warning me about him the other day? And calling him an ex-con just now?"

Nancy shrugged. "I'm not advising you to go ring shopping, but someone needs to clear out your cobwebs. Might as well be a fine-ass man who knows his way around a vajayjay. A woman can only survive on a vibrator for so long."

"It hasn't been *that* long." It'd been over five years. At this point, so much time passed she'd been intimate with a man she'd probably have a full-on panic attack if she tried.

"Don't even. Your vibrator called me the other day sobbing. It was sobbing, Brooke. It was all, 'Nancy, please find her a man. I'm exhausted. She keeps replacing the batteries instead of giving me the rest I need. The rest I deserve.'"

Brooke sat up and blinked at her friend. Then she burst out laughing. "You are insane."

Nancy grabbed a chip, loaded it up with guac, then lifted it as though toasting. "Never claimed otherwise."

They spent the next few hours alternately swimming, laying by the pool, and playing with the dogs. Brooke stopped herself after the second margarita. With Curly due in the evening, she needed her wits about her to keep from doing something stupid like telling him what she hadn't been willing to admit to Nancy. And that was just how irresistible she found those tattoos and all that hair.

And the muscles.

Lord, the muscles.

"Ugh," Nancy groaned as they air-dried on the lounge chairs after their recent cooldown in the pool. "David will be here soon, which means I have to leave. I don't wanna go. I'm too comfortable." There was a distinct whine in her voice.

Curly

Suddenly, Ray's head popped up, and his ears stood at attention. Then, he let out a loud woof and took off like a shot across the yard toward the gate. Of course, once he started running, the rest of the dogs grew interested, and soon the entire pack was yipping and yapping by the gate.

"Looks like your chariot has arrived."

"Waaah. Do you think if I throw a tantrum, he'll let me stay and play longer?" Nancy sat up, as did Brooke just as the gate opened. "Hey, bab—well, well, well, look who it is." Her grin radiated with evil glee.

Curly strode into the backyard, utterly unfazed by the dogs' attention. And it was pretty enthusiastic. Jack stuck nudged his head into Curly's hand while a pug puppy Brooke was pretty sure she would never be able to part with tugged at the laces on his boots. The rest of them ran circles around him, jumping for his hands in a shameless bid for affection.

"Ladies," he said with a lifted hand before crouching down to give the dogs love.

"Holy orgasmic wonderfulness," Nancy mouthed as she fanned herself.

Brooke peeked at her phone. "He's two hours early," she whispered. "Hand me my towel, I need to cover up."

"This towel?" Nancy asked as she reached for one of the towels folded at the bottom of her lounge chair. "Oops."

Brooke's eyes widened as she watched the towel flutter into the pool.

"My bad," Nancy said in the most insincere tone Brooke had ever heard. "It just fell from my hands."

"I hate you," she mouthed, only to be met with a shit-eating grin from her ex-best friend.

By then, Curly was making his way toward the lanai with the crew of dogs in tow. He walked with the kind of confident swagger that bordered on arrogance but never crossed the line. The man was truly a treat to look at. Thick thighs, toned arms, tanned skin, tattoos, and that curly hair falling almost to his shoulders. "Sorry, I'm so early. I was close by and took a chance you'd be home. I can scram if I'm interrupting."

Brooke stood, wearing nothing but her damp bikini with no choice but to greet him or risk being awkward and rude. Oh, God, the sexiest man she'd ever met was about to glimpse more of her forty-one-year-old body than any man ever had.

"Hey! It's no problem at all. We're just hanging out." Whoa, the combination of alcohol and sun had her feeling a little tipsier than she'd realized. To say Nancy had was a heavy-handed pourer was like saying her dogs *kinda* liked bacon: major understatement.

The moment Curly's eyes landed on her, his steps faltered, and his eyes darkened. Beside her, wrapping a towel around her waist, Nancy, the traitor, snickered. "Someone likes what they see," she muttered from the corner of her mouth.

Brooke swatted her friend's arm. "Shut up."

A horn honked from her driveway. The dogs started barking and zoomed toward the gate once again.

"Oh! That must be David. Gotta run. Don't wanna keep my man waiting. Toodles, you two!" With a cheery wave, she practically sprinted out of the lanai. After gifting smooches and rubs to all the dogs in the yard, Nancy vanished, and Brooke was left alone with Curly, who hadn't taken his eyes off her.

His gaze traveled every inch of her skin, heating her flesh more than the scorching Florida sun. He wasn't attempting to disguise his blatant perusal of her. Beneath the damp cups of her bathing suit top, her nipples tightened, and she prayed there was enough padding in the suit to keep him from noticing. From the way his eyes lingered at chest level, she wasn't feeling too confident in the bathing suit's lining.

Brooke cleared her throat. "Um, just let me dash inside and get dressed. Then I'll gather everything you need to get your new baby home."

"Take your time. These guys can keep me company." He strode back out into the yard.

Curly

"Okay." She turned and speed-walked toward her house, aware of his gaze on her ass the entire time.

"Hey, Brooke?" he called out just as she reached the French doors leading inside her home.

"Yeah?" She turned.

"Nice bathing suit."

"T-thanks," she squeaked.

Oh, my God. Oh, my God.

She scurried into the house and rested against the door with a hand over her pounding heart. Was it fear? Excitement? Who the hell knew? All Brooke knew was that the man sent her heart racing, her stomach fluttering, and her head spinning.

But it wasn't in a bad way. More in an overwhelming, tingly kind of way.

Ten minutes later, fully clothed and appearing much more professional, she'd gathered all the supplies and paperwork Curly would need for his first few days of puppy parenthood.

"You know," he said as she emerged back outside. "You didn't have to change on my account." He winked.

Her stomach flip-flopped as she waved away his comment. "Oh, no problem. I was done anyway since Nancy was about to leave. Okay, so here is her current vaccination—"

"Long as you didn't change for me. I was enjoying the view."

How the hell was she supposed to respond to that kind of comment? Was he flirting? Being kind? Being creepy? Gah, she was beyond out of practice. "Uh, thanks. So as I was saying, here's her shot record."

Curly chuckled and, thank God, let her get down to business. They ran through everything quickly since he mentioned this wasn't the first dog he'd owned.

"My phone number is on there. Please feel free to call or text if you have questions or problems. And I'm more than happy to help with training or anything. I've been working with her a bit, so she knows basic commands, but she's still a little gal who needs a ton of reinforcement."

"Thanks, Brooke. I might do that."

Her stomach flipped again. Not because she was excited, he might call her. Too much liquid in her belly. Had to be.

He sat on the concrete floor of her lanai with his new puppy crawling all over him. When he smiled, his face transformed from cautious and untrusting to open and happy.

"My pleasure. So what are you going to call her?"

"I'm gonna keep her as Harley. Don't wanna confuse her since that's what you've been calling her, and it fits pretty damn well." The puppy discovered a frayed string on his jeans and went to work attacking it. He laughed and scooped her into his arms, staring her straight in the face. She licked his nose. "Right, Harley? You like that name, don'tcha, girl?"

The dog yelped as though she understood him, and they both laughed.

So often, she related to her abused and neglected fosters, but never before had anyone looked at her with the instant love and adoration Curly shared with Harley. While she found nothing more fulfilling than matching a pet with its perfect owner, she couldn't help the stab of jealously she experienced when those animals found their loving forever families. Especially as she'd never find hers. The dogs were so much more adaptable than she was. They had the incredible capacity to trust again when shown consistent love and respect.

Brooke didn't think any amount of love would work to soften her toward a relationship.

Ugh, none of that.

She cleared her throat. "Think she approves. All right then, Harley it is. I always recommend keeping the name they are used to, but sometimes owners insist on a new one. It can help them connect and bond with the dog, but it can make training trickier."

He rose to his feet, still cradling the big puppy to his chest as though she were a lapdog instead of a big ol' girl, and Brooke's heart melted. There was nothing sexier than seeing a tough man be tender with something or someone smaller and vulnerable.

"Come on, Harley. Let's get you settled at home." He set the dog down, clipped on the leash she'd gifted, then hefted the bag of supplies Brooke provided to all new owners. "Oh, before I forget. Tomorrow night my guys will be going to a bar where Jinx will try to make a connection with Prick. Pulse'll be with him. Guys' night out. Me and the rest of them are gonna go hang there too so we can observe. We'll keep away from Jinx and Pulse, so Prick doesn't suspect we know each other. We may rile shit up a bit to throw him off and get Jinx on Prick's good side."

Brooke's heart sped up. Yes. This was the first step in ensuring she didn't end up with any more injured dogs. Though part of her worried one of the men would get in trouble on a mission she'd initiated, the majority of her couldn't wait to get the inside scoop on Prick's operation. "Yes! I want to be there."

Curly laughed. "Ain't happening. Especially since Prick knows who you are."

Brooke jammed her hands against her hips. Gone were the days when she blindly followed a man's orders. Now, the only one to direct her actions was her. Curly was about to find that out. She had as much right as he did to be at that bar. And she wanted to see Prick go down in the worst way. "I'm going," she said with finality.

Curly's eyes narrowed, and he stepped closer. She had to tip her head up to find his eyes. Without the gleeful puppy at his side, he'd have been intimidating as hell, but the adorable dog softened his edge.

Until he spoke.

"I get that you're independent as fuck, and I respect the hell outta it, but there is no way in fucking hell I'm letting you anywhere near that bar tomorrow night."

This man was about to reap all the benefits of Brooke's therapy and hard-won control over her own life. Poor man.

She gave him the sweetest smile she could muster as she said, "You think so, huh?"

Chapter Twelve

Curly alternated his death glare between Jinx and Pulse over at the bar and Brooke seated next to him, sipping her beer and yakking with Ty. He still had no idea how she'd gotten the upper hand in their argument. One minute he was in complete control, refusing to let her anywhere near this shitshow, and the next, she was wearing a sugary smile and sweetly telling him to fuck off.

Two minutes later, she had Ty on the phone—of course, she'd known he owned the tire shop, goddammed small towns—and Ty was spilling the name of the bar and time they were meeting. When Curly had shown up at the tire shop ranting and raving at his cousin, Ty just laughed and asked how it was possible for him to be pussy-whipped without having access to the pussy.

Asshole.

Now the two of them chatted and laughed like they were fucking besties without a care in the world while Curly stewed over the five million ways the night could go wrong and harm could come to Brooke.

Fucking stubborn woman.

"Will you relax?" Tracker murmured from the other side of him. Loud rock music made it difficult to hear the man's muffled comment. "You're tense as fuck and gonna draw attention to us. Ty isn't gonna home in on your territory, man."

That had Curly scowling Tracker's way. "What?"

"He's not trying to move in on your girl. Trust me, she ain't his type. He goes for the soft little bunnies. She's got away too much spit and sass for him."

"He can do whatever the fuck he wants. She's not mine."

Tracker snorted. "Okay, tell that to your pissed-off face."

He flipped Tracker off. "I just don't want her in the same room as Prick. Too much could go wrong."

They had a table in the bar's back corner, shielded by dim light and hordes of patrons noisy. Seated at a high-top table, they managed a fair view of the bar once they craned their necks to see around the Saturday night crowd. Jinx and Pulse drank at the bar, conveniently seated next to Prick and his buddy, but had yet to engage him.

"Hey." Tracker nudged his foot under the table. "You know we won't let anything happen to her, right? If shit goes south here, I'll get her out, promise. Your woman's top priority."

"She's not my woman." Maybe if he said it out loud enough times, he'd stop acting like she was his. Probably not. That wouldn't happen until he stopped fantasizing about her while he was in bed, and in the shower, and once that afternoon on the couch. He was helpless to stop imagining all that feisty attitude turned into sexual desire. It gotten even worse after seeing her in that skimpy bikini.

Rolling his eyes, Tracker lifted his beer to his lips. "So you keep saying," he whispered before taking a long swallow.

With a defeated sigh, Curly stared at the condensation running down his beer. "Thank you."

Tracker nodded. "Got your back, prez. Always."

Their gazes met, and Curly saw the sincerity in them. "You mean that."

He hadn't posed it as a question, yet Tracker answered. "Hundred fucking percent. When your own family is shit, your chosen one is important. I did some research on the Hell's

Handlers. Impressive club. Exactly what I'm looking for. This shit is serious to me."

Curly held out a fist which Tracker tapped against his own.

And just like that, he gained a true brother. Felt damn good. Exactly what he'd been searching for.

"Look," Brooke said, nudging him with her elbow. "Jinx is talking to Prick."

He followed her gaze to the bar in time to see Jinx toss his head back and laugh like a look at something Prick said. Then he slapped Prick in the back and flagged down the bartender. After ordering another drink for Prick, the two seemed to get into a serious discussion.

"Let the games begin," Ty muttered.

The four of them sat silently at the table, watching the interaction between Prick and Jinx. For his part, Pulse stayed on the outskirts of the conversation, interjecting occasionally but not playing a significant role.

Jinx was a natural. Where Pulse came across stiff and slightly uncomfortable, Jinx might as well have known Prick his entire life.

After a few minutes, a waitress appeared beside their table. "Such serious faces," she said with a bright smile. "Something not to ya'lls' liking?"

"We're good," Curly barked, which made Brooke roll her eyes.

"Another round please," she said, sweet as could be.

"You got it, hon." Their waitress, who had a high ponytail with purple hair hanging down to her ass, collected the empty bottles while eyeing him with suspicion. She returned within minutes, passing out the drinks and a dropping bowl of pretzels in the center of the table. "Flag me down if you need anything else, guys."

"Thanks, darlin'," Tracker said, shooting her a wink. She fluttered her eyelashes at him and flounced away to tend to the next table.

Curly grunted.

"Are you trying to draw attention to yourself?" Brooke asked as she popped a pretzel between her glossy lips. "Because being the grumpiest person in the bar is a good way to do that."

"Maybe if you'd stayed away like I wanted, I'd be in a better mood." And maybe if she'd stop drawing attention to her mouth, he could stop imagining it sliding up and down his dick, leaving a shiny pink trail.

She snorted at that, completely unphased by his shit attitude. "You are a sore loser."

Tyler burst out laughing. "Oh, man, does she have your number, cuz. Keep giving him hell, honey," he said as he clinked the neck of his bottle against Brookes.

With a self-satisfied smirk, she tipped her fresh beer to her lips and sipped a few times. Pissed as he was with her presence, even he could admit he enjoyed the woman's company. And he sure as fuck enjoyed looking at her. Especially that throat working as she swallowed the beer. Gave him all sorts of filthy thoughts of her swallowing something else.

Namely him.

After a few more minutes of silently observing the interaction at the bar, Brooke began to drum her nails on the tabletop. When she added a leg bounce, Curly had to intervene.

"Hey," he said, sliding his hand on top of hers. She immediately stilled and twisted to face him, wide-eyed. "Relax. It's going good. If this is stressing you—"

Her eyes narrowed to slits. "Don't you dare suggest I leave."

With a chuckle, he shook his head. "No, ma'am. I learned my lesson there, and I value my balls too much." Earlier, she'd threatened to unman him if he pulled any stunts to keep her from joining them. So he'd had no choice but to drop Harley off at Brooke's house to hang out with her boyfriend, Ray. Then he'd given Brooke a ride to the bar. "I was gonna say if you need a minute you can run to the bathroom and splash some water on your face."

"Clearly you've never worn make-up," she said with a laugh, "but I think I might take a minute to breathe. Watching them is making me want to crawl out of my skin. I keep waiting for the signal."

Once he'd gotten an invite to a dog fight, Jinx was supposed to slap Prick on the back twice before making his way to the parking lot. Then they'd know this had been a successful venture. And they could get the hell out of there.

"Want me to come with you?" he asked, which make Ty crack up.

"Pretty sure she can find her way to the potty by herself, man. Who the fuck knew you were such a mother hen?"

He expected to see the same mocking humor in Brooke's gaze, but instead, he found the warmth of appreciation. "I've got it," she whispered, squeezing his arm. "But thank you. Be right back, boys."

As she walked away, he could still feel the heat of her small but strong hand on his skin. Brooke was a simple woman. So different than most women he'd spent time with. Granted, it'd been years since he'd had one, but the women who hung around the Outlaws dressed to attract the brothers' attention. That meant tiny tops that had most of their tits on display. Short, tight skirts that gave a man a glimpse of what waited for them when they bent over. Heels sky-high worn to make their legs appear longer and shapelier no matter how hard they were to walk in, and enough make-up to make them look like flawless dolls.

Brooke wore distressed jeans, a black fitted tank top, and flip-flops. Her toes had a light coral polish, but her fingernails were bare. He'd yet to see her wear a piece of jewelry beyond stud earrings. Yet she had his dick harder than any of those sweet butts at his club ever did. Of course, it didn't hurt that the soft denim cupped her ass like it was making an offering to him.

There was an innate confidence in the way she carried herself. Who knew he'd be so attracted to a self-assured woman? Yet he was. Though a few times, at her core, he glimpsed a vulnerability he wanted to squash so no matter the situation, she could remain the kick-ass woman he'd met. He'd never understand men like her husband. Who would want to squash all that made her the rockin' woman she was?

"If you stare at her ass any harder, you likely to pop a blood vessel," Ty said with a laugh.

"Fuck off. Just making sure she gets there okay."

"Mm-hmm. Whatever you say, cuz. It is a treacherous journey."

"So I've been thinking," Tracker said. He set his beer down and rested his elbows on the table.

"That's not like you." Ty shot back.

"Aren't you just hilarious tonight? I'm fucking serious, though. You own the lot next to your shop, don't you?" Tracker asked Ty.

With a nod, Ty said, "Yeah, I snatched it up years ago when it went up for sale. Didn't want something shitty opening up next to me. Haven't had the capital to do anything with it, though."

Well, now Tracker had Curly thoroughly intrigued. "What are you thinking?"

"Car wash. It deals in a lot of cash and can be fucking profitable as hell on its own. If we're gonna be lending money, we may have to wash some on occasion, and having access to a cash business will make that easier. And it goes along well with what Ty already has going. We can offer full detailing too, not just car wash. Fuck, maybe mobile detailing. That shit's popular right now."

"Well, look at you with the fucking good ideas," Ty said.

Curly stroked his lower lip as he pondered Tracker's proposal. It was a damn fine idea, and he had more than enough capital to get it up and running without putting a dent in his finances.

"Good shit, right?" Tracker, the cocky fucker asked. But he'd give credit where it was due.

"Damn good shit. Fuck, Tracker, this could be perfect."

"I'll do some research and run some numbers for you so we can see what we might be looking at to get up and running."

"Thanks, brother," Curly said. Then he glanced back toward the bar, and his heart leaped to his throat. "Shit. Where the fuck's Prick?"

Tracker and Ty swiveled toward the bar and cursed as well. Jinx and Pulse sat side by side, speaking back and forth, but Prick was nowhere to be found,

"Texting Jinx," Tracker said as his fingers flew over his phone.

Damnit, how could he have been so fucking careless? Curly scanned the bar for any glimpse of Prick, but the place was too packed now and the lights too dim to properly search.

"Jinx said Prick went to take a leak," Tracker announced as he looked up with a grim expression.

"Fuck!" He shot out of his seat and began to shoulder his way through the crowd, ignoring the surprised cries of dismay whenever he checked someone.

"Shit, Curly, wait!" Ty shouted behind him, but fuck that. He should never have taken his eyes off Prick, and now that he had, Brooke could be in danger.

If that fucker had come within three feet of Brooke, this entire plan would have been a waste of time. He'd be putting an end to the dogfighting right then and there by wrapping his hands around Prick's throat and squeezing until he crushed the bastard's windpipe.

Chapter Thirteen

Of course, the ladies' room was out of paper towels. Wouldn't be a bar restroom if it was fully stocked. At least they'd had toilet paper, and the stalls were clean. And by clean, she meant they didn't make her shudder in horror. Brooke peered at her reflection while shaking her hands dry. Curly had been right. A few moments away from the table where she couldn't stare at Prick had calmed her nerves.

She wanted this plan to work with every cell in her body. She wanted to bust up the fighting ring, arrest every jackass involved, and arrange whatever help necessary for the mistreated dogs. But most of all, she wanted to see the look on Prick's face when his entire operation blew up. If another dog ended up on David's operating table in the middle of the night needing an emergency amputation, she couldn't be held responsible for her reaction. Men like Prick with such little regard for living creatures didn't deserve leniency. They deserved whatever the hell they got, whether it was a jail sentence or a pine box.

The vehement reaction was over the top, even for her animal-loving self. But she couldn't help it. Those animals suffered every day, even when not fighting. They were isolated, trained with harsh methods and punishment, taught to fear and attack other animals. It was sickening. The psychological impact of isolation, constant condemnation, and absence of affection was a hundred times harder to overcome than the physical injuries.

She knew firsthand. After Evan's one physical assault, her bruises healed within weeks, whereas she still bore the wounds of his emotional abuse.

Now, on top of her hatred of Prick over the dogfighting ring, she'd had to process the fact that the man helped send Curly to jail for a crime he didn't commit. She'd thought about it way too much since she found out, and each time, her heart cracked a little more.

And that was something she was terrified to delve into further. She barely knew Curly. Sure, she could feel sympathy for the rotten hand he'd been dealt, but she feared it was more than that. She wanted vengeance for him. Wanted someone to pay for what they'd done to him. Brooke was tired of assholes getting away with treating others like shit.

Assholes like her husband and Prick shouldn't get to move on with a smile on their smarmy faces. It just wasn't fair. And while years of therapy had tried to help her accept her freedom and happiness as a satisfying replacement for revenge, there were dark moments when it wasn't enough. Once in a while, when her hard-won independence felt more like loneliness than liberation, she wanted her husband to hurt as she'd hurt for so long, to fear as she'd feared, and to know the true meaning of helplessness. A state she vowed to never be in again.

Curly knew it, and her secret desire for retaliation extended to him as well. Destroying a significant source of income for Prick would be a fantastic start.

She rested her hands on the counter and gave herself a good internal assessment. Since leaving Evan and adopting Ray, she'd developed a protective streak a mile wide. Sometimes it got the better of her, and her reactions were a little over the top. Brooke blew out a breath and shook off the negativity as best she could.

Then she yanked the door open, strode into the hall, and slammed right into a large man.

"Shit, sor—" She nearly swallowed her tongue as she glanced up into the face of an irate Prick.

"You," he snarled down at her.

Every instinct she had told her to bitch him out, but one grain of sanity prevailed, making her hold her tongue. Thankfully that one morsel of self-preservation was hardier than the rest of her brain because, truth be told, he could squash her like a bug. So instead of giving him the verbal blasting he deserved, she just said, "Excuse me," and stepped to the side to move around his broad body.

"Not so fast," he said, scooting into her path.

"My friends are waiting for me." This time she moved in the other direction, but again he blocked her retreat.

"Found something out about you," he said, voice laden with venom.

Brooke sighed. "What's that?"

"Turns out your property borders mine."

She stiffened as she glared at him. Only her continued moving, beating out a rapid pattern. "And?"

He advanced on her, forcing her to stumble backward or have his protruding stomach bump her. Eventually, she encountered a wall. Trapped.

Shit.

He wasn't touching her, but the threat was there. Rancid breath wafted down, causing her to wrinkle her nose and breathe through her mouth. Had the man ever heard of a toothbrush? Maybe a stick of gum? If the yellow tinge to his teeth were any indication, he wasn't well acquainted with oral hygiene.

"It'd be a damn shame if something happened to all those cute little dogs you keep."

Brooke's spine snapped straight. Oh, hell no. Threatening her was one thing. Back her into a corner to show her he had the physical advantage? Fine. She could weather that storm. But threaten her babies?

Mama bear came out to play.

She drew herself up to her full five-feet-six inches, a solid half foot or so shorter than Prick, but screw it. "If you know what's good for you, you'll get the fuck out of my way. And if I ever catch you anywhere near my property, you'll be hobbling home with broken kneecaps." The thought of physically harming anyone, even this piece of shit, had her stomach roiling, but she'd do it to protect her brood.

How dare he threaten her dogs.

Prick let out a loud, obnoxious laugh. He grabbed her upper arms and shoved her against the wall so hard, she bit her tongue. Tears sprung to her eyes, but she'd die before letting him know she hurt. She'd learned from her husband that men like him got off on wielding power, so she became a master at hiding her true feelings.

"Get your fucking hands off me," she seethed despite the metallic taste filling her mouth.

"Or what? You gonna break my kneecaps?" he laughed again.

"No, but I sure as fuck will." Curly's enraged voice came from behind Prick, and Brooke wasn't ashamed to admit she sagged in relief.

Goading Prick might have been a mistake. For a second there, she'd worried she'd gone too far.

As soon as Prick turned, she darted around his girth and hustled to where Curly stood with Tracker and Ty. Even with his eyes spitting fire, Curly's touch was gentle as he took hold of her arm. "You're bleeding," he said as he swiped his thumb across her lower lip.

"It's nothing. Just bit my tongue."

"Go stand with Ty."

Normally she'd have bristled at the order, but she'd run out of steam and felt shaken to the core. When she reached Tyler, he slung an arm around her shoulder and pulled her close.

"What'd I tell you about keeping that bitch on a leash?" Prick said with a smirk she'd have loved to see Curly smack off his face. But they were in public, and a trip to jail would be the cherry on this shitty sundae of a night.

"Can't remember. I don't listen to a thing that comes out of your fat mouth. Now you wanna come at me, go right the fuck ahead. You know where I live as well." He spread his arms wide and gestured for Prick to come at him.

Brooke sucked in a breath.

"Nothing's gonna happen," Ty whispered down at her. "Prick's too much of a pussy to take on Curly."

Maybe, but the thought of him getting hurt because she ran her mouth had her feeling sick. Her husband always accused her of not thinking before she spoke. He'd hated it and berated her for it. Maybe it was one thing he'd been right about.

"Hey, everything okay down there?"

Brooke peered behind her to find Jinx standing at the opening of the hallway.

"Prick, you need an assist, man?" Jinx cracked his neck and stood with fists clenched as though ready to brawl.

Her eyes widened. Jinx's antagonistic attitude toward Curly was the absolute perfect way to get on Prick's good side, but if she showed her recognition of him, it'd be game over.

"Nah, this fuckface ain't worth getting kicked outta the bar. Not done drinkin' yet." Prick rammed his shoulder against Curly's as he stormed by. Curly's torso twisted, but he managed to keep his feet planted on the floor. The second Prick passed him, Curly spun, and the murderous look on his face had Brooke clutching Ty's shirt. She fisted the material at his waist to keep herself steady as she held her breath.

What was coming? Would Curly lash out and attack Prick, putting himself and the rest at risk for arrest, or would he swallow his pride and keep his cool?

With nostrils flared, Curly marched two steps forward.

"Are you going to stop him?" she whispered to Ty.

Before he had a chance to answer, Prick's voice rose again. "Thanks for the offer of backup, my man," he said presumably to Jinx. "Got something you might be interested in going down in two weeks. Let's have another drink at the bar, and I'll give you the details."

That stopped Curly in his tracks. Pissed as he was, he wouldn't screw up the reason they were there in the first place.

Prick slapped Jinx on the back, and they walked back toward the crowded bar together.

With a sigh of relief, Brooke released Ty's shirt and walked over to Curly. "Mission accomplished," she whispered with a slight grin. Excitement pumped through her veins, replacing the fear, and on impulse, she threw her arms around Curly in a victorious embrace.

He didn't return the hug. Instead, his body remained rigid as a stone pillar.

Jerking back, Brooke could have kicked herself for the impulsive gesture. What the hell was wrong with her, jumping him like they were best friends. "I'm sorr—"

"We're leaving. Get the fuck outside and into my truck."

"Excuse me?" she drew back as though he'd slapped her.

He took one step forward, causing her to tilt her head back or be staring at his chest. "I said, get the fuck outside the bar and into my truck." Then he dodged around her and stomped toward the exit. "Walk her out, Ty."

Brooke whirled around. "He did not just order me around."

A strangled sound came from Tyler's compressed lips. Tracker, who'd remained a strong, silent presence, didn't bother to suppress his laughter. "You better get out there, missy," he said through his chuckling. "Daddy's mad."

"Oh, I'm going out there," she snapped, surprised they couldn't see smoke rising from the top of her head. "But not because he freaking told me to. Because I'm done with this shithole." By the time she finished with him, Curly wouldn't command her to do another goddammed thing as long as he lived.

As she tromped past the guys, Tracker halted her with a hand on her shoulder. "Go easy on him," he whispered down to her. "He lost his fucking mind when he realized you might be alone with Prick."

That took some of the wind out of her sails, but not all of it. Curly had pushed the wrong button when he'd barked his harsh order. Now that she knew it was out of fear, she didn't want to rip his head off—she'd just knock it around a bit. Shaking off Tracker's hold, she marched her way through the crowd toward the door.

"Shit," Tracker whispered to Tyler as they rushed after her. "Hope Curly has plenty of ice at home. I have a feeling his balls are gonna need it."

Brooke's lips quirked. Damn straight he'd need some ice.

CURLY GRIPPED THE steering wheel so hard the leather creaked beneath his palms. Twice now, he had to witness Prick lording his height and strength over Brooke. And was she smart enough to back down?

Fuck, no.

The stupid woman had cajones the size of goddammed melons and got right up in Prick's face with her fucking attitude. Had she no sense? One clock of Prick's meaty fist and that jaw she flapped with her sass would be wired shut for weeks. And that was the least of what that bastard could and would do to her if she goaded him too far.

Brooke ripped the passenger side door open and climbed into the seat beside him.

"Good luck, cuz," Ty yelled.

She slammed the door closed, cutting off Ty's laughter, then buckled her seatbelt with exaggerated aggression. Had he not been so on edge, he'd have had to hold back his laughter at the way she didn't even pretend she wasn't pissed as hell at him. Once secure, she folded her arms and stared out the window.

They made the fifteen-minute trip to her house in heavy, tension-filled silence. Not once did she glance his way or shift her rigid posture.

Before he had the chance to fully brake in her driveway, she was out of the car and stomping to her front door.

Curly sighed. After the adrenalin-pumping fear he'd experienced less than thirty minutes ago, he wasn't looking forward to an impending argument. Nevertheless, he walked up behind her just as she unlocked her door and pushed it open.

"What the hell do you think you're doing?" She asked as she whirled on him. "I did not invite you into my house."

He cocked his head. "Does that mean you're kidnapping my dog?"

Brooke blinked, clearly forgetting Harley had been hanging out with Ray while they'd been at the bar. As she stood there with a surprised expression, the dogs in question came barreling around the corner.

Both clambered to him first, begging for affection. Ray rolled onto his back and presented his belly for a rub which Curly gladly gave while Harley jumped up licked all over his face.

"Fine. Get your dog and go," Brooke said.

Shit, even the sight of the dogs with him hadn't softened her. This was going to take the big guns.

"Brooke," he said to her back as she'd already started for her kitchen.

Her back remained stiff. "What?"

"Can I talk to you for a moment?"

Her shoulders slumped. After a few seconds, she turned and folded her arms across her luscious chest. "Say your piece and go. I want another beer and a swim in my pool. Originally I was going to ask you to join me, but now you are no longer invited to either."

Damn, the woman was cruel. And cold. Tempt him with another glimpse of her in that sexy bikini, then rip it away.

He walked to her, accompanied by the dogs, who seemed oblivious to the tension in the room. When he reached her, her stubborn chin lifted, and her eyes shone with anger.

Brooke was prepared for battle.

And she'd never looked more beautiful. That fiery defiance made his dick harder than it'd been in years. He could only imagine what she'd do with all that passion in bed.

"I'm sorry," he said.

She blinked. "What?"

"I took my eyes off Prick for a minute, and Jinx texted to say he'd gone to the bathroom right after you did. I freaked the fuck out. Then when I saw him cornering you and you getting in his face, I lost my shit. But it's no excuse for the way I barked at you. I'm sorry I was a dick to you."

Watching her anger melt away, only to be replaced by confusion, made his heart ache. Brooke had been married to an asshole who'd belittled her, controlled her, and dominated her life.

He may not be a saint, but he wasn't a motherfucker either. He was man enough to own it when he fucked up.

And hopefully, she just realized that.

Chapter Fourteen

"You're sorry?"

He's sorry?

He'd apologized?

Just like that?

Her head spun. Curly wasn't exactly the type she'd have expected to own his mistakes without being forced to. He was a biker. An outlaw. Physically, there wasn't anything soft about him, and she'd assumed it'd be the same emotionally.

But she was wrong.

"Yes." He stepped even closer, wrapping those big, callused hands around her upper arms. She tried to keep from shivering in delight, but the feel of those fingers on her skin made her want to sink to her knees and show him just how good he made her feel.

Since when do you have thoughts like that?

"Yes. I'm sorry. Brooke, I'm a man. Not a little boy pretending to be a man. I'm big enough to admit when I fuck up. Can't promise I won't do it again, but I'll try. And Brooke?"

"Yes?" Not only did the man apologize but he did a damn sincere and stellar job of it too. Who was he?

His face hovered close. Too close. So close she could smell his aftershave. Something she couldn't describe with words, but it drew her like she was a fish he'd reeled in. So did the stubble lining his jaw. Goosebumps erupted all over as her disobedient mind imagine the scrape of that stubble on her skin. She'd never had that nor wanted it, yet suddenly it seemed like the most decadent experience she could have.

"I admire the fuck outta you. You're strong, independent, and not afraid stand up to anyone. You're as impressive as you are beautiful."

Her breath caught. Holy shit. He thought she was beautiful? And impressive?

Her husband would have berated her for hours over being dumb enough to get herself in a precarious situation in the first. He'd have accused her of running into Prick on purpose and goading him. Curly was impressed with her ability to stand up for herself. Damn, that felt good.

Brooke searched his face for signs of insincerity or patronization but found none. Never, not once in their entire marriage had Evan apologized. He'd believed all the things he said to her, felt he had the right to demean her in any way he chose, and expected her to follow him without question just as these dogs did.

She wasn't unrealistic. Everyone fucked up from time to time. She certainly did and antagonizing Prick could have easily turned into one of those major fuckups if Curly hadn't come along to rescue her.

Twice.

"Thank you," she whispered then cleared her throat. "I have some triggers, so..." She shrugged as though it was enough to justify her overreaction.

A soft huff of air left him. "You don't need to explain. Got a few of those myself."

She was sure he did, and though she shouldn't, she wanted to learn more about them. "Uh, it's only nine. Care to join me for a beer and a swim?" Seemed like a good way to make nice.

His lips turned up in a wicked grin that had her knees wobbling. "That depends."

"On what?"

He still had his hands on her arms, but they'd creeped their way up, cupping her shoulders. Leaning in, he sent a puff of warm breath wafting across her ear. "Depends on whether I'll get to see you in that bikini again."

Don't shiver. Don't shiver.

She closed her eyes closed. No, she sure as hell hadn't been planning to wear the two-piece bathing suit, but the husky timbre of his voice and the hint of desire had her caving in an instant. "Yes, I'll wear it."

"Well then, the kids and I will be waiting for you out by the pool." He pulled back with a wink, then strode toward her French doors as though he'd been in her home a million times before.

The second his stellar backside disappeared from view, Brooke darted to her room to change. Standing in front of the bathroom mirror in the bikini once again, she saw an extra few hundred flaws she'd somehow managed to overlook when Nancy was there.

Even with the push-up from the top, her breasts could stand to be an inch or two higher. She also had this little—maybe medium—paunch right above the bathing suit bottom. Then there were those faint white lines on her inner thighs. Stretch marks. Evan had never been satisfied with her weight. She'd yo-yoed for years fluctuating up and down at least twenty pounds, but he'd always had a quick criticism. As a result of the fluctuations, she'd developed the lovely stretchmarks.

"You're acting ridiculous," she told her reflection. "What makes you think he even wants you? He probably has a whole harem of young biker-chasing women ready to service him anytime he snap his fingers."

With one last plump of her breasts, she rolled her eyes at the ridiculous forty-one-year-old in the mirror and left the bathroom. At least it was dark outside and while she had patio lighting, the night would still be dim enough to hide most of her flaws.

She found Curly standing in the shallow end of her pool with his arms stretched along the patio. Both dogs already snoozed on a lounge chair. He'd turned on the string lights that crisscrossed above the pool, casting a romantic glow through the lanai.

His gaze met hers and it was then she realized he didn't have a bathing suit so the dark fabric she glimpsed under the water must be his underwear.

This was a mistake. Why the hell had she invited him? Letting a man into her life was not in the plan. Never again would she be beholden to someone or give someone control over her life. She'd never done the casual sex thing, and while she told herself *that's* what this night could be, she had no idea how to do that.

His eyes widened as he noticed her approach and he let out a low whistle.

Her face heated under his blatant perusal.

"Get that fine ass in here. Feels fantastic." He pushed off the wall and waded toward her.

"Yeah. It's heated so it stays warm even at night."

Wow, Brooke, great conversation skills.

Even if the water were ice cold, the man currently making his way toward her would have heated it to boiling. He'd pulled those curls away from his face with a band though a few escaped. Tattoos were scattered across his naked chest and those pecs...God, those pecs. Though as sexy as they were, they had nothing on his biceps. For whatever reason, she'd always found a man's arms particularly sexy and Curly's were about as perfect as they came. Tanned and smooth, a vein ran diagonally across each one. She scraped her teeth across her tongue to stem the urge to lick the barbed wire tattoo ringing his right bicep.

On embarrassingly wobbly legs, she walked down the steps into the three-foot shallow end. Only a body's length separated them. Normally the warmth of the water would have her relaxing within seconds, but she couldn't seem to calm her racing heart and mind.

Did he think something would happen between them? Did he want something to happen between them?

Did *she* want something to happen between them? Did she have what it took to satisfy a man like Curly?

Not according to her husband who'd cheated on her for most of their marriage, blaming her, of course.

Ugh, this was why she steered clear of men. Too many mind games, even if they were all in her own head.

"Want to see my skills?" he asked as he sent a gentle splash her way.

"Your skills?" She arched an eyebrow.

"Yep. Betcha can't do this." After shooting her a wink, he dove beneath the water and kicked his legs up into a crooked handstand. When he toppled over after about two seconds, Brooke burst into laughter.

"Those were your skills?" she asked with a smile. "Impressive."

"Hey! That was just the warmup. You ready for the real thing this time?"

"Bring it on. Can't be worse than the last one."

Another surge of water came her way, this time with much more force behind it. The spray left her laughing and sputtering at the same time. Where on earth had this playful side of Curly come from? Though were she honest, she wasn't often carefree herself unless working with the dogs. They never judged her. Never criticized. Just loved and accepted her as she was, and she did the same for them.

Once again, Curly flipped upside down. This time he managed to hold his balance which gave her a chance to check out his ass in the, yep, those were boxer briefs. Wet ones that clung to him like a second skin.

He began to walk on his hands, turning around and suddenly she was no longer face to face with his muscular ass, but the very impressive outline of his cock. Nothing was hidden as the wet fabric molded to every inch of him.

"Holy shit," Brooke muttered on an exhale. She squeezed her legs together as an achy emptiness she hadn't experienced in ages made itself known.

"Boom!" Curly shouted as he surfaced, throwing his arms in the air. "What'd I tell ya? Skills."

His gaze landed on her face and his goofy grin morphed into something dark and wicked. Oh, God, what did he see in her eyes? Was her desperate need to be touched scrawled all over her face?

Whatever he'd used to tie back his hair failed under the water, and a wild array of wet curls hung down past his chin. Beads of water dotted his sculpted chest and suddenly Brooke was hit with a tremendous thirst only those drops would quench.

One of Curly's eyebrows took a slow journey upward. "Something catch your eye?" he asked, coming closer to her. The smooth water rippled around him sending small waves through the pool. Beneath the lights, his tanned skin shone, slick and bronzed. He looked feral, predatory, dangerous.

Delicious.

Shit, she was in so far over her head, she didn't even know how to respond to the flirty comment. "Um, no, I just...I was admiring your tattoos." Brooke took a step back. Then another. And one more until she hit the side of the pool. She probably sounded like an idiot.

"Is that right?"

That voice rasped over her skin like the light scraping of nails, sending shivers through her despite the warmth of the night.

"Y-yes," she said, breathless as her heart raced.

He dragged a wet hand across the left side of his chest where the tattoo of angel wings and a halo resided. "Would you like a closer peek? You know, so you can get the full view."

She nodded.

He kept wading through the water until he stood only inches away. Close enough to touch. Close enough to taste.

Her breath came in rapid bursts, and when his hands landed on her waist, she nearly moaned at the tingly heat.

Without a word, he hoisted her up and set her down on the edge of the pool before settling his hands on her thighs. He pushed them wide enough to step between. "Look your fill."

This was the most intimate thing she'd done with a man in years. *Years.* Her breath caught and she felt a little dizzy as his warmth and scent registered. Part of her was terrified of where this would lead, but she was helpless to do anything but let the tide pull her along.

As though commanded by an invisible force, her gaze went to his chest. It was then she realized the halo was actually made up of tiny letters and numbers. She lifted her hand to stroke over the skin but pulled back at the last second.

"You can touch me. Anywhere you'd like."

When her gaze jumped to his, he winked.

The ball bounced in her court. They hadn't so much as kissed, yet Brooke knew if she put her hands on him, something would happen between them tonight. Her body craved him while her mind warned against getting involved with an alpha biker. How could she every hold the attention of a man like him, even for one night, when she couldn't hold her husband's? A man more potent, powerful, and dangerous than her husband could have ever hoped to be. A man who'd committed crimes, served time, and had a mountain of baggage. Despite the field of red flags, Curly drew her with a compelling force she'd never experienced and didn't fully understand.

She had no intention of ever tying herself to a man again. Would never give a man power over her money, her friendships, her life, her heart. Just the thought of it made her sick to her stomach. But she was also forty-one years old and had never had a hot and heavy affair. She'd never felt explosive chemistry with a man like she did with Curly. Never felt the kind of sexual satisfaction novelists wrote about.

The intense desire bordered on need. As though she'd crumble if he didn't touch her. So against all her mind's sensible arguments, she traced the angel wings with her finger.

The moment her hand brushed his skin, he sucked in a harsh breath. Though inked in only black, they were done with thin lines giving them the most delicate of appearances. Every detail was perfect as though whoever tattooed this knew if was vitally important to him. His skin was smooth and warm beneath her finger. She wanted to press the other nine to him as well and soak up all that strong heat.

"Is this for Joy?" she asked in a low voice as she rubbed the halo between the wings.

He covered her hand with his, pressing her palm to his chest. The strong, rapid beat of his heart fluttered beneath her fingers. She lifted her gaze and met the darkened swirl of Curly's eyes.

"Yes. Along with the name, the halo has the date she died."

So many words danced on the tip of her tongue. How sorry she was for what he'd endured. How tragic the loss of a child's life was and also the loss of so many years of his life. But there'd be time for sorrow and comfort that later. Right then, beneath the stars and twinkling lights, she couldn't disrupt the magic brewing between them.

Curly lifted her hand off his chest and with his gaze locked on hers, pressed a long kiss to her palm. His tongue snuck out, tickling the skin, making her gasp. Then he took a step closer and kissed her wrist.

His broad frame stretched her legs even wider.

Next, his lips landed on her forearm, then the crook of her elbow, the sensitive skin of her upper arm, her shoulder...

Everywhere he made contact a spark of electricity buzzed along her nerve endings.

Brooke lifted her chin a fraction, inviting him to continue to her neck.

Curly

He hummed his approval then slid his tongue along her collar bone, drawing a shocked squeak from her. She curled her trembling fingers around the edge of the pool, holding on for dear life.

He kept going, kissing his way up her neck to her chin. Goosebumps erupted all over her body and she held her breath, afraid she'd miss something spectacular if she breathed.

After one final peck to the tip of her nose, he lined up their mouths and paused only a fraction of an inch away. He gripped the outside of her thighs and his eyes sparkled with roguish delight.

"Yes?" he asked in a whisper.

Finally, Brooke released the breath she'd been holding as she nodded. "Yes."

She'd barely gotten the word out when he swallowed it with his mouth. His lips crashed against hers, hungry and hot. She opened for him, wanting everything he was willing to give. They groaned together as their tongues teased and played. The taste of the dark stout he'd drunk at the bar lingered, making her crave more of his flavor.

As he attacked her mouth like he was starving, his hands flexed against her thighs. She wanted them to reach behind her. She wanted to feel them gripping her ass and grinding her into him. But she'd never ask for it. She walked through life confident and sure thanks to years of therapy, but one area where she hadn't conquered her insecurities was the bedroom.

Years of being told she was boring, unskilled, and unattractive had her afraid to truly let go. She'd worried about how she looked, if Evan was enjoying himself, if she was doing things right, if he was sleeping with someone else. Having an orgasm, or even enjoying the sex became impossible because her head never shut up and let her focus on the moment.

But now, she could think of nothing else but the man between her legs. Never had she been kissed like this. Like the man nipping her lips, delving his tongue into her mouth, and stealing her air couldn't get enough of her. Like he loved her taste, her moans, the feel of her lips on his.

The longer they kissed, the needier she felt. An ache developed between her legs, intensifying with each sweep of his tongue. Finally, she gave into the urge to slide her hands into his curls and grip the damp strands. She'd never been able to do this with a man, and she freakin' loved the way his hair felt between her fingers.

Curly groaned a long, tortured sound.

Emboldened, Brooke wrapped her ankles around his back and jerked herself forward against his body. Her stomach met the very hard length of his erection. She gasped into his mouth, making him chuckle.

Despite the urgency of his kiss, she hadn't realized he'd been as turned on as she was. Guess she needed the firsthand evidence.

Curly rested his forehead against hers as he caught his breath. "Christ, you can kiss."

The little compliment was like a straight shot of confidence to her soul.

"Pretty sure I've got nothing on you." Oh, God, her hands were still clutching his hair as though she'd fly away if she let go. How embarrassing. "Uh, sorry," she said with an awkward chuckle as she released him.

"Don't be. Fucking love your hands in my hair," he said, drawing back enough to see her face. "Why do you think I keep it long?"

"Well, I love your hair. It's so soft." The memory of her fantasies about his hair had heat rushing to her cheeks.

His eyes narrowed. "What was that?"

"Huh?"

"Your face got all red. You having naughty thoughts, Brooke?"

If there was enough room between their bodies, she'd have slid down into the water and never come up. Instead, she squeaked out a "No."

Curly chuckled. The husky sound only made her want him more. "Liar. Tell me."

She pressed her lips together, shaking her head.

"What happened to the ballsy chick who was ready to take down Prick?"

"That's different," she whispered. "This is so...personal." Intimate. Embarrassing. Once she'd confessed a fantasy to Evan and he'd laughed until she excused herself, went into the bathroom, and cried on the toilet, dying a little from the shame.

"All right." He ran his hands up and down her thighs. "Hmmm, you got all red when you mentioned liking my hair so I'm guessing it had something to do with that. You imagining something dirty involving my hair?"

She was going to die.

"Maybe pulling it while I'm fucking you?"

She gasped.

"Because I gotta tell you," he continued in that growly voice, "I love the fuck outta that idea."

The warmth of embarrassment had nothing on the incendiary heat of his sex-voice.

"T-that wasn't it."

"How about this? You tell me what you were thinking, and I'll give it to you."

I'm not going to survive.

Brooke sucked in a breath. "But—"

"Whatever it is. Nothing is off fucking limits. I'll make it happen."

Shit, she was going to tell him. She'd lost her mind. *He* made her lose her mind. Made her act in a way she'd never acted before, and part of her loved it. Because he didn't look at her with judgment or disgust. He didn't criticize her or fuel her insecurities. He seemed to genuinely want to make her fantasy a reality.

Whatever it is.

"I-you were, uh, sucking on me," she whispered, staring at his chest to avoid his crystal eyes.

He cupped and lifted her chin, taking away her ability to hide. "Your tits?" His gaze had darkened until it matched the night sky.

"Yes," she whispered.

He groaned. "I'd kill to get my mouth on those babies. What else?"

"When…" He liked her courage and confidence. He'd told her more than once. So she gathered it and held his stare. "I had my hands in your hair, holding you against me and when I wanted you to switch sides, I yanked your head back and pulled you to my other breast."

A groan ripped from him. "Jesus, fuck. I don't think my dick has ever been harder." He reached in the water to adjust himself. "Do you want it?"

She nodded.

"Say it."

"I want it." God did she ever. Now that the door had been unlocked, she was ready burst through and make up for the years-long dry spell.

Curly hooked reached behind her to the tie of her bathing suit. Shit, he was about to see her. No longer perky or twenty-five. Up close and personal. As personal as it got.

"Wait."

He froze.

"I-I'm forty-one," she said, holding his arms.

His forehead scrunched. "I know."

"No, I mean, I'm forty-one as in not twenty-something. So I look like I'm forty-one." Her face burned. "I wasn't a bombshell at thirty, so I can't imagine it's gotten any better." She tried for a nervous laugh but ended up with a half-choke, half-laugh.

Curly grunted. "That fucker did a serious number on your self-esteem. For that alone he deserves Hell. Brooke, you are beautiful. This body you seem to dislike has made me hard every time I've been around you. I've thought of little else than getting my hands on you. My mouth on you. Your husband was a not only an asshole, he was as stupid as they come. Let me show you what I think of this forty-one-year-old body. Please?"

Please? As if anyone would say no after that.

Biting her lower lip, she nodded and dropped her hands. He untied her bikini top then slide it down her arms. As predicted, her breasts didn't exactly stay up where they'd been with the support of the suit. Yet Curly didn't seem to care in the least. His gaze was riveted to her heavy breasts and pointed nipples. She couldn't blame the puckering on the chill from the wet bathing suit. No, it was one hundred percent arousal and need.

"Beautiful," he whispered as he cupped both breasts and lifted. As he did, he brushed his thumbs across her nipples sending a shock wave through her gut.

Brooke cried out and clung to his biceps.

"You're beautiful, these tits are beautiful, and I never want to hear a negative word about this sexy-as-fuck body from you again, you hear me?"

She let out a breathy laugh. "I'll try but I make no promise— aah!"

He sucked a nipple into his mouth, and she nearly came on the spot. God, it'd been so long since a man pleasured her in this way, she'd forgotten how amazing hot suction could be. After the first year of marriage foreplay vanished. "Holy shit," she whispered as she lifted her hands. When they reached the level of his head, his gaze shifted up to meet hers.

"Do it," he said, before drawing her back into the wet heat of his mouth. She dove her fingers into his hair and clutched the ringed strands as she held him against her breast. His groan and the increased pull on her nipple had her crying out.

It felt so unbelievably good. She closed her eyes and let her head tilt back as she absorbed the bombardment of sensations. Soft strands of wet hair weaving through her fingers, electric shocks shooting from her nipple, the throb of emptiness between her legs. She loved every single part of it.

After a few moments of being driven wild by his bold mouth, her other nipple began to ache from neglect. She needed that mouth over there more than she needed to breathe. So she did what she'd gotten herself off fantasizing about. She tugged on his hair.

It didn't work. He stayed firmly latched to her breast but gave her a smoldering look full of devilry.

He wanted more.

He wanted it harder.

This time she pulled his hair with a strength she thought would have hurt, but he growled a "fuck yeah," as he popped off her breast. They stared at each other for half a second before she roughly pushed his face to her other breast.

He needed no further guidance, attacking her nipple with a sharp nip.

Brooke shouted his name as she realized something.

Not only did Curly take her fantasy and make the reality better than she ever could have imagined, but he seemed to be loving it just as much.

A smile crossed her face as her eyes nearly rolled back in her head. This was how sex should feel. Hot, breathy, a little out of control, needy…and so damn good she wanted it to last forever.

Two people getting lost in each other. If nothing else, for the rest of her life she'd cherish Curly for giving her this moment.

Chapter Fifteen

Brooke tugged on his scalp with a strength bordering on pain, and fuck if it didn't make his dick leak. Hell, each time he sucked harder, her grasp tightened and he came close to coming in his jeans like a fucking fifteen-year-old watching porn for the first time. She was fire in his arms.

So responsive.

So sexy.

So open to him despite her insecurity.

After another minute of listening to her gasps and mewls, she again yanked on his hair. This time, she drew him to her mouth and claimed his lips with her own.

Fuck, he loved her boldness. Clearly, her douche of an ex-husband had fucked with her self-image and confidence in the bedroom, but with each passing second, she let those hang-ups go and allowed the assertive woman he knew to rise up.

She nipped his lower lip, drawing a grunt from him. He squeezed her ass in response and ground her against his aching cock.

She cried out and aided him by rocking her pelvis along his length.

When he finally needed air, he tore his mouth from hers, grazed his teeth along her ear lobe, then whispered, "You wanna come?"

Her eyes widened, and she sucked in a breath.

"Yes?"

A slight nod was all he got.

Part of him loved how she could be so shy here and so fierce otherwise, but damn, he'd give anything to see her tip past the point of no return and forget all her uncertainty.

"Say it. I want to hear you say it. Tell me to make you come."

"Y-yes," she whispered. "I-I want you to make me c-come."

Brooke was unlike any woman he'd been with in the past. Mostly, he'd fucked club girls who'd do any damn thing he asked. They'd been there for his pleasure, the security his club had provided, and with the hope of becoming an ol' lady one day. As president, he'd had his pick of any woman willing to bend over or drop to her knees as soon as he snapped his fingers. There was no challenge, no connection, no giving a shit about her.

Crude, but true.

Even when he'd had an ol' lady, something had been missing. He'd loved her, yes. And they'd worked for a while, but their connection wasn't as deep as it should have been.

Brooke challenged him. She took no shit, lived the way she wanted, and, with a little prodding, would be demanding the pleasure she deserved. Curly found he wanted nothing more than to watch her shatter and hear her scream his name as she came.

He wanted it even more than he wanted relief for his hungry dick.

Keeping his gaze locked with hers, he slid his fingers beneath the swatch of fabric covering her sex. She sucked in a breath and sank her teeth into her lower lip as she braced her hands on the pool deck, reclining a bit. Her face was flushed, part embarrassment for sure, but hopefully also from desire. Wariness filled her gaze, but she nodded for him to continue.

The angle allowed him easy access to her slippery pussy, not wet from the pool but his fervent sucking on her tits. He played with her for a moment, lightly fingering her entrance until she was panting and his knuckles turned white on the edge of the pool.

"Something wrong?" he asked with a chuckle as she scowled at him.

"Y-yes." Her tone was a blend of arousal and frustration that he could listen to for hours, knowing he was the one driving her out of her mind. "You're teasing me."

Laughing, he shook his head. "No, baby. A tease would walk away right now. I'm just playing a little bit, but I promise to deliver. I'll have you screaming in no time." As he said those last words, he gently thrust a finger into her, making her eyes flare.

"Oh, my God," she whispered as she shut her eyes tight.

"Feel good?" Sure felt good on his end. Hot, wet, tight…fuck, he could only imagine how his dick would erupt if it had the honor of being where his lucky finger was.

Brooke nodded, and he took that as a sign he'd made her speechless.

Nothing wrong with that.

He gave her a second to adjust since he assumed it'd been a while for her, then he curled his finger and stroked along her inner wall. Brooke moaned and lifted her hips an inch before dropping them back to the patio.

"Good?"

"Y-yes. Good. So, so good." She stared at him with wonder in her gaze.

She wanted more. He could tell by the subtle way she squirmed, but she didn't know how to take it or demand it. Well, she was about to learn. He'd give her whatever the hell she wanted. She just had to ask.

Or take.

"You want more?"

"Yes," she said as she bit her lip again.

"Stop holding back," he ordered.

"What?"

Fuck, she looked terrified for a second. As though he was about to criticize her. Like he ever would. There wasn't a damn thing to complain about. No way in hell would he send her scurrying into her shell.

"Let go, Brooke. You're incredible. Burning me alive. I want to hear you. Anything you want, anything you do will be perfect." She watched him for a moment as though trying to decide whether she believed him.

He added a second finger and slowly fucked her with them.

She made a noise in the back of her throat. After a few seconds, her eyes darkened, and her mouth fell open. A breathy moan left her lips.

"That's it. Hell yes. Give me more."

She lifted her hips, testing her ability to move on his hand. He grinned. Damn, he was a lucky bastard. It didn't take but a moment to find a rhythm. With each thrust of his hand, she lost some of her inhibitions.

When he added a third finger, she whimpered and pushed hard into his hand, looking like a sacrificial offering with her bark arched and hips pumping. Her lips were swollen from his kisses, and her nipples red and drawn so tight his mouth salivated for another taste. "T-touch me," she whispered as she thrust against him again.

"Fuck yes. Anything." He grabbed her tit, giving a rough squeeze before plucking at the nipple while he fucked his fingers in and out of her.

She groaned. "Y-yes. Keep going," she encouraged. "Oh, God."

Her hips moved faster, as did his fingers. Arousal coated his hand, allowing him to glide with ease. When he slid a slicked thumb across her clit, she cried out and pitched forward, grabbing his arms for support.

"Holy shit, do that again."

Only a fucking fool would refuse a demand like that, so he thrummed her clit as he fingered her. She curled her nails into his nails as she humped herself on his hand.

Fuck she was beautiful chasing her pleasure. Eyes screwed shut, mouth partway open, face flushed.

"You're close," he said as he fingered her harder.

"I-I'm really close."

"Open your eyes."

She did as he asked, and the minute her unfocused gaze found his, he pinched her clit between his thumb and first finger.

She went off like a shaken bottle of soda.

"Curly," she shouted as she clutched his arms and quaked against him. The tremors lasted for long seconds until she eventually slumped. Her forehead rested on his chest while she gulped in air. He stroked her back, her limbs, her ass, any expanse of skin he could reach while she rode out the climax.

When her breathing finally evened, she straightened, and he saw the uncertainty in her eyes. Now that it was over, her brain would retake control, reminding her of what a foolish idea this had been.

He was having none of that shit. Not after the way she'd just burned alive in his arms. He withdrew his fingers, causing her to tremble. Then, as she watched he brought them to his mouth and licked them clean.

Her pussy tasted even better than her mouth.

A gasp left her lips and her eyes widened comically. Once he'd finished his treat, he grabbed the back of her head and brought her in for a sloppy, unrestrained kiss.

When it ended, she still had that shy, slightly glazed-over look to her. "That was, uh…"

"The hottest fucking thing I've ever seen? Shit, Brooke, I could watch you come all day."

She let out a nervous laugh while pressing a hand to her chest.

If her heart was anything like his, it still raced with the thrill of the moment.

As though she suddenly recalled her nudity, she began to cross her arms over her tits, but he caught her wrists and planted them at her sides.

"No way you're hiding from me now. Those babies and I are good friends."

That got a much more authentic laugh from her.

His phone chimed from her lounge chair. He kissed her mouth quickly, then said, "That'll be Jinx. We're supposed to meet up to discuss what he learned tonight."

"So you have to go?"

He groaned at the renewed vulnerability in her voice. "Trust me, I don't want to. But yes, they'll be expecting me."

"But, you didn't…" She waved toward his impossible-to-miss hard-on.

His chuckle sounded more like a grumble. "Trust me, I'm aware." Grabbing her hand, he guided it to his still hard cock. The second her palm made contact, even with the wet boxer briefs between them, he clenched his teeth to keep from groaning in agony.

Brooke sucked in a breath, and her hand tightened around him.

"Shit," he said, then leaned in to whisper, "next time." And there would be a next time. He wasn't finished with the sexy dog trainer. If he were intelligent, he'd walk away. A woman like Brooke—smart, fierce, beautiful—deserved so much more than he was able to give. After coming off a marriage to such a piece of shit, she deserved love, she deserved a partner, she deserved forever. All Curly had to give was his cock and some hot nights between the sheets. But after getting a taste of her tonight, he knew he'd be back for more. What man could be expected to resist her?

Curly

After stealing one last kiss in which she slid her tongue into his mouth and turned what he'd expected to be a peck into a full-on make-out, he pushed up and out of the pool. Brooke remained where she sat, observing him as the water ran down his body. He snagged a towel from the lounge chair and wrapped it around his waist. Harley hopped down from the chaise and lapped at the water droplets on his bare feet. Her little butt wiggled back and forth with the speed of her wagging tail. Fuck, he was already head over heels for the pup.

"Will you fill me in on what happened with Jinx and Prick?" she asked while slipping her bikini top back over her head. In some mind-boggling feat of female contortionism, she managed to secure the tie behind her back.

He wanted to tell her no. To keep her far away from anything potentially harmful, but that wouldn't fly with Brooke. And for reasons he had no plans on delving into, he had a hard time denying this woman.

"I will. How about breakfast? Pick your favorite spot." Fuck, he was already making plans to see her again. It wasn't smart. "It'll be easier to catch you up in person."

With a nod, she said, "Okay. There's a place nearby called Biscuit Bistro that has the best breakfast."

"Meet you there at nine?"

"I'll be there. They have an outdoor seating area where they allow dogs, so feel free to bring Harley. Ray loves it."

Always thinking about her four-legged friends. "Will do." He slipped his T-shirt over his head and stepped into his jeans, wet underwear and all. The discomfort would keep his dick in check for the drive home.

He started for the gate with Harley trotting along beside him when he thought better of it. Then, spinning on his heel, he marched back over to where Brooke now stood with a towel around her waist, cupped the back of her head, and planted one last doozy of a kiss on her. "Best night I've had in more than fourteen years," he said to her shocked face.

He left her standing there dazed and pressing her fingers to her lips.

Once he had Harley settled in the front seat of his truck, he responded to Jinx. Sure, it was ten o'clock on a Saturday night, but he'd be the guys' president soon, and that meant they said how high when Curly told them to jump. Sure enough, Jinx promised to be at Curly's house in twenty minutes along with the rest of the soon-to-be Hell's Handlers Florida Chapter.

At least having a house full of bikers would prevent him from jerking off to memories of Brooke all night.

"That guy is about as stupid as they come," Jinx said the moment Curly opened the door.

"Who, Prick?" Curly asked. "Come in," he said, waving the guys into his house as Harley tried to worm her way around his feet and out the door.

"Oh, man, who's this?" Tracker crouched down and rubbed Harley under her soft chin. "Hey, pretty girl."

The pup hopped her front paws up on Tracker's thighs and licked sloppy kisses all over his face. "That's right. Give Uncle Tracker all the love. Who's the prettiest girl?"

Curly bit back a laugh as the muscled and extremely tattooed badass melted into a pile of goo around a friendly puppy.

When Tracker finally stood with Harley in his arms, he took one step forward then stopped with a wrinkled forehead. "What?"

The rest of them stood gaping at the transformed Tracker.

"Dude," Jinx said with a chuckle. "Who knew you were such a softie?"

With a scowl that didn't fit the gentle way he cradled the puppy, Tracker flipped them all off. "Thought we were here to talk about shit with Prick?"

"Don't you mean the stupid motherfucker?" Gabe muttered as they filed their way into Curly's kitchen.

Fuck, they needed a clubhouse. Ever since Lock had mentioned Prick's farm would be the perfect spot for their headquarters, Curly couldn't get the idea out of his head. He liked the option so much, he'd canceled his realty appointments and hadn't scouted another property in days. The farm needed a shit-ton of renovating, but he could certainly afford it. The location worked perfectly as well. On the outskirts of town, secluded, easy to keep secure.

The fact that it bordered Brooke's property had nothing to do with his desire to acquire the land.

Nothing at all.

One thought of her name and he recalled how good her skin tasted and the way her moans of pleasure had gone straight to his dick.

He also remembered how he hadn't come. That would be happening as soon as he got the info he needed and got rid of these assholes. A shower and his fist would suffice for the night, but next time…

Next time he'd be coming inside Brooke.

Once the guys were crammed around Curly's table drinking beer and Harley was happily snuggled up to Tracker, Jinx lifted his bottle. "To the easiest information gathering mission on the face of the planet."

"Really?" Ty asked. "He coughed up the info?"

Pulse snorted as Jinx said, "Coughed it up? He practically begged us to come to the next fight. It's two weeks from tonight. He keeps the exact location private until the afternoon of the fight but has used his farm a number of times."

Nodding, Ty said, "Makes sense. He hasn't done jack shit to the place since he moved in. Still looks abandoned. He can easily have spectators park out in the fields out of view of the road."

"Pretty sure the cops know about it and let it happen. For a cut, of course," Jinx added.

Well, Brooke would be ripshit when she learned that bit of news. Learning Prick was still in bed with the cops didn't surprise him in the least, but she'd yet to be slapped in the face with just how corrupt the system could be. "You have any idea how much he's earning at this shit?"

With a nod, Jinx said, "Yeah, he couldn't brag loud enough. Get this, at the last fight, Prick walked away with ten Gs. He takes half the pot. Rest is for winners."

"Shit, he made ten thousand dollars in one night of fighting dogs?" Tracker's voice hardened to a murderous degree. "That's some serious cheddar."

"Yep. Said it's even higher sometimes," Pulse chimed in.

The entire setup turned Curly's stomach. He'd love nothing more than to dump Prick's body in the ring with his dogs. Give him a taste of what those poor animals went through.

With the cops in his pocket, it's no wonder he's so willing to blab about his operation," Ty said. "He's not worried about getting busted."

"All I had to do was convince him I had money to burn, and he was practically salivating. Told him I used to bet on shit like this when I lived in Alabama. Gave him my number, and he's going to text me the location afternoon of. Boom." Jinx grinned a victorious smile as he mimed a mic drop.

"All right," Curly stroked a hand over his rough cheek. Shit, he'd probably given Brooke a wicked case of beard burn. Not that he regretted it. The thought of sitting across from her at breakfast with his mark on her skin had the cock he'd managed to control on the way home acting up again. "Sounds like we've got two weeks to figure out how we want to play this shit."

Maybe he'd give Copper a ring to ask his advice. It'd been a long time since Curly had been in charge of anything or anyone but himself. Copper had a way of leading his men through difficult situations successfully while weeding out the bullshit and commanding fierce loyalty.

Yes, the Handlers had experienced loss, devastating loss, but Copper was a smart man whose club members would follow him to hell and back a dozen times.

Curly

"Let's give it some thought over the next few days and meet up on Wednesday night. That work for you guys?"

When they all nodded, Ty said, "When are we thinking about making this club official? Patching in, getting cuts and shit?"

Curly smiled. "I've ordered cuts and patches for everyone. They should be in soon. Once they're here, one of the guys from Tennessee will ride down to swear you all in with me. You'll be taking the same oath they do up there. Same one I did. We'll be following their club bylaws but can amend them as necessary. There'll be a chance to back out first if you change your mind, but once you patch in, you're committed." He focused on Pulse as he delivered that little pep talk.

"Nah," Pulse said, lifting his beer in salute. "Think we're all locked in now."

"Good deal," Curly said with a single nod. Pulse talked a good game and had done his job well tonight, but something about the man still niggled the back of Curly's mind. He wouldn't be surprised if that man never wore a patch.

They hung out for a while longer, until well past midnight, and Curly was ready for some quiet time. This was why they needed a clubhouse. A place for them all to hang but where he could disappear when he needed a break.

Finally, somewhere around two a.m., Curly crawled into bed naked, wrapped a fist around his aching cock, and jacked himself to a bone-rattling climax with memories of the way Brooke shouted his name ringing in his ears.

Chapter Sixteen

One of Brooke's favorite things about living in Florida was not freezing her ass off during the early morning trudge out to feed her foster babies. She could make her way to the kennels at seven in the morning dressed only in her sleep shorts and a tank and be perfectly comfortable almost all year round.

"Who's hungry?" she called out as she did every morning when she emerged into the bright sunshine. The yips and yaps of excited dogs never failed to draw a smile from her. Who wouldn't love to be greeted with extreme enthusiasm every time they walked in the room?

Ray strolled along beside her until nature called, then he veered off to take care of business. Already the morning sun warmed her skin, and the dew had her feet wet inside her flip-flops.

"What the..." she said as she reached her kennels only to find a folded piece of paper nailed to the center of the door.

She yanked the small nail out of the wood with a frown. Had one of her clients left it yesterday, and she'd somehow missed it? As she unfolded the paper then read the scrawled words, her heart plummeted to her feet.

Cute dogs. Be a shame if something were to happen to them.

Curly

Her stomach lurched, and she nearly vomited the half cup of coffee she'd sucked down before venturing outside. Beyond the door, the dogs continued barking. No doubt they were confused as to why she hadn't come to greet them yet. Heart in her throat, she whipped her head around, scanning the expanse of the fenced-in yard.

Someone had been there. But when? Brooke was ninety percent certain this note hadn't been there when Curly was over.

The hairs on the back of her neck rose to attention as a shiver ran down her spine. Another scan of the yard revealed no one beside her and Ray. They were alone. Ray's presence allowed her to blow out a tense breath. If someone were in the backyard with them, they'd never escape his remarkable nose.

Prick. This had to be Prick.

Jesus, had he just waltzed into her backyard while she'd been sleeping? Never before had she given much thought to security. She lived in a fairly rural area with plenty of space between neighbors, quiet streets, and minimal crime. From the first night she'd stayed there, she felt safe alone, probably because Ray snoozed right beside her and would alert her if danger came too close. In addition, she had a heavy-duty lock on the gates and deadbolts on her doors. Those minimal safety measures had always seemed adequate when combined with the protective German Shepherd.

Could she have left the gate unlocked the night before?

No. She distinctly remembered securing the fence lock as she did every night after a final check on the dogs. During the days, she often left it open, but only when she was home. With the bolts still intact, someone had scaled her fence to deliver this early morning warning.

Prick, not someone.

Or maybe they'd broken the lock. A quick glance over her shoulder confirmed the gate and the lock to be fully intact.

The dogs' barks turned to desperate whimpers and hungry whines. With a sigh, she shoved the note in her pocket. It'd have to wait until later. There were hungry pups to feed.

She set about her morning chores, feeding, and watering the dogs, letting them out to relieve themselves, then making sure the kennels were clean. As she worked, her mind drifted back to the note. After her breakfast with Curly, she'd make a quick trip to the hardware store and purchase some security cameras.

Curly.

Should she tell him about the threat?

Would he want to know?

His hatred for Prick ran deep, rightfully so, but she'd already involved him and his friends in a situation that had nothing to do with them. He and his new club members were putting themselves at risk to help end the dogfighting ring. Telling him about the note would only anger him and possibly make him go after Prick.

Besides, she handled her issues.

Always.

She didn't need anyone solving her problems, holding her hand, or taking over. Didn't need it or want it. Been there, done that, and had thick emotional scars to prove it. As it was, she loathed the fact she needed Curly's help to take down Prick's operation, but it was admittedly a task she'd have difficulty accomplishing on her own, especially since the police refused to do their job.

But she didn't have to like it. And she didn't have to involve Curly in her personal affairs any more than he already was. Given what had happened last night, mind-blowing as it was, she needed boundaries. The very last thing she'd allow in her life was some tough biker thinking he had the right to tell her what to do and how to do it. Since they hadn't discussed it last night, she'd have to make her position clear at breakfast.

Should be a fun conversation.

Curly

Many people would consider her a control freak, but after a decade and a half long marriage to Evan, she'd earned the right to regulate her own life. While married, the few decisions she been allowed to make were always wrong, always stupid, always criticized, always punished. After a while, kowtowing to everything Evan wanted became easier and safer, including giving him power over what she wore or ate. No more.

She valued the ability to make her own choices and govern her own life above all.

So, no, she wouldn't be telling him. She'd pick up some security cameras, install them herself, and take care of the problem. The police might be able to look the other way on a dogfighting ring, but if a citizen came to them with camera footage of someone scaling their fence in the middle of the night, they'd be forced to act.

Right?

Shaking off the negative start to the morning, Brooke spent the next hour playing fetch, running with the dogs, and focusing on basic obedience skills her fosters had never learned. Once the pack was panting and tuckered out—her included—she returned the pups to their kennels so she could grab a quick shower and head out to meet Curly.

Forty-five minutes later, hair still damp, she sat across from Curly in her favorite breakfast spot. He wore an outfit similar to every one she'd seen him in thus far. Dark T-shirt and jeans with boots. How he didn't melt into a sweaty puddle every time he walked outside, she'd never understand. Still, the simple attire suited him, and he wore it well.

Well, ha, he wore it like the shirt had been painted on and the jeans custom fit.

Shit, she'd made a grave error in judgment.

How on earth had she expected to share a meal with the first man to give her an orgasm in over five years and not feel awkward as hell? Chalk it up to lack of experience, or so much time having passed since she'd been with a guy she completely forgot about the goddammed morning after, whatever. Moral of the story…she had no idea what to say to the man who looked like he just walked off the cover of some Harley magazine.

He, of course, came off totally at ease as he perused the menu. Probably had a different woman in his bed every weekend.

God, he must think her such a fool.

"So what's good here?" he asked, finally breaking the silence.

She could have kissed him—only for breaking the silence, not because she remembered how intoxicating his kisses were.

Wait? What had he asked? "Um, sorry? What'd you say?"

His eyes sparkled over his menu as though he had a secret insight to her thoughts. "What do you recommend?"

Oh, food, right. "I always get the spicy chicken biscuit. It's incredible. A huge piece of spicy fried chicken with pepper jack cheese and bacon all on a homemade biscuit. And I promise these are the best biscuits you'll ever eat. And I'm not just saying that because the owner, Koryn, is a friend."

"That's high praise," he said with an open grin that helped put her at ease. "Don't forget I grew up here in the south, so I've had my fair share of biscuits."

She gave him a sassy smirk. "I stand by my statement."

"You like it hot, huh?"

"What?" she asked, nearly choking on her saliva. Where the hell was their waitress?

"Your food? You like spicy food?" The way he pressed his lips together said he knew exactly what he was doing to her.

"Oh." She needed to get out more. Go on some dates, so she didn't make such a fool of herself. "Yes. I do."

"All right," he said as their waitress walked over.

She seemed to be in her late twenties, early thirties at most. Her friendly smile and casual dress of denim and a company T-shirt fit with the welcoming environment.

"Mornin', folks. I'm Sally, and I'll be takin' care of ya'll today." She was adorable in short denim shorts, a fitted T-shirt, the smooth skin of the youthful, and the kind of figure Brooke had only managed when practically starving herself at her husband's behest. "Can I start ya'll off with some coffee?"

"Yes, please," she said.

"Make that two," Curly added.

"Perfect. Ready to order?" She faced Curly as she spoke, which had Brooke's hackles rising. Now that she'd told him her favorite meal, he'd probably order it for her, and there wasn't anything that irked her more than when a man ordered her food as though she couldn't speak for herself.

"I believe..." Curly started as he shut his menu with a charming smile or the waitress.

Brooke resisted the urge to roll her eyes, but it was tough.

Really tough.

"I believe I'm going to let the regular decide for me since this is my first visit." As he handed the menu to Sally, his amused gaze fell to Brooke.

She blinked at him. This wasn't the first time the man surprised her, and she had to admit, she loved it. "Spicy okay with you?" she asked him.

"Pretty sure you know the answer to that by now." He winked, and Brooke swore Sally swooned.

Face hot as the coffee she'd soon be drinking, Brooke forced herself to look at their waitress. "We'll each have the spicy chicken biscuit. And can we get some sweet rolls as well?"

"You got it. Excellent choices. Be back with that coffee in a shake." She spun and flounced toward the kitchen. Even Brooke couldn't help but take a peek at her ass as she walked. Every man in the room seemed to be doing the same, but when she faced forward again, she found Curly's intense gaze on her and her alone.

She unfolded then refolded her napkin, needing something to do with her hands. "So, Jinx?" she asked. Easier to dive right in rather than obsess about what he was thinking. Or to wonder about what he wanted from her. Or remember the way those hands felt on her. Or his mouth.

Ugh.

Last night had been the stupidest thing she'd done in ages. Okay, the second stupidest. Confronting on her own won that award. Last night had been the most fun and pleasurable, but one of the most foolish as well. She'd spent hours staring at the ceiling, bouncing between questioning her sanity and replaying their encounter in her head before she finally fell asleep. She'd even pulled out her trusty vibrator as soon as she'd awakened and relived the moment in her mind yet again.

"The next fi—party," he said as Sally returned with their coffee. "Is in two weeks."

"Here ya'll go." Sally set down their oversized mugs, a small ceramic pitcher of cream, and a basket of sweeteners. "Food'll be ready in a few. Ya'll good?"

"Yes, thank you," Brooke answered immediately and probably with too much bite. She'd apologize, but all she wanted to know was more about the dog fights.

"Two weeks?" she clarified in a low voice after Sally strutted away again. Was it her imagination, or was she wiggling just a little extra this time?

"Two weeks from last night. So not next Saturday, but the following."

Two weeks was good. That gave her—them—time to figure out how to take Prick down. "At the farm?"

He shrugged. "Not sure."

She frowned, and he gestured her closer. As she leaned across the table, he took hold of her folded hands. After prying them apart, he began to play with her fingers. "They've held them at the farm a few times, but not always. Prick texts the location to the attendees on the afternoon of to keep shit as secret as possible." He practically whispered the words, but to anyone observing them, they probably looked like a couple lost in a close conversation. Which was a ridiculous thought, right?

Was he *interested* in her? There was no way. Sure, maybe for sex, but not for cozy breakfasts and dates. Maybe he was just starting with some kindness before he told her how he regretted the previous night. Or how she wasn't what he'd expected. That she could believe.

And if he was interested?

Her stomach fluttered. It didn't matter. She couldn't—wouldn't—become involved with him or any man. She wouldn't risk herself that way again.

Focus. Dogfighting. In two Saturdays.

"Well, shit," she whispered once she had control of her thoughts again. "How the hell are we supposed to figure out a way to stop it if we don't know where it is?"

His grim expression told her what she didn't want to hear. Yet he said it anyway. "We may be just observing at this one."

"No!" she said, straightening.

Several customers glanced her way at the outburst.

"Sorry," she said, speaking quietly again. "But there is no way we can let another one happen without doing something about it." As she spoke, she shook her head, imploring him with her eyes. He had to understand how important this was to her. Having the fights occur while she was ignorant of it was one thing, but now that she knew exactly when it was happening and would soon know where, she couldn't possibly sit back and allow it.

Curly's expression held sympathy and a bit of pity. Telling him about her past was a mistake. Now he probably saw her as some unfortunate creature comparing herself to these imprisoned dogs.

Wasn't she, though?

"Babe," he said, stroking circles on her palm with his thumb. If he meant the move to calm her, it was working, damn him. "I get that this fucking sucks. But we've got two weeks to work on it. Jinx is gonna continue to kiss Prick's ass. Maybe he'll find out the location early, but if not, I need you to prepare yourself that we may have to use this one as recon. We need to know how they run, how many people are there, if they have security, weapons, all kinds of shit."

Well, damn. She hadn't thought of a single thing beyond her worry over another dog or dogs being injured or killed.

His grim expression matched how she felt inside. "As much as I detest what's going on, I can't risk my guys. I won't have them injured or arrested."

Regret hit her hard. "No," she whispered. "Of course not. I'm sorry. I get kinda crazy about this."

He lifted her hand, pressing a kiss to her knuckles. "One of the best qualities about you is your passion, Brooke." Then he winked. "In its many forms."

This man and his silver tongue were going to be the death of her. But at least it was a good segue into the conversation she was dreading but needed to have. "Um, about last night…"

His smile turned dark and dangerous. The exact one that had led to last night's insanity.

No, no, no.

"Look, I just want to be upfront with you."

"Okay." He released her hands and settled back against the vinyl of their booth.

Well, if that wasn't a withdrawal, she didn't know what was. Of course it was. She'd known from the start he'd pull away from her. A man like him and a woman like her made no sense. Even for a fling. Still, being rejected stung. Even if she had no plans for any kind of relationship with him or anyone.

Brooke straightened in the seat as well. It was time to get out in front of this conversation instead of letting him call the shots. "I'm not interested in any kind of complication." She gave him the benefit of eye contact, so he'd know she wasn't playing games or using this as some kind of passive-aggressive ploy to actually draw him in. "What I mean is that I don't want a relationship of any kind. I refuse to be beholden to a man ever again, even as a girlfriend or a casual date. I make my own decisions, run my own life, and have no plans for that to change."

There. Direct and to the point, in case he was thinking they'd be starting something. Not that she'd be opposed to a repeat of last night in the physical sense, but even that could eventually lead to screwed-up emotions and hurt. Though now that she knew how he tasted and how that mouth could melt her brain, he'd be hard to resist if he wanted another go.

"Works for me," he said, making her frown.

Just like that?

That wasn't disappointment she felt.

It wasn't.

"Why are you frowning?"

"Oh, no reason. Just surprised you agreed so easily. I thought maybe after last night…"

"What? That'd I'd start picking out china and searching for wedding venues?" He laughed.

Well, when he put it that way, she just sounded stupid. "No. That's not what I meant at all."

"Look, babe, I think you're hot as fuck. I respect the hell outta you and think you seriously kick ass. I'm down for a fuck any time you want, but like you, I'm not interested in anything more. Ever. You know I had an ol' lady before I went to prison?"

A what? Her expression must have shown her confusion.

"An ol' lady is basically the equivalent of a wife."

Her jaw almost hit the table. "You were married?" How did she not know that? Oh my God, was he still?

"No. Not legally, but in the MC life, an ol' lady is like a wife. A serious relationship."

"Wow. I had no idea. Is she still…" She couldn't even ask the question without her stomach souring. Never would she have considered Curly the cheating type, but she'd die if she found out some poor woman was waiting at home for him while he'd been driving her wild last night.

"Shortly before the police arrested me, I caught her getting done from behind by Prick at our clubhouse."

Brooke winced. "Shit."

"It wasn't the relationship people make movies about, but I loved her and we were committed. Or supposed to be." He grunted, then took a sip of his coffee. "I ended it with her and stripped Prick of his title as Sargeant of Arms in the club. A few weeks later, I was arrested. I don't know if she played any part in that, but the back-to-back betrayal is all twisted together in my head. I trusted her. I trusted Prick. I don't trust anymore. Not easily."

"Oh, wow." The things this man had lived through.

"Yep. Pretty sure that's why Prick was so eager to help the cops frame me. Payback's truly a bitch."

"Holy shit," she breathed. The story made her heart hurt.

"So I get it, Brooke. I get why you don't want to tie yourself to a man again. Feel the same way about relationships." Wrongfully imprisoned, and he lost his girlfriend to the man who helped put him there. What a mind fuck.

"Well, we're quite a pair of headcases, aren't we?" she asked just as the waitress arrived with their breakfast.

"Yeah, so no offense," he said once she'd delivered the food, "but I'll never trust a woman with anything besides my dick."

Brooke flinched at the harsh declaration, but it was the same thing she'd said to him, only cruder.

So how come it hurt to hear him say it?

Chapter Seventeen

Curly's phone rang Wednesday morning as he stepped out of the pet store with Harley, who was more interested in his boot laces than walking toward the car. He'd loaded up on toys, a dog bed, enough food to last this little girl a while, a bin to store all the food, and a bunch of other shit he didn't need but ended up buying.

"Hello?" he said without checking who it was. At the same time, Harley simultaneously tugged the laces on one boot while managing to shimmy right in the path of his other. "Fuck," he shouted as he did some sort of ninja move to avoid falling on his ass or squashing his new baby. Once steady with one hand on the shopping cart and the phone nestled between his ear and shoulder, he scooped up his rascally pup and deposited her in the cart's child seat.

"Having some trouble over there?" Scott's amusement came through loud and clear.

"Scott. Good to hear from you, man. Don't get a puppy. They're more trouble than a jealous club whore."

Scott's booming laugh caught the attention of Harley, who tilted her head and stared at Curly.

"You're lucky you're so damn cute," he muttered as Scott still laughed.

"A dog, man? Seriously? What'd you want, a bitch that wouldn't talk back to you?" Though joking, Scott already spoke more like a biker than he had when Curly first met him months ago.

Curly snorted. "Something like that." He'd shoot himself in the foot before admitting he couldn't stand the quiet around his house. After living in prison with hundreds of other men, he'd expected to want nothing more than peace and silence, but it turned out he'd become so accustomed to a level of constant noise and the company of a cellmate, the silence drove him up a wall. It was either find another living creature to inhabit his house and time or become an alcoholic. "How's shit going with you?"

"I'm out. Free and clear of Uncle Sam. Been hanging at Chloe and Rocket's for the past few days."

"Shit, congrats, I think. How's it feel?" He opened the tailgate of his truck and started loading his purchases.

"Thanks." Scott laughed. "Feels weird as fuck. Keep thinking I'm on leave for a few days, and I'll be back on base before I know it. Then I remember I'm basically homeless, jobless, and totally without purpose in life."

"Well, man, I can give you some purpose in about five seconds." They could use him and his expertise in planning and conducting covert operations. Curly had no doubt Scott would have a few suggestions on how to put an end to Prick. Or at least his dirty fucking business.

Scott's laugh came quick. "Shit, man, you making trouble already?"

While Harley watched his every move from her throne at the top of the cart, he finished loading up the truck. "Yeah, well, there are motherfuckers messing shit up everywhere you go."

"Ain't that the fucking truth." Gone was the teasing and relaxed quality of Scott's voice. "When do you need me?"

"If you need time to decompress and get your head straight after such a big change, there's no rush." Hell, Curly took half a year to hang out with Holly and the Hell's Handlers crew in Tennessee before he made any move toward a plotting future. "But if you're ready to rock and roll, I'd be grateful to have you now."

"Don't need time. I'm better when I got something to focus on. Shit goes downhill when I'm idle." Scott cleared his throat. "I'm good to get my ass to Florida whenever."

If he'd known Scott better, Curly might have tried to dig around in his brain a little. After being a Green Beret in the army for over a decade, he was bound to have scars both mentally and physically. Like many in the military, prisoners often experienced symptoms of PTSD. It'd be better to know upfront whether Scott had any triggers that could potentially be an issue for the club. For now, he'd keep a close eye on the guy. If shit hit the fan...well, they'd cross the bridge when it happened.

"I'm gonna clue Chloe in on my plans tonight. Figure I'll need a day or two for her to get over her being mad at me not sticking around Tennessee, then I'll ride your way. So, expect me maybe Saturday? Sunday at the latest."

That'd still give them a week until the dog fight. They could work with a week. Maybe Scott could help them come up with an idea to shut it all down without having to wait until the next fight.

"Sounds perfect. I'll text you my address. Crash at my place until you get your shit sorted. Seriously, brother. As long as you need."

"Thanks, Curly. Appreciate that. Anything you need from me right now?"

"Nah." He scooped Harley up, enduring an attack of slobbery puppy kisses as he walked to the driver's side door. "Enjoy the time with your sister. I'll fill you in when you get down here." The guy deserved at least a bit of a break before jumping into his new life as the enforcer of a budding MC.

"Perfect, bro. Think Copper mentioned he'd be calling you for an update in the next day or two, so be on the lookout for that."

"Thanks for the heads up. Got a bunch of stuff to run by him as well." He wished Scott a good trip then hit the road back to his house. Since arriving in Florida, he'd been so busy fixing up the house and yard, most of his traveling had required his truck. He was itching to get on a bike ride until his mind cleared. Maybe within the next day or two, he could drop Harley with Brooke and take a ride along the gulf coast.

Or, better idea, maybe he could leave Harley with her boyfriend Ray, and Brooke could join him for a half-day ride. She'd feel damn good plastered along his back as he cruised the sunny coast. They could stop for some mouth-watering seafood and see where the day took them.

Only problem with that plan was it sounded like a date. And he had no interest in a date. Then again, neither did Brooke. Still, the idea of cruising the coast with her was almost too good to resist. Her company was as appealing as her body.

A loud whine behind him had him checking the rear-view mirror. "Fuck my ass," he muttered as flashing lights drew closer by the second. What were the chances they were their way to an accident a mile up the road?

Curly pulled over to the right, and the cop followed.

Zero. Then chances were zero.

What the fuck had he done to warrant them pulling him over? Sure, he'd been lost in his head thinking about Brooke, but he hadn't been speeding or blown a stop sign.

As he gripped the steering wheel in the optimal ten-and-two position, Curly blew out a frustrated sigh. After what he'd been through in his life, no one could blame him for his hatred or distrust of the cops, but this guy certainly wouldn't give a fuck. Counting to ten, he willed himself to keep from mouthing off and making shit worse for himself.

The cop took his sweet time walking from his department vehicle to Curly's truck. He hooked his thumbs in his belt loops and walked in a slow swagger like he'd stepped out of some wild west movie. All the while, Curly watched through his side mirror, sitting there like an idiot waiting. Aviators blocked the officer's eyes, but something about the slightly crooked set of his nose and the divot in his chin rang familiar.

After what seemed like a solid five minutes, the officer made it to Curly's window. He rapped against it and made an old-fashioned roll-down motion with his hand. Resisting the urge to roll his eyes, Curly hit the button once, and the window slid open. "Afternoon, officer. Something I can help you with?"

So there was a bit of sarcasm in his voice, he wasn't a damn saint.

"Was behind you for a bit there. Think you got a taillight out."

The fuck he did not. He'd owned this brand spanking new truck for a grand total of three months. "You sure about that? Truck's new."

"You saying my eyes don't work right?"

Stay cool. "Nope, just be surprised if my light is out. That's all."

"Huh. Sounds to me like you're mouthing off. Am I gonna have to ask you to step out of the vehicle?"

The fuck?

It was then the officer pulled his sunglasses off.

Fuck, fuck, fuck.

Curly squeezed his steering wheel hard enough to leave permanent indents in the leather.

"Travis fucking Bryant," the cop said with a smug, self-satisfied grin. "Heard you were back in town. Long time no see."

"Officer Gaines," he said in response as his stomach soured. This guy had been a rookie cop with something to prove the year Curly was arrested. He'd been mean as a fucking junkyard dog and just as willing to sink his teeth into any part of Curly he could. He'd been loaned to the homicide department from patrol as an extra set of hands for the investigation. When everything unraveled for the department last year, no one had been able to prove Gaines had anything to do with framing Curly, but he wouldn't be a bit surprised to find out this fuck-bucket's hands were dirty. "I see you haven't moved up from traffic stops in the last thirteen years. Shame. Seemed like you had such a promising future."

His beady little eyes narrowed, reminding Curly of a nasty rodent. He folded his arms, resting them on the open window. "Actually, I just got promoted to detective last year. But, enough about me. What have you been up to since I last saw you?"

Christ, how he wanted to seize this asshole by his collar, yank him in the car, and bash his face against the steering wheel until he bled. Just because he didn't want to live the same violent, sometimes brutal lifestyle he'd had as a younger man didn't mean those parts of him had died. Now, he hid them behind the desire to remain out of prison and make up for losing thirteen years of his life. Instead of acting on the fierce impulse, he asked, "Since I'm guessing my taillight is just fine, you wanna get to the real reason for this little circle jerk?"

"Oh, just wanted to welcome you back to town properly, is all. Let you know we got eyes on you." His white teeth flashed as he smiled, the perfect target for Curly's fist.

"*Officer* Gaines, you have heard that I was framed by someone in your department, haven't you? Or did you miss that particular memo?"

The cop's lips thinned and his nostrils flared. Curly didn't give a shit about taunting the bull. Let him charge and see just what happened to his horns.

"Think I can let you off with a warning this time. Get that light fixed." Gaines straightened and tapped his fist against the windowsill. "Good seeing ya, Travis. 'Spect it won't be the only time." As he began another slow stroll, this time back to his car, he called over his shoulder. "Little birdie told me you were planning on getting the old MC back together. Sounds like a *great* idea."

Motherfucker.

How the hell did he learn about the MC? Curly would bet his new pup none of his guys blabbed. That left Prick. It'd explain how his old SAA got away with letting dogs maul each other without concern from the police.

Goddammit, once a traitor, always a traitor. As though sensing his distress, Harley climbed into his lap and lapped at his chin.

Thirteen years in prison for a crime he hadn't committed, and to someone like Gaines, it meant nothing more than a weapon to use against him. No sorrow, no regret, no apology for what had happened on behalf of a department that jackass still worked for. Nothing but smug superiority.

Not that he'd expected anything else. Running into the local PD for the first time since they'd locked him behind bars hadn't been on the day's to-do list.

He clenched the steering wheel until his arms shook. "Fuck!" he shouted, making Harley jump.

If Curly didn't get some release, he'd crawl right out of his skin. He had to get on the back of his bike. And he knew himself. He needed someone around to make sure he kept his head straight.

Instead of turning left toward his own home, he kept on straight to Brooke's. Fuck it. It wasn't a goddammed date. It was therapy.

And he needed it.

Not her. Just someone to join him.

That's what he told himself over and over again as his excitement grew with every mile he drove closer to her home.

Chapter Eighteen

Four days and three notes.

Brooke sighed Wednesday morning as she set each strip of paper side by side on her kitchen island. Each had a similar theme, but this one was downright bone-chilling.

Nice try.

Two simple words, but it sent a spike of fear through her bloodstream.

The security cameras she'd installed the morning before lay in pieces on the ground beneath the note. Someone crushed them. Probably stomped on them with a boot. A biker boot just like the ones Prick wore both times she'd seen him.

Her options were to take these notes and the broken camera to the police, but if she shared her suspicions about Prick, that was likely to get her nowhere. Another option would be more cameras, maybe inside the house so no one could rip them down, but none of her windows had a great view of the kennel entry. She had no idea where Prick was hopping her fence, and it'd be insanely expensive to monitor the entire expanse. That left a third option.

Asking Curly for help.

Everything in her rejected the idea. Especially since she already found herself thinking about him way more than was wise. If she went down this path, before she knew it she'd be calling him every time she needed help opening a jar, and she'd be right back to the woman she hated. The woman who too timid to fight her own battles and waited on her man for everything decision.

Okay, maybe her fears were slightly dramatic, but bottom line, she would fight to the death for her independence. That meant she needed to solve her own problems, even the frightening ones. Besides, she had no plans to go near Prick anytime soon. Once the man felt confident she wasn't a threat, he'd back off.

Just as she was about to brew a third cup of coffee and brainstorm some more, a pounding knock had Ray barking and scampering toward the door.

"Hold up, buddy," she said, and the obedient boy immediately plopped his fuzzy butt down. His tail still wagged hard enough to create a wind tunnel behind him.

Bam, bam, bam.

Brooke frowned. She didn't have any training clients that afternoon, and Nancy never knocked like the hounds of hell were chasing her down. So who the hell was it?

A shiver of fear ran down her spine. Prick?

No. He wouldn't be brazen enough to confront her at her house in broad daylight.

Would he?

Bam, bam—

She yanked the door open to find a scowling Curly with his fist raised for another attempt at busting down her door.

"Seriously?" he practically snarled. "You don't check who it is?"

Harley, who'd been at his feet, shot inside and pounced on an elated Ray. Together they darted off and out the dog door into the backyard, where the rest of the pups were running around.

"It's eleven in the morning. I wasn't exactly worried." She told him the white lie as she waved him in. "Plus, I have Ray."

He snorted. "Trust me when I tell you Prick is a piece of shit at all hours of the day."

Her stomach turned, but she waved away his concern and avoided eye contact. "Prick's not coming after me."

Liar.

Curly barely seemed to hear her. He prowled into her foyer and began to pace. Agitated energy wafted off him in strong waves. Dressed in his typical jeans and T-shirt, he looked irritated and hot as hell.

Big surprise.

"Everything okay?" she asked as she shut the door and leaned her back against it. Any other time she'd been around him—aside from the bar incident—he'd been entirely in control, and now something seemed off. He came across as a ticking time bomb ready to blow. "You having trouble with Harley or something?"

Or had Prick done something? Shit, had he somehow found out about the notes? She could imagine him losing his shit over that.

Stopping his movement, he faced her. "What? No. Harley's fine."

He stalked toward her then boxed her in against the wall.

Immediately her pulse shot through the roof, and her body recalled the last time they'd been so close. When he'd had his hands on her. And that sinful mouth.

Ugh, why did he always have to smell so good?

"Ever been on a bike?" he asked.

She blinked. "What?"

He chuckled as though he saw beneath her skin to the rapid heartbeat and breathlessness caused by his proximity. "A motorcycle. Ever ridden one?"

"No. I haven't." Did he want to take her on a ride? Did she want to go on one? Pressed against him. Having to hold onto him.

Her insides fluttered.

"Well, throw on some jeans, and let's get out of here. Nothing better than riding along the coast. We can stop and grab some lunch."

Good God, did that sound like the perfect way to spend her afternoon. But it also sounded like a date. She eyed him as her brain whirred, trying to interpret his mood and why he'd popped up to take her out like this. Especially after their conversation at breakfast a few days ago. She hadn't seen or spoken to him since.

Though she'd sure thought about him a lot.

Too much.

The idea of sitting pressed against him as the wind blew her hair and the salty gulf air tickled her nose was almost too much to bear. It'd be a giant step in the wrong direction of resisting him. "Actually, today isn't the greatest." She had about two seconds to come up with a credible excuse.

"Brooke," he said in an antsy tone that didn't fit the man she knew. "My head's a little fucked right now. I need to ride. Need to clear some shit from my mind. When I'm like this, it's better if I'm not alone."

The word no hung on the tip of her tongue. Couldn't he ask one of his new brothers to join him? But it was eleven on a workday. They'd all be busy. His troubled gaze pleaded his case and proved his word. Frustration, maybe even anxiety, hovered in those dark orbs. They held a wealth of pain he masked every day.

Of course they did. When she tried to imagine what the past thirteen years of his life must have been like, she could only stand to think about it for a moment or two before the sorrow and indignation took over. In some ways, she understood the horror of being trapped where you didn't want to be, but she eventually had the power to escape. He was at the mercy of others until the day someone finally discovered the egregious act that put him there.

So she found herself saying, "Give me twenty minutes to get all the dogs settled," instead of declining his perilous offer.

In the end, it only took ten minutes with Curly's help to wrangle the foster pups into their kennels. Brooke changed into jeans as he'd suggested while Curly waited. Ray and Harley were curled up on Ray's dog bed, snoozing away when they locked the door and left.

They drove to his house in his truck. "Hold up," he said after parking in the driveway.

Fifteen seconds later, he was opening the truck door for her.

She did not find that charming.

"I could have gotten it," she said.

"I know. But then I couldn't have done this." He reached in and grabbed her waist, then pulled her to him.

She yelped and grabbed for his arms as he lifted her off the seat. Their gazes locked. Slowly, he lowered her to the ground, letting her brush against his body the entire way.

Oh, my God, was he hard? It took everything in her not to shiver in delight.

"There, wasn't it more fun my way?" he asked with a wink before walking to the garage.

She sagged against the truck.

As the garage door slid open, his motorcycle came into view. Up close and personal, the bike was huge. Much bigger than she'd expected. Was he sure this outing would be safe? While she pondered whether this would be her last day on earth, Curly wrapped a hand around her waist from behind. Why did he have to feel so good?

"Sweetheart, I've been riding since I was eight." He spun her then plopped a helmet on her head with an amused grin. "Promise you're safe with me." He winked while securing the helmet.

Brooke snorted out a laugh. "Eight? Come on. Pull the other one."

"Started on dirt bikes as a kid. Man, we'd spend all summer on them. I remember my mama throwing a fit nearly every night when I came home covered in mud and muck from riding around the swamps." He chuckled at the memory. "Life sure was simpler then."

No kidding. She'd spent her childhood summers at the local lake and gobbling down popsicles with her friends. Not a care in the world beyond the next time she could get in her bathing suit.

"All right," he said once she was all set. Finally, he gave her a lopsided grin. The first genuine smile since he'd walked into her house. "You look cute as hell." After flicking her on the nose, he swung a thick muscular leg over the seat of his bike, leaving her standing there feeling like a teenage girl on her first date with the coolest guy in school.

Not a date.

Not a date.

As long as she kept repeating that, she'd be good. This was nothing more than her doing him a favor on a bad day. Least she could do to repay him for saving her bacon more than once.

And for that stellar orgasm.

"So what do I do?" she asked, trying to keep her voice even.

"Just climb aboard and hang on tight." He pointed toward what looked like pegs sticking out from the sides of the bike. "You can rest your feet there. Just relax and enjoy. Let your body follow mine when we lean into turns. You'll get a feel for it in a few minutes. And you'll love it."

She eyed the bike until he burst out laughing.

"How about a bet?"

Raising an eyebrow, she asked, "A bet?"

"Uh, huh.I If you do not love it by the time we hit the restaurant, lunch is on me. If you fucking love it, you're buying."

Well, that certainly went a long way toward making her feel like it wasn't a date. "You're on," she said, holding out a hand. He shook it then tugged her to him.

"Brooke?"

"Y-yes?" she asked as his musky, slightly leathery scent made her shiver.

"Get on the bike."

"Right." She did as asked, lightly placing her hands on his sides. Even that was too much physical contact. But when he grabbed her wrists and pulled her flush against his back, her eyes rolled back in her head. The warmth of the Florida sun had nothing on the heat radiating off this man.

"Right there, babe," he said, as he rooted her hands against his obscenely rippled stomach.

Oh, Lord.

"Ready to ride?"

"Let's do it," she said with more enthusiasm than she felt. This day was going to wreak havoc on her mental fortitude.

Curly let out a loud whoop before he revved the engine, making her jump, then laugh. Already he appeared in a better mood for just having sat his ass on his bike.

Beneath her, the bike rumbled, and between her legs, the man did the same. She held tight, maybe too tight, but falling off wasn't on her agenda for the day. Blowing out a breath, she tried her damnedest to ignore the way his muscular back felt beneath her breasts. And the perfect fit of his ass between her spread legs. She pretended he didn't smell like the ocean and sunshine wrapped in a woodsy blanket because if she did smell it, she might lean forward and bite him.

This ride might kill her in a different way than she'd been expecting.

Twenty minutes into the ride, Brooke conceded she'd be buying lunch, and she was totally cool with admitting her defeat. This was one of the best experiences she'd had in years, if ever. And she one hundred percent understood why Curly craved this when his head felt scrambled. She could sum it up in one word.

Freedom.

Curly

The open air. The ability to smell, feel, see, and be a part of the world as they traveled through it. Nothing holding them back. No one lording over them. Every sense felt heightened as she inhaled the salty air, absorbed the combination of sun and wind on her skin, soaked up the delicious heat from Curly, and listened to the engine purr.

The rest of the world faded away, and though they didn't try to speak, she'd never felt more connected to another person. An ease entered her soul she hadn't experience in years. Well over an hour passed before he finally pulled into the parking lot of what could only be described as a shack. A sign boasted the best fried grouper sandwich in Florida, and that was saying something of the state's specialty.

"Well?" Curly called over his shoulder after he killed the engine.

She wasn't even a bit mad about losing the bet. Grinning so wide her cheeks hurt, she said, "Guess lunch is on me today."

Laughing, he climbed off the bike. His face held an ease and joy, which was the opposite of the tension he'd worn when he showed up at her house. "Nah," he said with a wink. "My invite, my treat. Besides, I knew you'd love it, so it was an unfair bet."

Brooke opened her mouth to argue with him, but he stole the words with a quick but hard kiss. As she sat there stunned, he removed her helmet and extended a hand. "Let's go. I'm starved. Something about being near the water always makes me hungry."

While she wanted to argue that she was perfectly capable of paying for her own lunch and would prefer it that way, his elated mood was infectious, and she hated to kill the buzz with an argument. So, she took his hand and allowed him to lead her to the outdoor order window.

"The food at this place is out of this world," he said, still holding her hand.

She wiggled her fingers, but he seemed to have no plans to release her, so she sighed and went along with it. Besides, she'd be lying if she didn't admit, at least to herself, how great it felt to have her smaller hand wrapped in his big one.

Only one person waited in front of them in line. Then, before she knew it, they were at the counter.

"Trust me to order?" he asked, which immediately had her spine straightening.

Her knee-jerk reaction was to say, "hell no," and order for herself. Her husband always ordered for her when they'd gone out to eat. And by ordered for her, she meant chose her meal no matter what she wanted. Every time it was a salad or something equally unsatisfying. And heaven forbid she try to get some dessert.

But the look on Curly's face showed nothing of a desire to control her. And he'd asked rather than do it without her approval. He seemed so excited to introduce her to his favorite eatery, so again she found herself compromising her normal actions and nodding. "Go ahead."

"All right." He rubbed his hands together as the teen behind the counter asked. "Welcome to Fredia's Fish Shack, what can I getcha today?"

"Two grouper baskets and two lemonades," Curly said. "You are gonna love this. Fish, potatoes, grease, and ice-cold lemonade. It's heaven in a basket."

Her mouth watered at the sound of it. The incredible smell of fried fish wafting from the restaurant had her stomach rumbling in the most attractive way.

Not five minutes later, they were seated on the beach with piping hot fish sandwiches, watching the gentle waves of the Gulf.

"Thank you," Curly said after swallowing his first monster-sized bite.

"Mm-hmm," she managed as she bit into her sandwich. Damn, that was delicious. Seasoned perfectly, crispy, with fresh lettuce, tomato, and tartar sauce. "Wow, that's so good."

"Right?"

"Why did you thank me?"

Though they sat side by side, they both turned their heads toward each other. "I was in a shit mood. You could have easily told me to fuck off, but you tagged along. I appreciate it. Turned my foul morning into a perfect day."

An odd tightness entered her chest. Or maybe it was warmth. Something squishy and not entirely comfortable. "Well," she said as she lifted her sandwich. "I did it for the food."

When he didn't laugh as she'd hoped, she nudged his shoulder with hers.

"Wanna talk about whatever had you all spun up?"

He shoved a fry in his mouth then chased it with a long sip of lemonade. Just when she thought he'd completely ignore the question, he spoke. "Got pulled over on my way home from the pet store. It was a bullshit stop. Some cop who was around during the investigation and my trial who wanted to let me know he'd be keeping an eye on me."

"What?" she said, dropping her sandwich in the basket. "Well, that is bullshit. He does know you're innocent, right?"

"Asked him that very same question. I have no proof, of course, but I always suspected he had some hand in my framing. Even if he just looked the other way. Pretty sure he knows Prick."

Well, that explained the douchebaggery. "I'm sorry."

"Eh, it just brought up some unpleasant memories and shot my attitude to shit. A good ride always helps that." He nudged her shoulder back. "Good company even more."

Brooke swallowed down a bubble of emotion that welled. It felt nice to be needed by someone. To know her mere presence had helped soothe his soul. "Was it as awful as I imagine it would be?" she asked.

He understood she meant being in prison without her having to elaborate. "No. It was worse."

"To say I'm sorry for what you went through seems so inadequate. I suppose there aren't any words to make it remotely acceptable." She'd admired his muscles and how strong they made him, but his true strength came from with. No everyone could endure what he had and not be a bitter, miserable person.

"No, there aren't," he said with a sigh as he gazed out over the watery horizon. Then he faced her way again. "I imagine you know a little about that."

Shaking her head, she bit into a crisp fry. "No. Our situations were nothing alike. I willingly walked into my marriage. The stupid mistake was my own."

"So you deserved it?" His expression darkened.

"No. Of course not. I just don't want you to think I'm trying to compare being in a loveless, abusive marriage to being jailed for a crime I didn't commit."

"It's not a competition, babe. You were dealt a shit hand. I was dealt a shit hand. It's all shit in the end."

Yeah. It was. But some shit stank worse than others. He had every right to wallow in anger and hatred. It spoke to the type of man he was and the strength of his character that he chose not to. The more she learned of him, the more he appealed to her in a way she'd never intended. She'd assumed so many things about him at first, including that he'd be a bossy, possessive, controlling man, and all of them were proving to be wrong. He had many layers, and each one she peeled back revealed a man she was drawn to.

She needed to be careful around him. As much as she liked him, she couldn't let a man get past her defenses. Evan hadn't a monster in the beginning, either. Though if she were honest, she knew she'd ignored a host of red flags with her ex-husband.

"You ever hear from him?"

"Who?"

"Your fuckwad of an ex."

"Oh. God, no. Not anymore. Not for about three years or so. He still lives in Silicon Valley. Or at least he did a year or so ago. I assume he's still there. The house we owned was gifted to him by his parents when they decided to downsize." She picked up a fry, twirling it with her fingers. She'd never liked the house. Too gaudy and ornate for her tastes. She preferred simplicity, comfort, and function. The home they'd lived in was practically a museum to affluence.

"Anyway, after the divorce, he used to call every once in a while. The calls would start with apologies and all kinds of sweet promises for a better future if I'd just come back." She grunted, recalling the final phone call where she'd recorded him and threatened to share it with everyone he knew. "He'd always call from a different number, so I couldn't just block him. Then he'd turn ugly when I refused him or threatened to hang up. After a time, I stopped answering calls from any number I didn't recognize, and he'd leave furious voicemails. Eventually the calls grew less frequent, and then they stopped." She shrugged. "Last I saw from the one mutual contact we still have on social media, he'd found some other poor woman to fall for his bullshit. Someone new to torture. Gave him something to focus on besides me. I haven't heard from him since." She popped the fry in her mouth and chewed slowly. "Although who knows. Maybe she was the picture-perfect trophy wife he'd been searching for all along, and they're living happily ever after. God knows I never lived up to his expectations."

She sipped her lemonade and let the sweetness wash away bitter memories.

Curly grunted. "You can't possibly believe that bullshit." His voice was like iron. He stared at her with the intensity of a man who shouldn't be trifled with. "Men—no, he shouldn't even be called a man—assholes like him aren't happy with anything or anyone they have because they're rotten at their core. Spoiled babies who always think they deserve more or better. He already had the best, and that fucker couldn't appreciate her for shit, so whoever he's married to now will only disappoint him even more."

He bit into his sandwich and gazed out over the water once again as though his words hadn't rocked her. He spoke the sweet words so casually she almost didn't believe she'd heard them.

He already had the best…

Her. He'd meant her, right?

How else could she interpret it?

He'd already been sweeter to her than her husband had been for most of their marriage. Imagine being married to a man who thought she was the best? Would it have been different than what she'd experienced, or would it have soured in the end anyway?

She should thank him for the compliments, but with each passing second, she grew to like the man more. That was fine as long as those feelings stayed confined to friendship which she feared would be difficult. If he wasn't so damned sexy, if he didn't appeal to her every buried desire, if their chemistry wouldn't have made the gulf water boil, it'd be so much easier to keep the lines from blurring.

But he was all of those things and their chemistry was off the charts. She wanted him. And she liked him. A very dangerous combination that once led to her losing her dreams, her friends and family, and her identity.

Never again.

So instead of thanking him and possibly treading on dangerous ground by deepening their connection, she said, "Heavy topics." Then she cleared her throat. "So, how's Harley doing at home?"

He grinned, and the weight of their personal issues lifted. "Great. She's cute as fuck." Then he winced. Not sure your stance on dogs sleeping in the bed since you're a trainer, but she snuggles right next to me all night." He chuckled. "Thought I'd hate sharing a bed with a woman after sleeping alone for so many years, but she doesn't hog the blankets or put cold feet on me, so it's all good."

Curly

Brooke laughed. "No judgment here. Ray sleeps with me every night, too."

And just like that, the conversation flowed into lighter topics. As they finished their meals, they chatted and laughed. Brooke shared hilarious stories of working with ridiculous pet owners, and Curly shared some tales from his misspent youth. They watched kids playing in the gulf and lovers strolling hand in hand. By the time Curly announced it was nearly four in the afternoon, her stomach ached from laughing, and they'd probably both gotten enough sun to be uncomfortable tomorrow.

The hours had flown by, turning the day into one of the most enjoyable she'd had in a long time. It was official. She needed to get out and socialize more. Nancy and her four-legged companions shouldn't encompass her entire social circle.

Neither should outlaw bikers. But at least they were safe and allowed her to be herself without judgment.

"Well," he said after an uncharacteristic lull in the conversation. "Guess we better get back before the dogs mutiny."

"Yeah, they'll be wanting dinner and some playtime soon. Thank you for this. I don't think you're the only one who needed some beach therapy."

"And the ride." He winked. "Don't forget the ride."

As if she could. The fact that she got to get back on that motorcycle in a few minutes had her practically giddy with anticipation.

They tossed their trash then walked back to the motorcycle in pleasant silence. Once again, he took care of the helmet for her. She felt his heavy gaze roaming her face as he buckled her up but couldn't bring herself to meet his gaze. If she saw the same needy lust she was experiencing, she'd likely make a huge mistake.

But then his fingers clasped her chin, and she gasped as she looked into his eyes. A slow smile curled his lips right before he kissed her.

It was a soft kiss. Gentle and teasing as opposed to the scorching hot make-out session from a few nights ago. But the tenderness made it even more powerful. Curly led, taking his time to work his tongue into her mouth. She sighed against him as they explored each other. No one had ever kissed her like this. As though she was precious. As though she was special. As though she was perfect.

When it ended, she kept her eyes closed for a moment, terrified to open them and find she'd read too much into the sweetest kiss she'd ever received.

"I needed this." he whispered. "The day and the kiss."

What did that mean? Where did that leave them? Because that wasn't a this-is-just-physical kiss. It was deeper. It was…more.

"Ready?"

"Yep." Hopefully, she sounded normal and not like she was about to melt into a puddle of goo.

After he settled himself on the seat, she placed a hand on his shoulder to steady herself as she climbed behind him. The muscles under her fingers tensed, and she was powerless to keep from kneading her fingers into them a tiny bit. As soon as it happened, she yanked her hand back, mortified, but he was having none of that. He grabbed her hand and put it right back on him.

It wasn't long before they were cruising back home. As with the first trip, she had her arms wrapped around his waist, only this time the vibrations of the bike and warmth of his back lulled her into a relaxed, sleepy state. Soon, holding her head up took too much effort, so she rested her cheek against Curly's back. With the helmet, finding a comfortable position took some effort, but she eventually settled into a spot that worked perfectly. Once she stopped wiggling, he took a hand off the handlebar and gave her thigh an affection squeeze.

Was this what it'd feel like to sleep next to him at night? To wrap herself around him and cradle all his strength and power in her arms? Or would he prefer their positions reversed where he held her?

Maybe he'd be like her husband and despise anyone touching him in sleep, leaving her cold and alone even while a warm body lay inches away.

But something told her that wouldn't be the case. Curly had lived the lonely life of an inmate, and as he said, steel bars might not have blocked her cell, but she hadn't been free.

Chapter Nineteen

They arrived at Brooke's home shortly after five. Curly accompanied her inside to fetch Harley, then ended up sticking around and playing in the yard with all the other dogs while she loaded them up with food and water.

When Brooke hollered, "Dinner time," the dogs, including Harley and Ray, charged toward the kennel.

"I should get her home to eat," he said as he strolled over to where she stood outside the kennel.

"There's plenty of food. She's fine to eat here," Brooke answered, smiling at the dogs chowing down at their food bowls as though they'd never eaten.

The slurping and crunching sounds of famished dogs filled the room.

"Unless you need to go. Don't feel like you have to stick around, but you're welcome to stay until she's finished. Or longer. Whatever."

Brooke was cute when she got flustered, and lately, he seemed to fluster her more and more. Her mistrust of men and relationships made perfect sense—hell, he wanted to fly to California and beat the fuck outta her shit-stain ex—but she had nothing to fear with him. Not only did he have no desire to control her in any way, but he also had no plans for any complicated commitment. Okay, maybe there was one way he could imagine controlling her, but he had a feeling she wouldn't like to be dominated in bed either. Though seeing her submit to him would be so sexy, his heart would likely give out. Then again, having her boss him around while naked would be fun, too.

Shit, he was starting to feel pretty damn hungry himself.

"Nah, I'm not in a rush. Don't have any scheduled plans until the weekend. Guy who's gonna be our enforcer just got out of the military and will be rolling into town this weekend. He'll be crashing with me until he gets all his shit sorted. You'll have to meet him. Think you'll like him."

What the fuck? She had to meet Scott? What the hell did he care whether she met his people? If he wasn't careful, she'd start thinking he was some sappy fucker who wanted to bring her home to meet the fucking fam.

He nearly shuddered at the thought of that potential disaster. Who remained of his family hadn't spoken to him since his arrest. Now that he was out, he had no plan to reach out to them, and none of them had made any attempt to contact him. Fuck 'em all for refusing to stand by him when he proclaimed his innocence. He had a brother, a set of parents, and a handful of cousins besides Tyler who'd never know a thing about his life.

Their loss.

Brooke glanced his way. She'd gotten some sun today, deepening her tan. The tips of her shoulders were pink, along with her nose. Her ponytail had loosened throughout the day, and strands of hair now hung free. The woman was downright stunning in her natural state. He'd never given much thought to all the primping women he'd been within the past had done, but with Brooke, he loved how she didn't cover herself up or alter her natural beauty.

"You want a beer or something while we wait for them to finish up? Or maybe something to eat?" she asked.

"An ice-cold beer sounds perfect."

"It does. Follow me." Smiling, she waved him into her house.

It was a picture-perfect Florida evening. The surprising lack of humidity for the time of year made for a pleasant warmth. Evenings like this made him want to live outside, watch the sunset, and do nothing but soak up his freedom.

Enjoy life the way it was intended to be enjoyed.

He couldn't help but imagine Brooke at his side, enjoying life's simple pleasures. A sense of peace washed over him. It was a nice vision, as though they belonged side by side.

Crazy thoughts.

"Here you go," Brooke said as she handed him an uncapped bottle. Her cheeks were pink, and she wouldn't meet his gaze, which seemed odd. If she wanted him to leave, why hadn't she let him go when he'd offered to grab Harley and get outta her hair?

Then he glanced down at the beer bottle, and her bashful reaction made sense. She'd given him his favorite beer. One that came from a local microbrewery. The same kind he'd had at his house.

What the fuck did that mean? Had she purchased it, hoping he'd be around to share it with her? He almost laughed out loud.

Way to make it about you.

More likely, she enjoyed the brew and wanted some or herself. Why was that option disappointing?

"It's good," she said, voice slightly defensive as though she'd heard the direction of his thoughts. "I hadn't had it before. Now I'm hooked."

Well, that answered that. But she still wouldn't make eye contact.

Interesting.

"Wanna sit outside?" she asked as she collected two more beers from the fridge.

"Yeah, I was just thinking how it's a sin to be inside on evenings like this."

"Definitely." She filled a small bucket with ice, then stuck the extra drinks in it. "Let's do it."

They sat in silence next to each other on a pair of lounge chairs near her pool. Whatever comfortable intimacy they'd shared earlier at the beach had dissolved into a thick tension where neither seemed to know how to fill the silence. It'd happened the moment she called the dogs for dinner. As if she'd realized he was invading her personal private sanctuary, though she hadn't seemed to mind it the other night.

He bit off a groan. Last thing he needed to be thinking about was the other night and how incredible she'd looked coming apart for him.

"Can I ask you something?" she said right after draining her first beer.

He'd polished one off as well and reached for a second the same time she did. Their fingers brushed, sending a jolt of electricity straight up his arm and somehow to his dick. "Anything."

"What's the appeal of forming a new motorcycle club after all you've been through? I mean, from what you've said, you were specifically framed because the father of the murdered girl hated MCs with a passion. Doesn't that make you think twice about doing it all over again?" Then as though she only realized the personal nature of the question once the words were out there, she shook her head. "Shit. That's such an invasive question. Please don't answer. The beer must be loosening my lips."

He chuckled at her embarrassment. "Nah, it's all good, babe. You know where I went as soon as I got my head on straight after being released?"

She shook her head. The twilight hour made her tanned skin almost glow. With her wind-blown hair in a high ponytail and the simple outfit of a red T-shirt and denim shorts, she was natural, casual, and so goddammed appealing his dick got hard just looking at her.

"I went to see Holly."

Her jaw unhinged. "Wait, isn't she the twin of the girl who was murdered?"

With a nod, he took a long drag of the beer, wishing it was something a bit stronger. The past was something he couldn't avoid. Hell, it had dominated thirteen years of his life, but that didn't make it easy to talk about.

"Yes. They were twelve when Joy died. I'd met Holly a few weeks before Joy's murder. She'd been late leaving a friend's house and was racing home on her bicycle. The front tire hit a rock, and she flew over the handlebars. Scraped herself all the fuck up and mangled her bike. I saw it happen, so I stopped and gave her a ride home. Then I called one of my prospects to pick up her bike. We fixed it for her, and I left it in her parents' driveway."

Brooke's forehead wrinkled as though she didn't understand what any of this had to do with her question, but she stayed quiet.

He appreciated the silent moment to gather his thoughts.

"Of course, since she was Joy's twin, she was questioned as a witness during the investigation. Her parents had no idea what had gone down the night I helped her out, but when the cops asked if she or Joy had ever encountered any members of my club, she told them about it. She also told them I was kind to her and how she hadn't felt uncomfortable or threatened in my presence. That little girl stood up for me and said I could never have killed Joy. My own family didn't have my back like she did. Even after I was arrested, Holly stuck to her belief that I couldn't have done it." He shrugged, attempting to shake off the hatred and disgust that always accompanied these memories.

Betrayed by his ol' lady.

Betrayed by a club brother.

Set up by the police.

Abandoned by his family.

So many had turned on him, but not Holly. The only one standing at his side had been a twelve-year-old girl. What did that say about his life and the kind of man he'd been?

Nothing good. But now, he had a second chance to write his story. It'd be better this time around. He'd do better.

He cleared his throat. "But she was a kid, so her opinion meant dick to anyone. Especially once they found *evidence* that I'd done it."

Brooke sat up, swinging her legs over the side of her chair, so she faced him. Her beer dangled from her hands, and her face was a mask of disbelief and sorrow. "God, Curly, I had no idea..."

"Anyway, after I got out, I took a few months to get my head right, then went to see her. She'd hooked up with a guy in an MC, if you can believe that shit," he said with a chuckle. To say he'd been shocked to find that out was the understatement of the year. He'd been fucking floored. Her father had nearly disowned her before she'd discovered his corruption. "He's a good man. She's a great girl. Twenty-five now." He snorted. "Fuck, I could be her father. Kinda feel like it now."

Brooke gave him a soft smile. "You spent time with her?"

"Yeah, right up until I came here. Their club is great. They live the life I always wanted when I patched in with the Outlaws. They're a true brotherhood. One that cares less about profit and power and more about family. A family of damn good men and damn amazing women. I wanted it back then to make up for my own shit family, and I still want it now. It's in my blood or something. So I'll be opening an extension of their club here and running it the way they do."

"Do they..." Her nose wrinkled. "I mean, are they an, what do you call it? An outlaw club?"

He met her gaze. Lying would be easy. Probably smarter. It didn't matter if she accepted him for that aspect of his life. She'd never be a part of it, but he found himself eager to find out if she'd look at him differently once she knew. "They are."

"So you could go to jail. Again."

With a slow nod, he said, "I could. It's always a risk."

Her mouth turned down. "I don't understand why you would risk your freedom again. Not after what you went through. Doesn't the idea of going back scare you to death?"

"It does. But the Hell's Handlers aren't into what the True Outlaws were. No drugs. No guns. No prostitution. So the risk is much lower. I'm a biker. I thrive in that brotherhood. My own family, whoever is still alive, is uninterested in me. Chosen family is what I get. Club life is who I am, and living without it scares me more than the other possibilities."

"But it's still there."

Again, he wouldn't lie to her, so he just shrugged. "I've never quite been able to conform to society's rules and the way people think I'm supposed to live. Club life lets me be who I am."

"I understand that," she whispered. "God, how I understand that."

"Living for yourself?"

She nodded, gazing at him with an almost tender expression that had his chest tightening nearly as much as his dick. Is this what a future with Brooke would look like? Peaceful evenings outside as the sun set and dogs scampered about. A brotherhood at their back. Retiring to their bed to spend hours getting lost in pleasure. Living by their own rules.

Damn, that sounded just about perfect.

But a fantasy was all it was. He knew firsthand life didn't play out like a storybook.

By now, the dogs had long finished eating. Most sprawled out in her yard, enjoying their food comas while a few still ran about, chasing each other.

He shifted his focus back to her to find her watching him with a darkened gaze. Christ, he hoped to fuck it was lust and not just fatigue.

"Thank you," she whispered.

What the fuck did she have to thank him for? "For what?"

Curly

The smile she gave him transformed her face. "For today. For my first ride. For being honest with me."

Even in the dwindling light, he saw her cheeks turn pink. Fuck, he loved that damn blush and how easy it was to bring it out of her.

"I think I've been in a bit of a rut. It was nice to break out for a day."

It wasn't a rut, but it was her safe place. She used her routine, small social circle, and job to keep her protected from further hurt. Who could blame her after what she'd been through? But they'd talked about enough serious shit for one night, so he just said, "It was my pleasure."

That one word, pleasure, seemed to spark something in Brooke. She bit her lower lip, then gazed out at the darkening yard. This time, when she turned back to him, there was no mistaking the desire written all across her face.

She stood, set down her beer, then closed the two-foot distance between their chairs until she stood above him, peering down. That lower lip still rested between her teeth. He wanted to suck it into his mouth, soothe it with his tongue, see it stretched around his cock.

As though grappling with the sanity of her options, she continued to watch him. For his part, he remained silent and still as fuck. There wasn't a goddammed thing he could do to keep his cock from hardening, but other than breathing, he waited for her to make her next move.

Either she'd walk away, or…

When she turned and began walking, disappointment surged so strongly, he nearly whimpered like one of those fucking dogs. But Brooke didn't go into the house. No, she headed out the screen door into the yard, where she called the dogs to the kennel. After disappearing inside for a few moments, she emerged again with Ray and Harley at her heels. The dogs ran ahead of her when she reopened the screen, beelining straight for him.

"Ray, go to bed," she said in a firm voice.

Instead of jumping on the lounge chair, Ray scampered into the house with Harley hot on his trail.

Brooke didn't follow the dogs.

She sauntered straight toward him. Those bare legs of hers, smooth and sleek, had him envisioning all kinds of dirty scenarios with them wrapped around his waist, thrown over his shoulders, squeezing the fuck out of his face as he feasted on her.

Christ, why was he torturing himself this way?

She kept moving his way until she once again stood next to his chaise. Unable to resist the urge to feel her silk skin, he slid a hand up the back of her thigh and held on. She gasped, letting her eyes flutter shut as he stroked her incredibly soft skin. When her eyes opened, indecision warring with desire stared down at him.

Then for whatever reason, she made up her mind. She threw one leg over him and settled down on his body, straddling him.

He cupped the back of her legs, slid his hands up and under the frayed edges of her shorts until he met her curvy ass cheeks. Then he filled his hands with them and squeezed.

Brooke moaned like his touch was the most amazing sensation in the world. If it wasn't for her panties, his hands would feel even better. They needed to do something about those panties.

But first…

"Be sure, Brooke," he rasped out as she slid her hands under his shirt and found his abs. Fuck, he wanted those hands wrapped around his dick. "Be fucking sure because if we start this, I'm not gonna be satisfied fingering you off and leaving with a hard-as-fuck dick. Not tonight."

Her smile was slightly shy as she whispered, "You didn't have to the other night."

"Gotta be a gentleman once in my life," he said with a wink.

Her laughter was music to his ears. She scraped her thumbnails over his nipples, and he grunted. When the hell had that ever felt good? Damn, this woman just did it for him. She could probably get him off by sucking his finger.

"I'm sure," she whispered as she leaned down until her lips were a breath away from his. "I'm sure I want you to take me into my bedroom and fuck me."

Fucking hell. He tightened his grip on her ass, swung his legs over the side, then stood in a smooth series of moves that had her clinging to him. The second those ankles of hers crossed behind his back, he took her mouth in a searing kiss that left them both breathless and panting.

This was a foolish idea that would only deepen the tie between them then end in disaster at some point, but right then and there, nothing short of the end of the world could have kept him from having her.

"Point me toward your room," he said against her mouth. "And I hope to hell you're ready for the fucking ride of of lifetime."

He'd deal with the consequences later. It was how he'd lived most of his life.

And when had that ever worked out for him?

Chapter Twenty

Was she ready? Was she sure?

The only thing she was sure of was that she'd lost her damn mind. Spending such a chill day with Curly had done something to her. Unlocked a long-buried well of yearning she couldn't ignore. The pull to him had intensified throughout the day, not only the physical desire to be close to Curly, but a cerebral desire as well. She wanted to know what went on in his head. To understand him. To learn all there was to discover about the gruff man who'd hadn't lived an easy life.

As luck would have it, he'd given her a wide glimpse into his psyche today. Into the man beneath the sexy muscles, commanding presence, and fearsome scowl. To the wounded soul searching for his place in a world that had turned its back on him. A world in which he didn't quite fit. Not now and maybe not ever. She could only imagine how much tougher it must be for him to find his footing following betrayal, years of wrongful incarceration, and the loss of his club family. Despite its faults, his MC had been the one thing that made sense before everything went to shit.

No wonder he wanted that part of his life back.

Brooke knew what it was to exist in a universe where she didn't belong. Her ex-husband's world had been a dark, lonely, abusive place disguised by the glitz and glamor of high-society money and backstabbing friendships. For years, she'd tried to mold herself, to force herself into the rigid slot her husband had carved for her, and she'd failed spectacularly. Because, like Curly, she couldn't live while suppressing her true identity. Wearing designer dresses every day when she preferred to live in jeans, styling her hair to fit her husband's desired image of her, attending gossipy brunches with women she despised because they needed to be seen in certain circles, never owning a pet because it had the potential to dirty the house. That life had nearly destroyed her.

She wasn't a woman who could thrive in a man's shadow.

She wasn't someone who could keep her mouth shut when she saw something she disapproved of.

She wasn't a woman who took orders without question.

And she sure as hell wasn't some trophy to be stored on a shelf, polished, and shown off at will.

No, she was a woman who spoke her mind, fought for what was important to her, and took what she wanted.

Tonight, she wanted Curly.

Even if she shouldn't. Even if no one from her husband's world would ever understand the appeal of a man like him.

Hell, maybe because of it. Perhaps it made her a horrible person, but there was something about choosing a man so opposite her staid, refined, and pretentious husband as the first man to have her since her divorce that had her blood zinging with excitement. It was the ultimate show of defiant autonomy.

"Brooke?" he asked in a rasp.

She blinked, "Huh? What?" They stood in the middle of her kitchen with his hands cupping her ass and her legs wrapped tight around his trim waist. She clung to his shoulders for balance.

His eyes narrowed, giving him a roguish look. "Where did you go?" He held her with ease, as though she weighed no more than Harley. His strength excited her. Not so much because she wanted him to use it on her—though that'd be hot as hell—but she had the insane notion of bringing all that strength to heel. Of being the one to make him quiver and beg while she steered the boat.

Fuck, that'd be the most erotic thing she'd ever participate in. But it probably wouldn't happen with a powerful man like him.

"Nowhere. I'm here. All here." It'd been a day or so since he'd shaved and rough stubble dotted his strong jaw, calling to her. She tightened her legs around him as she leaned in and enjoyed the scratch of his scruff against her cheek.

"My room is the last door at the end of the hall," she whispered against his ear.

His hands flexed on her ass, drawing a shudder from deep within in her. The way he held her with possessive authority as he marched them toward her bedroom had her wishing they were already naked.

Sex with her ex had been mediocre at best and humiliating at its worst. After the first few years, getting aroused for a man she'd grown to hate hadn't been an easy task. Of course, he'd noticed her body's lack of response and blamed her for being *frigid* despite being disgusted by the one fantasy she'd shared with him. She'd taken to disappearing into elaborate fantasies in her head to tolerate his advances, but even those only went so far when the actual man inside her was complaining about her being a cold fish in bed or how she'd embarrassed him at the latest company function.

There was nothing cold or frigid between her and Curly. His lips attacked her neck, and she swore her entire body heated twenty degrees. They were going to burn the house to the ground with their chemistry.

"Fuck," he ground out as his teeth raked across her pulse point. "I want to fucking mark you everywhere." Then he sucked hard on her collarbone, ensuring she'd have a bruise in the morning.

Curly

When the sting grew too intense, she squeaked, grabbed his hair, and yanked his head back. His eyes flared with primal desire, making her pussy clench.

He liked that. Liked it when she got aggressive with him. At least, it seemed that way.

Maybe she needed to test the theory.

Hand still filled with his silky hair, she brought their mouths close. "Kiss me?" she asked.

"You never have to ask, Brooke. Just take it. Or fucking demand it of me." He filled her mouth with his skillful tongue. They moaned into each other, then he was gone, shouting, "Ouch, fuck!"

Her heart stopped in her chest. Had she gone too far?

"My foot," he grumbled. "I kicked the fucking doorframe."

Brooke giggled.

"You think that's funny?" he asked as he maneuvered them into her bedroom.

Biting her lower lip to keep from laughing more, she nodded.

He growled and kissed her again with even more passion this time. She squeezed, wrapping her arms around his neck as they devoured each other in a sloppy kiss that was more about need than finesse. Tongues clashed, teeth clanked and nipped, and lips sucked for long, heated minutes. As amazing as kissing him was, Brooke's arousal grew with each passing second until she was practically humping his stomach to get some relief from the ache between her legs.

She needed more.

The next thing she knew, he was dropping onto her bed and she was straddling his lap. He still held her ass, grinding her pelvis against the hardness between his legs. She cried out as frustration neared its tipping point. This felt remarkable, the kissing, the touching, but she needed more.

She wanted skin.

With a little snarl, she tried to lift Curly's shirt, but the tail was stuck under him.

He chuckled as he shifted to give her the access she demanded. "Someone needs it bad, huh?"

Nodding, she yanked his shirt up and off his body.

Finally! Yards of warm, delicious skin. Even though she'd seen his bare chest when they'd been in her pool, the sight of all those tanned and inked muscles took her breath away. The need to rub herself all over that enticing skin had her hopping off his lap and ripping her own T-shirt over her head.

Gazes locked, they each went to work, shedding their own pants. The second her shorts pooled at her feet, she kicked them away along with her panties, then her attention snagged on the hard cock fisted in his hand and her knees nearly buckled.

He lounged back on one elbow as he stroked himself with a self-satisfied smirk. The man knew what he was doing to her and he loved it. "You do need it bad. You need this cock, baby?"

Her insides clenched. Whether it was his thick hard-on, near purple and angry from the surge of blood, or the pet name, it didn't matter. All she could think about was filling the emptiness inside her with that length. "I need it," she said as her heart thudded and her belly quivered.

Just as she was about to climb on the bed next to him and lie on her back, he smirked. "Then come take it."

She froze. "What?"

Still wearing that sexy smirk, he scooted back until he lay with his head on a pile of pillows and legs spread wide enough, she could see his heavy sac resting on her comforter. Then he resumed playing with himself as though he did this in front of a woman every day. Hell, for all she knew, he did.

"You've been on two rides today. Isn't there a saying about good things *coming* in threes?"

Her tongue dried up, so she nodded. They did say that. Though she was pretty sure they were on the hundredth good moment of the day.

"Wanna go for your third ride? I guarantee this will blow the first two out of the water." His husky, strained voice had her head spinning.

Did she want to climb on top of him and ride him, both of them, to an explosive finish? "Y-yes." God, did she ever want that.

Could she do it? It was the ultimate in vulnerable positions. Letting him see everything, touch anything, trust he wouldn't criticize.

He spread his arms in offering. As he released his cock, it slapped against his stomach. Nothing short of a gun to the head could have forced her attention elsewhere. "Then I'm all yours. Do with me what you'd like."

Her gaze snapped to his. Holy shit, she might come on the spot from the idea of being in control of a man like him. Even before her marriage had gone bad and her husband had revealed his true colors, he had no tolerance for what he called "an aggressive woman." She was there to be fucked by him, not to do any fucking. Eventually, she recognized it was another way of controlling her. God forbid a woman exert herself in bed or have her own needs.

Day by day, Curly was introducing her to a different type of man. One confident in his masculinity and not intimated by a strong woman. At least for now.

And the here and now was all that mattered. If he meant it, she'd explore every inch of his body with her hands, lips, and tongue until he was strung tight with need and begging her to take his cock. Shit, she was lightheaded just at the notion of it.

"I can do anything?" she whispered. Her voice shook as she tried to suppress her eagerness.

"*Anything*." Once again, he fisted his dick, resuming the show. "Brooke, when it comes to fucking there isn't a goddammed thing I wouldn't want you to do to me."

"Holy shit." She spoke so low, he probably didn't hear her, but his grin expanded to something almost daring. After swallowing down a spike of nerves, Brooke breathed in a burst of confidence. "Stop touching yourself. Only I get to touch that cock."

One of his eyebrows rose, but he immediately did as she asked, settling his hands on the comforter at his sides.

"You're so gorgeous," she said as she knelt in the space between his feet.

"I've got nothing on you, Brooke. Do you have any idea how much time I've spent thinking about this over the past few weeks? Thinking about seeing you naked and hungry for me? All your tanned skin. Those tits I tasted. Your drenched pussy."

If it was anywhere around the number of times she'd imagined him—hundreds.

"Hands stay there," she said. "No matter what." This newfound boldness and confidence with her nudity came from him. From the appreciative way his gaze raked over her nakedness. Maybe he needed glasses as he didn't seem to notice the cellulite on her thighs or the roundness of her belly. She kept her lacy bra on, not quite ready to have her forty-plus-year-old breasts drooping over him yet she had a feeling he'd be blind to her flaws there, too.

He grunted and she swore his entire body trembled. Chill from the air conditioner? Desire? Anticipation? "Yes, ma'am."

As proud of herself as she was for the hard-won independence she'd never relinquish to a man, as much as she loved her life and had grown to love herself, she couldn't deny the thrill of having a man express admiration for her body.

On hands and knees, she crawled forward until she was between his thighs. Then she smoothed her hands over the hairy skin there, loving the way his quads flexed at the contact. "I love your strength," she said, continuing to pet him.

"Spent a lot of time working out in prison. Fuck, I like your hands on me."

"Mmm." She bent forward and nuzzled her nose against his flat stomach, trailing it downward. When she reached his erection, she inhaled and Curly cursed. He smelled of soap, and the beach, and something uniquely Curly. It was his own fragrance she found so intoxicating. She pressed a quick kiss to his inner thigh, loving the way his breath caught and his leg jerked. Then, unable to stop herself, she bit him.

"Jesus, fuck," he shouted.

She glanced up to find his neck corded with tension. "Too much?" she asked as her heart thundered. Was her ex right? Did all men despise a woman getting aggressive?

"Fuck no, it's not too much. Put your teeth all over me. I fucking love it."

Well, in that case...She bit his other thigh even harder. Leaving a crescent shaped mark this time. Out of the corner of her eye, she caught his hands fist the comforter.

Sitting up straight, Brooke gazed down at his cock which was now leaking. "You're so incredibly hard."

"Your fault," he said through clenched teeth, making her smile.

"I have no problem taking the blame for that." She gently stroked him in a hand-over-hand motion as he shifted on the bed. The skin over his erection was silky smooth and rigid with full veins.

"Those hands...shit it's so good."

After a moment, she grew curious and cupped the heavy sac beneath his dick.

Curly stiffened and bit his lip, punching his pelvis upward.

With a mischievous smile, she gave a little tug and his back arched off the bed. Damn, she loved this. Torturing him one sensual touch at a time. It was all on her timetable, her way, her decisions. He was a buffet of sexy fun spread out for her to play and pleasure. She could grow addicted to this kind of power.

Her own need continued to expand exponentially. Aching nipples pointed his way through the thin lace of her bra, drawing his attention. He licked his lips, and she lifted a hand to her breast. "You like?" she asked, thumbing her nipple.

"Fucking love your tits. Let me see 'em. Take 'em out."

She shouldn't love his use of words like tits and pussy, but God, she did. It was raw, primal, dirty. Nothing flowery or schmoopy. Those sentiments were too easy to fake. Reaching behind her back, she quickly opened the clasp and let the bra slide down her arms. Cool air from her room pebbled her nipples even more.

"Yes," he hissed as her breasts came into full view. "So sexy. So beautiful. All woman."

This man's approval shouldn't make her insides melt as it did, but she loved the way he looked at her. She felt his words rather than just heard them. She felt sexy, pretty, desirable as a woman and not a piece of property. "What else do you like?" she asked. Later, she'd be mortified at the blatant way she fished for compliments but in the moment she couldn't get enough of his praise.

"Your mouth."

"This mouth?" she asked as she bent down and took the head of his dick between her lips.

His harsh cry had her smiling around him.

Immediately his salty flavor coated her tongue and assaulted her taste buds. She'd never much cared for giving head but found she loved pleasuring him and seeing how she turned him on.

A hard suck had him shouting. "Yes! Fuck, that mouth."

He made her want things she'd never imagined enjoying. He made her love being in control of his body. His pleasure. She wanted to take him deep as she could and tell him to let loose. To use her.

She trembled. What the hell was happening to her?

When Brooke released him after only a few more seconds of strong suction, he shouted, "No," and arched up as though trying to get his dick back in her mouth.

"Tsk tsk," she said, wagging her finger at him. "Let's not be greedy. I have so many areas to explore. Can't spend all my time in one place."

Curly groaned. "Who knew you'd turn out to be such a sadist?"

That made her laugh. It came out as more of a giggle, a sound she'd never had cause to make in bed. "I promise it will all be worth it in the end." When she took him into her body and rode him until he roared. "But for now, you will man up and take it."

He mumbled something that sounded like "evil woman" right before she licked a long line up is abdomen.

"Shit." He shook and squirmed. Beneath her stomach, his cock twitched.

She continued her journey, kissing, licking, and nibbling at his firm abs. All the while he panted and tugged on the comforter so hard, it'd probably tear. When she reached his nipples, she lashed one flat disc then the other with her tongue. Sweat broke out along his torso, adding a salty flavor to his warm skin.

Next, his throat got her attention. She absolutely loved the way his neck muscles bunched and flexed beneath her wandering tongue. She bit his earlobe, giving a tug.

"Fuck," he whispered in a tortured tone.

"Time to make my way back down," she whispered before nipping his jaw.

"No." He shook his head on the pillow, sounding like a man close to the edge. "Fuck, Brooke, you're killing me."

Power surged through her at the agonized look on his face. She sat up and worked her way up until she straddled his chest. "Do you need something specific?" she asked in an innocent tone.

He narrowed his dark gaze. "Your pussy. I need your goddammed pussy. You're fucking dripping on my chest. Put me out of my misery and fuck me."

Shit. This big, strong, intimidating biker was begging.

Her.

Never before had she felt so powerful. So desired. So strong.

"Please, baby." He groaned when she pinched and twisted his nipples. "Please fill yourself with my cock. You know you need it as much as I do. To feel me stretching that soaked pussy."

Now it was her turn to groan. "You don't play fair." She'd meant to drag this out even longer but the idea of having him inside her was too tempting.

He winked. "Never claimed to."

Giggling, something she'd never imagined doing during sex, Brooke stretched until she could reach her nightstand. That's where she'd stashed the condoms she bought after their night in the pool.

"Jesus," Curly whispered as she fished one out of the drawer.

"What?"

"Your ass is so fucking sexy."

With a smile, she shimmied back down his body. "That comment just might get you laid, sir."

"Fucking better."

Brooke ripped the condom open and rolled it down his straining erection. His entire body jerked the second she touched him as though the light contact sent an electric shock surging through him. Once they were protected, she lined herself up and teased him a little more, rubbing the tip of his cock against her opening.

Of course, it had the effect of teasing her as well and within seconds she was ready to slam herself down on him. How the hell had he withstood her torture for so long? If the tables had been turned, she would have cracked long before he did.

Their gazes locked as she slowly began to lower down onto him. As badly as her body wanted to be full of him, she took her time, savoring every delectable second.

He was big, and it'd been so long for her that he stretched her almost to the point of uncomfortable.

"Fuck," he whispered when the tip disappeared into her body. "Fucking tight as hell."

Curly

She trembled, her head whirled, and her chest worked to draw in enough air. She began to feel like she was about to spin out of control and fly off into space. "Curly," she cried in a desperate need for something she couldn't voice.

"Travis," he said, gaze boring into hers. He finally released the comforter and grabbed onto her hips. "It's Travis, and I've got you, baby."

Her hands flew to his and as though they'd planned it, they interlaced their fingers and together guided her the rest of the way onto him. As soon as he bottomed out inside her she gasped. "Travis," she whispered.

"Heaven. Fucking heaven, baby." Heavy lidded eyes met her gaze and a full-body shiver ran through her at the possessive gleam of adoration in his eyes. Maybe she was only imagining it or wishing for it.

Either way, it was a problem because she loved that look and wanted it as much as she wanted this next orgasm.

And that meant she was already in over her head.

Chapter Twenty-One

Curly had thought he might die from the slow, sensual torture Brooke dished out like she'd been born for it. Drenched in sweat, he'd been a quivering mess while he waited for her to put him out of his misery. So many times, he wanted to release his knuckle-aching grip on the comforter, slam her to the bed, and pound inside her until she was screaming his name.

But then he caught the look of wonder on her face as she explored his body and the power she had to bring him to his knees. He'd have given her anything she wanted at that moment. And she'd wanted to take the reins. So he'd endured the sexual agony.

And now, he reaped his reward: the tight, scorching hot clasp of her pussy as she engulfed his entire length. The sight of a naked Brooke enjoying his body was almost as hot as her pussy surrounding his dick. Her tits hung heavy, swaying as her chest rose and fell. He'd abused her lips with wild kisses, and they shone red and swollen as they parted on a sigh. Every inch of her appealed to him. He couldn't wait to return the favor of driving her out of her mind with his hands and mouth.

He'd have his turn.

He dug his fingers into her hips, trying to keep himself from plunging up into her. But, fuck, it felt so good, and he needed her to move on him before he blew his load without a single thrust. The way her hands clutched his told him she was just as affected.

They stared at each other as she adjusted to his size with tiny rocks of her pelvis. Then, after a moment, her grip on him relaxed, and she rolled her hips. They both gasped, him because lightning shot straight from his dick up his spine.

"Feels good," she whispered as if she was fighting to keep her voice level.

Good didn't come close to describing the feel of her around him. "Ready for it to get even better?"

She nodded then an impish smile broke out across her face. "Let's ride."

Curly laughed until she lifted her hips and dropped back down on him, then he shouted a filthy string of curses that had her eyes widening.

But she wasn't disgusted. No, she breathed out and said, "Why is it so hot when you talk like that?" Then she did it again, and they stopped speaking.

He kept his hold on her hips, helping her move over him. With each passing second, she grew more confident, moving faster and harder. Her hips gyrated in an innately sensual rhythm that squeezed and tugged his cock in all the right ways. Each time she slid down his length, his eyes tried to roll back in his head. Only through sheer force of will was he able to keep his gaze on her.

When he bridged his hips up, she cried out and launched forward, bracing her hands on his shoulders. The angle changed the way he hit inside her pussy. She squeezed him impossibly tight until he swore he saw stars.

She swiveled her hips. "So good, so good," she chanted as she pumped him.

"Jesus." It was the only word he could get out. Her tits dangled, swinging back and forth in an arc above his face and making his mouth water. "Gimme a taste," he commanded as he drew his knees up. The change in position drove him even deeper into her and shifted her tits closer to his mouth.

He captured a nipple between his lips then gave it the good, hard suck she'd seemed to love the last time they were together.

Brooke whimpered then began to rock faster and harder as she chased her orgasm.

"That's it, baby. Fuck yourself on that big cock," he said before going for the other tit.

"Travis," she called as she moved with frenzied purpose. "I've never…this is so…" She squeezed her eyes shut as she moaned and arched her back, feeding him more of her tit.

Working together, they shuttled her hips at an outrageous speed. Eventually, he needed to breathe and released her from his mouth. She sat back up, and he straightened his legs. Her tits bounced, as did her ass against his thighs. With her head tipped back and mouth open, she was the picture of sexual bliss.

One of her hands smacked onto his thigh as she arched back then ground her clit against his pelvis. Gone were her reservations about her body or how he viewed her. Instead, she lost herself in the giving and taking of pleasure. Fuck, it was the sexiest sight.

Curly inhaled oxygen to his starving lungs. The smell of her arousal filled his nose. She'd taken over every one of his goddammed senses. He could spend the rest of his life surrounded by her gorgeous body.

But his balls had another idea. They ached and throbbed with the need to unload. If she didn't come soon, he was going to die from holding back.

All of a sudden, Brooke's eyes flew open, and she shouted as she drove down hard then shattered around him. "Travis!" Her nails dug into his leg. Her thighs trembled as she clamped down on his hips while forcefully grinding against him. Her pussy spasmed around his cock in excruciatingly tight pulses as though coaxing him to join her.

The sight alone of her coming would have done it for him but combined with the way her body milked his dick, and he had no hope of hanging on.

"Fuck!" He shouted as he surged upward, wrapping his arms around her. Together they rode out the intense orgasm, writhing and whimpering under the strength of it.

It'd been years since he'd come like that, if ever. Beneath his skin, his nerves buzzed with excitement though the rest of him grew lethargic and sated. Brooke had sagged heavily in his arms, and if it weren't the occasional tremor of aftershocks, he'd have wondered if she fell asleep.

After pressing a kiss to her damp temple, he eased them back down onto her bed. He grunted, and she whimpered as his over-sensitive dick slipped from her. At some point, he needed to deal with the condom still covering his softening cock, but it could wait a few minutes.

Brooke didn't pull away, but she didn't look at him either as they settled. He kept his arms around her, stroking her back. Hopefully, it'd ease any tension or awkwardness she might be feeling. She had to know he wasn't about to make professions of love or ask for a relationship, but he didn't want to be the asshole who hopped up and left the second his balls were empty.

At the very least, she deserved him sticking around for a half hour or so. Maybe until she fell asleep.

With a soft sigh, Brooke shifted. One of her legs lay across his thighs, and her head was cradled in the space between his arm and his chest while her palm rested over his heart. "It's pounding," she whispered.

With a chuckle, he stroked back the hair that had stuck to her cheek. "You gave this old guy a workout. Hope you're not expecting a repeat anytime soon because I'm forty-six, babe. Gonna need more than a few minutes or maybe some jumper cables to get some life back in him," he said, pointing to his spent cock.

Brooke laughed as she propped her chin on his chest. The joke had done precisely what he'd hoped and helped skip past the post-orgasm tension. "Don't worry, old man. I'm only a few years behind you, and I definitely need a nap after that. Could stand a shower, too."

Oh man, that sounded good. Warm water, soap, a slippery Brooke. A shower sounded perfect. But way too intimate. But it was the perfect segue into him leaving. "Gotta take care of that," he said, pointing toward the condom.

"Oh, right." Brooke sat up, and as she did, the sheet slipped down. She folded her arms over her chest, and her face turned red as a cherry.

With a sigh, he reached for her crossed arms. "No point in it now, babe. I've seen, touched, and tasted it, and I gotta tell ya, I'm not sure I've ever seen better."

A bark of laughter left her. "That's some smooth-talking bullshit right there."

With a grunt, he stood, then pulled off the condom as he walked toward the bathroom. "I'm not one to give out unwarranted compliments. If I tell you your tits are perfect, they're fucking perfect." He tied off the condom and tossed it in her trash can before washing his hands. When he emerged from the bathroom, she was wearing an oversized T-shirt and a smile.

"Thank you," she said, and he had a feeling it was for more than the words.

Still naked, he snagged her wrist and pulled her against him. "I'm pretty sure I should be thanking you. You blew my fucking top off."

Her shy smile got him every time. How she could be so ballsy in life and timid in an intimate setting was a testament to her ex's shitty job as a husband. But he'd get her there...

Well, some man would.

He kissed her then hunted down his clothing. Brooke sat on the edge of her bed and made no attempt to hide how she watched every move he made. Something about her gaze on him filled him with warmth. Been a long time since he'd spent time with a woman in this way. Hell, before the arrest, he and his ol' lady didn't exactly have the type of relationship where they enjoyed quiet peace with each other. He'd been an MC president, and she wanted to be the queen. She'd been a hot, good fuck, understood the life, and promised loyalty. She'd been just what a hot-headed outlaw president wanted. Every man in the club envied him.

Too bad she'd been a lying, cheating bitch who'd betrayed him in the worst way, setting off a chain of events that permanently altered his life.

Now, with more than thirteen years of hindsight, he understood the relationship had been a train wreck waiting to happen. A hard lesson he'd never need to relearn.

Once fully dressed, he pulled her up to stand with him. "Gotta grab Harley before I take off."

For a split second, Brooke stiffened against him then seemed to shake it off.

Had she thought he'd stay? Did she want him to stay?

She nodded. "I'm sure Harley is snuggled up with her boyfriend."

Grinning, he pressed a final kiss to her lips to keep himself from saying something stupid, like how incredible he found her or asking when they could do this again. But when he pulled back, he said something even more foolish. "I'm getting all the guys together Sunday night to work on our plans for the dog fight. You wanna be there?"

Her eyes lit. "You'd want me to come?"

Oh, that was a dangerous question. He was finding he wanted her around a lot of the time when he shouldn't. "You deserve to be there."

Some of the light dimmed. "Well, then, yes, thanks. I'll be there."

With a nod, he kissed her forehead. "I'll text you the details." He couldn't resist brushing her hair back from her shoulder. "Come lock up after me."

Something close to discomfort flickered in her gaze when he said that, but it disappeared as fast as it came.

"Right behind you," she said.

As he collected his puppy, Brooke went to the front door and opened it for him. Arms full of squirming dog—he really needed to start using her leash—he stopped in front of Brooke.

No surprise, her attention went right to the pup. "Bye, Harley," she crooned. "You're such a sweet girl," she said as she rubbed the dog's head.

"She's not the only sweet one here."

Brooke blushed but kept her gaze on the dog.

"Thanks for today. Best day I've had in more than fourteen years."

"For me too," she whispered without looking at him.

He snagged her chin, kissed her quick, then left her staring after him as he tucked Harley across his lap so she could ride with him on the bike. They'd tried this a few times, and she'd loved it.

Though he didn't turn back, he felt the weight of Brooke's gaze on his back as he rode down her street. If all went according to plan, he'd be getting his hands on the land that abutted her property.

They'd be neighbors.

What else would they be?

Friends?

Fuck buddies?

It seemed all either could give.

It was certainly more than he'd had in the past decade and probably more than he deserved.

Even if a rogue part of him wasn't convinced it would be enough.

Chapter Twenty-Two

Sometime around noon on Sunday, while Curly was finishing up painting the exterior of his house, the rumble of motorcycle pipes alerted him to Scott's arrival. After wiping the sweat from his forehead with his shirt, Curly climbed off the ladder just as Scott pulled into the wide driveway.

"Damn, it's hot as fuck here, brother," Scott announced as he yanked his helmet off. His hair stuck to his forehead until he ran a hand through it. "Thought I'd melt off my bike before I got here."

With a large smile, Curly met him halfway between the driveway and the house. They embraced, slapping each other's backs. His excitement at having Scott there was genuine. He was a link between the Tennessee and Florida Hell's Handlers, and Curly needed that connection. Scott knew Rocket best, but also Copper and many of the other guys. Scott understood how the club worked and shared Curly's vision for this charter.

When his sister, Chloe, first hooked up with a biker, Scott had flipped his shit. She'd been horribly assaulted by a madman, which set her special forces brother off. Though Rocket had been the one to save her, Scott couldn't wrap his head around the idea of her tying herself to someone who often walked on the wrong side of the law. The past few years had changed Scott's opinion on the club, and leaving the military brotherhood left a void Curly hoped to fill.

"Damn, it's good to have you here, man. Come on in. House is cool. Beer is cold."

"Perfect. I'll grab my shit later," Scott said as he walked next to Curly into the house.

Five minutes later, they were back outside, this time with a few beers and a bag of pretzels between them.

"Were you telling me you stumbled on some trouble already?"

With a grunt, Curly settled back in one of the new chairs he'd purchased for the porch. His home wasn't nearly as impressive as Brooke's, but it suited for now, and he planned to move soon anyway. He'd build himself a house on whatever property they ended up acquiring as a clubhouse—hopefully Prick's farm.

"Yeah. Got a motherfucker running a dogfighting ring and dumping the bodies near the house of a friend of mine." Calling Brooke a friend left a strange and unpleasant taste in his mouth. "She's tried going to the cops, but you can guess how that went."

"All talk, no action."

"Pretty much."

"Why you so invested in this?"

It took a few minutes, but Curly caught Scott up on the details of what had happened around his arrest and the role Prick played.

Once he had all the details, Scott shook his head. "Fucking bastard," he said with a surprising amount of venom. He shoved out of his chair and whipped his empty beer bottle over the fence. It crashed into a tree, splintering into a million piercing shards. Then he stood staring after it with his hands on his hips.

Curly raised an eyebrow. Apparently, Scott had quite the quickfire temper. They were casual friends, soon-to-be brothers, but he and Scott hadn't exactly spent a lot of time together. Scott's immediate and furious outburst wasn't exactly expected.

"Sorry," he said as he turned back. "I'll clean it up. I just fucking hate assholes like that."

"You and me both, brother. Listen, I got the rest of the guys coming by around six tonight so we can put our skulls together and come up with a plan. Next dog fight is in six days, but we won't know where until the day of."

"Have any of you guys gone to one yet?"

Curly shook his head.

"Hmm." Still out in the middle of the yard, Scott stared off into space for a minute. Curly could practically hear the operational gears turning in Scott's military-trained brain. "Much as it sucks, your best bet is to get some guys in there for recon this time. It'd be stupid to try something without knowing what you're dealing with."

Much as Brooke would hate it, Curly had pretty much come to that same conclusion. Without police backup, they needed a creative way to take down Prick's operation that wouldn't land them all behind bars. Charging into an unknown situation, guns blazing, would do just that. "Yeah. I'm of the same mind." He rubbed his jaw. "Gonna suck walking in and out without doing a damn thing to help those the dogs, though. Some of them will end up injured or fucking killed that night."

"Well, pretty sure *you're* not gonna be walking in or out of anything."

Curly raised an eyebrow.

"This guy knows you. You can't be there." Scott reached into the bag and came out with a fistful of pretzels.

Fuck. He was right. Prick would spot him and have him tossed out on his ass in a heartbeat.

Curly stood. "Why don't I show you the spare room and let you get settled. We'll sort this shit out when the rest of the guys get here tonight."

"Sounds good. Let me grab my stuff."

After Scott retrieved his bags from his bike, Curly showed him to the spare room. They shot the shit for a few more minutes, then he left Scott alone to chill before the meeting. Ever since he'd brought him up to speed regarding Prick, Scott seemed agitated. He had trouble standing still, frequently rubbed at a tattoo on his right forearm, and cracked his neck every few minutes. Maybe he needed some downtime, or perhaps he was still getting on solid ground after such a significant change like leaving the military. Hopefully, he'd settle soon.

The guys began arriving around six, as expected. He'd texted Brooke earlier, and she'd be joining as well. He tried not to look too deeply at why he'd wanted to do a backflip when she confirmed she'd be there. It'd been a few days since he'd seen her, and fuck if she hadn't been on his mind at least once an hour since. Hell, part of him wanted to cancel with the rest of the guys and spend the night alone with Brooke.

A big part of him.

"Piping hot pizza!" Tracker announced as he strode into the house without knocking. Fuck, they needed a clubhouse. Curly had no problem lending his place, but was a knock too much to ask for? What if he and Brooke had been—

Nope. He needed to stop going there. She wasn't his woman, and who knew when and if she'd want a repeat of the other night?

Though he sure as fuck wanted it.

"You can take those out to the backyard, Tracker," he said of the five pizza boxes the man carried. "I got a table on the patio out there. Getting too crowded in here."

"Got it, boss."

He followed Tracker outside to where Ty and Scott were already getting to know each other. Laughing, Scott slapped Ty's shoulder as Ty told a story. Off to a good start.

"Tracker, this is Scott. His sister is a Hell's Handlers ol' lady up in Tennessee, and he just got out of the military. Scott, this is Tracker. He's a tattoo artist and does SAR."

Tracker set the pizzas down on the table then stuck his hand out to Scott. "Welcome to town, man. What branch?"

Curly

Scott stood and shook Tracker's hand. "Army. Green Beret."

With a low whistle, Tracker found his own seat. "Spec Ops, huh? Impressive. Mind if I call you Spec?"

Scott's eyebrows shot to his head, but Tyler nodded. "Shit, that's a good handle. What do ya think?"

With a grin and a nod, Scott said, "Spec, huh? I'm down with that."

"All right." Tracker rubbed his hands together. "Dig in. There's plenty. Lock's bringing the booze."

The rest of the crew arrived, and introductions were made. Harley ran around, soaking up all the attention she could from each of the men. When they thought Curly wasn't looking, they'd sneak bits of crust and pepperoni her way.

"Knock it off," he said as he whacked Tyler on the back of the head. "Brooke'll have my ass if you keep feeding my dog that shit."

Jinx snorted. "What was that about Brooke and your ass?"

Busting out in a laugh, Lock jumped in, "Sounds like she takes it out on his ass when he does something she doesn't like. Who knew Brooke was into that shit?"

The guys laughed until they all heard, "What am I into?"

Lock choked on his mouthful of pizza. His eyes bugged so wide they almost fell out of his head and onto the table. "Nothing," he mumbled as he tried to hide behind his beer bottle.

Slapping him on the back, Jinx gave her an innocent grin. "Putting the hurt on Curly for letting Harley have table scraps. You should see all the pizza he keeps sneaking her."

"What the fuck, man?" Curly threw his hands in the air as the rest of them laughed. "That's not true. It wasn't me." He gave Brooke a pleading look as she shook her head and rolled her eyes. Ugh, how was it possible a simple ribbed tank top and denim cutoffs could make a woman look so seductive?

Jinx winked at Brooke.

She stood in the open sliding glass doorway leading to his patio with a scrunched forehead. "Why do I feel like I'm the butt of some joke?"

Crickets. All of a sudden, this chatty bunch of bastards had nothing to say. But they all stared at him as though any of this was his fault. "Assholes," he said, pointing around the table. "All of you."

Scott, God love him, leaped to his feet. "I don't know about the rest of these fuckers," he said, flashing Brooke a charming smile. "But my momma taught me to stand when a beautiful woman walked in the room." He came around the table, hand extended. "I'm Scott, though apparently these guys are gonna be calling me Spec. Nice to meet you."

The rest of the guys grumbled and jumped up, each accusing the others of being rude and boorish.

Curly rolled his eyes. For Christ's sake.

Brooke burst out laughing as she took Scott's hand. "Brooke," she said. "Curly's been looking forward to having you here." She glanced at the rest of the guys now standing around the table in an awkward stare-off. "Can you idiots sit down?" she said with a roll of her eyes.

"Oh, thank God." Jinx plopped down in his chair. "Felt like we were greeting the queen or some shit."

With a snort, Brooke set a Tupperware container in the center of the table. "Had some time this afternoon so I made some peanut butter chocolate chip cookies. Dig in."

"Fuck yes!" Pulse ripped into the container as Brooke came around the table to the only empty seat, which of course, they'd left next to Curly.

As she approached, he nudged the chair out with his foot so she could sit easily.

Brooke ran her hand across the back of his shoulders as she passed behind him. That was all it took to have his dick filling with blood. One touch and a quick hit of the fresh citrusy scent he'd come to associate with her, and he was ready to kick the guys out and drag her to bed like a caveman.

"Hey," she said, slightly breathless as though she felt the same intense pull.

"Hey." He winked, trying to tamper his reaction. The guys would never let him live it down if they saw him slobbering over her worse than Harley with the pizza. "You didn't have to do that," he said, inclining his head toward the table where the guys were chowing down on the cookies as though they hadn't just eaten ninety pizzas. "You'll spoil them."

Damn, it got him right in the feels to know she thought of his guys and took steps to do something sweet for them.

She blushed as he'd come to expect while waving away his thanks. "It was no big deal. They're fun."

With a grunt, he said. "That's one word for 'em."

"Hey, Brooke, I'm grabbing another round of beers. Want one?" Tyler asked. He stood and snatched a cookie out of Tracker's hands before the man could take a bite.

"The fuck, man?"

Grinning, Brooke nodded. "I'd love one, thanks."

She looked good sitting there around the table with his men. Comfortable, as though she fit with them. Hell, she did fit with them. Her strong personality had the guys respect the first time they met her, and her quick wit made them love bantering with her. He had a feeling they all appreciated the way she gave them shit right back when they were ribbing her. No one had to tiptoe around or worry about offending her with their crass language or vulgar jokes.

Brooke could handle these guys with ease.

She'd make a damn good ol' lady.

For someone looking, of course. And that disturbing thought had him studying the faces of all his men. They better keep their dirty fucking hands to themselves when it came to Brooke. He had no plans to claim her or any woman, but fuck if he'd let one of these jokers at her.

"Hey," she whispered in his ear. "You okay?"

Curly blinked. Shit, he'd totally zoned out. "Yeah, I'm good. Just thinking."

Thankfully everyone else was still fighting over Brooke's cookies. They laughed and stuffed their faces. Damn, he had a good group here. They meshed well already. Copper would like this crew, and they'd like the Tennessee Handlers as well. Finally, shit was coming together as he'd hoped. All they needed to do was get rid of one prickly thorn in their side.

"So what'd I miss?" Brooke asked. She'd directed the question at him, but it quieted the rest of the group down.

Another thing he appreciated about these guys. They were chill as fuck but knew when to get serious and quit bullshitting.

Tyler returned, handing out beers. "We were about to discuss the plan for Saturday," he said.

Nodding, Brooke accepted a beer then focused her attention Curly's way.

"Hold up," Tracker cut in. A smug grin curled his lips. "Guess the fuck what I found out."

"What?" Curly said.

Tracker leaned back in his chair, still smirking. "Prick doesn't own the farmland." He dropped his pizza to his plate. "Tell me I'm amazing."

Curly's heart seized. "What?"

"You're shitting me," Ty added.

Shaking his head, Tracker said. "Damn honest truth. Met this chick last night. Banged her at—" He flicked a quick glance at Brooke, then winced. "Uh, I made love to her at my house."

Brooke rolled her eyes. "Seriously? You *made love* to a woman?"

"No, fine, you're right. I was trying to be respectful. I banged her good. Damn, she had an *ass*."

Curly cleared his throat.

"But I digress. Turns out she's a realtor and knew all about the property because her company had it on the market for fucking years. Owner's this old guy who lives in Georgia now. He finally agreed to rent it out to Prick about five months or so ago since no one wants the place."

Curly wanted it. And he just got about ten steps closer to owning it. Without the obstacle of Prick, he'd get his hands on the place so much easier. He was confident he could make the man an offer he'd never turn down. Who even cared if he paid too much for the property?

"Shit, man, that's damn good news. Thanks." Curly extended a fist to Tracker, who bumped it. The guys were already looking out for the club.

"No problem. Happy to fuck a wild chick in the name of the club any time you need." He winked at Brooke, who snorted.

"Okay," Jinx said. "Let's get back to Saturday."

Curly sighed. She wasn't going to like this shit one bit, but it was the most intelligent way to play it. "We've gotta use this fight to gather intelligence. We can't go in blind and expect to get anything done. Jinx met up with Prick at the bar again last night, and the guy won't give up info about where this fight will be."

She gripped the arm of her chair so hard; her knuckles were white. "There's gotta be a way—"

Placing a hand over hers, he shook his head. "We have no idea what his security is like, if any. For all we know, half the guys who attend will be armed. We know the cops are in his pocket. Maybe some of them are there. If we bust in thinking we're gonna shut shit down, one of us could end up with a bullet in our ass or behind bars."

Brooke paled.

Everyone remained quiet, letting her process. After a few moments, her shoulders slumped. "It makes me sick to think we might find another injured or dead dog on the side of the road Sunday morning, but I do understand. I'm not blinded by my need to rescue the dogs. I'd kill me if something happened to any one of you. I'm the one who put this on your plate."

Like the dogs she rescued, time seemed to have Brooke slowly relaxing and letting others into her orbit.

She turned her hand over and linked her fingers with his. Curly pretended not to notice the curious stares from his soon-to-be brothers. "We'll nail his ass to the wall, Brooke. I promise you. We just have to be smart about it."

After blowing out a breath, she said, "I'd love ten minutes in a room with him. Tie him up and give me ten minutes, and he'd never hurt another dog again." Her tone was low, deadly, and serious as a heart attack.

Fuck if it didn't make him even harder to hear her threaten Prick with violence.

From across the table, Tracker tried to suppress a laugh, which made him snort instead.

Jinx whistled. "Damn, woman, you're fierce. Do not let me get on your bad side."

That brought a small smile to her lips.

"Tell you what," Scott said from her left side. "You trust us to do this our way, and I'll get you your ten minutes with him."

The fuck?

Scott held his hand out to Brooke. She studied him for a moment before slipping her hand in his. "Deal."

There was no fucking way that'd be happening. What the hell was Scott thinking? Sure, Brooke was a kick-ass woman, but she did not need shit like that fucking with her head. And it would because that's what it did. He'd lived surrounded by men accustomed to violence for his entire life. Brooke wasn't like that. She talked a damn good game, but she was a rescuer, a healer, a nurturer.

Not a torturer.

But they could deal with that later. "So here's the plan." Neither he nor Brooke had let go, so they sat at the table still holding hands. "Jinx and Pulse are obviously going since they set this all up. They can take Scott and Lock with them. Their objective is to learn as much as possible about the setup and security and to find any weaknesses we can exploit. Don't worry so much about the specifics of the building because the next one might be somewhere different, but try to find patterns in how they guard the place." He looked at the three who'd be in the thick of it. "We have one night to come up with a definitive way to end these dog fights."

He wanted Prick's property as well, but that was a secondary problem.

"The rest of us will be close by as back up just in case something goes—"

"I'm going too," Brooke announced.

"Uhh…" Scott's attention shifted to Curly, as did everyone's.

He was hit with instant and consuming nausea at the idea of Brooke being anywhere near the dog fights. She'd lose her mind and probably try to release each of the dogs right then and there. Not to mention Prick would take one look at her and know why she was there.

"There's no way in fucking hell I'm letting you anywhere near those fights," he said as he tightened his grip on her hand. Did she have any idea what Prick would do to her if he saw her there? He'd nearly attacked her in a crowded bar. Get her on his turf, and there was no saying what would happen to her.

Brooke's mouth dropped. "Excuse me?" she asked with an incredulous laugh.

"You heard me."

"It's on now," Jinx whispered.

"Uhh," The rest of the guys stood and began shuffling toward the house. "We're just gonna go over uh, yeah…" Tracker nodded once then chased the others into the house. After letting out a yip of excitement, Harley bounded after them, stranding Curly alone with a furious Brooke in the backyard.

So much for brotherhood. Bunch of traitors.

"You're out of your mind if you think you have any right to tell me what to do. I don't take orders, Curly, and if you think fucking me once gives you any right to tell me what to do, then you're delusional." She yanked her hand from his, then stood and stalked across the yard.

Something deep inside him surged with pride at the way she wasn't afraid to stand up for herself. The way she didn't think twice about telling an outlaw MC president and man who'd spent more than a decade surrounded by murders behind bars to go fuck himself. The other part trembled in fear because that take no prisoners attitude would get her in a world of trouble in the wrong situation. Only one of the reasons she wasn't setting foot within a mile of Prick.

He needed to see the guys out, so he left her for a minute to collect herself. She stood in his yard, hands on her hips, back rigid as she stared into the late evening twilight. Was she comparing him to her douchebag ex who'd controlled her every moment? With any luck, she'd realize he acted out of fear for her safety, not some sick need to have her bend to his will.

Hopefully, they could speak about it after the rest of the club left.

Because one thing was for sure, Brooke wasn't setting foot near that dog fight.

Chapter Twenty-Three

So, she might have overreacted.

Okay, fine, she'd completely lost her shit.

But who could blame her? With both feet, Curly had stomped right on her hot button issue. Then he'd ground his heel down for good measure.

With a sigh, she stared up at the darkening sky. Stars were just beginning to pop out everywhere she looked.

Damnit. She'd acted like a child, hadn't she? Thrown a fit and stormed off in a huff. Apologizing wasn't easy for her. She'd spent so much of her marriage apologizing for who and what she was, along with trying to change both those things, that now her knee-jerk reaction was to balk at the idea of apologizing for her actions.

But as her therapist had reminded her on more than one occasion, she wasn't, in fact, perfect, and accepting her own imperfections was critical on her path to true joy. She nearly snorted out loud.

No shit, she wasn't perfect.

But what her therapist had meant was that she needed a reset on her insight. She would screw up on occasion, as everyone did. She would hurt someone else with her words or actions. She would lose her temper, be in a cranky mood, or even be a bitch.

That was a natural part of humanity, and those who got burned in her fire deserved an apology. It wasn't the same as being criticized for being who she was. It wasn't the same as being told she was inadequate.

This was one of the many reasons she had a small social circle and avoided relationships like the plague. Not that she and Curly were in a relationship, but they were…something more than fuck buddies. Even she could admit that terrifying fact. Evan had messed with her head, and who knew if it'd ever be screwed on exactly right again?

"Prick knows your face."

Curly's voice came from only a few feet behind her, calm and steady. Harley scampered around her feet then shot off to investigate a rustling in the bushes.

"I know," she said as she turned. He wasn't far, standing with his hands in his back pockets and a patient expression.

"He wouldn't hesitate to hurt you. It's the same reason I'm not going in. I'm too recognizable. I need the guys in there focused on recon, not worrying about you or me getting noticed and needing backup."

Meeting his gaze was difficult as shame for how she'd yelled at him washed over her. "I know."

"But I'm sorry for the way I just demanded you not go. I know it's a trigger for you."

"Stop," she whispered. Why the hell did she feel like she was about to burst into tears? He was such a good man. Caring and patient with her even when she didn't deserve it. So different from her husband. So tempting to want to pull him close and never let go. "I'm the one who should apologize. I didn't even give you a chance to explain before I lost my shit. I'm embarrassed. Please don't say you're sorry."

He held out his arms, and she walked into them, burying her face against his muscular, warm chest. As soon as his arms closed around her, she sighed and melted into a man's comfort in a way she'd promised herself she never would.

"Babe, I'm a grown-ass man. Not some spoiled, piece-of-shit mama's boy who can't admit when I fuck shit up. I know your triggers. Next time I'll go straight to the explanation and skip the barked orders."

Her husband had never apologized. The man didn't know how. He'd never thought he'd done anything he had to apologize for.

Pompous jackass.

"Well, I didn't help anything by flipping out. The guys must think I'm crazy."

He snorted. "Are you kidding? Pretty sure any one of them would get on a knee and propose to you tomorrow if you wanted it."

Brooke laughed. "Now that's a scary thought."

"But it made you laugh," he whispered. "See, I know you."

He did know her. He knew exactly what to say to talk her off the ledge. It unnerved her because, first, he wasn't supposed to be anything more than someone helping with a problem. And second, he also wasn't supposed to be anything more than some physical stress relief. Now he was holding her and guaranteeing things for *next time.*

"I promise we'll stop him, Brooke. And I promise we won't leave you in the dark. But I need you to trust me. Depending on how ugly this gets, at some point, I may have to shout an order at you. If I can avoid it, I will. I'll always try to approach you with an explanation first, but I need you to know that I'll only tell you what to do if I have no choice."

His big hands moved from her back to her head. He drew her back, framing her face and forcing her gaze on his.

"It's not because I don't think you're smart, or capable, or amazing. You're all those things and so much more, Brooke. Remember that and do not apologize for it. I'm asking you to stay away from the dog fight because I can't stand the thought of something happening to you. Put your trust in my guys and me. Can you do that?"

Her heart skipped a beat as she stared at the sincerity in his eyes. If she were a smarter woman, she'd tell him yes, kiss his cheek, and head back to her house. But standing there under the twinkling lights of the stars, she was anything but intelligent. Telling him she trusted him seemed insufficient. Showing him became imperative. She let her emotions and her body overrule her brain and slowly sank to her knees in front of him.

"Brooke," he rumbled. "You don't need to—shit."

She popped the button on his jeans then slid the zipper down.

"This isn't what I—oh fuck."

Brooke snickered. She'd tugged his jeans and boxer briefs down at the same time. She'd given plenty of blowjobs to her husband. It was something he'd loved and frequently demanded though he always had a critical comment or ten about her performance. After a while, it had become a chore she never looked forward to, but right then and there, face to face with Curly's erection, her mouth watered.

It salivated at the thought of tasting him and feeling all that hardness against her tongue. Maybe it was the way his eyes burned with lust or the fact he hadn't expected it, but she couldn't wait to drive him out of his mind.

Right there in the middle of his darkening backyard, she closed her hand around his cock and gave a firm stroke.

Curly hissed as he clenched his fists at his side.

Holding him near her lips, she licked a slow circle around the head.

"Fuck," he ground own, staring down at her. "You want it, don't you?"

Brooke nodded, letting his dick brush her lips.

"You want my cock in that pretty mouth?" His hand came to her face, where he cupped her jaw.

Another nod. She did want it. So much that her nipples ached, and her panties felt soaked through with arousal while she knelt fully clothed and untouched. This was so different than the last time they'd had sex. She'd been on top, in charge, and so powerful. Now she was on her knees before the man, something she'd have expected to trigger an adverse reaction, but the opposite was true. She still held all the power. As the one in charge of his pleasure, she'd command his every sigh, every grunt, every groan.

And it sent a thrill through her as she'd never experienced.

He tapped the hand around his cock, and she released him, allowing him to grab himself. "Open up, baby. Let me see how gorgeous you with your lips stretched around my cock."

So slowly he might call her a tease, she let her lower jaw relax. Part of her wanted to keep her eyes on the stiff dick hovering in front of her mouth, but she couldn't tear her gaze away from the blaze burning in his blue eyes.

"Suck me, Brooke." His voice dipped even lower and gruffer than usual. Curly sounded like a man close to the edge. "Show me how much you love that cock."

Never would she have imagined such filthy words turning her on. But they did. So much that she had to squeeze her legs together or go insane with need. At the same time, she closed her lips around the head of his cock and sucked.

Curly jolted as a string of curses left his lips. He grabbed her head but didn't force himself down her throat. A deeply buried part of her wanted him to, but it'd been so long since she'd given head, she'd probably embarrass herself if she tried to deep throat him right away.

However, this was about trust and demonstrating to him that she trusted him not only when it came to dealing with Prick but with her body. She'd resigned herself to never trusting a man with her heart again, but Curly had proven he wouldn't harm her body, so she met his gaze and gave a single nod at the same time she rubbed her tongue under the tip of his cock.

"Shit, you're perfect," he whispered in a strangled voice. Then he tapped the side of her jaw.

She widened her mouth, and he slid his cock deeper. With a gentleness she wouldn't have expected of a man who'd lived a life of violence and power, he glided his cock in and out of her mouth. Within a few seconds, she found her rhythm alternating strong suction with teasing licks and flicks of her tongue.

The smooth skin of his erection felt incredible, slipping back and forth across her tongue. She couldn't believe how hard he was and how he filled her entire mouth. Her lips stretched to accommodate his girth. Each time a salty drop of precum met her tastebuds, every time he cursed and groaned, her desire and pride flared. And when he tightened his grip on her hair and muttered, "fucking heaven," she almost popped off and begged him to fuck her.

She'd done this. She was the one bringing this strong, dangerous, yet incredible man so much pleasure he was mumbling about heaven. He wanted her, and she fucking loved it.

Rising higher on her knees, she gripped the backs of his thighs and forced his cock deeper into her mouth. After a few small gags, she was able to relax her throat enough to take him to the back.

"Shit, Brooke," he shouted. Beneath her hands, his leg muscles began to tremble. "Fuck, babe, I can't hold back."

"Do it," she said, around his cock right before he bumped the back of her throat. She curled fingers into his flesh and swallowed.

"Goddammit," he roared as he flooded her mouth with come. His abdominal muscles flexed hard, rounding his upper body. He held her hair so tight, her scalp ached, and his hips jerked forward in quick little punches. The man had lost control of his body, consumed by what she hoped was a phenomenal orgasm.

As he began to calm, she let his softening cock slip from her lips, but she couldn't resist one final lick to the crown. He hissed and jolted, which made her smile.

Shyness began to set in, which was ridiculous because he'd made no attempt to hide how much he'd loved what she'd been doing to him.

She moved one aching knee, ready to rise to her feet when he suddenly dropped down and kissed the ever-loving hell out of her.

There was no chance to catch her breath. No time to wonder if he felt squeamish about kissing her while his taste still lingered on her tongue. The world tilted, and the next thing she knew, she was flat on her back in the grass with two hundred pounds of ravenous biker on top of her.

He devoured her mouth with bruising kisses and an aggressive tongue. She shivered, loving the way his weight pressed her into the ground. She was helpless to do anything but receive his hungry kisses and squirm beneath his roving hands.

"I want to hear you scream," he said against her mouth.

Then he was gone.

"Wha..." With her head spinning to catch up with the runaway train of the moment, his words barely registered.

The next thing she knew, he was tearing at her shorts like a man possessed. They were open and down around her ankles before she knew it. Once he'd yanked them off and tossed them somewhere in the yard, he came back for her panties. They were given the same rough treatment but didn't hold up as well as the denim. A tearing sound had her glancing down her body to find him throwing the tattered material over his shoulder.

The glint in his eye sent a shiver of dark desire racing down her spine. Never had a man looked at her as though he wanted to destroy her, consume her, and own her all at once.

Her breath caught as he bent each of her knees up one at a time then placed his callused hands on her inner thighs. They trembled beneath his fingertips. With a grin, he must have stolen from the devil, he stared her straight in the eye as he pushed her legs wide with a rough shove.

"Shit." She covered her eyes with her forearm as heat flooded her face. She could count on one hand that was missing a few fingers the number of times her ex had gone down on her. God, he'd had a million excuses for why he'd found it so repulsive, each one more insulting than the next.

Curly seemed to want this for himself as much as for her.

She was beyond exposed, lying in the grass with her wet sex completely on display. But she only had a half-second to worry about it because Curly was a man possessed. He dove straight for her clit, teasing it with his tongue.

Fireworks shot through her limbs. She cried out and arched her back, which only drove her pelvis against his face. As though her flavor drove him insane, he grabbed her ass, held her down, and buried his tongue in her pussy.

Again, she shouted loud into the quiet night. Her vision blurred as the pleasure became so intense it was almost unbearable. "Travis," she said on a moan as she wriggled against him. She wasn't sure if she was trying to get closer or pull away. All she knew was that her mind was overwhelmed to the point of being unable to think.

He licked and sucked and fucked her with his tongue, occasionally letting out a little growl that vibrated through her system. Brooke writhed in the grass, moving with him to enhance the sublime feelings coursing through her body.

"Fuck, you taste so fucking sweet," he said against her.

His hands held her ass so tight she'd have marks for sure. The idea of seeing his finger marks on her bottom sent a filthy thrill through her. This was the most depraved act she'd participated in. Any of his neighbors could hear her, peek over the fence and see her, or call the police. She had to be violating the noise ordinance with all her moaning and yelling.

Curly sucked her clit between his lips, and her stomach coiled into a tight knot. She couldn't believe it. It'd been mere minutes, and she was already going to—

"Oh, my God," she screamed as stars floated in front of her eyes. She clawed at his head, grabbing handfuls of his thick hair as she held his face against her and rode out the most epic orgasm she'd ever had. It seemed to go on for hours, the tingling, the tremoring, the flood of chemicals making her float among the clouds. Eventually, her muscles relaxed, and she sagged into the stiff grass. "Holy shit," she managed to croak even though she needed a gallon of water to quench her thirst.

Curly cleared his throat. "Babe?"

"Yeah?" she asked, breathless. Above her, the sky twinkled with millions of stars, witnesses to one of the best moments of her life.

"You gonna let me go?"

"Huh?"

She glanced down at the same time her brain retook control of her body. She still had her hands tangled in the long strands of his hair, and she still held his face against her sex. "Oh, God, I'm sorry," she said as she released him. The poor man probably had two bald spots now.

He raised his head and gave her a satisfied, slightly smug smile. As much as she wanted to praise him for taking her to the moon and back, all she could see was the wild rat's nest of hair she'd created while he ate her out. She snorted, trying to hold back a laugh.

One of his eyebrows rose, and Brooke lost it. She flopped back on the grass, laughing so hard, her stomach ached.

"Not sure you're supposed to laugh after I give you my best moves," he said with a fierce frown she wasn't buying for a second.

"I—I'm sorry," she said between laughs.

"Are you?"

That had her dissolving into giggles all over again. "No! Y—your hair!"

He rolled his eyes at her as he sat up. Once steady, he tied his hair back with the band on his wrist. "Stay the night?" he asked, extending a hand to her.

Her heart lodged in her throat. Stay the night? That sounded like a colossal mistake, but the idea of waking up to him was almost too tempting to resist. Still… "I have the dogs."

"Oh, right. You fried my brain, and it's not one hundred percent recovered yet." He winked. "I could stay at your place."

No.

Nope.

Not gonna happen.

Danger!

"Yeah. I'd like that."

And she'd done it. What a fool. This was step one down the relationship highway and the path to compromising her identity.

Curly helped her to her feet. Then he knelt and grabbed her denim shorts. "Madam," he said, holding the shorts at her feet. It was an odd Cinderella moment that had her face heating. No one did things for her. Sure, Nancy and her husband helped her out if she needed assistance with something major, but day-to-day, it was all her. After leaving her husband, she'd set it up that way, and that's how she liked it.

Having Curly do something as simple yet sweet as helping her into her shorts after sex messed with her head. She needed to take back control before she slipped up and handed a piece of herself over to him. He couldn't be allowed to have power over her. To have the ability to hurt her.

But as he held out her flip-flop like her very own Prince Charming, she slid her foot in the sandal and chuckled along with him.

Once she was all set, he held out a hand to her. "Let me grab Harley and a change of clothes, then I'll follow you home."

She almost told him she'd head out while he gathered what he needed then meet him at her house, but as she kept doing in his presence, she broke her own rule and followed his lead. "Sounds good," she said.

He smiled as he squeezed her hand, then pulled her in for a quick kiss.

Fifteen minutes later, when she glanced in her rear-view mirror, she found herself smiling at the sight of his truck behind her.

Curly

There was something nice about not having to travel across town in the dark alone. Nice to have someone at her back.

Nice, yet terrifying.

Chapter Twenty-Four

What a fucking joke.

Curly could have run this operation better blindfolded and gagged. For fuck's sake, he'd waltzed right into the packed barn on Prick's property as though he belonged there. Security consisted of one monster-sized brute at the door acting as a gatekeeper who was too busy drooling over a big-titted woman with candy apple lipstick and skunk stripes in her hair to do more than extend his meaty hand for the cover charge. After all his bluster about Brooke staying far away, she could have joined him, and no one would have noticed her either. However, Curly was more than happy to have her tucked away at home.

He'd spent every night in her bed for nearly a week and couldn't think of any place he'd enjoyed more. Ever. He'd be lying if he said he would rather be at the dog fight than stashed away with Brooke, but some things they couldn't avoid.

Just because Prick's meager security allowed him into the dog fight without a single issue didn't mean his luck would hold out. Aside from his guys milling around, at least fifty other people, primarily men, filled the barn. The place was as shitty as it'd appeared the day he'd found Brooke sneaking around. Faded planks and rotted roofs made it seem as though one hefty breeze take out the entire structure. The run-down state of the interior matched the exterior.

Six stalls, which must have been used for horses at one point in time, now served as makeshift kennels for snarling fight dogs who were about to be used as money-making props for their sick owners. The urge to casually stroll past each stall and release the dogs clawed at Curly's stomach, but he'd never make it past the first without getting busted, so he remained where he was in a dark corner of the barn where no one paid him any attention.

As he scanned the crowd, trying to get a feel for the players and who owned the dogs, Curly's gaze met Scott's. His enforcer cocked his head and arched an eyebrow before shaking his head and heading Curly's way.

So much for flying under the radar. He'd secured his hair in a knot at the base of his scalp before putting on a black hoodie. The damn curls made him identifiable to almost everyone who saw him. While the disguise worked with the distracted beast at the door, he should have known Scott wouldn't fool so easily. His new enforcer had some well-developed observation skills.

"Thought you agreed to wait outside in the truck," Scott said with a wry grin as he settled his back against the wall next to Curly.

"Why do I feel like you were specifically looking for me?"

"Because I knew you couldn't stay away." Scott shrugged. Though he came off as chill with a relaxed posture, his sharp eyes told a different story. Scott, the special operations soldier, was one hundred percent attuned to everything happening around them.

If Curly had to place bets, he'd wager Scott already tagged every dog owner, the highest bidders, and how much Prick stood to earn tonight.

"I'd do the same. Not much for sitting on the sidelines. You see that?" Scott asked as he discreetly pointed toward a lean man chatting with Prick.

Curly followed his friend's gaze, and sure enough, Officer fucking Gains, the same damn motherfucker who'd pulled Curly over the other day, laughed with Prick as he stuffed a full envelope into his back pocket.

A payoff for sure.

That explained the shitty security. Fuck, the complete lack of security. Why bother if they had the cops on their payroll? "Fuck," he whispered. "I knew that asshole had an in with the cops, but I didn't think they were fucking besties." And he'd known Gains was dirty as three-day-old underwear.

"Mm-hmm," Scott agreed while still riveted to the room. "Makes our job harder." Then he flashed Curly a grin that would have had him writing out a will if they weren't on the same team. "Lucky for me, I love a challenge. You sure you just don't want me to kill him and be done with it? Be easy enough to make it look like an accident."

Curly snorted out a half-laugh but one glance at Scott's face, and he realized the man wasn't joking. He'd do it. Kill Prick in cold blood without an ounce of remorse. Hell, the gleam in his eye said he'd probably enjoy it. "I'm not afraid to do what has to be done as self-defense, or if there is no fucking way out," Curly said, making his voice like ice. "But I ain't sanctioning you killing a man in cold blood cuz we got beef with him." He'd killed before and had a feeling he would again, but he sure as fuck wouldn't be stupid about it, and killing Prick would be stupid. Too many people, Officer Gaines included, would turn their investigative gazes toward him the second they found Prick pulseless.

Scott shrugged. "Works for me. Guess we're going with plan B." He lifted a paper bag and jiggled it in front of Curly's face.

"The fuck is that?" They spoke in low tones to keep the attention off themselves though everyone there seemed more interested in drinking, placing bets, and checking out the dogs than noticing random two men chatting in the corner.

Curly

"I had a brilliant fucking idea. Came to me right as I was making some grub this afternoon." He shook the bag again, eyes sparkling.

"Think you've drawn it out long enough? What the fuck's in the bag?"

"Hot dogs."

Curly frowned. "Hot dogs?"

With a nod, Scott's gaze tracked Prick as he crossed the humid as fuck barn to green a man with a hand slap and a laugh. "Hotdogs and Xanax."

"Come again?"

"Man, I'd love to, but, no offense, you're not really my type. Dick just doesn't do it for me."

"Jesus, cut the shit. What the fuck are you doing with hotdogs and Xanax?"

"Saving the dogs, brother. Your woman was stressed as fuck about not being able to rescue all the dogs tonight, right?"

"Right..." Stressed out didn't begin to cover it. Last night, after they'd sated themselves with food, wine, and core-shaking orgasms, Curly had passed out only to be woken by the sound of Brooke's tears sometime late in the night. She's apologized a hundred times only to unravel when he finally got her to admit what had her so upset.

She'd been lying awake consumed with worry not only for Curly and his men but for the dogs they wouldn't be able to save that evening. More than likely, one more would die, and, for sure, some would be injured. Possibly severely.

Knowing what would happen to the dogs tonight so close to her home and not being able to do a damn thing to prevent it was killing her. One thing he'd learned about Brooke over the past few weeks, besides her love of Thai food and early morning sex, was her absolute hatred of being helpless. Brooke was the type of woman who'd try to move a mountain then berate herself for not being strong enough if the peak wouldn't budge.

If Scott had a plot that would spare her anguish over the fate of these dogs, Curly was more than happy to entertain it.

"That got me thinking," Scott said.

The music grew even louder, which he'd have considered impossible five seconds ago.

"I'm gonna stroll around and casually drop them in the kennels, then get the fuck outta here. In twenty minutes, those pups will either be snoozing like babies or stumbling around like drunk frat boys. Either way, they'll be useless in a fight. A hamster would be a fiercer competitor by the time I finish with them." A sinister smile transformed his face into a scary mask of deviance. "What do you think?"

Fuck, Scott was a damn genius. Not only would this prevent any of the dogs from being fatally harmed, but it'd fuck with Prick's business and wallet. There'd be no fight tonight. Curly wasn't naïve enough to believe it'd be adequate to end the dog fights for good, but it'd undoubtedly derail this one. Damn, that was an exciting thought. Then his guys could use the info they gathered tonight to devise a plan to shut this shit down permanently.

"You sure you can be stealthy enough?"

"You kidding, brother? If I can sneak in a Taliban village, slide my knife deep into the gut of their leader, then slide back out without a goddammed soul knowing, I can feed some dogs on the sly." The former Green Beret seared him with a look that had him lifting his hands in apology.

"Sorry, stupid question, brother. Do it. But then I want you out of here. After the initial panic, Prick will probably realize someone sabotaged him. He might ramp up security for next time."

Nodding, Scott said, "Won't be a problem. I have some ideas for that, too."

"All right." He gripped Scott's shoulder. "Be careful as fuck."

"Will do. This shit's easy." With a wink, Scott smiled as though the thought of jumping into danger excited the hell outta him. Maybe it did. Years of living in constant peril didn't appeal to everyone, but it certainly drew Scott. Was he just an adrenalin junkie? Or was there more to his apparent enjoyment of violence?

Adjusting his hoodie, he shoved that question aside for another day. "Meet you at Brooke's later?" She'd insisted they come straight to her house and let her knew every detail they'd learned. He was more than happy to oblige if it kept her away from this shitshow. Besides, he'd be going to her house anyway, seeing as how he'd spent the last six nights in her bed.

Stupid, he admitted that, but he couldn't tear himself away from her. She was sexy, fun, kind, funny, compassionate, and the list went on. She was just a fucking unicorn among women, and she'd ensnared him in her magic trap.

"Yep. Midnight. I'll be there." Scott gave him a final nod, then faded into the rowdy crowd.

If he were smart, Curly would take his own advice and get the hell outta there, but the idea of exiting before he learned Scott had been successful didn't sit well. He'd hang around until Scott finished dosing all the dogs, then head over to Brooke's.

Within seconds, he'd lost sight of Scott in the mob. The guy was as stealthy as a goddammed ninja. As he scoured the faces of the men and women treating this sick event some kind of fucked-up house party, Curly came across Pulse and Jinx chatting with Prick.

Something Jinx said had Prick laughing and slapping him on the back. He had to hand it to Jinx. The guy had a personality that would draw his worst enemy to him. Had to make him lethal with the ladies. Pulse had mentioned something about Jinx drowning in pussy every time they went out.

Now it made sense. The younger man could charm the habit off a nun.

While he'd never been one people flocked to for his charismatic or easygoing nature, Curly hadn't had a problem picking up women when he'd been Jinx's age. Being president of an outlaw MC drew them from all around. Women looking for nothing more than the chance to wrap their lips around the dick of a powerful man. No commitment, no promises, not even the exchange of names most of the time. Back in the day, he'd loved that shit.

But by the time he hit thirty, he'd grown tired of the game. The responsibilities of running the True Outlaws MC had worn on him, and the stability of having an ol' lady became more appealing. Joke was on him when she turned out to be a special brand of bitch.

Once he officially had the MC up and running, women would come crawling out of the woodwork once again. That was just how it went. Get together a group of single bikers who loved to party, and the women would be knocking each other over to get in the clubhouse doors. If he pleased, he could snap his fingers and have as many as he wanted ready to drop their knees or bend over and hike up their mini skirts for him. He could go back to living large and being a king.

The first few years he'd been in prison, he'd dreamed of it. Being back at the head of the table with hordes of women ready to fuck him or suck him on command. Now, the idea held no appeal. Whether age, experience, or circumstance, he'd long since lost interest in letting social climbers get their greedy hands on him.

All he wanted was to crawl into bed with Brooke at the end of the night and wake to her each morning. Hers was the only body he craved, the only smile he cared about, the only woman he wanted touching him. At first, he'd assumed it was just one of those things that happened with age, but fuck, he'd known plenty of old-timers in the Outlaws who'd had a different twenty-something bouncing on their dick nightly.

Since his dick only got hard for Brooke these days, he was either staring down the barrel at a prescription for Viagra, or she meant a whole lot more to him than he was ready to admit.

Or think about.

Curly

And that had disaster written all over it.

As the song changed from something recent to nineties alternative rock, Curly caught sight of Scott out the corner of his eye. The soon-to-be enforcer stood next to one of the former horse stalls, laughing with a man who owned the dog in the stall. The guy was a few teeth short of a complete set and walked with a pronounced limp. He didn't look like he weighed enough to handle a chihuahua on a leash, let alone eighty pounds of ferocious brawl-hungry pitbull.

As they talked, presumably about the dog's fighting record and training, Scott slyly worked his arm up until he'd propped it on top of the horse stall.

Curly zeroed in on Scott's hand. Palm opened and turned down, he gave off a relaxed and chill vibe. But it was all an act designed to throw the dog owner off his scent. Scott wiggled his fingers as though fidgeting. Then he pulled his arm back and folded it across his chest, and Curly just knew.

He'd dropped a piece of hot dog laced with Xanax into the dog's pen right in front of its oblivious owner. Those were some enviable double-o-seven stealth skills.

Shit, if MC life didn't do it for Scott, the devious bastard had a career as a sleight of hand magician.

Five minutes later, Scott strutted his cunning ass right out the entrance, whistling along with Nirvana as though he didn't have a care in the world. The only acknowledgment of a successful exercise was a chin lift in Curly's direction. But it was enough. Scott wasn't one to be underestimated. If the man said he'd dose all those dogs, he'd get it done.

And he had.

A glance across the room found Jinx and Pulse grabbing a beer from the impromptu bar. With heads tilted close as they spoke, they seemed deep in an intense conversation for their ears only.

After checking on those two members of his new MC, Curly slipped out the same way Scott had gone. Since he didn't have the training and skill Scott did to make himself invisible, he pretended to take a phone call as he walked by the bouncer. Once again, the lazy man barely paid him or any of the other people coming and going a lick of attention.

Part of him wanted to stick around until the dogs began to conk out, but a bigger, more dominating part needed to see Brooke. Hopefully, she and Nancy wouldn't mind him crashing their girls' night early. Even if they wanted their time together, he was more than happy to hang outside while they watched a movie or guzzled wine. All he wanted, all he needed was to be in Brooke's presence.

Ladies and gentlemen, I believe we call that whipped.

Chapter Twenty-Five

"So, he stayed the night, then?" Nancy asked as she pushed her oversized sunglasses up her nose. They wouldn't be necessary much longer as the sun had begun its journey below the horizon.

"Mm-hmm." He'd stayed Sunday night. And Monday. Tuesday too. Oh, and uh, all the other nights. One week was all it had taken for his absence to be noticed and his presence to be missed.

Greatly.

"Mm-hmm," Nancy said in a mocking tone. "What's that mean? Why are you acting weird?" She swung her legs off the side of the lounge chair, pulled her sunglasses off, and narrowed her eyes. "What aren't you telling me?"

"Nothing." Brooke kept her gaze on the pool. Ray lounged in the dwindling sun out in her yard while the rest of the dogs scampered around, playing.

"No. There's something going on." Nancy tapped the end of her sunglasses against her pursed lips. "Is he bad in bed or something?"

Brooke snorted. "Uh, no." As if.

"Ohhh, really?" Nancy waggled her eyebrows. "I feel as though I'm going to need more deets on that part, but first... what is it? Does he poop with the door open or something?"

Brooke barked out a laugh. "Ew, no, he does not. There's nothing bad."

"So what is it that has you avoiding eye contact with me and lying there all tense when you should be relaxed and sucking back your margarita?"

She sighed. "You're like a dog with a bone sometimes. You know that?"

With a smirk, Nancy said. "I prefer to call it tenacious. Now spill."

"Fine," Brooke grumbled. Then she passed a hand over her mouth as she said, "He's stayed every night sinceSunday."

"I'm sorry, what was that?" Nancy inclined her head. "Couldn't hear you. Your hand was like, blocking your mouth. Almost as though you didn't want me to hear something." Her lips quirked. Smug bitch was enjoying the hell outta this.

Brooke rolled her eyes. "God, you're annoying. He's stayed here every night since Sunday. There. Are you happy?" Admitting it out loud had her stomach twisting with the stupidity of her actions.

Nancy clapped her hands as she bounced on the chair. "Happy? Yes, Brookie, I'm ecstatic! Brookie has a boyfriend!" she sang in the most obnoxious way possible. "A hot as fuck, bad boy, growly boyfriend." Now her eyebrows were waggling.

Glaring at her friend, Brooke shook her head. "No. I do not. There is no *boyfriend*," she said, mimicking Nancy's tone. "I'm forty-one, not fifteen. There's just excellent sex that's been a *long* time coming. I'm finally enjoying a hot sex life, that's all." A hot sex life and night spent falling asleep in Curly's arms. Breakfasts together. Sunsets by her pool. Sharing of life stories.

Ugh, she was screwed.

She picked up her margarita. After a long sip where she avoided looking at her friend, she finally glanced in Nancy's direction. "Seriously. Sex. That's it."

"You, honey, are full of shit," Nancy said with complete conviction. "You've mentioned him about two thousand six

Curly

hundred and seventy-three times, and each time you say his name, these little hearts float above your head. It's quite sickening." She pressed her lips together in a failed attempt to keep her smirk under control.

Brooke pulled the lime wedge off the rim of her margarita glass and threw it at her friend. "You need therapy."

Laughing, Nancy managed to dodge the flying fruit. "That's a separate issue, which has nothing to do with your heart emoji face. Let's stick with one topic at a time."

With a roll of her eyes, Brooke said, "Okay, fine. Bottom line, I like him a lot. He's intelligent, funny, a little rough around the edges, and, well, you have eyes. He's hot as Hades. The sex is off the charts, and I enjoy his company."

Understatement of the century. She found herself wanting to be in his presence all the time, which was why she forced herself to set limits on their time spent together. Soft limits, clearly, as he'd spent every damn night in her bed.

"I fail to see the problem here," Nancy said with a frown. "Sound like perfect *boyfriend* material to me."

"The problem is that I'm not interested in having a boyfriend." The word tasted bitter on her tongue. "Now or ever. I've played that game before, given up my independence, made myself vulnerable, and I came out of it as a weak, pathetic woman I didn't even recognize anymore." She shuddered. "Never again."

With a glare a parent might give a petulant child, Nancy rose. "This conversation is not finished, but we need more margaritas, and I need to put something on this mosquito bite on my ankle before I start scratching my skin off."

Ahh, saved by the blood-sucking insect. She'd take it. "There's a stick of bug stuff in my kitchen junk drawer. The one next to the dishwasher."

"Thanks, sweetie." Nancy blew her a kiss as she sauntered off toward the house, completely comfortable strolling around in her bright blue bikini. Not that she shouldn't be. Her athletic body was the envy of women everywhere. With her tanned skin and bleach-blond hair, she was the picture of a Florida native. "Be back in a jiff. Don't run away. I'll track you down." She pointed to Brooke with a perfectly manicured pale pink nail.

The second she disappeared into the house, Brooke blew out a breath. A moment of reprieve. She'd invited Nancy over to keep her distracted while Curly's men were at the dog fight. All day, she'd been dreading these hours where the guys would potentially be in danger. She liked them, the men who would make up the motorcycle club. Though brash and a little unruly, they already seemed loyal to Curly and a close-knit group. With any luck and some time, those bonds would strengthen, turning them into a true brotherhood. A family. Exactly what Curly wanted.

A pang of something she refused to call jealously hit dead center in her chest. It'd been a long time since she had family to count on, blood-related or chosen. Sure, Nancy and Daniel were close friends, but they were married and had their own families she wasn't a part of. Though they always invited her, she'd spent holidays alone since leaving her husband. Crashing her friends' family gatherings because she had none of her own never sat right with her. Witnessing the closeness of siblings, aunts, uncles, and parents as they laughed and shared stories she couldn't relate to sounded more like a root canal than holiday merriment.

The whir of the blender sounded from inside. Another drink or two should help calm her nerves. Hopefully, it could turn off the incessant spinning of her brain as well.

What was Curly doing at that moment?

Was he safely far enough away from the dog fight?

Were the rest of the guys safe?

Were they gathering useful information?

Hordes of questions had been driving her insane all evening.

An earlier text from Curly let her know that the dog fight was taking place right at the farm. It was so close yet might as well have been on another planet.

Curly

Not being on the front lines was killing her. Worry for the guys' safety combined with straight-up curiosity had been eating at her insides all day. She'd invited Nancy for a night swim and hang out to keep her mind occupied, but every lull in the conversation led her right back to stressing.

"Um, what the fuck is this?" Nancy's stormed out of the house with a fistful of papers and a dark expression.

Oh, shit. A wave of dread washed over her.

She'd had stashed the notes from Prick in her junk drawer and completely forgot about that when she offered the bug cream to Nancy. "Um...it's nothing. I'll take them."

Nancy came to a halt next to Brooke's lounge chair. "Seriously, Brooke," she said, shaking the papers in front of Brooke's face. "What the fuck are these? Don't you dare say it's nothing. Is someone threatening you?"

She hadn't told Nance or David anything about how she'd been investigating the dog fights or how she got busted snooping around Prick's property. And she certainly hadn't mentioned involving Curly or the new MC. But the jig was up, and she had to come clean. At least about some of it. She'd omit Curly and the MC's role from the story. Last thing she wanted was to make trouble for them for helping her.

She sat up straight and ran a hand through her damp hair. "Okay, um, sit down, and I'll tell you what it is."

"I don't think I can sit. Seriously. What the fuck, Brooke? Why haven't you told David or me about this? Why haven't you called the cops?"

"Please sit. I promise I'll tell you."

With a huff, Nancy flopped down on her lounge chair. The backyard lights illuminated the fierce frown on her face.

"I was pretty convinced the injured dogs were coming from the farm that borders my property."

"Okay...David mentioned that theory to me. And to the police."

Brooke snorted. He'd wasted energy on that task. "The cops aren't interested in helping, so I went out there to do a little investigative work myself."

"What?" Nancy sprang to her feet. "You went by yourself?"

With a wince, she nodded.

"Are you out of your mind? Why the hell didn't you ask David to go with you? Shit, Brooke."

Brooke inclined her head.

Sighing, Nancy nodded. "Because my rule-following husband would have tried to talk you out of it. Damnit, Brooke, you are too independent for your own good. There's independent, then there's just plain stupid. Can you guess which one you were?"

She lifted her hands. "I get it, Nance. I'm well aware it wasn't my most intelligent idea."

"So what happened?" her friend asked as she slowly sat back down.

"The guy who owns the farm caught me trying to peek in the barn. His name is Prick, and he's a real shithead."

Nancy pinched the bridge of her nose. "Keep talking. I'm trying not to strangle you."

Brooke couldn't help it, she huffed out a small laugh.

"I'm sorry? Is this funny?" Nancy asked. "Because I fail to see what is so humorous about my friend putting herself in harm's way."

Duly chastised, Brooke shook her head. "No. It's not funny. I realize now how unsafe and foolish it was. Anyway, Curly was there because he and Prick have a bit of an...ugly history." Another understatement, but she refused to divulge Curly's private business to Nancy. "Anyway, he defused the situation, but Prick now knows I'm determined to put an end to his dogfighting ring."

"And he's been leaving you threatening messages."

She hadn't phrased it as a question, but Brooke said, "Yes," anyway. "At least I think it's him. There isn't anyone else who'd want to scare me. I've found five notes all nailed to the kennel door."

Nancy's eyes widened. "Jesus, Brooke, he's coming in your yard?"

"Sometime in the night. I got cameras, but he destroyed them."

"What is Curly saying about all this? What is he doing about it? I can't imagine he's the type to idly sit by while his woman is threatened."

Brooke pursed her lips. It wasn't the time to point out yet again that she wasn't *his woman*. What a stupid possessive statement of ownership.

"Oh, my God, you haven't told him either, have you?" Nancy threaded her fingers through her hair, pulling at the strands as she sat there with her mouth open. "What the hell is wrong with you?"

"Hey! Nothing is wrong with me!" At first, she'd been sympathetic to Nancy's shock and outrage, but now her friend was acting borderline rude.

"Um, your actions prove otherwise. Jesus, Brooke, what if he breaks into your house one night? What the hell are you gonna do then? Hit him with a skillet, for fuck's sake?"

Placing her hands on her distressed friend's shoulders, Brooke said, "Look, the notes have stopped. I haven't received one all week. Not since Curly started staying here. Prick is just mouthing off. It's just bluster. He's a bully who only wants to scare me. And like a bully, as soon as someone bigger and stronger comes along, he runs away. I refuse to let him scare me away, so I'm going about my life business as usual."

"Oh, yeah? Must be nice to be such a pillar of courage. It's scaring me. And none of this explains why you haven't told Curly."

"Why would I tell him? It's my problem, Nance. It has nothing to do with him."

"Okay." Nancy pressed the heels of her palms to her eyes and blew out a breath. "I'm not sure if you're terminally stubborn or just straight-up self-destructive."

Ouch. Who knew Nancy could be so cutting when freaked out. "Hey! You've been insulting me quite a bit tonight. Wanna lay off?"

"You would tell Curly because he is a man that cares about you. One you share your thoughts and feelings and body with."

"I—"

"Nu-uh." Nancy held out her hand. "I'm still talking. He's a man you are close to and would want to know if someone was threatening you. He would want to help you take care of the problem. Hell, he could probably take care of the problem himself in a half hour. You know that man's gotta have some scary connections."

"I don't want him to take care of it," Brooke said. Her voice rose to a near yell. "I can take care of it by myself. Why is that so hard for everyone to understand? I don't need a man to take care of my troubles for me. I'm a fully capable, independent, grown-ass woman, not some weakling who needs a man to do shit for me." She stood and paced away from the lounge chairs, then spun back to face Nancy. "Shit. I'm sorry I'm yelling at you."

Nancy walked over to her and gathered her in a hug. "Sweetie, being independent doesn't mean refusing to accept help when it would be smart to have it. Sharing this burden with Curly wouldn't take anything away from who you are and all you've fought for. You'd still be a badass bitch who escaped a toxic relationship. You'd still be the amazing woman who started her own business. You'd still be you, and you'd still be independent. No one can do it all, and no one should have to."

Brooke's shoulders sagged. "I've done it before," she whispered. "I let someone in. I shared my weaknesses with someone and lost myself. Bit by bit, he took control of everything until I couldn't choose what I wanted to have for breakfast. Or what socks to wear. The day I met Evan, a guy was hassling me

270

at a party. The jackass kept hitting on me and wouldn't leave me alone. Evan stepped in, took control, and had the guy tossed out of the party. My dependence on him started right then, the second I met him, and continued until I was a shell of myself. Only it took me years to realize what was happening. There isn't anything in the world that will put me in that position again. Not a man who gives me earth-shaking orgasms, not pressure from my friends, and definitely not empty threats from some asshole."

Nancy pursed her lips then said, "You realize you're more afraid of letting Curly in than you are of a man who is threatening you?"

Nancy straight-up didn't understand. The pity in her eyes made Brooke want to turn away, but her friend didn't allow it. She cupped Brooke's face between her hands. "Do you think I'm weak?" Nancy asked.

With a gasp, Brooke said, "What? No! Of course not." She tried to shake her head, but Nance held her firm. "God, no. You're super strong. You have an incredible job, hobbies, friends, you don't take shit from anyone. Nothing about you is weak."

"Thank you. That's sweet of you to say. Did you know that I asked David to open a jar of pickles at lunch today because I couldn't get it? And about twenty minutes after that, a wasp flew into the house. I screeched and went running into the bedroom, squawking about how he had to go kill it. How about now? Do you think I'm weak?"

"No, of course not, but—"

"And then in the afternoon, David asked me to proofread an email for him because he sucks at grammar. Then a light bulb burned out in our ceiling fan, and David asked if I'd change it because our ceilings are high, and he's so afraid of heights he can't even climb up a ladder. Do you get where I'm going with this?"

A heavy sigh left her. "Yes. You both do things for each other."

"Brooke, in a healthy relationship, you accept each other's limitations and are happy to let your partner help you through yours. You're also happy to help your partner navigate theirs. That doesn't make you weak. Doesn't mean you can't grow or improve on things you feel are your inadequacies, but it means you feel safe enough to share them. Because in a healthy relationship, your partner won't make you feel ashamed of yourself. No one is perfect. No one is an island. No one can do it all on their own. Not even you, my friend. And I hope that someday you realize it's okay to let someone in, to be vulnerable in front of the right person, and to let go of your rigid control. Because when it's the right person, it's not only a relief to have someone to share life's burdens, it's beautiful."

Tears prickled at the edges of Brooke's eyes. When she met Evan, she'd wished for what Brooke described. She'd hoped life with him would be exactly that. But it'd all gone so incredibly wrong.

Nancy pulled her close and kissed her forehead. "Come one, let's get the dogs settled, go inside, get drunk, and watch a movie. David isn't picking me up for another few hours."

"Sounds good," she said, and if Nancy noticed the tremor in her voice, she kindly ignored it.

They queued up Bridesmaids, their all-time favorite, but Brooke found she couldn't concentrate on a single minute of the hilarity. Her friend's words ran through her head over and over. Could she do it? Could she let a man into her life, her mind, and her heart?

Not just a man, but Curly. If she were candid, she'd have to admit she'd already let him in more than anyone in five years.

Sometime after the first half of the movie and one more margarita, Brooke fell asleep with a terrifying truth bouncing around in her head.

It didn't matter how hard she denied it. She'd already fallen for the biker with the curly hair and the tragic past.

Chapter Twenty-Six

Incessant barking reverberated through Brooke's foggy head. "Ray, quit it," she mumbled as she tried to roll over but almost fell off the bed.

"Seriously, buddy, what the hell?" Nancy groaned.

Nancy? Why was Nancy in her bed?

As she fluttered her eyes open, then blinked into the dark space. This wasn't her bedroom. After a few seconds, the glow of the television jogged her memory. They'd been watching a movie in the den and had both passed out on the couch before it ended. It couldn't be too late because David hadn't shown up to collect his wife yet.

Ray's barking continued, loud, aggressive, and unrelenting. The hair on the back of Brooke's neck rose along with a twist of unease in her stomach. That wasn't a normal, squirrel-sighting bark. It was a something's-very-wrong bark.

Nancy sat up, pushing a hand through her hair. "What is going on with him?" she yelled over Ray's continued and furious barking. "He never acts like this."

No, he didn't, which explained the sudden heaviness of dread in Brooke's heart. Something had to be very off for Ray to be in such an alarmed state.

He stood at her French doors with his ears pointing straight back, his body poised as though ready to tear across the yard if she opened the door. His bark morphed into a snarl as though there were an intrud—"Oh, my God!" The last vestiges of sleep vanished in an instant as Brooke shot to her feet and raced toward the French doors. "Maybe he saw the person who's been leaving notes."

It couldn't have been Prick himself since he was at the dog fight, but that asshole could easily have paid someone to scale her fence and tack a note to her kennel. In fact, he'd probably hired someone to leave all of them so he could claim innocence.

The chicken shit. And now whoever it was had been spotted by Ray. "Good boy," she said, patting his head as she reached for the door handles.

"Are you crazy?" Nancy shrieked the second Brooke yanked the doors open. "Don't go out there if you think someone might be in your yard." She darted over.

"I have to. This is my home. Ray, heel," she ordered, and for the first time more than five years, he disobeyed her stern command. Barking like a maniac, Ray shot out the door into the lanai, then through the doggie door into the backyard. He raced toward the kennel, growling so loud he'd wake the neighbors.

"Ray, stop!" She shouted as she ran after him. What if the trespasser was still out there, and they hurt her baby? Or any of the dogs? The thought had her pushing faster. She'd never forgive herself if Ray encountered someone who hurt him.

Without thought to her safety, she sprinted through the lanai. Nancy continued to rail at her to come back. Not a chance until she ensured Ray and the others were safe.

As soon as she reached the screen door leading to the backyard, she saw it. Or smelled it. Maybe she heard it first.

"No," she whispered as her chest seized.

She'd never remember what came first, but the acrid stench of smoke filled her nostrils, and an orange glow flickered from her kennel, and the panicked wails of terrified dogs tormented her ears.

"Fire!" she screamed as she tore out the door at top speed.

"Brooke! No!" Nancy shouted so loud her voice cracked. "It's too dangerous."

"The dogs! I have to get the dogs." Her feet crunched over the stiff Florida grass and something stabbed into her foot, but she ignored the pain.

"Brooke!"

Nancy's voice sounded a million miles away over the roar of pumping blood in her ears.

She glanced over her shoulder at her friend's stricken expression. "Call nine-one-one! I'm going to get the dogs." Then she whipped back around, stumbling from the momentum.

"Shit," she yelled as she landed on all fours. Then, without assessing if she'd cut herself, she scrambled to her feet and pressed on. She trusted Nancy to get help, so she focused all her attention on saving her babies before the fire consumed them. The thought of them perishing in a fire had her stomach cramping so hard she nearly doubled over, but there wasn't time for fear. There wasn't even time to make it across the yard, but she pumped her arms and legs as hard as possible as she charged.

Heat radiated off the kennel, scorching her skin when she drew near. She recoiled, gaping with her jaw open at the mesmerizing horror show.

It seemed as though the fire was contained to the roof for now, but that could change at any moment, and the ravenous flames could consume the entire structure.

How long until the roof caved in, trapping anyone in the kennel under a fiery blanket of death?

Minutes?

Seconds?

Even less time?

It didn't matter. If there was a fraction of a chance of saving the dogs, Brooke would take it. Her heart pounded, and she panted from the sprint, making her dizzy. Or maybe it was the smoke, which already burned her lungs. God, she wished she wasn't alone. Wished Curly was there to help her. Wished he could lend her his strength to accomplish this herculean task.

Quickly as possible, she tapped her hand against the door handle. Thank God it wasn't hot yet. She wrenched the kennel door open only to be bombarded by a hot cloud of smoke. With a choked gasp, Brooke held her arms up to shield her face, but the blistering smoke was no match for her. Her eyes stung. Her lungs ached. She coughed violently. The roar of the fire couldn't drown out the terrified shrieks of the trapped dogs. Behind her, Ray continued to bark.

With each passing second, thick plumes of black smoke flooded her yard. If she didn't release the dogs soon, she'd have a full-on tragedy on her hands. How would she look at herself in the mirror if she failed to save the dogs?

Coughing as though she had a brutal case of pneumonia, Brooke yanked her sweatshirt off then dropped to her knees. As best she could, she covered her nose and mouth with the fabric then tied the sleeves around the back of her head. Left only in a T-shirt and yoga pants, she crawled on all fours into the nightmare that used to be her pride and joy.

You can do this.

Despite the blazing orange of the fire, inside the kennel was dark as night. Her eyes stung as though she'd poured chemicals directly into them. Tears washed down her face, trying to expel the toxins. Her vision blurred, making it that much harder to find her way around.

You've been in here a million times. You can find the kennels by feel. Move your ass.

Hot ash riddled the floor. Brooke ignored the searing pain in her palms and knees as she blindly crawled to the first kennel.

Muffin made a pitiful, high-pitched whine of panic behind the metal bars.

She wanted to reassure the puppy she was there to help, but every time she opened her mouth, smoke rushed in despite her makeshift mask.

Slapping her hands against the heated cage, she worked her way up toward the latch. The second she had the door open, something brushed against her leg. All she could do was hope Muffin made it outside and far enough away as she moved onto the next dog.

How much time did she have before the building collapsed? Was the fire department on the way? She had to be running out of time at a perilous pace.

God, it seemed like hours had passed since Ray woke her when in reality, it'd been only a few minutes.

Glowing chunks of roof rained down all around her, searing her bare arms with burning pain as they pelted her. She was no stranger to discomfort, physical or emotional. But this was on another level. Fear ramped up every sensation but also motivated her like the mothers who lifted cars to save their children.

These dogs were her children.

Keep moving.

Though it felt like she was moving through peanut butter, she inched from cage to cage as fast as possible, pausing only when forced to by her lungs, purging the poison in a painful series of violent spasms. She worked down the left side of the kennel, then crossed to the right when she reached the back. All she had to do was head toward the door, opening a few more cages before the building collapsed or completely succumbed to the flames.

Move faster.

By the time she'd opened five of the six cages, her head spun, and her lungs screamed for relief. If she didn't get out of there very soon, the roof was either going to crush her or she'd pass out, then the roof would crush her.

Still on hands and knees, she scrambled to the final cage. There was no way of knowing whether the dogs had gotten out into the fresh air or not, but she'd given them the best chance for escape.

Breathing became near impossible as every breath only filled her lungs with sludge. Her vision—limited as it was—tunneled, making panic rise to the surface.

As she fought to remain conscious and control the amplifying anxiety, a tremendous pain crashed into her back. Brooke cried out as she fell flat out on the ground. With a groan, she twisted, shoving whatever had hit her, probably a burning piece of lumber, to the ground.

Once she was free of the debris, she felt for the cage again. Her heart sank. Where the hell was the kennel? Oh, God, she'd gotten turned around trying to remove the wood. Terror nipped at her heels as she waved her hands in wild arcs only to encounter smoky air and ash.

"No!" she cried, then crumpled into a fit of coughing. Her back throbbed, and her palms burned, but she ignored the intense discomfort. She had to save the final dog, or she'd never survive herself.

A loud bang next to her had her jolting in desperate fear. Time was out. The roof would cave in seconds. She needed to find the final latch and get the hell out, or they'd both die.

Suddenly, a strong arm, banded around her waist, hauled her off the ground and through the air. "No!" she screamed, but it came out as strangled rasps between the forceful coughs. Seconds later, she hit the grass. Someone ripped the sweatshirt off her mouth, and fresh air flooded her lungs making her hack even harder as her body fought to expel the toxic smoke.

Curly lay spooned around her, also coughing, but not nearly as hard as she was.

"The cage," she tried to say, but her voice box ceased to make any sound more than a strangled croak.

As she went to push herself up, the entire roof buckled, sending flames shooting yards into the sky.

Brooke screamed a soundless howl and tried to clamber toward the building, but Curly's arms kept her immobile.

Sirens wailed so close they drowned out the dogs barking.

Brooke fought like hell against Curly's hold. How could he possibly hold her back when she hadn't rescued all the dogs? "Please," she whispered as a crushing sense of defeat pressed down on her.

"Baby," Curly whispered against her ear.

Or maybe he yelled it. Her head was a muddled mess, pain radiated from her entire body, and noise came from every direction, making it impossible to process. All she knew is she wouldn't stop struggling until she had a chance to save the final dog.

"Settle." His embrace tightened, keeping her flailing limbs from catching his face. "I released the last one. Carried him out with you. They're all out. Six dogs plus Ray. All safe, baby. They're all safe."

As soon as she heard the words, Brooke burst into tears. Choked sobs made her jerk and tremble. She turned into Curly's heat, burying her face against his chest the fear, pain, and trauma came to a head.

He wrapped her in a gentle hold and rocked her as he kissed the top of her head over and over. Ray ran over and flopped down next to them. He'd always been able to sense Brooke's distress. Once again, he'd saved the day. Actually, the title of hero went to Curly tonight.

All around them, the sounds of firefighters taming the blaze rang out. Brooke couldn't look. She couldn't bear to see the devastation and destruction of the one thing in her life she'd been so damn proud of. The thing that had saved her from spiraling down a dark, lonely pit after her divorce.

It was gone. Everything she'd worked for was gone in a matter of minutes.

Prick had taken it from her.

Despite all her professions of independence and capability, she hadn't been able to protect what was hers.

She'd failed, and had it not been for Curly, the catastrophe would have been fatal.

Chapter Twenty-Seven

Curly's insides vibrated with a combination of terror, panic, fury, and relief.

Did Brooke realize she'd been seconds, *seconds* away from an agonizing death?

Less than twenty seconds after he pulled her and a small pug from the inferno, the entire roof caved in. Had he not happened to show up at the exact right moment, Brooke would be dead.

Dead.

Christ, his skin felt too tight, as though it was trying to shrink-wrap itself around his bones and drive him mad.

Stupid, selfless, amazing woman.

He blew out a shaky breath as he clutched her weeping form in his arms. The feel of her tears seeping into his shirt drove home the knowledge that she'd survived. She was alive, pressed against him, not charred to a crisp in that damned kennel.

Still, he'd have nightmares about the moment he realized she was in that kennel for the rest of his life.

He'd arrived less than three minutes ago to find a frantic Nancy screaming at him from Brooke's front porch. With her cell pressed to her ear and make-up running down on her face, she half-yelled, half-sobbed out how the kennel was on fire. That'd been all he'd needed to hear to know deep in his gut Brooke was in terrible danger. The stubborn woman would never allow harm to come to her dogs while there was breath left in her body. If that meant charging full force into a burning building, so be it.

He'd driven over the grass and rammed his truck straight through her fence. Then, he'd practically flown across her yard, weaving around a bunch of terrified dogs to get to the burning kennel.

He'd always assumed the moment he'd stood in the courtroom, listening to the guilty verdict being read, would forever be the worst of his life. How could anything come close to the horror of being sentenced to life in prison for a crime he hadn't committed? It'd been unfathomable.

He'd been dead wrong.

The second the flaming kennel came into view, and he realized they had mere seconds before the structure crumbled on top of Brooke beat out his conviction tenfold. He'd never shake the stark terror that slammed into him at the sight.

By some miracle, he'd found her on hands and knees close to the open door. She'd been groping the air, with her eyes squeezed shut and her T-shirt over her mouth as she hacked and coughed. As much as he loved animals, Curly hadn't given a shit about anything but rescuing Brooke at that moment. But she'd never forgive him if he saved her only to let a dog die. So, he'd flipped the latch on the final kennel and scooped up the pug before dragging Brooke shirtless and filthy into the night.

That span of sixty seconds had shaved ten years off his life.

"Excuse me, sir?"

Curly glanced up into the sympathetic face of a paramedic. His buzzed black hair and round face made him look too young to drive, but the uniform and gear bag spoke to his legitimacy.

"May I check her out?" the paramedic asked.

Last thing he wanted to do was disturb Brooke, but red welts dotted her back along with one nasty-looking mark at the base of her spine. Once the adrenaline wore off, pain would set in, and

she'd be miserable. At the very least, he wanted the paramedic to get some pain medication into her.

"Baby," he whispered against the top of her head. "The ambulance is here, and the paramedics need to examine you. Okay?"

Her heart-breaking sobs had quieted to a soft sniffing with the occasional body-wracking cough. She nodded against his chest. Curly helped her sit, biting his lip as she winced with the movement.

"Ma'am, I'm Brody. Mind I take a look at you?"

"Go ahead," Brooke rasped as she wiped her damp eyes. The scratchy voice ate at Curly's heart.

The paramedic worked with quick efficiency. Once he'd assessed Brooke's oxygen level, he placed a mask over her nose and mouth to provide fresh oxygen. Then he went about checking her burns, explaining his process in a soothing voice. A flashlight gave him a better view of Brooke's injuries, but it was still difficult for him to fully evaluate the damage.

Brooke sat silently through the exam, only speaking when asked a direct question, but she kept looking around the yard as though counting the dogs. Her hand sifted through Ray's fur. He was her steadfast anchor in the chaos as he'd been before.

"They're all there," Curly said. He ran a hand over her dirty hair. "All the dogs are safe. David just got here. Looks like he and Nancy are rounding them up."

Speak of the devil. As the paramedic continued to do his thing, Nancy strolled over. "Sweetie?" she asked in the same soft tone she used when soothing a frightened animal at the clinic.

Brooke shifted her devastated gaze Nancy's way.

Crouching down to Brooke's eyes level, Nancy ran a hand over her friend's back. "We're gonna take the dogs to the clinic to check them all out, okay?"

Before she had the chance to respond, the paramedic interrupted. "Brooke, I'm going to recommend you come to the hospital. Your wounds need proper cleaning and dressing, and you should really be monitored overnight for effects of smoke inhalation."

As Brooke opened her mouth, Curly shot her a look that hopefully conveyed his opinion on the matter. She'd be going to that hospital if he had to tie her up and toss her in the bed of his truck.

Her shoulders sagged, and a sigh left her, but she didn't argue. "Okay." The scratchy rasp at the back of her throat caused another fit of coughing.

"We'll keep the dogs as long as you need," Nancy said. "I don't want you to worry about anything but feeling better." She shifted her attention to him. "We can take Harley and Ray for the night as well if you're okay with that." Brooke shouldn't be required to make any decisions right then. Shock always made logical thinking difficult.

"Thank you, Nancy," Curly said, sparing Brooke from having to answer. Instead, she nodded her gratitude. It'd been a long while since he'd had people in his corner. Trusted friends he could count on in a crisis. In prison, friendships shifted like the tides, and no one could ever be fully trusted. He'd seen the closest of men stab each other in the back over a carton of cigarettes—literally.

After blowing a kiss, Nancy walked back to her husband, who sat in the grass holding an oxygen mask over the pug's mouth and nose.

Another two paramedics wheeled a stretcher into the backyard. "Ma'am, let's help you on here so we can get you to the hospital. Sir, you're going to have to drive yourself."

He almost told them to fuck themselves but settled for a murderous glare. When his glower didn't faze the paramedic, he grunted. "I'll meet you there, okay, Brooke? I'll be right behind the ambulance."

Again, Brooke nodded.

Probably for the best anyway, he needed a moment of privacy to give Tyler a call. Maybe he'd ring Pulse as well since he was a trauma nurse. At the very least, he could translate whatever doctor speak the hospital was about to dish out.

He stuck to Brooke's side until they loaded her into the ambulance. Holding one of her singed hands was out of the question, so he kept a hand on her shoulder. Touching her reminded him she was alive and kept him from spiraling into a panic.

"I'll meet you at the hospital, babe," he said before kissing her temple.

She nodded but didn't respond. The vacant stare in her bloodshot eyes had a hollow pit of fear forming in his stomach. Hopefully, once he had a moment alone with her, he'd be able to remind her the dogs were safe, she was safe, and the kennel was fixable. Fuck, he'd fork over whatever cash necessary to build her one ten times as big. She'd be able to house every stray dog in Florida by the time he finished. Anything to see her smile return.

Once the paramedic slammed the door, Curly jogged to his truck.

Instead of opening the door, he let his forehead thunk against the window.

His hand shook. His heart tapped an erratic rhythm, and for fuck's sake, his eyes fucking misted. Christ, it had been close. So damn close. He almost lost her. After spending the past week in her bed every night, he'd almost lost her in the most traumatic way possible.

Despite all his protests about not wanting an ol' lady, losing her would have pulverized his heart into nothingness. She was everything a man like him needed in his life. Smart, driven, ambitious, sexy, sweet. Brooke was the entire package and then some.

Oh fuck, he'd done it.

He'd gone and fallen for the woman.

A throat cleared behind him. He whipped around.

David stood there with a mixture of distrust and resignation on his face. Black soot covered him from head to toe, probably rubbed off from wrangling the dogs. Curly imagined he looked just as messy.

"You need help with the dogs?" Curly asked. *Ugh, please say no.* All he wanted to do was get to the hospital so Brooke wouldn't have to be alone.

"Nancy gave me these," he said, holding out a few small squares of paper. "She said she found them in a drawer. Looks like it's been going on for a while."

With a frown, Curly took the papers. "What is this?"

"Read them," David said before sighing.

"What the fuck?" he muttered after reading the first one.

Threats. Five in all, each a little more ominous than the last. Fury like he'd only known one other time in his life began to bubble in his veins. The fire was an escalation of these threats. Someone was going to die tonight.

"Looks like it's been going on a little while."

"Christ." He scrubbed a hand down his grimy face. Why the fuck hadn't Brooke mentioned someone was threatening her?

"Figured you didn't know about it. You don't seem the type to let someone get away with threatening your woman."

As he was about to tell David Brooke wasn't his woman, he met the other man's grave gaze. He could say whatever he wanted, but both of them knew it was bullshit.

Brooke was his woman, and David was right. He sure as fuck wasn't the type to let some fucker get away with harassing her. "Thanks, man," he said, working to keep the fury from spilling out. "I'll take care of this."

With a single nod, David said, "See that you do. She's important to us." Then he went to his wife, who was just as dirty and waiting beside their vehicle full of unhappy dogs.

Curly watched them drive off with rage simmering just beneath the surface of his skin.

Brooke had some serious explaining to do.

Curly

Two hours later, he wasn't any less livid. He'd come close to punching a doctor and tossing a chair out the ER's waiting room window. They wouldn't allow in the treatment room while the staff attended to Brooke's burns, but at least she'd authorized them to speak to him about her injuries. He'd learned the fire scorched her palms and knees when she'd crawled over the hot ash. Her arms had multiple burns from falling debris, and her lower back had one hell of a bruise from a hunk of wood that had landed on her.

Christ, what if it had hit her head instead of her back? She'd be in here with a different set of problems.

All in all, she'd been lucky. None of the burns were worse than second degree. No surgery or skin grafts would be required, and she'd heal without significant scarring. The news should have settled him, but with each injury, the ER doctor ticked off, Curly only grew more agitated. The only thing keeping him from ripping the waiting room to shreds had been the arrival of his guys. Pulse stood by his side, asking all the right questions and helping to explain whenever the medical lingo flew over Curly's head.

"You think it's Prick?" Tracker asked below his breath after the physician had hustled off. Everyone in this place seemed to walk at top speed all the time.

Curly had called Tyler as soon as he'd been on the road to the hospital. Ty informed the rest of the guys, and they'd all met up at the hospital.

Brotherhood.

Fuck, it was good to have these men at his back. Knowing they'd always be there was even better. Knowing they'd have his back in destroying the fucker who hurt Brooke was the icing on the cake.

"Gotta be," Curly answered as he cracked his knuckles. If he didn't keep moving, he'd claw off his own skin. When he'd been released from prison, he'd vowed to never be in a position of helplessness again. Though his insides churned with the same turmoil he'd experienced when convicted, he wasn't helpless now. He needed to remember that. He could take action, it would only have to wait a short while. Until he'd spoken to Brooke. "She antagonized him to his face. Told him she'd do whatever she needed to put him out of business. This is his way of keeping her in line."

Though on the quieter side, Lock's deadly gaze told them all they'd need to know. He was pissed and ready for battle. "What're we gonna do about it?" he asked in a deadly voice.

"If these fucking nurses would let me see her," Curly yelled.

Scott snickered.

A nurse hustled by, glaring at him.

He glared right back.

Yeah, you're one of the ones keeping me from my woman.

Unfortunately, nurses were made of tough shit, and none of them cowered or gave in to his bullying.

"Soon as they let me see her, I'm gonna ask her exactly what the fuck went down with these fucking notes. Long as she hasn't crossed anyone else recently, I'm going after Prick."

Ty and Tracker shared a look. "Think someone else might have it out for her business?"

"Who the fuck knows," he grumbled. She'd kept the threatening notes from him, so who knew what other secrets she'd been hiding? He'd been down the road of having a woman lie to him and couldn't believe he was there again.

"Go easy on her," Pulse said. "She's been through a lot of shit tonight."

"Fuck, you say?" Curly snapped, rising to his feet. "You got a problem with the way I handle my shit? With the way I treat my woman?" He got in the shorter man's face.

Pulse's eyes bugged as he shook his head. "What? No! Fuck no. I just meant—"

Ty tugged his sleeve. "Sit the fuck down, cuz. You're attracting unwanted attention." He gazed left where a few others in the waiting room had begun to watch them with guarded expressions. "Take a goddammed breath. Pulse is right. She's not gonna tell you shit if you walk in there like a bomb about to explode."

Christ, they were fucking right, but he felt like a climber dangling from the side of the mountain, watching his rope fray one strand at a time. It wouldn't be long before the final thread snapped, and he did as well.

Yanking his arm from Tyler's hold, Curly spun to take a walk, but a pinched-face nurse met him three steps in. "We're finished with Ms. Williams," she said in a haughty tone as she stared down her nose at the group of rough bikers. Curly, especially as he soot and dirt covered him from head to toe. "I can take you to her now."

"'Bout fucking time," he muttered.

"We'll hang around, prez," Scott said. He was the only one whose ire seemed to match Curly's. He'd stayed quiet since arriving, but that didn't mean he wasn't a hair's breadth away from combusting. A deadly volcano resided deep within Scott, just beginning to wake. What would happen when it finally blew?

He had enough on his plate without worrying about Scott.

"Here we go," the nurse said. "Room four. We'll be moving her upstairs to her room on the floor in a little while." She pushed the sliding door open. "Okay, Brooke, I have your gentleman here. Push the blue button on the side of the bed if you need assistance *with anything*," she said to Brooke before casting Curly some serious side-eye as she left the room.

Brooke lay on her back in the reclined bed. Both hands had crisp white bandages resembling mittens. A clear tube under her nose provided oxygen, and some kind of fluid dripped into her left arm through an IV. Someone had given her a hospital gown to cover her and replace the destroyed clothing she'd arrived in. Nobody had bothered to help wash her face or hair, which still had streaks of black and flakes of ash. Lying under the plain white hospital blanket with minor burns on her arms and a sad smile aimed his way, she appeared so small and vulnerable. So unlike the Brooke he'd come to know and lo—

Know and respect.

Lying there injured because she'd been too goddammed stubborn to ask for his help.

And there went the final strand of his rope. Snapped like he'd love to do to Prick's fucking neck.

"Hey," she said in a ravaged voice.

He gripped the foot of her bed hard enough to make the plastic creak. Then he pulled the notes from his pocket. "What the fuck are these?"

Brooke's eyes widened, and her mouth parted, but no words came out.

"What?" he asked as he stepped closer tossed the papers onto the bed. "Did you think I wouldn't find out? That some asshole would threaten you, set fire to your fucking property, and I'd just go on living in the dark? Christ, Brooke, somebody almost killed you!"

If he'd been two minutes later, fuck thirty seconds later, the outcome would have been very different. If he'd stopped at that yellow light instead of blasting through it Brooke would be dead. He'd have arrived to find her burned and broken body lying beneath flaming rubble.

His stomach lurched, and his chest ached so bad he might need to check himself into the next room.

He was going to be sick.

He was going to lose his mind. All he could see in his mind was the image of Brooke, shattered, scorched, dead.

He needed to hurt someone. To make someone pay for the agony of the past few hours.

"The dogs—"

"Fuck the dogs!" he shouted. "You could have died, Brooke!"

Even the tremble of her lower lip didn't break through the fog of fury. He was too close to the edge of his sanity to stop now.

"Is this Prick? Did he fucking do this?"

"I-I think so. But—"

"Fuck!" He struck out, slamming his fist into the cheap vinyl recliner next to the bed, making Brooke jump. With his eyes closed, he asked, "How long has this been going on?"

She met his gaze, defiant and bold as though daring him to call her out on her foolishness.

Oh, he'd call her out all right.

"Started shortly after Prick caught me at the farm."

"Fucking hell." He pinched the bridge of his nose. "Why the fuck didn't you tell me?"

"Because I handle my own problems," she said as though he were short a few brain cells. "I don't need someone to do things for me."

Curly wasn't one to pray. He'd long ago given up on the notion of a God who loved him and answered his pleas, but at that moment, he peered up at the ceiling and prayed for the mental fortitude to resist reaching out and shaking Brooke until whatever was loose in her brain settled into place.

God, give me strength.

Chapter Twenty-Eight

"I was handling it."

Brooke squared her shoulders and tried to appear the competent adult she claimed to be despite the wounds, tubes, and filth. Screw him for marching in her room all big and muscly and capable of taking on the damn world while she lay there weak, uncomfortable, and heartsick.

Thankfully, the pain medication had dulled the worst of the discomfort to an annoying throb, but it also made her head foggy and had her riding an emotional fine line.

Her kennel was gone. What she'd worked so hard to achieve burned up in a matter of minutes. It hurt so much more than the burns on her hands, knees, and arms. And that was saying something because those hurt like a sonofabitch. She'd hit her mental limit. If only she could curl into a ball, squeeze her eyes shut, and wake up to two weeks ago before she'd so stupidly antagonized Prick. To top off the horrible night, the one person she'd been dying to see since she arrived at the hospital stormed in spewing judgment and without so much as asking how she felt.

God, she was going to cry again and humiliate herself further. How could she convince him she didn't need someone managing her when she broke down every time life got bumpy?

"You call this handling it?" he asked, waving toward her bed. "For real?"

Agitation rolled off him in palpable waves.

Brooke narrowed her eyes. "Obviously this is an extenuating circumstance."

With a snort, he said, "Obviously." Then he returned to the end of her bed, glaring at her while he gripped the footboard. "Do you not see the problem here, Brooke?"

"I'm not blind." She coughed as she'd been doing ever since the fire. "I realize Prick is a huge problem."

"Jesus Christ." Curly threw his hands in the air. "I'm talking about the problem with you. How your stupid need to be *independent* no matter what nearly cost you and the dogs your goddammed lives!" He said the word independent as though it scored his tongue.

The words were a direct hit. They stole her breath. Brooke blinked her eyes as fast as possible to keep the tears from rushing forward. She loved those dogs with all her heart, and the thought that her actions could have placed them in harm's way gutted her.

"This is exactly the reason I chose to live without a man," she said, waving a bandaged hand in his direction. "All you assholes do is pass judgment and call me stupid. I lived through ten years of that garbage from my good-for-nothing-husband. I will not tolerate it from you or anyone ever again." Another fit of coughing seized her. Damnit, she couldn't even reach for the cup of water because of her stupid hands.

A straw appeared at her lips. For just one juvenile second, Brooke considered turning her head. But she was insanely thirsty and not a masochist, so she sipped the water. "Thanks," she mumbled, casting a glance at his face.

Yikes, he is mad.

The glare he leveled her with would have sent her running if she wasn't attached to so many damn machines, and if she wasn't a hundred percent certain he wouldn't kill her as his scowl suggested.

"I didn't call you stupid, Brooke," he said in a deadly calm tone. "I called your inability to admit you can't do everything alone stupid. You aren't a goddammed miracle worker. None of us are. What the fuck do you think MC life is all about? It's about brotherhood. Fucking family. Because we're all smart enough to realize that sometimes we fucking need other people to help us handle our shit."

"I had it under control," she said through clenched teeth though as soon as the words left her mouth, she realized the absurdity of sticking to that story. Her kennel was gone, the dogs had nowhere to go, and she was injured.

Why was she still clinging to the idiotic notion she'd been right in keeping the information from Curly? Why couldn't she just admit she'd been terrified tonight and wished to hell he'd been there? Why couldn't she tell him she wanted to go back in time and show him the very first note five seconds after she got it?

Because still, after he saved her life and her dog's life, she was afraid of losing herself.

"You know what?" he asked as he pushed off the bed. "I've got shit to do tonight. Someone I know is in hot water over their head and needs a life raft. Now, it's my turn to *handle their shit*. Why don't you give me a call if you ever pull your head out of your ass?"

How dare he…

As he wrenched the door open and started to storm into the hallway, Brooke called out, "I'm fine, by the way. Thanks for asking. In some pain, but it's nothing major. I'll be going home tomorrow. By my fucking self!"

Not her most mature moment, but he'd pissed her off.

Back to her, he paused. Brooke held her breath, wiling him to turn around even if she couldn't say the words aloud. His shoulders drooped. "If you'd take a minute to let go of your stubborn pride, you'd realize that I do care, Brooke. I care so much, I'll do goddammed anything to make sure you're all right. Even piss you off by taking over." He marched into the hall just as Nancy was coming in.

"Whoa!" Nancy said as a Curly tornado blew past her. She blinked, watched after him for a second, then turned back to Brooke. "I take it he's mad?"

With a snort, Brooke shook her head. "Something like that."

A heavy sigh left Nancy. "How are you feeling, sweetie?"

"See," she muttered. "It's not hard to ask someone in the hospital how they are doing?"

Nancy pressed her lips together. "Um…"

Waving her friend in, Brooke shook her head. "It's nothing. Come on in."

At some point, Nancy had been lucky enough to take a shower and rid herself of all the remnants of the fire. She'd shoved her still-damp hair in a messy pile on top of her head. Brooke would kill for a shower; hell, even a bucket of water would be great. The doctor told her to keep her hands dry for the next forty-eight hours, which sounded like an absolute treat.

Her friend stepped into the room and took the seat next to the bed. "What are the doctors saying?" She looked much more comfortable dressed in loose linen shorts and an army green T-shirt than Brooke felt.

"I have some second-degree burns on my arms, hands, and knees. My back is bruised and sore as hell thanks to a chunk of wood that landed on me."

"God, Brooke." Nancy blinked rapidly as though chasing tears away.

She nodded at her friend. "I know. I'm very lucky."

"I'm not sure you're even aware of how lucky you are. I saw Curly pull you from that building seconds, *seconds* before it collapsed, Brooke." Nancy shuddered. "That sight will be in my nightmares for a long time to come."

Never would she have imagined her decision to ignore the notes would have such far-reaching implications. Curly, Nancy, Daniel, the rest of the MC, and the dogs. All affected by her choice. "I'm sorry," she whispered to her friend.

Nancy placed her hand over Brooke's thigh. Usually full of spunk and sass, her friend's expression remained grim. "He's angry about the notes?"

"Pretty sure they don't have a word for how angry he is. He rode in here on his high horse spewing accusations and telling me how dumb it was to keep the threats to myself. Can you believe him?"

Huffing out some of her frustration, she glanced at her friend.

"What?" she asked when Nancy only tilted her head and pressed her lips together. "Don't tell me you're on his side here? He was an ass!" She began coughing all over again. Damn, her chest ached liked she'd run a marathon in the freezing cold.

Nancy lifted her hands in surrender. "Brooke, if David did what you did, he'd be in a hospital bed because I'd be the one who put him there. And can you imagine if I kept such important information like that from him? It'd destroy him."

"I guess," Brooke said as her resolve began to waver and ice slithered into her stomach. "But you're married."

"And you *are* in a relationship with Curly. Maybe you two haven't defined it yet or whatever because you're both too stubborn and prideful for your own damn good, but you are in a relationship."

"N—"

She leveled Brooke with a shut-the-hell-up stare. "Brooke, he's in your bed every single night."

She sighed. Nancy and her logic were going to crumble Brooke's thick walls.

"Look, the man may not have expressed himself in the best way, but he's right. I'm sorry. He dragged you from a burning building with seconds to spare. Try to imagine how he feels. If he'd been a minute later, you'd be dead and all because you were too obstinate to talk to him." She leaned in, so Brooke had no choice but to look her straight in the eye. "Needing someone else once in a while doesn't make you weak. Letting a man help you, participate in your life, and share your burdens doesn't mean you are giving up your independence or losing your identity."

It sounded so easy when Nancy said it. "While I was in the kennel, scrambling to save the dogs and trying not to get hurt, I wished he was there to help me. And then I got mad at myself for being weak." She shrugged and averted her gaze. Admitting her internal struggles wasn't an easy task. After spending a decade with a man who ridiculed her for her thoughts and actions, being vulnerable to anyone, even her best friend, was as daunting as scaling Mt. Everest.

Her friend's gaze held sympathy. "I can't even begin to imagine what it's like to live with abuse for so long like you did, so I'm not judging you, Brooke. Nor am I suggesting it will be easy to let Curly have an important role in your life or that it will be perfect if you do. But I can tell you that when a relationship works, it's worth every ounce of effort you put into it."

"My husband almost broke me, Nancy." Her throat tightened as a sob threatened to burst free. "Not physically, but my spirit. I don't think I'm strong enough to start over again if I need to."

"Sweetie, I never met your husband, but I've met men like him. Boys, really, who think the world owes them whatever the hell they want from it. Curly is a man, not a selfish boy. He's drawn to your independence and confidence. Anyone who is around the two of you together can see that in under a minute."

Brooke let Nancy's words wash over her. She had some thinking to do. Some soul searching. Burying her head in the sand wouldn't work.

"Besides," Nancy chirped with a smile that was both evil and cheery. "This time, you have me, and if Curly is a shit to you, I'll take him out. Can't be much harder to euthanize a six-foot plus man than it is a large dog."

Brooke snorted out a laugh that made her cough. "You're a little scary right now."

"Damn straight," Nancy said with a nod. "Okay, enough of the man talk. Who do we have to bribe around here to get a basin of water and some soap? No offense, but you're kinda nasty. I'll help you wash up so you don't risk getting your new fancy gloves wet."

"No, I can manage it—" She caught Nancy's fierce glare and snapped her mouth closed. Shit, she really didn't let anyone help with anything beyond caring for the dogs. And then it was only because Nancy and David owned a vet clinic and performed services she couldn't. Come to think of it, she'd never so much as asked for a small favor. Brooke would rather drive an hour to a store to buy something she needed than borrow from her best friend.

And why?

Because she was afraid of trusting others. Afraid to let herself need someone and end up hurt, alone, and scared all over again. Afraid to lose what she'd built for herself and who she'd fought so hard to become. Afraid she wasn't good enough, that she was too needy, that she was all the things Evan accused her of.

She'd nutured that fear and allowed it to grow into a monster that no longer recognized reason. And she'd nearly gotten her dogs killed because of it. Because her idea of independence belied sense.

Years had passed since Evan had any say in her day-to-day, yet he still had control over her. Everything she accomplished in her daily life, from the simplest of tasks to the monumental she did with demonstrating independence in mind. She'd spent years proving again and again that she didn't need him when walking away from the marriage should have been enough to send that message.

At some point, she had to live *with* the fear, not *under* the fear. She had to climb out and move forward despite being afraid. Wouldn't that be true victory? Actual independence?

Curly

What a fool she'd been. It was long past time to pry Evan's talons out of her brain and let people into her mind and heart.

Starting with a biker named Curly.

Chapter Twenty-Nine

"Let's roll," Curly barked as he stormed across the emergency room lobby.

Instantly on alert, his men bolted to their feet. All through the waiting room, wide-eyed would-be patients stared with awe and a bit of fear in their gazes.

"It's him?" Scott asked with a hungry gleam in his eyes.

"It's him."

Curious whispers trailed them as they left the ER waiting room as one fearsome unit. Curly didn't attempt to stem his fury. It rolled off him in waves, no doubt reaching the innocents waiting for their turn with the physicians. They'd survive—maybe not their illness, but they'd survive the rough group of pissed-off bikers storming past them.

"What's the plan?" Tracker asked as they burst out into the muggy night—or rather early morning air. Last time Curly had seen a clock, it'd been shortly after two. Couldn't be more than two-thirty at that point.

"Fuck the plan," Curly growled. "This ends tonight."

"Back to Prick's?" Scott asked, nearly giddy with glee. The same excitement that had Curly beginning to question his sanity.

Curly

"Yes, and we're not leaving until the motherfucker gives us his farm and agrees to get the fuck outta town and fucking stay there."

"Put him six feet under. Takes care of both," Scott muttered.

Tempting as it was, Curly couldn't risk them murdering Prick in cold blood. And he didn't have the patience tonight to make it look like a fucking accident. Prick had friends on the police force who'd love nothing more than to send Curly back to prison for good this time. Hell, Office Gibson had already approached him. Any undue harm that came to Prick would be like putting a flashing neon sign over his head saying, "I killed him."

However, fucking the guy up until he agreed it'd be in his best interest to leave town would do the trick.

"We split up," he announced as he reached his truck. "Scott, you okay to leave your bike here so you can ride with me? Ty, you too."

"Sure thing, prez," Scott said as Tyler nodded. "Jinx, Pulse, Locke, you three give it five minutes then leave. Want you three guarding the farmhouse. Check the barn for stragglers. Call if anyone gets close."

"We sure the dog fight's over?" Scott asked as he faced Jinx.

The other man nodded. "One hundred percent sure. It never happened. Scott's plan was fucking perfect. Prick was furious, and most of the handlers took their wasted dogs and stormed out. Everyone else left once they realize there wouldn't be a show."

"Good." Scott slapped Curly on the back. "Let's go make sure your woman stays safe." His grin grew feral. "And get us a clubhouse."

His woman.

Curly was pretty sure he'd destroyed any chance of that. Fuck. Goddammed stubborn woman.

She'd take on the whole damn world if it came gunning for her.

He yanked his truck door open, wishing he could just rip the thing off. A murderous surge of adrenaline coursed through his veins, giving him enough energy to run the ten miles to Prick's farm. He wanted to smash his fist into the man's face, wrap his hands around that fat throat, and press his knee into Prick's chest until he gasped and struggled for air in the most satisfying display of panic. He deserved nothing less than to experience the same near-death fear Brooke felt only hours ago.

"Prez?" Scott asked.

"Huh?" He jerked his gaze away from the windshield.

"Need me to drive? You haven't started the truck. We're just sitting here."

"Fuck. No, I'm good." He was so far from good it was laughable.

"Brooke holding up?" Ty asked once they were on the road speeding toward the farm.

"She's tough." He didn't want to talk about this. Or anything.

"Sure as hell is," Ty said with pride in his voice. "Gotta tell you, brother, she'll make a fantastic ol' lady. Hope you're not stupid enough to let that shit pass you by."

Christ, they needed to shut the fuck up.

Curly's anger expanded as the miles flew by until it filled the truck and seeped out the windows. All he could see was Brooke's devastated face stained with tears and soot. All he could hear were agonizing sobs. All he could think about was how different this night would have ended if he'd been two minutes later.

By the time they reached the long stretch of road that led to Prick's farmhouse, Curly was vibrating with so much repressed fury Scott and Ty exchanged multiple troubled glances.

"I'm fine," he barked when their concern reached annoying. "I'm not gonna kill the fucker. You can stop worrying."

With a snort, Scott checked the clip on the nine-millimeter he wasn't willing to be more than three feet from. "That's why I'm worried. I wish you would kill him." Once satisfied, he rested the weapon on his lap. "Or give me the green light to take him out myself. He's the kind of scum that I get a hard-on putting down."

Ty frowned. "You're not in the military anymore, Spec. We kill him, and we're going down for murder. Anyone who knows Prick knows Curly hates his fucking guts. He'll be hauled in before the body cools."

"Relax, Mom, I said I'd restrain myself." The smirk Curly was coming to think of as Scott's *homicide grin* appeared.

Curly met Ty's gaze in the mirror. His cousin's lips pressed into a thin line of disapproval. Last thing he needed was his VP and his enforcer differing on such a basic topic as how kill-happy the enforcer should be. Tyler had the balls to do what needed to be done regardless of the task, but he also had no desire to be part of a gang of trigger-happy thugs, whereas Scott seemed ready, willing, and eager to pump anyone who crossed him with a gut full of lead.

Once the rest of this shit settled, he'd grab a beer with Scott to see where his head was at. Maybe he'd give Rocket a call and pick his brain. If anyone would be on the up and up about Scott's mental state, it'd be Rocket. As Scott's sister's ol' man and former black-ops assassin, he'd have some solid insight.

Curly slowed the vehicle as the ramshackle farmhouse came into view. A dim light shown from one window to the right of the front door. Otherwise, the rickety house sat dark and silent. He killed the engine about a hundred yards out. They'd complete the trip on foot to keep from alerting Prick of their arrival.

A fission of excitement zinged through his veins. This moment had been a long time coming. Prick had countless sins to atone for, and Curly couldn't wait to dine on the man's fear. He sucked in a breath to settle the violence rising from a long-buried place. A place he hadn't visited since he'd been in prison.

Dark. Dangerous. Vengeful.

Ty didn't need to know, but Curly would love to let Scott loose on Prick. Fuck that, he'd love to kill the man himself. He'd do it slowly so he could enjoy watching the life leach from the man's eyes one breath at a time. It'd be so damn sweet.

But he wasn't that man anymore. He didn't have the backing of a long-established MC behind him, and he'd always be front and center on the cops' minds. When the "truth" about his conviction came to light and the entire nation learned of the man who'd been sentenced to thirteen years in prison for a crime he hadn't committed because the police department mishandled the investigation, the entire department felt the sting of that humiliation. Cops in the entire state were bitter and would love nothing more than to nail him for anything from jaywalking to pissing in public. So as much as he'd love to take this shit to the limit, he had to be smart.

There was no way in hell he'd go back to prison.

The three of them convened at the front of Curly's truck. Though around three in the morning, it was a clear night with an almost full, bright-as-fuck moon. He could plainly see the faces of both his men. "I want Prick shitting himself," he said, rolling his shoulders. "Rough him up, fuck up his house, threaten him within an inch of his life, but he remains breathing when we walk out that door, understand?" he asked as he pinned Scott with a harsh glare.

Raising his hands, Scott grunted. "Got it. Fuck, I'm not a sociopath, I can control myself."

"Guess we're about to find out," Ty muttered, but he also drew a weapon. Difference was Ty wasn't chomping at the bit to fire his and only would if necessary.

Curly didn't carry a gun. Not anymore. Another adjustment to keep the cops from finding a reason to bust him.

Scott flipped Ty off with a smug gleam in his eye.

"Let's roll."

Together they made their way up to the farmhouse. Curly considered going in stealthy and sneaking around to different entrances, but in the end, he decided, fuck it. They'd bust in the front door and make as much fucking noise as they damn well pleased.

Three steps led to what was probably once a beautiful wrap-around porch but now held only rotting boards. An impressive wasp nest bulged from the overhang.

"Shit," Ty whispered with a shudder. "Glad those suckers aren't out now."

They clomped up the steps.

"Here we go." Scott rubbed his hands together, then flicked a glance at Curly.

He nodded right before Scott lifted his huge, booted foot and power kicked right next to the doorknob with a loud war cry.

No surprise, the wood splintered with ease, and the door flew open. The forceful kick dislodged the entire doorknob, and the old brass fixture skittered across the floor with a loud clatter. Gun drawn, Scott swaggered into the house like the football captain arriving at a frat party.

"Well, shit, had I known there'd be porn, I'd have brought my lube."

A feminine shriek followed by a man's shout and another high-pitched cry met Curly's ear.

Scott whistled, then let out a laugh.

Stepping into the house, Curly found two naked women scrambling off Prick. The man sat on the only chair in the room, a threadbare recliner, with his jeans open, shirt off, and dick out.

"Ladies, collect your shit and get the fuck out," he announced. The second Prick realized who'd barged into his house, he growled and began to rise.

"Uh-uh," Scott tsked. He aimed his gun dead center on Prick's chest.

Ty lingered back near the door, also prepared to fire if no alternative presented itself.

As the women clambered around, gathering clothes and heels, Prick dropped back down. Fifty bucks said he didn't know either woman's name or give a single shit what happened to them once they left his house.

"Aww, buddy," Scott crooned with mock sympathy. "Why don't you put that little guy away?" He waved his gun toward Prick's soft cock. "Pretty sure I saw bigger ones on the dogs tonight."

That got a reaction out of Prick. As he tucked himself in his jeans, his eyes narrowed, and his jaw ticked with anger. He'd clearly had no idea any of Curly's men had attended the dog fight, and it fucking riled him to know he'd been played.

Damn, they hadn't done a damn thing yet, and Curly felt fantastic.

The second the women disappeared through the open door, Curly strode forward until he stood a few feet in front of Prick.

"How much money did you make tonight?"

"Fuck you," Prick said as he spat at Curly's feet.

Curly looked to Scott, who grinned, then surged forward. He cocked his arm back and smashed the butt of his gun across Prick's face so fast the asshole never saw it coming. He cried out, then snarled as he glared up at Curly with hatred burning in his gaze. Already his right cheek swelled and changed to an ugly shade of purple. Blood trailed from the corner of his mouth. He spit again, this time a mouthful of red.

"How much money did you make tonight?"

"Ten grand," Prick said.

"Not bad. Enjoy it. It's the last you'll ever make from fucking dog fights."

"Fuck you," Prick said again. "That little bitch of yours send you here? She's a hot little thing. Bet she sucks a mean dick." He shifted his gaze to Tyler. "He let you have a run at her? Maybe you get to tap her ass while he—"

Curly again signaled Scott, who produced a switchblade from fucking thin air. A quick flick of his wrist and the knife was soaring toward Prick. One second later, it found a soft place to land in man's meaty thighs.

Curly

"Fuck!" he screamed at Scott as his hands went to the handle.

"Don't touch it." Scott held his gun as steady as anyone ever had.

"Jesus, you're fucking crazy." Sweat ran down Prick's face, which had turned a light shade of green. He groaned and flopped back against the recliner.

"You have no idea," Scott said with a toothy smile that validated Prick's accusation.

"You like terrorizing women, Prick? Leaving 'em notes in the middle of the night?"

"Fuck you," Prick said, but his voice had weakened. "Fuck that bitch."

"Should I tie you to that chair and burn this place to the ground like you tried to do to Brooke's dogs?" Fury had Curly speaking through clenched teeth and squeezing his fists in tight balls.

Prick's eyes widened. "What? I didn't do that? I didn't start a fucking fire. You-you gotta believe me. I just wanted to scare the bit—"

Curly snarled.

"I-I just wanted to scare the b—uh, her off."

"Fucking chicken-shit liar. Can't even own it. What? You think I'll let you off with a pat on the back if you somehow convince me you didn't do it?" Curly grunted. "Funny. Guess what I found out, Prick?" Curly asked, calm as could be even though his insides were a jumbled mess of contradicting needs. His right hand twitched with the desire to grab that knife handle, yank it from Prick's leg, and plunge it into the fucker's neck.

"W-what?"

"You don't own this land. You're renting the house from an old man who has owned it for year and hasn't been able to sell. You still got family in Texas?"

"Y-yes," Prick answered, sweating profusely now. Blood soaked through the denim over his thigh. "A-a sister."

"Here's how we're gonna play this. You're done here in Florida. Tuck your tail between your legs and hobble off to Texas. Go stay with your sister if she'll have your dumb ass. I'll be putting an offer on this place and making it my club's home base. Kinda poetic, isn't it? Feel like we've come full circle or something."

Prick groaned and rocked back and forth.

"After you leave, we'll never see you again, and you'll never see us. However, I'll be keeping tabs on you. If I hear you're still running dog fights, I'll kill you. If you show your face here in Florida, I'll kill you. If you come near or hurt Brooke again, I'll torture you before I kill you. You get where I'm going with this?" Part of him would love Prick to break those rules so Curly could fulfill this promise.

Prick had gone pale, and his eyes shone with a glassy confusion.

"Prick, you with me?" Curly snapped his fingers in front of the guy's face.

"I got it," Scott said.

Curly stepped back, assuming another hard slap was coming Prick's way when a gunshot rang out, followed by Prick's high-pitched scream of agony.

"What the fuck!" Prick screamed as he reached for his foot. His gut kept him from cradling the injured appendage, so he rocked back and forth in his chair, moaning.

With a grunt, Curly faced Scott. "Seriously?" He'd shot a hole straight through Prick's bare foot. Blood gushed from the wound.

"What?" Scott shrugged. "He wasn't paying attention."

Fuck. It was time to split before Prick bled out, and they ended up with a body on their hands.

"Prick!" Curly clapped his hands in front of the sniveling man's face.

"W-what?" He continued to rock with all his attention on Scott, waiting for the man to strike again.

Curly

Scott blew him a kiss.

"Hey!" Curly clapped again, and this time Prick jolted then faced him. He was shaking as shock began to set in. "What are you gonna do?"

Prick sent Curly such a scathing look for one second he almost told Scott to finish the bastard off. There wasn't a doubt in his mind that Prick had hired someone to terrorize Brooke.

And they'd been so damn close to killing her.

"L-leave," he said, trembling. "I'll l-leave."

"For good?"

"Y-yes."

"And the house?"

"Y-yours."

"Generous of you. And only the tip of the iceberg as far as what you owe me, fucker."

"D-doctor. I n-need a—"

Curly leaned in. "You scared?" he whispered. The sour scent of Prick's fear singed his nostrils. "Scared you might die? Maybe lose your foot? Can you feel your life draining as the blood seeps out?"

Prick couldn't seem to speak anymore, so he just nodded. Snot ran down his face, mixing with his tear. It was a beautiful sight.

"Good. I want you to feel what Brooke felt. Unfortunately for you, you failed. All her dogs survived, and so did she. And she'll rebuild bigger and better while you'll be slumming it in a room at your sister's house looking over your shoulder for the rest of your life because I will be watching and waiting for you to fuck up so I can take you out."

With that, he stood. "We're done here." Prick could do whatever the fuck he wanted once they left. Call a doctor, an ambulance, try to stem the blood flow himself. Even though he had friends on the force, Curly had no doubt he wouldn't be contacting the police. He might be dumb as a hunk of concrete, but even the stupidest of people had some sense of self-preservation.

Tyler went out the door first. Curly trailed his cousin. As soon as he stepped down the three porch steps onto the dirt, another gunshot rent the quiet night air followed by a familiar scream. His gaze met Ty's before they both started back for the house.

Scott appeared in the door, bringing Curly up short. His face must have shown his utter shock because Scott's eyebrows winged. "What? I didn't kill the mother fucker. Just shot his other foot." He shrugged then jogged down the three steps. "Couldn't leave it asymmetrical. Blame my OCD." Then he began to stroll toward the truck whistling a jaunty tune as though he hadn't just stabbed a man then shot him twice. Curly watched him for a few seconds before following.

Scott was out of his fucking mind, but he'd be lying if he didn't admit the thought of Prick flopping around the house with two bullet holes in his feet gave him great pleasure.

It was only a fraction of what the asshole deserved, but already Curly felt the pressure release in his chest.

One problem fixed, one very big, very beautiful, very furious problem to go.

If only that one would be as easy to solve.

Chapter Thirty

Someone repaired her broken gate.

The broken gate Curly had rammed his truck through in his frantic rush to save her sorry ass.

Brooke sat in the driveway with an ache in her chest as she stared at the newly fixed fence. She'd been out for the past five hours and in that time someone had repaired the gate and two fence panels that had been destroyed.

She sighed and wiped at her sweaty forehead. Despite the blasting air conditioning, her idling car heated from the sun's intense rays beating down on her windshield.

Curly did this. It had to have been Curly. Maybe he hadn't been the one out there with the hammer and nails sweating in the midday heat, but he'd set the ball in motion.

Damn him.

She wanted to be mad at him. A few days ago, she would have been furious at him for going above her head to get the task completed, especially when they were on the outs, but everything had changed.

And after chatting with Nancy in the hospital two days ago, she viewed herself through a new lens, which wasn't necessarily positive. When she looked in the mirror, she no longer saw an admirable liberated woman who didn't need anyone in her life.

Instead, she saw a stubborn ass hellbent on self-sabotage. A woman so consumed by her past she might have destroyed her future with an incredible man who not only appreciated her for who she was, he celebrated it.

Curly didn't have someone repair her fence because he thought she was weak, incapable, or stupid, he did it because he cared about her and wanted to make her life easier. Even when she'd been a complete bitch to him.

"Ugh," she groaned as she bonked her head against the headrest a few times. Introspection sucked sometimes.

Fatigue hung around her shoulders like a weighted blanket. Since the night of the fire, she hadn't slept much. Her to-do list had approximately six hundred tasks, and she spent the long, lonely nights obsessing over everything she had to get done. And scowling at her stupid, burned hands, which were making life ten times more difficult.

And berating herself for the way she'd treated Curly.

And missing him with a gut-wrenching force. No one who knew her would ever believe how many hours she'd spent staring at her cellphone and willing damn thing to ring.

Scheduling fence estimates had been one of the first things she'd accomplished the morning after the fire. The soonest any of the companies had been able to fit her in her was three weeks out. Curly had gotten it done in two days. She was beyond grateful to have a closed-in yard again. Now she needed to find a way to kennel the dogs until the insurance check arrived and she could rebuild a permanent structure. Nancy and David were generous enough to keep the dogs for her, but every kennel filled by one of her dogs was lost money for them and added guilt for her.

With a heavy sigh, Brooke reached for the door handle. A stinging pain shot from her palm as she curled it around the handle, making her flinch. It was the hundredth time already that morning that she'd forgotten about her burned hands. All things considered, the wounds were minor and healing beautiful. The occasional spike of pain was an annoyance more than anything else. Brooke didn't appreciate being hindered in any capacity.

Humidity assaulted her the second she stepped into the late summer morning. The air was so thick, sweat coated her forehead from the short walk to her front door. After a quick battle with the key, she pushed her front door open. "Oh, that feels so good," she said on an exhale as the cool air of her home washed over her.

Ray bounded toward her with his heavy tongue lolling. He stopped and plopped his fuzzy butt down at her feet.

"Hi, baby boy," she said, holding her dressed hand out for him. As he'd been doing the past two days, he sniffed before allowing her to rub the gauzy bandage over his head. "Let's go upstairs, bud. I need a bath." Showers were out of the question until the bandages came off. Nancy had stopped by the night before to wash her hair in the sink, but a full-body soak sounded like heaven at the moment, especially since her back ached like a mother.

Fifteen minutes later, Brooke sank down into the large soaking tub with a moan of appreciation. She kept her hands resting on the ledges of the tub, safe and dry.

"I could live in here," she announced to Ray, who lounged on the rug next to her tub. His only response was a twitch of his ear.

She'd spent the morning on the phone with the insurance company. They claimed a check would be mailed out in a few weeks, which made her heart sink. A few weeks felt like an eternity when she needed a place for her foster dogs yesterday. After she'd finished with the insurance company, she'd called the contractor who'd built her kennel to discuss plans for a rebuild. The only good thing to come of this whole fucking mess was being able to add a few touches to the kennel she wished she'd done the first time around.

That tiny sliver of positive news didn't come close to outweighing how shitty the entire situation was.

After what felt like hours on the phone, she'd gone to David's clinic to spend time with her foster dogs. They'd been thrilled to see her and whiny when she left, which broke her heart. She might have to find a way to keep them all in her house until the kennel could be rebuilt.

Another sigh left her. She seemed to be doing that a lot the past few days, trying to expel her overwhelming stress with her breath. She closed her eyes and attempted to clear her mind so she could enjoy the warm water lapping at her skin. The warm water did wonders for her stiff and knotted back.

As the warmth of the water lulled her into a sleepy state, a low growl sounded from next to the tub,

"I don't think so, Ray. So not in the mood."

He growled again. Louder this time.

Brooke opened one eye and peered over the edge of the tub just as Ray sprang to his feet and began to snarl in earnest. She frowned as her heart began to pound with memories of the other night when he'd reacted similarly. Given that he'd saved her life and the lives of the other dogs, she wasn't inclined to ignore his distress. "What's wrong, bud?"

His ears stood at attention, and his tail had dropped between his legs. He shifted forward as though ready to pounce at any moment. This time, when he growled, his upper lip quivered, baring the sharp teeth that inflict do some serious damage.

Brooke's stomach knotted. Over the years, she'd learned to trust Ray's instinct. The night of the fire marked the second time he'd saved her life. "Okay," she whispered. "I'm coming." Quiet as possible, she climbed out of the tub. She didn't bother with a towel but grabbed her fluffy lavender robe from a hook next to the tub. Water cascaded everywhere, slicking the tile floor. She ignored the discomfort of the now-soaked robe against her skin as she grabbed Ray's collar.

"Okay, buddy, let's go slow."

Curly

With a loose grip on his collar to avoid harming her injured hand, they started forward. Ray continued to growl but didn't lunge or drag her forward.

"What is it?" she whispered. "What do you hear?" Straining her ears didn't help. The house was silent. Still, Ray stayed on alert and her gut churned with fear. Something wasn't right. She knew it. *Felt* it.

With a light tug on Ray's collar, she stopped as she shoved her free hand in her pocket.

Dammit!

She'd left her phone downstairs.

Right then, all she wanted was to hide in her bedroom and call Curly. Like the night of the fire, she craved his calm, capable presence. Whenever he was in her home, she felt safe.

God, she wished he were there with her now. She'd drop to her knees and beg for forgiveness. Plead with him to have patience with her while she worked to open herself up to another person.

She loved the way he made her feel protected without being overbearing.

She loved the way he allowed her to be herself and supported who she was.

She loved the way he touched her and held her.

She loved—

It all came crashing down on her like a ton of bricks.

She loved him.

Loved him.

Oh, God, she'd been so stupid pushing him away when she should have held him close.

Ray quieted, which had her relaxing as well. Together they took another step.

"Broooke?"

She froze dead in her tracks. Ray did the same, but only for one second. Then he went nuts, barking and lunging forward, trying to break free of her grip. Pain tore through her palm as she struggled to subdue him. She bit her lower lip to hold back a cry as she managed to keep her grip on the collar tight.

"Brooke? I know you're up there. There's no point in hiding. Your phone is down here, so you can't call anyone." Evan's sing-song voice had chills running down her spine.

She straddled Ray, trying her hardest to keep him under control, but he continued to bark and growl so loud she almost couldn't hear Evan.

Evan. What the hell was he doing in her house?

"Here's how this is gonna go, sweetheart. You're gonna put the mutt in your bedroom with the door shut so he can't bite me again. Then you're gonna come downstairs and talk to me. If you're not down here in forty-five seconds, I'll come up there. And I'll start shooting. Understand?"

Shooting?

She gasped and nearly collapsed to the ground as fear pelted her. Immediately, she recognized the changes in herself. Her posture slumped, her eyes cast down toward the floor, and she ignored the instinct to fight back. The sound of his voice had her falling back into the scared submissive mouse she'd been for years.

"Answer me, sweetheart."

"Y-yes, I u-understand," she called back.

As though on autopilot, she wrestled Ray into her bedroom. "It's okay," she whispered to him as she shut the door behind them. "We'll be okay."

She wanted Curly. Wanted to tell him she loved him before Evan did whatever the hell he was there to do. Drag her back to a life in California.

She wretched, clutching her stomach as the muscles contracted with extreme force. She'd rather die than live one more day as Evan's thing.

"I'll be back," she said to Ray, though it was more to reassure herself than the agitated dog.

As she turned to leave the room, her gaze drifted over her freshly made bed, catching sight of her iPad.

Her iPad!

Holy shit, she could contact Curly.

She could do this. Get help. Save herself and Ray by being smart and reaching out for help. A surge of confidence rose in her. Fuck Evan. There was no way in hell she'd bow to that man again. She'd go down fighting.

But she didn't have to do it alone.

She scrambled across the room and dropped to her knees beside the bed. Her right hand throbbed from restraining Ray, and she had a feeling if she removed the bandage, she'd find blood, but she managed to use her cramping fingers to unlock the iPad.

Quick as humanly possible, she opened Curly's name in the messaging app.

"Time's up, sweetheart. I'm coming up."

Evan's voice had her heart slammed against her chest so fast, the iPad wavered before her eyes.

911. My house. Please.

There wasn't time to explain. After shoving the iPad under the bed, she ran from the room. "I'm coming down!" she screamed. "I'm on my way."

Ray's whines and frantic barks broke her heart, but she left him closed in the room. He scratched the door, and she could only pray he didn't injure his paws in his desperate attempt to get to her.

When she reached the top of the stairs, she drew up short with a sharp gasp.

Even stood below with a gun in his left hand and a familiar appalled gleam in his eye. Other than that, he looked...different. Unwell. He'd lost a considerable amount of weight since she'd last seen him. Gone were the gym-honed muscles, replaced with a gaunt physique that had him swimming in his hunter-green polo. The hair he'd never let be out of place had receded a few inches and grayed. Dark smudges beneath his eyes drew her attention to his pasty face.

"What the hell happened to you?" he practically snarled. "You look like a cheap whore."

Her? He was the one she wouldn't have recognized if she'd passed him on the street. Though she probably looked shockingly different as well. The second she'd left him, she'd ditched the designed duds for tank tops and denim shorts. She'd sold the pearls and diamonds and left her neck bare. She'd burned the four-inch heels and moved into flip-flops.

And she'd felt terrific. So fuck him. "What happened to me?" she asked in as snide a tone as she could pull off. "I left my husband. He was a controlling asshole who made me wear clothes I hated. So now I dress for myself. If it makes me happy, I wear it. The fact that you hate it is a bonus."

Damn that felt good. They'd never had it out after she left. She'd refused any contact and conducted all communication through her attorney. Getting a chance to tell him off now, after all these years, just might set her free in a way she hadn't been before.

His upper lip curled in disgust. "Do you know what you've done?"

"Hmm," she tapped her finger against her lips. As long as that finger didn't tremble and as long as her voice didn't waver, she could disguise how afraid she was of that gun he held. "Moved away from you? Started a career I love? Created a fantastic life for myself without you? Found a man who curls my toes? I'm not exactly sure which you're referring to."

"Get down here."

He brandished the gun at her in a wide, uncoordinated arc. Some of her brash confidence vanished. But she shoved the flutter of nerves behind a haughty smile as she took the steps slow enough to earn a deeper scowl.

"Hurry the fuck up!"

Curly

She forced her legs to remain steady and kept the pace of a turtle. Anything to give Curly a few extra seconds to receive her message and send help. When she reached the ground level, he pointed toward her couch with the gun. "Sit."

Mouthing off was one thing, flat out refusing him when he held a gun mere feet from her face was another. She didn't plan to give him any reason to shoot her.

All she could do now was obey and pray Curly came through.

If he'd blocked her number in anger, she was screwed.

Once she sat on the couch, stiff as a board, Evan began pacing the length of her den, mumbling to himself.

She had to do something. Sitting on her ass waiting for the cavalry to possibly show up wouldn't cut it. For all she knew, he wouldn't receive her message for hours, if at all. She had to try at least to free herself. "Evan, why are you here? We haven't spoken in years," she said in as calm and placating a voice as she could muster. How many times had she worked with volatile animals over the years? Countless.

This was no different.

Keep him calm. Keep him steady. Don't do anything to make him strike.

Earn his trust.

"You ruined me," he mumbled, more to himself than her. Then he stopped walking and stared at her with desperation in his gaze. "Ruined me. I have nothing." He gripped his hair with both hands and muttered, "Nothing," as he continued pacing.

She frowned. He was unraveling before her eyes. She'd never seen this side of him before. The closest had been the night Ray attacked him, but even while he'd been in a rage, he'd had complete control over his actions. Control was his thing. The bastard lobbed insults like horseshoes while remaining calm, cool, and collected. That Evan, she understood. This ragged version was a mystery to her. And that made him dangerous. She couldn't predict how he'd react or when he'd snap.

How the hell was she supposed to play this?

"Um…" She cleared her throat in an attempt to keep it from quivering with fear. "Last I heard, you had a, uh, really great fiancé."

"She left me." He whirled around, swinging the gun in another of those wild arcs.

Brooke kept her gaze on the weapon as she said, "I-I'm sorry to hear that." Even to her ears, the sentiment sounded fake as hell. She gripped the couch cushions until her blistered palms screamed in agony.

"You're not. You're not sorry because you made her leave. *You!*" He shouted the last word, making her jump. "She told me you were right about me. That *you* talked to her and warned her away from me."

Shit. As soon as she'd learned he was seeing someone, she'd contacted the woman via social media and told her about what life with Evan had been like. When she hadn't received a response, and they'd remained together, she assumed one of three things happened.

The woman hadn't received her message.

The woman hadn't believed her.

Or Evan treated her better than he had Brooke.

Looked like it'd been the second option, at least for a while. The woman had come to her senses eventually. Luckily for her, she hadn't lost a decade of her life to the asshole known as Evan.

"I-I never talked to her, Evan. I'm s-sorry if her leaving hurt you." The bullshit lies were nearly impossible to speak when all she wanted was to tell him what a piece of trash he was.

"My parents cut me off. They took back control of my trust because I couldn't keep a wife, and it embarrassed them. My father told me not to come back to work until I got my personal life in order." He marched over to her until she had to crane her neck to see his face and the very serious barrel of the gun which pointed directly at her head. "This is all your fucking fault. You were a shitty wife, and you're still fucking up my life five years later." Bloodshot eyes met her gaze.

Curly

When was the last time he'd slept? Or eaten?

Brooke swallowed a burning throatful of bile. "W-what can I do to h-help you, Evan?"

He laughed a high-pitched hysterical whoop that sent a chill down her spine. "I don't want hour help. I want you to hurt. I want you to suffer. I want you to lose everything as I did. I want you to watch as I finish the job and burn down the rest of your life."

Her jaw dropped, and she gasped as her stomach plummeted. A sense of impending doom overrode all other sensations.

This wasn't going to end well for her. She could see it now.

Evan had burned down her kennel.

Chapter Thirty-One

Curly had crammed a month's worth of bullshit into the past two days.

Using an attorney Scott recommended from his military days, they were able to push through closing on the property in record-breaking time. He'd charged a fuck-ton for the service, but Curly was more than happy to fork it over.

Now the club owned the farmland and renovations could begin. He'd met with multiple contractors who'd listened to his vision and would be sending bids over the next few days. Along with that, he'd had Tracker put pressure on a fence company, and by now, Brooke's fence should be good as new.

Jinx, tasked with keeping an eye on Prick, reported the asshole had left town that morning. One of the losers he rode with helped load his truck and drove since Prick would be riding a different set of wheels for the foreseeable future.

Life seemed to be moving in a positive direction or once, but Curly wasn't holding his breath. He knew shine could turn to shit in the blink of an eye and tended to err on the side of caution. Ty teased him relentlessly about being a pessimist.

Fuck that. He'd more than earned the right to be skeptical of the world.

Curly

He'd spent thirteen years behind bars for a crime he hadn't committed, for Christ's sake. He wasn't a pessimist; he was smart.

On top of all the running around over the past few days, he'd spent a solid chunk of time obsessing about Brooke. She'd get one final day of reprieve before he sought her out. Thankfully, her friend Nancy was on his side. She'd been keeping him apprised of how Brooke was healing. Though she'd sustained minor injuries, he still worried.

He expected to receive a furious phone call the moment she discovered her fence had been repaired behind her back. It didn't matter how much she railed at him, he had no intention of apologizing.

He cared about her, and the idea of her not being able to house her dogs for weeks because of a fencing issue he'd caused wasn't acceptable. Having her pups home would be her number one priority, and if he could make that happen, he'd do it without an ounce of remorse. She could kick him in the nuts for all he cared. At least that would mean she was touching him.

What did it say about him that he wanted to be around her even if she felt bloodthirsty? After spending every night in her bed, not speaking to her for three days sucked. It reminded him of the few times he'd been in solitary confinement early on in his imprisonment. This sense of extreme isolation and frustration twisted together. A phone call, a text, a wave as she drove by, hell, anything would be better than nothing at this point. He'd about reached his limit, and tomorrow would put an end to the separation.

Hopefully, the few days apart had given her time to think and process. Curly wanted her. He wanted more than sweaty nights and occasional dates.

He wanted her independence.

He wanted her smiles.

He wanted her stubbornness and intelligence.

He wanted that soft heart hellbent on saving every canine in sight.

He wanted her love.

And he wanted to give her his love. Turned out, it didn't matter if he'd told himself he couldn't have a relationship, wouldn't let a woman get close to him, wouldn't fall in love. It had happened anyway without his consent and out of his control.

Now when he envisioned his future, he couldn't see anything but Brooke at his side, leading their new family through life.

His phone rang through the Bluetooth in his helmet, making his heart jolt in anticipation.

"Hello?"

"Curly! Hi! It's so good to hear your voice. How's Florida?"

Not Brooke, but his second favorite lady. "Hey, little miss. Florida is hot as balls. How are you and your ol' man doing?"

"We're good," Holly said with excitement in her voice. "I only have a minute, but I wanted to let you know that I'm coming down for the patch-in ceremony. Actually, I think the majority of the club will be making the trip to celebrate your charter."

A genuine smile spread across his face. "No shit? That's awesome, Hols." Copper and Zach had mentioned they'd come down to help him patch the guys in and formally establish the charter, but he hadn't expected more than that. Having the entire HHMC supporting him meant the fucking world.

"So, who's Brooke?" Holly asked with a teasing tone.

"Who told you about Brooke?" What the hell? MC gossip spread through the ol' ladies faster than juicy tidbits at an old-fashioned hair salon.

"It was Chloe. Scott told her."

He rolled his eyes as he steered his bike into the parking lot of a coffee shop where he planned to meet with Scott, Ty, and Pulse.

"Hey, hon, I gotta go. But I can't fucking wait to see you."

"Me either! And don't think you're getting out of the question. I want to know who Brooke is."

Curly

"Goodbye."

"And I better meet her!" Holly yelled right before he disconnected the call.

Chuckling, he pulled off his helmet. Holly would love Brooke and vice versa. All the HHMC women were tough as nails. Each had their own difficult histories, some truly tragic and some terrifying. They'd survived hardships, trauma, and loss and came out shining, just as Brooke had.

His phone chimed. After pulling it out of his pocket, his eyes widened at the sight of Brooke's name. Just seeing her text on the screen had his heart going crazy in his chest. Here it came, the anger over his high-handedness with her fence. He couldn't wait.

Chuckling, he opened the message. The lighthearted mood faded in an instant the second he read what she'd sent.

911. My house. Please.

Something was wrong. For Brooke to send an SOS message like that, something was terrifyingly wrong.

Curly glanced up to find Ty and Pulse waving at him from a window seat in the café. His face must have betrayed his devastation because Ty frowned and tapped Scott on the shoulder, then the three of them were racing of the café.

"Brooke's house," he shouted over the firing of his engine as they emerged from the building. "Something's fucking wrong."

Without question or comment, the other three sprinted for their bikes. Curly didn't bother to wait for them, he shot out of the parking lot like his motorcycle had a rocket engine. The others would only be a moment behind, but it was a moment too long to linger.

Though he broke every speed limit ever enacted, the five-minute trip to Brooke's felt like hours. As he sped down the highway at a dangerous velocity, every horrifying scenario possible played through his head.

Prick didn't leave. He was at Brooke's.

She was hurt and bleeding.

She'd been robbed.

Ray was injured.

The worries got more and more gruesome from there. He tried to calm his mind and body, but concern for Brooke consumed him.

Why the fuck hadn't he put a man on her house until Prick was securely in Texas? What a fucking fool he'd been. If Prick dared to set foot on her property, the man would die today.

Fuck the consequences.

He screeched to a stop in front of Brooke's house and practically leaped from the bike. It crashed to the ground, but he didn't give a fuck. Ty could fix whatever damage he'd just caused. The urge to bust through the front door was nearly impossible to resist, but Curly forced himself to slow down. He had no idea what he'd be walking into and needed to be smart despite the burning need to see Brooke alive and well.

As he reached the front door, he caught the sounds of motorcycle pipes in the distance. Ty, Scott, and Pulse would pull up any second. They'd be pissed he didn't wait for backup, but he fucking couldn't.

Quiet as possible, he turned the knob on Brooke's front door then eased it open. He slipped inside and plastered himself against the wall.

Ray's frantic but muffled barks had him frowning. Where the hell was the dog? His desperate cries seemed to come from the second floor.

As Curly took a step toward the stairs, he heard Brooke's stunned whisper. "You? You burned down my kennel? Why?"

A voice he didn't recognize responded. "I wanted you to feel what I felt. Why should you get to keep your life when mine is gone? Why should I be the only one who suffers? You took what I love, so I took what you love."

Who the fuck?

Brooke had to be terrified.

"Evan, I didn't take anything from you, you narcissistic psychopath."

Evan? Her fucking piece-of-shit ex?

So much for fear. Brooke was fucking pissed. Pride flared in Curly. Fuck, his woman was amazing. Did she cower and tremor? Fuck no, she stood right up to her tormentor.

The click of a gun cocking had ice forming in Curly's veins.

Fuck. She better not push him too far.

Showtime.

He stepped out from behind the wall into clear view of Evan and Brooke.

"Curly," she said on a gasp. Her eyes were wide and frantic with fear despite her strong words and aggressive posture. Fuck she was beautiful.

Evan swung the gun his way, which was fine by Curly. He'd much rather the weapon focus on him. The man looked about ten cheeseburgers shy of a healthy weight. His skin had a sickly yellowish pallor to it, and his clothes hung too big. Maybe he'd been handsome once, but no longer. Between the unhinged gleam in his eye and the twitchy way he couldn't stand still, the guy was either on something or losing his shit.

"Back the fuck up. This is between my wife and me."

Curly lifted his hands to shoulder height but grunted. "She's not your wife. Not anymore. You fucked that up too much for her to stay with you."

"Shut up." Evan's upper lip curled in a snarl similar to Ray's.

"Curly, don't…" Fear was etched all across Brooke's face.

He winked at her.

"Brooke has a real man now. One who doesn't need to control how she dresses, who she talks to, or what she does to overcompensate for having a small dick."

"Shut your fucking mouth." Evan's face turned beet red. Best thing that could happen right then would be for the guy to stroke out and keel over. But he'd take the attention on himself until Brooke could escape or his guys burst in. "I gave her everything, and she ruined my fucking life."

Ray continued to bark. A thumping came from upstairs as well. Probably the frenzied dog throwing his body against the door. Brooke would kill Evan six times over if Ray injured himself.

"You know who blames their shit on their woman?" Curly asked, calm as could be on the outside though his insides were screaming at his men to hurry the fuck up and get in there with some weapons. "Spoiled little boys."

Brooke snorted out a laugh that made Curly want to kiss her.

"Fuck you!" Evan lunged toward Brooke, grabbing her by the hair.

Brooke yelled in pain as she sunk her fingernails into Evan's hand.

A loud bark drew all of their attention. Ray tore down the stairs snarling, snapping, and baring his teeth is a ferocious display of protection. He skipped the last five steps, then a streak of black and tan dashed toward the den.

The next three seconds seemed to happen in slow motion. Evan released Brooke and spun toward Ray with his finger on the trigger. Brooke sprang forward, trying to grab the gun. Ray jumped, flying through their air as he made for Evan, who pulled the trigger.

Curly reacted without thinking. He threw himself to the right, slamming into Ray's airborne body. Pain ripped through his side, fiery and intense a second before he hit the tile floor.

Brooke screamed as glass shattered then another gunshot rang out. From his position wrapped around Ray on the floor, Curly watched Evan collapse in a heap. The gun fell from his limp hand with a clatter.

"Curly! Ray!" Brooke ran to them, dropping to her knees. "Oh, my God, there's blood." Her expression revealed the horror she felt inside. "There's so much blood."

"Ray's okay, baby. He's fine. He's not hurt." As though to prove his point, Ray hopped to his feet and ran toward Scott who'd just entered the room with a rifle in hand. He nodded once to Curly, then held his hand out for the dog.

"Ray's okay? She glanced over at the dog then down at him. So then you…" She paled.

"Shit, prez, you're hit?" Pulse ran in and dropped down next to him, lifting his shirt. He studied Curly's side with a competent, clinical expression. "I'm pretty sure this is just a graze. It's bleeding like a mother fucker, but it doesn't look deep at all. I got supplies in my saddlebags. Be right back."

"Yeah, I think it's only a nasty scratch." A scratch that hurt like a fucking bullet had ripped through him. But, for Brooke's sake, he played it down. She seemed about two seconds from melting down.

A bubble of hysterical laughter left a wide-eyed, shocky Brooke. "A scratch? Shit." She folded over. Her forehead hit his shoulder, and she began to sob.

"Shhh, baby, it's okay." He cradled her head against his shoulder, kissing the top of her head. "It's over. He can't hurt you."

Her tears soaked one side of his shirt while blood seeped into the other. It burned as though someone held a white-hot poker against his torso, but the perfection of having Brooke alive and in his arms exceeded the relief any pain medication could provide.

"He burned down my kennel. It wasn't Prick."

"I know, baby. I'm so sorry."

"I was so stupid." She lifted her head. Tearful eyes met his gaze. Even devastated and terrified, Brooke was the most beautiful woman he'd ever seen. "I thought I had to do it all myself. I convinced myself needing you and wanting you made me weak. That I would lose something of myself by giving my heart to you. Then today, when I discovered Evan in my house, I couldn't think of anything besides how much I needed you.

Instead of holding me back, you give me strength. You allow me to fly. Together we are better than either of us are alone. Curly, I love you. And if you can be patient with me, I promise I will work on my trust issues and let you in."

He took her face between his hands. "Brooke, I think I fell in love with you the first time I heard you tell Prick off."

She choked out a watery laugh and lightly slapped his shoulder.

What he was about to say could be the most important words of his life, so he kept her focus on him. "I will never block the light that shines from you because basking in that light is where I belong."

"Curly..." she whispered.

"Brooke, I love you. I want to create a life with you and stand side by side as we rebuild your kennel bigger and better than before and grow this new MC into our family. I want your hand in mine and the head of our family table."

She sucked in a breath the nodded. "I love that. All of it."

It'd been too long since either of them felt the love and acceptance of family. She didn't need to put into words how significant this moment was for her. He felt it in her soft smile, her gentle touch, and the love in her gaze.

"Kiss me," he said.

"Thought you'd never ask."

He slid his hand from her face to the back of her head, drawing her down to his mouth. Brooke kissed him with the same passion he felt for her. The pain disappeared, as did everything else. They were no longer lying on the floor in her den with her dead ex-husband on the opposite side of the room. He wasn't waiting for Pulse to return and dress his gunshot would. They didn't live in a world where someone had set fire to Brooke's home.

It was just the two of them in a bubble, connecting, pleasuring, loving.

Curly

He licked into her mouth and reveled in the moan that ripped through her. The sound had his dick hardening. Fuck, it'd been too many days since he'd had her naked, and he needed to connect with her soon, or he'd lose his fucking mind. With his favorite destination in mind, he stroked his hand down her back. Once he had a handful of her ass, he squeezed, making her moan again.

"For fuck's sake. If there's enough blood in your body to tent your jeans like that, I'm pretty sure you'll survive." Scott's humor-laced comment stuck a pin in their bubble.

Brooke squeaked and jerked back. While her lips were swollen from his kisses, her cheeks were pink with embarrassment.

Curly flipped Scott off.

Laughing, Scott turned to deal with the body. If only he'd known Curly hadn't meant the gesture as a joke. Idiot couldn't have given them a few more minutes of privacy?

"Think you can keep your lips off each other long enough I can make sure you don't bleed out?" Pulse asked as he knelt next to Curly.

"For fucks sake. Dramatic much? It's a damn scratch," he said at the same time Brooke said, "I'll do my best, but no promises."

Pulse threw his head back and laughed. "Shit, woman, pretty sure you're a perfect match for our little family of misfits."

It was the first time Curly truly felt Pulse's acceptance of their club.

Brooke beamed a huge smile then laced her bandaged hand with his. "Thanks, Pulse. Now let's get him to stop bleeding."

As Pulse set about cleaning and dressing his wound, the rest of the guys arrived. There wasn't a way to avoid the cops in this situation, seeing as how Brooke had a dead body in her house. Soon as Pulse finished, they'd deal with it.

He noticed that Brooke hadn't once looked in the direction of the body. That was fine by him. She didn't need to see it and have it haunt her dreams. Evan was her past, and now they had a bright and shiny future to anticipate.

She was staring at his side with a frown on her face, so he lifted her hand to his mouth and pressed a kiss to the back. She smiled at him and mouthed, "I love you."

"Love you, baby," he mouthed back.

After more than a decade of incarceration, loneliness, and bitter anger, Curly finally gained the freedom he'd had stolen from him. It was something he'd never take for granted and couldn't imagine a more perfect way to live his second chance at life than with Brooke at his side.

Epilogue

Strong arms came around her waist a second before Brooke's favorite pair of lips found her neck.

"Mmm." She tilted her head to give Curly better access. He obliged, kissing his way up to her jaw before nipping at her earlobe.

"Have I told you how sexy you look tonight?" he whispered against her ear.

Warmth filled her. "At least ten times."

"It's not enough. You look incredible. I've been fucking hard since the moment you walked in here." His hard-on rubbed against her back, emphasizing his statement.

She turned her head to meet his gaze. "That was hours ago."

"Trust me, I know." With a grunt, he kissed her long and deep.

That was all it took to turn her on. She'd never had so much sex in her life. Ever since Curly moved in with her a few days after the incident with Evan, they'd been going at it like rabbits. She couldn't get enough of the man.

With a sassy grin, she spun in his arms until their chest's pressed together. He interlaced his hands at the base of her spine and kissed her as he walked them toward the room that would be his new office once construction on the farmhouse finished.

"Need to show you something," he growled against her lips.

With a giggle, she allowed herself to be led. "Pretty sure I've already seen it. This morning, actually."

He playfully growled and nipped at her lips, making her laugh. Never before had she felt so bright and free to be exactly who she was. Curly seemed to feel the same. Since confessing their feelings, he also had a lightness about him he reserved only for her.

She loved that side of him. The fun, lighthearted side most didn't get to experience.

Also the sweet side. He had one a mile wide when it came to her and her alone.

"Where the hell are you two going?" a man yelled into the crowded clubhouse. From head to toe, the man was covered in ink and had a snarky personality that had her in stitches seconds after meeting him.

Maverick. His name was Maverick. The entire Hell's Handlers club from Tennessee had come down for the weekend to celebrate the inception of a new chapter of their club. The guys had been partying for days and, man, could those boys put away some liquor.

"I have something I need my woman to take care of," Curly hollered back, making her eyes flare wide. "It's pretty hard so it might take a few minutes."

"Curly!" she said with a laugh as he attacked her neck again.

Within seconds they were in his office, behind a closed door and he was pressing her against that door. Even fully clothed, the feel of his muscular body plastered to hers got her going in a way nothing ever had before.

"Fucking love this easy access," he said into the curve of her neck as he trailed his fingers up her thighs and under her denim miniskirt. This was the first time he'd seen her in anything other than shorts, yoga pants, and hang-around clothes. His eyes had nearly fallen from his head when she strutted into the farmhouse wearing heels, a skirt, and a low-cut tank.

Curly

He'd gawked at her like she was the most gorgeous thing he'd ever seen despite her forty-one-year-old body. Best part about it was how he made her feel like she was the most attractive woman on the planet and there wasn't much of a better feeling than knowing she was desired by the man she loved.

"This is gonna be quick and dirty." His hot mouth sucked at her collar bone, making her knees weak.

"Love it that way," she said on a gasp as he yanked her panties aside.

"I know you do." He took her mouth in a scorching kiss.

Each time his lips found hers, butterflies exploded in her stomach. Instead of fading, the hunger she had for him seemed to grow by the day. Being so deeply connected to him on an emotional and mental level took their physical connection to levels she'd only read about in books.

As he ravaged her mouth, he fumbled with the zipper on his jeans. The second she heard the clicking stop, she shoved his pants over his ass and grabbed the smooth, muscular skin.

He hiked up one of her legs and drove into her without needing guidance. They were so in sync.

Brooke shouted when he bottomed out inside her.

"Shhh," he said with an arrogant smirk. "Lots of people partying out there."

"The music is super loud. No one can hear me," she said as he thrust deep making her moan loudly.

His lips trailed the shell of her ear. "I think you get off on the idea of someone hearing us."

She didn't confirm or deny his assumption because she could no longer speak. He fucked her with sharp, rapid punches of his hips.

Seconds later she was clawing at the leather of his brand-new Hell's Handler's cut. The scent of it tickled her nose. "God, yes. More, Curly."

He grunted as he fucked her faster and harder. Within mere minutes she was careening toward a powerful orgasm.

"Fuck, baby, can't hold on. You gonna come?"

"Yes. Yes. Yes, now," she chanted as she clamped her thighs around his waist. He powered into her one last time, then held himself as deep as he could go. Stars danced in front of her eyes as a full-body orgasm flooded her with immense, please. She gyrated against him, burying her face in his neck as he did to her.

They stood wrapped in each other until the trembling subsided.

"Fuck," he whispered. "That goddammed skirt is magic."

With a laugh, she unwrapped her legs. He let her down and helped right her clothes before fixing his own. It took a few minutes as they kept stealing kisses and running their hands over each other.

Once decent again, Curly smiled down at her. "Ready to go back out to our family?"

She ran her hands over the front of his cut as she peered up at him. Seeing him in the leather vest brought a huge surge of pride. Not only did it make him look hot and dangerous, but it bore a president's patch, letting the world know who he was.

Not everyone would support them, understand their life, or agree with it, but in the few days she'd spent with the entire HHMC crew, Brooke got it. This wasn't a gang of unruly bikers. It was chosen family of men and women who'd seen the darker side of life and decided instead of succumbing to their demons, they'd band together and create a wonderful life full of love, friendship, and joy.

It wouldn't be all sunshine and rainbows. Hell, it hadn't been even in the short time they'd been together. She'd had some difficulty dealing with the aftermath of Evan's break-in and death. Nightmares, anxiety being in the house alone, guilt. But Curly had seen her through it and the worst had faded. Hopefully soon it would all be a distant memory she never called up. She'd never expected or asked for an easy life. Just one where she could be accepted and loved for everything she was.

Curly

And she'd found that with Curly and the Handlers.

"I'm ready for all of it, Curly. I love you."

FOR SO MANY years, he'd thought the universe was out to get him. Amazing how he could feel like such a lucky bastard at this stage of his life after going through so much shit.

"Baby, I love you too," he said just as there was a knock on his office door.

"Gave you two as long as I could, but they're wanting the prez to make a speech." Scott's voice came through the door.

"Two minutes."

"He doing okay?" Brooke asked with a furrow to her brow. She'd taken the guys under her wing as she did with her rescue dog. They became her pups, men to care for and love.

As he zipped up his jeans, he shook his head. "Not sure, baby. Seems like his fuse grows shorter by the day. Planning to talk to his sister and Rocket about him tomorrow." Scott had become unpredictable and volatile, starting fights and drinking like a fucking fish.

With a smile, Brooke stretched up on her tip toes. "Then we'll worry about it tomorrow. Time for you to go talk to your men." She kissed him. "I'm so proud of you."

Had anyone ever said those simple words to him?

Not likely. Damn, they made him feel like the king of the world.

He held his hand out for Brooke. "Let's go. Stay right at my side, okay?"

Beaming, she nodded. "Nowhere else I'd rather be."

Hand in hand, they walked out into the partially renovated clubhouse. In a few short months the work would be completed, and he'd have a home for his family. Men slapped him on the back and women kissed both his and Brooke's cheeks as they wormed their way to the temporary bar.

A loud whistle ripped through the room, ending the chatter. All eyes of both the Tennessee and Florida chapters of the Hell's

Handlers MC focused on him. This was where he belonged. Where he'd wanted to be his entire life. He'd been here before but was too young and stupid to realize the many mistakes he'd made. Now, older, wiser, and harder, he was ready to resume his role as president of a motorcycle club. Having Brooke at his side made this moment a million times sweeter. He squeezed her hand as he smiled down at her.

"Listen up," he boomed through the crowd. "Wanna start off by thanking Copper and every one of you who welcomed me into your home in Tennessee. And I wanna thank you for trusting me to expand your family down to Florida. I promise to do right by all of you. As for the new patches of the Florida chapter, congrats. Can't fucking wait to see what trouble we can get into together."

All around the farmhouse, men and women cheered and hollered.

Curly lifted his hand to quiet them once again. "I don't want to drag this out, so that's all I'm gonna say. Keep drinking, have fun, and get laid!"

The music kicked up along with whoops and cheers as the crowd went back to drinking and dancing.

He glanced down at the remarkable woman at his side. "Took me forty-six years and multiple trips through hell, but I'm finally where I'm supposed to be."

Moisture shone in Brooke's eyes. She cupped his face between her soft hands. "Same for me, baby. And the next time we have to go through hell, we'll handle it together. Side by side. Hand in hand."

He kissed her, letting the world fall away as his new family celebrated life all around them.

After living so many years in misery, Curly would never forget the perfection of this moment.

Keep reading for a preview of **First Comes Loathe** by Lilly Atlas.

First Comes Loathe Preview

"SCARLETT, HEY SCARLETT. You gotta get up!" A voice whisper-yelled into the darkness as a hand shook her shoulder, making her brain rattle around painfully in her skull.

Michaela blinked, then groaned. "Fuck, stop!" Even after all these years of going by her stage name, her mind reacted with confusion to being called Scarlett first thing in the morning. The stage name had been her talent agent's idea after a series of crushing rejections early on. A name change and colored contacts, professional hair bleaching, shedding twenty pounds, and speech training to rid herself of the southern accent. He claimed the stage name gave her an allure of mystery.

Or some bullshit like that.

Sprawled on her stomach, Michaela lifted her head. "Becca?" she croaked. God, her throat felt dry as the freakin' Sahara. "Why are you here? Why am I on my couch?"

"Because you needed to be up about twenty minutes ago," her personal assistant whispered.

"The fuck?" she asked. "Why?"

"God, Scarlett, you're really out of it this morning. Today is the first day where you're filming the battle scene through sunrise. Remember? You've got a four thirty call time for the next five days. You're due on set in an hour, and based on the look of things, you're gonna need at least that long in hair and makeup."

"Oh, shit," Michaela said on a long groan. Now that she'd officially been awake for a few moments, unpleasant sensations bombarded her from all angles. Her head throbbed like a bongo drummer was whacking on it, her tongue felt like a dried-out slug, and someone might have actually rubbed her eyeballs with sandpaper before she'd passed out.

Not like she could remember.

What the hell had she gotten up to last night? Probably nothing more than her usual. This sure wasn't the first time Becca had to get her ass out of bed after a night of partying. Hell, she paid her good money to be useful.

"Jesus," she mumbled. She pushed up from the armrest until she was seated. Fuck, her neck hurt. She shoved the rat's nest of hair off her face. "That better be coffee I smell, or you're out of a job."

"Yes. Triple shot." Becca, her assistant of four years, shoved a monster-sized to-go cup in her face. "Want me to turn the light on?"

"Fuck, no." Just the thought of it had her head screaming in protest. "Give me five minutes to throw on my robe and brush my teeth. I'll meet you outside."

"Okay. Do you want me to grab you something to eat?"

The thought of food had her stomach turning. "What time is it?"

"Three-thirty."

Torture. "Ugh. No, coffee is all I want."

Even through the darkness, she saw Becca's mouth turn down. "Are you sure? I don't think you had anything for dinner last night." She still whispered, probably in blessed reverence to Michaela's wicked hangover.

"I had drinks." And Lord knew what else.

"Surprise, surprise," Becca mumbled.

Curly

If she'd had more energy, Michaela would have called her out on the snark. Naked as the day she was born, Michela shivered. "Damn, it's cold. Where the fuck's my robe?" Nudity, her own and others, didn't bother her. Hadn't for a long time. Not since that shitty slasher movie she'd done at twenty. It'd been the first she'd starred in to make it to the big screen as well as her first lead. And it'd been shit. Absolute garbage. She'd had a fifteen-minute-long scene where she'd run from the psycho killer in a towel that fell toward the end. After being naked through countless takes, she'd lost any shyness she'd once possessed.

Now she felt nothing, whether clothed or in the nude.

"I think I see it on that chair," Becca said as she maneuvered through the trailer. "Here." She tossed Michaela the silk robe. "I'll wait for you outside, Scarlett."

"Thanks, hon." After donning the robe, Michaela stood and stretched her arms over her head. Her shoulder cracked and her back ached. God, she felt older than her twenty-eight years. Especially this early in the morning.

A few sips of coffee cleared the cobwebs enough to have her stumbling through the dark trailer into the bathroom. She did her business and brushed her teeth by the light of her makeup mirror. No way in hell was she going to flip on the overhead light and rocket her hangover headache into a full-on migraine.

She didn't bother checking her appearance, either. That could wait until hair and makeup performed their magic and made it look like she hadn't spent the majority of the night partying. Or at least that's how she assumed she'd spent the previous night. The details were fuzzy at best.

Which reminded her. Coffee alone wouldn't cut it today.

She opened the mini medicine cabinet in her trailer's bathroom and pulled out the little vial she kept on hand for just this kinda day. Which unfortunately seemed like most days, lately. This would take care of the fact she'd only gone to bed an hour or two ago.

Michaela twisted the cap, pulled out the snuff spoon, then frowned. "Shit," she murmured. "I'm out? How can I be fucking out?" Dammit. A bump of coke would have been perfect. Now she'd have to suffer with nothing more potent than caffeine to get her through the early morning shoot.

It would have been painful with the coke; now it was going to be downright excruciating.

"What fucking choice do I have? I'm the goddammed star," she muttered as she left the bathroom. After shoving her feet in some sandals, she exited the trailer.

Becca waited with her back against the trailer, using two thumbs to type on her phone furiously. "Ready?" she asked without looking up. "We gotta book it. They've been ready for you for twenty minutes."

Michaela snorted then took a long sip of the tepid coffee. "They can fucking wait. Not like they're gonna start shooting without me."

"Yeah, but sunrise is—"

She shook her coffee cup in her assistant's face. "I'm gonna need another one of these as soon as this is empty, which will be in about five seconds."

"Okay, sure." Her assistant fell in step beside her.

"And I need to run an errand after we wrap up for today."

"I'll get you whatever you need." Becca's eager to please eyes came shining through even in the darkness.

"What? No, I said I'd do it." She never had her staff meet with her dealer, well, except for the ones who bought from him too, and Becca was definitely not one of those assistants. She was as gleaming as a recently polished shoe. "God, why the fuck is it so bright out here?" Michaela shielded her eyes as she passed under a lamp in the lot. "Fucking middle of the night."

Becca shot her a side-eyed frown but wisely kept her trap shut. The caffeine hadn't done shit to wake Michaela up, and, frankly, she felt like garbage. The walk to the hair and makeup trailer only took a few moments. Not long enough get her blood flowing and make her feel human.

When she stepped into the well-lit space, she flinched as the shocking bright lights assaulted her senses. "Fuck, can we turn a few of those down?" she asked without greeting anyone.

Ralph, her best friend and long-time stylist gave an elegant snort. "Uh, no, babe. We most certainly cannot." Then he frowned. "With the way you look this morning, I'm gonna need all the tricks in my bag, and I can't work my magic in the dark." Then he winked. "Well not the kinda magic you need, anyway. Sit that skinny ass down in my chair," he said as he spun the salon chair toward her. Then he tilted his head and gave her a long up and down look. "You losing more weight, Mick?" His voice took on a note of concern, matching the frown pulling down his lips. She'd known him since the first week she'd moved to LA. They'd climbed the cinema ladder together, and he refused to call her Scarlett in private.

"What?" She shuffled over to his station in front of the mirror and plopped into the chair. "No. I actually need to drop a few pounds." Someone had commented on a social media post from a few weeks ago that the dress she'd been wearing made her look fat. Last thing she needed was a viral post about how fluffy she'd become.

She leaned forward, examining herself in the mirror. Oh man, Ralph wasn't kidding. She looked rough. "My mane needs some serious help this morning, babe."

Coming to stand behind her, he placed his hands on her shoulders. "Yes, sweetheart. I have eyes. Speaking of eyes, Libby is gonna need to put about a gallon of concealer under yours. Wild night?"

Had it been? She shrugged. Maybe.

Ralph frowned as he switched on a hair straightener. "One of those again, huh? Mick, we've all had 'em, but maybe you could do me a favor and save the extra wild nights for days when you don't have to be on set at the ass crack of dawn, huh? Help a sister out."

"Yes, Daddy. I'll stay in tonight and do my homework."

Ralph laughed, but it didn't hold the normal joy he carried. "Thank you." He grabbed some clips and began sectioning off her hair but stopped after only a few seconds. "You okay, Mickie? For real? Because you've been worrying me a little late!
—"

Oh, *hell* no. They were not playing the I'm-worried-about-you game. She was fine. At the top of her game, richer than sin, sought by all for her skills and her appearance. Not a goddamn thing was wrong besides the lack of sleep. "Becca! Where the fuck's my coffee?" she yelled, holding up the empty Venti cup.

Ralph narrowed his eyes at her in the mirror but kept his mouth shut. Thank God.

"On it," her assistant called back.

It was going to be a long-ass morning.

Forty-five minutes later, Ralph had straightened her long, platinum locks into a sleek, silky waterfall, which he then gathered high on her head in a fierce power ponytail. She'd have to keep the look in mind for a future awards show. But for today, the ponytail would be braided with leather ribbons woven through. After snapping the metal cuff which accompanied her ensemble around the pony, his part was complete, and she was well on her way to resembling a movie star again. Libby took over once Ralph departed and used her makeup skills to produce the badass look her tribal warrior princess character required.

And now she was standing in the middle of the California desert at four thirty in the morning waiting for the director to call action. This post-apocalyptic movie had been a surprise offer. Not a typical dramatic role for her. But so far, she'd been enjoying the challenge of stretching her acting skills. Even if Charles Francola, the director, was a bit of a misogynistic asshole. They'd rubbed each other the wrong way from day one when she'd mistaken him for an intern and demanded a coffee.

The man held a grudge like a champ and had been growly with her throughout filming.

"Fucking finally," Francola grumbled from his chair under a tent as he stretched his arms overhead.

At least she wasn't the only one hating the early morning hour.

After a jaw-yawn that stretched out his stubbled face, Francola straightened the ball cap he was never without. "Let's get this fucking show on the road now that our star has decided to grace us with her presence."

Michaela resisted the urge to roll her eyes and flip him off. Damn right, she was a star. One who'd made forty million dollars on her last movie release, which was only one of many chart-topping films she'd starred in. Francola could bitch and moan all he wanted, but he knew his movie would sell on the clout of her name alone.

"*Sunrise Battle*, take one," the clap loader called out the scene name before the familiar snap of the clapperboard indicated the start of filming.

Despite an unyielding headache and increasing nausea— maybe she should have had a bite to eat—Michaela fell into the dynamic character like she was born to it.

And she was. Nothing gave her a thrill like delving inside the skin of a new character. Learning who they were and adopting their personality for a period of time. Especially a character like this one, a warrior who clawed her way to the top for everything she'd earned in life. Though not the commander of a post-apocalyptic army, Michaela understood the struggle and perseverance to be the best.

To be more accurate, nothing *had* given her a thrill like learning a new role. Lately, everything in her life had become muddled. A day-to-day rush of promos, interviews, meetings, stress, and drama.

"Charge!" Michaela shouted an hour and a half later, thrusting her golden sword in the air as she commanded her troops to attack the warring faction of Armageddon survivors. The small army of extras charged around her. Later, in post-production, thousands of additional soldiers would be added via CGI.

"Hold steady!" the director hollered, springing from his chair. He followed next to the camera panning her face, then shouted an irritated, "Cut!"

Michaela's arm dropped to her side. Damn, that blade was heavier than it looked. What the hell was Francola's problem now? This director wasn't satisfied with her scenes if she didn't shoot and reshoot them seventy times.

"Scarlett!" he bellowed as he waved her over. His gaze was fixed on the camera viewer, probably reviewing what she'd just performed.

"What's up?" she asked as she took her time, strolling to him. No way would she hustle just because he snapped his fingers. She hadn't been that actress since she'd made her first ten million. This director needed *her*, and she'd make sure he remembered it. "What has your panties in a twist this morning?"

"You. I'm unhappy with you." He stepped aside and indicated the camera with a snort. "You even bother looking in a mirror this morning, Scarlett?"

Michaela's spine snapped straight. "Excuse me?" Without bothering to peer at the screen, she rounded on the director. His disrespectful question pinged around in her head, dredging up one of the lowest moments in her life.

Francola scoffed. "Scarlett, you look like shit. You're so fucking skinny, you're like a bag of bones. Your hair is limp, and your skin is waxy and pale even with fifty layers of makeup. It's coming across like garbage on camera. You're losing the thing that made you a star, Scarlett."

Her blood ran cold.

Hell fucking no. No one spoke to *her* that way. Not anymore and especially not a man. Men dove in front of her to lay their bodies over puddles so she wouldn't get her designer shoes wet. They jumped to do her bidding with one sultry glance. They showered her with affection and tripped over their tongues to tell her how stunning she was.

And here was this nothing of a man daring to lecture her in the manner she'd been spoken to ten years ago. Back when she'd dumped a nine-dollar box of bleach in her hair and thought drug store makeup would make her magnificent.

Fuck him.

She'd spent fifteen hundred dollars at the spa yesterday on her hair, a facial, and body treatments. And this little elf had the nerve to comment on her *vibe*?

She squared her shoulders and advanced. "How dare you speak to me like that?" With the five-inch heels on her thigh-high boots, she topped out at six feet tall and towered over the little man.

Little in both stature and character. She may have been small once when she was a nobody living in a mining town in West Virginia without two nickels to rub together, but she wasn't now. She'd worked her ass off for a decade to make sure no one would ever look down their nose at her again.

He rolled his eyes.

"Have you forgotten who I am?" Michaela asked with venom dripping from her voice.

They'd drawn a crowd. It seemed the entire cast and crew stopped what they'd been doing to gawk at the escalating argument. Good, it'd be great to have witnesses to Francola's downfall.

No one could accuse her of not appreciating the value of a good audience.

Nostrils flaring and eyes narrowed to deadly slits, he met her head-on. The six inches she had on him forced his head back to meet her gaze, but he wasn't intimidated. "I know exactly who you are, *Scarlett*. A spoiled fucking diva who snorts her meals instead of eating them."

"Be careful, Charles. I'll walk." She smiled the kind of smile victors wore right before delivering the kill shot. The same one she during the last scene they film when her character led her arm to defeat a warring faction. "I'll walk, and this movie will swirl down the toilet where it belongs. The studio probably won't even fine me once they hear how you treated their favorite actress." She tossed the end of her braid over her shoulder for good measure, then took a few steps back to enhance the visual of her walking away from his shitty movie.

Damn, the view from the top of the world was spectacular.

He spread his arms, sneering. "Knock yourself out. You'll be doing me a favor."

"What?" Her heart skipped a beat.

Why wasn't he begging her to stay?

"That's right. Walk, princess." Now it was his turn for a smug, winner's grin. "And guess what? I won't even feel tempted to stare at your boney fucking ass while you go."

No, no, no.

This couldn't be happening. The studio had warned her of how important this movie was for her career. She'd gotten in hot water on the last set for allegedly causing too much drama and unrest among the cast by sleeping with her co-star. How the hell was she supposed to know he'd had a pregnant girlfriend? The chick had never once hung around the set. Besides, he'd come on to her, not the other way around.

Asshole.

Regardless, the studio warned her if she acted out on this set, it'd be the last time they worked with her.

And they were a big fucking deal. As in, career makers or breakers. Even at her level of stardom. In Hollywood, there was always someone above you on the food chain. Few could destroy the life she'd made for herself, but a major studio executive was one of those people.

And with the way his grin curled in sinister delight, Francola knew it.

"Charles..." She'd have died from the flood of panic without years of solid acting experience propping her up. To everyone watching, she stood tall, arrogant, indifferent to his idle threats. But her insides shriveled and died in the same way they'd done at her very first audition. Only then, she had the resiliency of youth to bounce back and charge forward. Now? Now all she wanted was to lock herself in her trailer with a bottle of vodka and some Xanax until the pain subsided.

"Please go, Scarlett. I'd hate to have to call security on you," Charles said, and then that motherfucker turned his back on her.

Fuck the studio and fuck Charles. She was the country's hottest movie star, for fuck's sake.

With the sun barely peeking over the horizon, Michaela let out a harsh laugh. "Enjoy the unemployment line, asshole," she said as she lifted both hands in a double middle-finger salute. "I'm a fucking star known through every household in America. Who the fuck are you?"

With that parting shot, she spun on her heel, making sure to present her widest smile as she sashayed toward her trailer. Despite NDAs, these photos would go viral in minutes. She'd be damned if she didn't look hot as fuck while leaving these losers in the dust. Her PR team would flip their shit, but fuck them, too. They worked for her, not the other way around. She paid them a shit ton of money to make her look fantastic, and they could earn their worth.

By the time her trailer was in sight, Becca had sprinted up next to her. "Okay, will do," she said into her phone before ending a call. Breathless, she nearly jogged her tiny legs to keep up with Michaela's long stride. "Soon as we get in the trailer, we'll call Tatiana and get moving on damage control." Her fingers flew over her phone screen. "Shit. I was hoping we'd a least have a few minutes before the videos started hitting social media, but no luck."

"I want that man ruined," Michaela spat as she marched forward.

Becca didn't respond.

Michaela's headache jacked up in intensity until the rising sun felt as though it were burning her brain. God, was it only just past five in the morning? Seemed as though an entire week had gone by since she'd woken up.

When she reached the trailer, Michaela wrenched the door open so hard it smacked against the outside wall. Of course, Becca followed her inside. Just as she was about to kick her assistant out, Michaela's gaze fell to her bed. She drew up short. "Who the fuck—"

Becca smacked into her back. "Sorry. Who are you talking about—oh."

Michaela gaped at the two men passed out face down on her bed. She turned to her assistant. "Who the fuck are they?" One of the guys slept on his stomach, sheet covering his ass, but fully tattooed back on display. The one next to him had smooth, bare skin, but lay on his back with the sheet covering, well, nothing. "Jesus, are they naked? What the fuck?"

Becca's nose wrinkled as she averted her gaze. Michaela knew that Becca had seen far worse while working for her and shouldn't be afraid of a little male nudity, but still, the sweet girl blushed and stared at the floor. "Um, you don't remember?"

"Obviously, I don't fucking remember. Would I be asking if I did?" She gripped the back of her neck and blew out a breath. The braid in her hair had to go. It pulled her scalp ridiculously taught, exacerbating the pain.

"Uh, they're extras." Becca still kept her gaze on the floor. "You were partying with them last night and, uh, invited them here."

"What?" She whipped her gaze back to the disheveled bed with a scrunched brow. "I did?"

"Yes."

Curly

"Shit." Had she slept with them? One? Both? Being that they were naked, and she'd awakened the same way, it wasn't a leap. The coffee soured in her stomach. How the hell could she have fucked two men and not remember it only a few hours later? Rubbing her tender forehead, Michaela fought for an unconcerned tone. "I need to use the bathroom. I want them gone by the time I get out."

"What? Me?" Becca squeaked. "You want me to get rid of them?"

One of the men stirred but didn't wake. If someone had offered her the exorbitant sum she'd earned from her last movie, she couldn't have recalled his name. Or the other one. Had they both touched her, kissed her, been inside her? Jesus, had she taken them into her mouth? She pressed a hand to her rolling stomach. Michaela wasn't shy when it came to sex, and this sure as hell wasn't her first threesome, but not remembering a single detail of the night, including the fact she'd had sex at all, well, that was a new low.

And frankly, it rattled her to her core.

Never let them see your weakness. You're going to be a star.

Her mother's advice rang loud in her ears. Michaela straightened her shoulders as she glared at Becca. "Yes, you. What the fuck do you think I pay you for?" she snapped as she stormed into the bathroom and slammed the door with enough force to shake the entire trailer. There, she'd done her part in waking the guys. All Becca had to do was kick their asses to the parking lot.

She blew out a breath.

Finally, alone.

Michaela rested her hands on the tiny sink and bowed her head. The empty cocaine vial still sat there, mocking her.

So she'd lost a few pounds recently. Since when had anyone in Hollywood complained about women being too skinny?

Fucking Francola.

The growls and curses of displeased men exiting her trailer had relief flooding her. She took a breath, closed her eyes, then raised her head. As she opened them, finding her reflection, Michaela let out a sharp gasp. A sunken-cheeked, sallow-complexioned skeleton with purple smudges under each eye stared back at her. Now that Francola had ripped her blinders off, she barely recognized the shell of a woman in the mirror.

Her hand shook as she lifted it to probe her gaunt face. Cheekbones that used to be the envy of women across the globe now jutted out in harsh lines.

Enjoy being a star, my beautiful girl. Just don't let them take away who you are.

Her eyes closed as she pressed a hand to her heart the way her ailing mother had done all those years ago when Michaela told her she planned to move to Hollywood. They'd both known the end was near for her mother, and Michaela wanted her to pass knowing her daughter would fulfill their dreams. At the time, she'd laughed off the advice, too high on the prospect of fame and fortune to recognize the true warning there.

Now, dozens of movies and millions of dollars later, she used chemicals and sex to chase that high. The one that had long worn off. And to fill the void of living a vapid, superficial life devoid of any meaningful human connection.

Last night she'd been too stoned and wasted to remember fucking two strangers. This morning she lost her coveted role in what was projected to be the next big blockbuster. And right now, images of her flipping off her director and sensationalized accounts of the encounter were popping up on every social media platform available. Stories of the temper-tantrum-throwing starlet would be trending within minutes.

But despite it all, only one problem dominated her mind and demanded immediate action. And that was the empty vial of cocaine. She longed for a hit to pull her from the crushing fatigue assailing her. If she couldn't have that, the half-full bottle of vodka she'd seen on the table in the trailer would do. Though it wouldn't energize her, it'd numb the pain and the voice in her head now screaming she was a failure.

And that was a serious problem.

Who had she become?

No longer able to look at the husk of a woman now crying in the mirror, Michaela jerked back from the sink. She hit the wall hard. The crash seemed to dislodge a sob wedged in her gut. She sank to the floor, weeping as despair washed over her.

She was tired. So tired her bones ached, and her soul held a heaviness that weighed down her entire being.

If she just had something to combat the exhaustion, she could think clearer and find a way out of this mess.

She crawled forward with tear-stained cheeks, opening the small cabinet beneath the sink. She'd often hidden her stash in a tampon box when visitors stopped by. Sure enough, a baggie peeked out from the tampons. "Holy shit. Yes." The relief at knowing she'd feel better had her sighing in pleasure.

It was crystal meth.

She swallowed as she held up the small bag. One of the guys from last night must have put it there. This would take the edge off and allow her to make it through the remainder of this miserable day. But it was one drug she'd never tried.

Growing up, she'd seen one too many toothless tweakers in the crappy apartment complex she'd lived in. She'd sworn to herself, no matter what, this was a line she would never cross.

She stared at the baggie with a sinking heart.

Today would go down as one of the worst days in her professional career. She needed a boost, just this once.

Desperate times called for desperate measures.

After setting up, she snorted a line, then leaned back against the door as the rush of endorphins fired up her blood.

"One more," she whispered, then repeated the process once again.

With her heart now racing, she finally felt alive and not like the zombie who'd woken up and stumbled through the morning.

Fuck, that's better.

She smiled, then eyed the baggie, which still held plenty more meth.

"Fuck it." After snorting two more lines, she was flying high. Now she was ready to talk to her team. To make a plan and fuck Francola good.

As she tried to stand, the room spun, and she stumbled. Giggling, she landed on her ass and hit the door with her back. "Let's try that again." She leaned forward only to have the left side of her chest seize up in a crushing pain that took her breath away.

With a gasp and a garbled shout, she grabbed her chest and slumped against the door. It felt as if the entire trailer had collapsed on top of her chest. Fire shot down her left arm. She tried to yell as panic set in, but it came out as a strangled cry once again.

"Scarlett?" Becca called out as she knocked lightly on the other side of the door. "Are you okay?"

"No," she croaked, throat tight and aching.

"What do you need? What can I get for you?" Even after being snapped at and treated like nothing more than a servant, Becca's sweetness won out.

"Help," Michaela whispered through the agony. "I think I need some help."

The knob jiggled, and pressure hit her back. "Scarlett, I can't get the door open."

"Call...call EMS," she managed as the room began to fade to darkness.

Please don't let me die here.

* * *

Thank you so much for reading **CURLY**. If you enjoyed it, please consider leaving a review on Amazon or Goodreads.

Other books by Lilly Atlas

No Prisoners MC
Hook: A No Prisoners Novella
Striker
Jester
Acer
Lucky
Snake

Trident Ink

Escapades

Hell's Handlers MC
Zach
Maverick
Jigsaw
Copper
Rocket
Little Jack
Joy
Screw
Viper
Thunder

Hell's Handlers MC Florida Chapter
Curly

Lilly Atlas

* * *

Audiobooks
Audio

Join Lilly's mailing list for a **FREE** No Prisoners short
story.
www.lillyatlas.com
Facebook
Instagram
TikTok
Twitter

Join my Facebook group, **Lilly's Ladies** for book previews, early cover reveals, contests and more!

Keep reading for a preview of Zach, Book One of the Hell's Handlers MC Series

About the Author

Lilly Atlas is an award-winning contemporary romance author. She's a proud Navy wife and mother of three spunky girls. Every time Lilly downloads a new eBook she expects her Kindle App to tell her it's exhausted and overworked, and to beg for some rest. Thankfully that hasn't happened yet so she can often be found absorbed in a good book.